MARKED

DAW Novels by S. ANDREW SWANN

Fantasy
DRAGONS & DWARVES
(*The Dragons of the Cuyahoga* | *The Dwarves of Whiskey Island*)
*
BROKEN CRESCENT
*
GOD'S DICE
*
DRAGON • PRINCESS
DRAGON • THIEF
DRAGON • WIZARD
*
MARKED

Fiction
ZIMMERMAN'S ALGORITHM

Science Fiction
THE HOSTILE TAKEOVER TRILOGY
(*Profiteer* | *Partisan* | *Revolutionary*)

THE MOREAU QUARTET: VOLUME ONE
(*Forests of the Night* | *Fearful Symmetries*)
THE MOREAU QUARTET: VOLUME TWO
(*Emperors of the Twilight* | *Specters of the Dawn*)

S. Andrew Swann

MARKED

DAW BOOKS, INC.
DONALD A. WOLLHEIM, FOUNDER
1745 Broadway, New York, NY 10019
ELIZABETH R. WOLLHEIM
SHEILA E. GILBERT
PUBLISHERS
www.dawbooks.com

Cover art by Chris Gibbs.

Cover design by G-Force Design.

DAW Book Collectors No. 1812.

Published by DAW Books, Inc.
1745 Broadway, New York, NY 10019.

First Printing, January 2019
1 2 3 4 5 6 7 8 9

DAW TRADEMARK REGISTERED
U.S. PAT. AND TM. OFF. AND FOREIGN COUNTRIES
—MARCA REGISTRADA
HECHO EN U.S.A.

PRINTED IN THE U.S.A.

For the new kid, Loki.

ONE

I NEVER TOLD my parents about the Mark.

Of course, they knew it was there on their adopted little girl's back. Some of my earliest memories are of the man who would become my dad taking me to strange places to have strange people look at the strange patterns drawn across his strange little girl's back.

My parents never learned the origin of the tattoo, much less what it might mean, and by the time I grew into puberty, I was too self-conscious in my desire for normalcy to ever allow the Mark to be uncovered in anyone else's presence, even those who loved me.

Much as I wished otherwise, I wasn't normal, and the Mark on my back was more than a simple tattoo. I was nearly an adult myself before I understood that, even on the the most basic level.

So I never told them.

FOUR days after my mom's funeral, the temperatures reached up into the mid-nineties and stayed there, the air pressing down on everything like a wet towel. We were on the road five minutes before the AC on the unmarked ten-year-old Crown Victoria cruiser sputtered and died, the air from the vents turning from barely cool to burning-asphalt hot.

Jacob Hightower, my partner, reached over from the wheel and tried to adjust the controls, to no effect. "Doesn't the garage ever check these before signing them out?" He shut off the vents, and the airflow died with a shuddering wheeze. He toggled the windows and they reluctantly slid down. "Makes you wish you worked for a city with a maintenance budget."

"Yeah."

"Want to take this back to the motor pool?"

"We can switch cars after we meet Mrs. Kim. After what she's been through, I don't want to make her wait." Right now I was too aware of what it was like when you lost part of your family. I didn't want to be responsible for dragging out this experience for her.

I turned to look out the open passenger window. The wind tore into the car, carrying the smells of diesel exhaust and hot tar. It made my eyes water.

Jacob said something that I lost in the sound of the wind. "*What?*" I hollered, still facing the Cleveland skyline rolling by past the freeway guardrail.

"*I asked, are you up for this, Dana?*" he yelled back at me, sounding very far away beyond the roaring wind.

"*I'm fine!*"

After working together for three years, he was probably aware that I was lying to him. Even so, he didn't press the point. I was grateful for that.

I was the junior member of the team, and Jacob had an irritating protective streak that I tried not to hold against him. He knew that I had just come back to work after saying goodbye to the only family I had left. He *should* have been concerned about me; it was part of his job.

It wasn't his fault if that type of concern grated against something very basic inside me. Even from him. *Especially* from him.

It was just past rush hour, and traffic moved quickly along the freeway as we headed toward the West Side. We were silent until we hit the exit and the wind died down, the stillness resurrecting the oppressive heat. Jacob squinted at the traffic light and said, "We should have taken your car."

"Oh, no. That baby is strictly for civilian use."

"I thought you got it because you liked the patrol cars in Solon."

"The places we have to park? No, thank you."

"I'm sure you could—"

"Jacob, you aren't going to get to drive my Charger."

He wove the car through the surface streets while I did my best to undo the violence the wind had done to my hair, getting the scary blonde halo back into a semicontrolled ponytail. It made me envious of Jacob's short brown military cut. By the time I had gotten my appearance a few notches back under horrifying, Jacob had parked the car in front of our destination.

The storefront was tucked between a liquor store hiding behind vistas of yellowing cigarette and lottery ads, and a payday loan office that was so antiseptic and sterile it looked like a set from an old *Star Trek* episode. Between them, *Asia FX* stood out like a drag queen at an Amish funeral.

The name loomed over the store, drawn in a chromed graffiti font three times the height of the sans serif gracing its drab siblings. Behind the window and unlit neon signs proclaiming "tattoos" and "piercings" were panels of artwork: skulls, Buddhas, tigers, dragons, and elaborate inscriptions in Kanji and Indian script.

Hanging on the door was a plastic sign apologizing for being closed—as if the yellow police tape wasn't enough of a clue.

I stared at the place and felt uncomfortably aware of the Mark on my back. I could almost feel phantom fingers tracing the black whorls and branches etched into my skin. I wondered if this had been one of the places my dad had brought me to when he was still trying to identify it, trying to identify *me*.

"Are you all right, Dana?"

I tried to laugh it off. "Just some déjà vu."

He looked at my face, and I couldn't help returning the look. He had a strong face, as if a confident artist had drawn it with just a few bold perfectly-placed strokes. He had a shadow of a beard, just enough to be masculine, not enough to look messy. His hazel eyes gave me the uncomfortable sense that he saw my emotions better than I did.

"You're due for some time off," he told me. "The funeral was only—"

"I'm fine," I snapped, too defensively. He turned from me, and my bitchiness made me feel even worse. I belatedly realized I was taking things out on him. "I'm sorry."

"I know. Don't worry about it." He faced *Asia FX*, squinting in the morning light. "Mrs. Kim should be here soon to let us in."

He was right. I *wasn't* up for this. I was just too stubborn to admit it to him—or maybe I had just become too accustomed to keeping uncomfortable secrets.

When I had come to work the Monday after Mom's funeral, I had honestly thought I could handle it. I wasn't a teenager anymore, not like when Dad had been shot.

But parked across from *Asia FX*, it felt as if the past ten years hadn't happened. I was a teenager again, and it wasn't my mom that had just been buried—it was my dad. I could feel the irrational guilt as a physical presence filling my stomach and my throat, making it hard to breathe. I rubbed my eyes and told myself that they still burned from riding with the windows open.

"Here she comes," Jacob said, stepping out of the car.

The victim's daughter looked like hell. She was a tiny Korean woman, about fifty. Rogue strands of hair trailed across her face. Her frown looked out of place, a foreign invader in unfamiliar territory. It was painful to watch it turn to a forced smile as she acknowledged Jacob's presence. "Detective Hightower?"

"Yes. Mrs. Kim?"

I spent a few moments composing myself as the two of them exchanged faux pleasantries. However I felt, I still had a job to do. I sucked in a few breaths, told myself to cowgirl up, and got out of the passenger side in time for Jacob to gesture my way and say, "And this is Detective Rohan."

"Thank you for meeting us, Mrs. Kim," I said.

"You're welcome," she responded, turning immediately back to Jacob. "What can I do for you?" she asked.

Some people of a certain generation, especially women of a certain generation, really had trouble accepting a female police detective. Over the three years since I'd become one, I had learned to let Jacob take the lead in questioning in those situations. Normally it irritated me, but right now I was grateful that Jacob bore the brunt of dealing with the grieving family member.

"Well," Jacob said, "I have a few more questions, and Detective Rohan would like to look at the scene."

They both turned to look at me, and I suddenly felt that I wouldn't like to see the scene of the crime, not at all. But I needed to. If I was going to bring my skills to bear, I needed to get the lay of the land, plan out how I was going to confront the suspect.

Everything I felt right now was beside the point.

Ms. Kim turned to me and said, "The officers took pictures already. They said we could clean up." There was almost a pleading tone in her voice. And I read in her face, *please, just let this part of it be over.*

I knew how she felt. It wasn't just the grieving; she probably hadn't even dealt with that part yet. There was the legal stuff, the insurance, tracking down all the bills, dealing with the incompetent funeral director, realizing that you were the one who had to tell all your mom's friends that she had gone into the hospital and no, she hadn't made it. . . .

Oh, hell.

I tried my best reassuring smile, mentally shoving away all the issues I had been dealing with. "I'm just looking at the physical layout of the scene."

"She's very good at what she does," Jacob said.

Mrs. Kim nodded, one of the stray trails of hair pulling free in the morning breeze. I could see the individual strands of white mixing in with the black.

While Jacob removed the crime-scene tape, she pulled a massive key ring from her purse and began a long ritual of unlocking the door. I glanced at Jacob, looking for a sign that he saw how rattled I was.

I decided I was being paranoid. Jacob was good at taking me at my word, perhaps even when he shouldn't have. He wasn't paying attention to me as he watched Mrs. Kim open the door to *Asia FX*.

I felt more comfortable studying him when he wasn't looking at me. I always had liked his face. He only had about six years on me, but he had begun getting a premature dusting of gray at the temples though his short brown hair was so light that it was easy to miss it. Rather than aging him, it gave him an almost subliminal air of authority that suited a cop.

I think that's why I liked working with him, liked *him*. He looked and acted the part of a cop—the kind of cop that I had wanted to be ever since the year Dad died. He wouldn't look out of place in a picture with Joe Friday or Eliot Ness.

Or my dad.

I hoped that at least some of that had rubbed off on me over the past three years.

Mrs. Kim turned around in the now open doorway and asked, "What do you want to see?" The interior was dark behind her, the shadows gaping like a hungry mouth.

"Where are the security cameras?"

"The officers took the tapes."

"I know," I told her. Back at the station, I'd reviewed the security footage with Jacob. The video of the shooting had a time stamp of 11:05 and showed a male suspect—white or Hispanic—wearing a gray hoodie and a pair of jeans with a hole torn in the right knee. The video was bad quality, probably because it was an ancient system that had been reusing the same VHS tape for years. "Can you show me where the cameras are?" I asked.

She nodded and led me into the dark. Even in the gloom, I could see her whole body tense as we walked into the place where her father had been murdered. The only light came from the morning sun leaking through the front windows, and that didn't penetrate very deep into the room beyond. In the gloom, she almost became a ghost herself.

Around us, gods and monsters covered the walls, watching.

She stopped in front of a counter, which bore the first visible sign of the tragedy that had happened to her family last night. It was a small, glass-fronted case like you'd see in a jewelry store. The front had been smashed and the contents emptied. A small cash register sat on top of the busted display case, turned toward us, the drawer half open.

Behind the case, a padded stool lay on its side next to a dark stain in the carpet. The air in here felt dry and still as a tomb, the only sound the buzzing of a few flies.

"What was in the case?" I asked, stepping around the broken glass.

"Nothing. It was all costume jewelry . . ." Her voice caught. She paused before pointing up into the darkness above the counter. "There."

I looked up at where a small security camera poked from the acoustical tile, covering the register and the entrance. The thing was obvious and bulky, probably at least twenty years old. I looked at the register again and realized that it had come from another decade as well. Mrs. Kim's father had been in business here for a long time.

"Is that the only one?" I asked.

"Yes," she waved toward the back, past a folding oriental screen that made a private alcove beyond the counter. I couldn't see anything past it. "He has a TV back there so he can see people come in when he is working alone . . . *was* working alone."

Mrs. Kim stood there and made a small sound somewhere between a gasp and a sob. I looked at her and could feel everything I had felt when I knew that someone had killed my dad, and there was nothing that could ever fix it.

"I know," I whispered to myself. In the still confines of the tattoo parlor, I might as well have shouted.

She turned to face me with an expression that looked lost in the shadows. "You know?"

"How you feel," I said, feeling very unlike the detective I was supposed to be at the moment.

"I suppose you do. You must see things like this every day."

"I—" *I lost my father, too. It was just as stupid and pointless. I just buried my mom and I'm still trying to deal with that. . . .* I didn't say any of it, but she must have seen something in my face.

"Detective Rohan, are you all right?"

"I'm fine. But you don't need to be here. Why don't you go and talk to Detective Hightower? I'm just going to look around here for a few minutes."

"Okay," she said uncertainly.

I reached out and touched her arm, saying, "I promise you, we will get the guy who did this."

She nodded, but from her lost expression, I could tell she didn't have any faith in my reassurance. She walked back toward the doorway, toward Jacob's silhouette. As I watched her walk away from me, I found myself gripped by an unexpected anger at the person who had done this to her father. She was right. I dealt with things like this all the time. This wasn't any different. No matter how I felt right now, this was just another armed robbery that had ended badly.

That's what I kept telling myself.

At the door, she turned around and pointed past me, toward the far wall. "The light switches are by the back door there."

"Thank you."

She vanished into the daylight with Jacob, leaving me alone in the tattoo parlor. I turned around and walked into the darkness.

Past the screen, I bumped into a padded chair and had to feel around to find the back door. After some fumbling, I found the switches.

When I flipped on the lights, I suddenly found myself facing a photo of a full back piece of a blue-skinned Shiva: fangs, bloody swords, skull necklace, and all. The picture's appearance was so sudden and violent that I took an involuntary step back.

That brought more pictures into my field of vision, dozens of them, photos of this guy's work. He was good. Very good. The intricacy of what he did was awe-inspiring at every level of detail, mandalas and Buddhas, tigers and dragons, abstract floral designs, and at least one demonic creature that must have come from a seventeenth century Japanese print.

I turned around and faced the alcove where he had done his work. There was one adjustable padded chair behind the screen, a magnifying lamp on a swinging arm, and a rolling cart with needles, ink, and various other tools laid out with surgical precision. It was spotless and orderly back here, and if it wasn't for the pictures on the wall, I could have been standing in a hospital's examination room.

I felt as if I stood in the heart of a man's life.

I glanced up and looked past the screen. It blocked the front of the shop, but I could see the shadows of Jacob and Mrs. Kim moving across the window in the front of the shop.

I was completely hidden from them.

I shouldn't do this now.

I felt raw and angry. Just being here, standing in this place, was driving splinters into my need to do something. The Mark felt it as well; I could feel it rippling across my skin, long hot fingers pushing at me, wanting to be used. I bit my lip.

Now wasn't the time.

Then my gaze fell on one particular picture. The image showed a unique tribal pattern across someone's back. The stark black pattern of the abstract lines stood out amid the other, more colorful pieces. I saw the swirls and arcs of a branching design that never self-intersected.

Ever since I had walked into *Asia FX,* I had felt the memories bubbling up, memories of my dad taking me to places like this, showing my back to men marked in their own ways. I remembered how my own Mark seemed to frighten and fascinate them.

Seeing that stark black pattern in the midst of all that color, I couldn't help imagining the artist being influenced by the bizarre pattern he had seen on the skin of a lost little girl. It was easy to believe that I had once stood on this spot while Mrs. Kim's father tried to give my dad some clue as to who had drawn the Mark on my back and where it had come from.

That man who had tried to help me now had his life taken as senselessly as my dad's had been. His daughter had been dropped without warning into the same chaos of grief and bureaucracy I had just gone through with Mom.

I wanted to deal with the punk that had killed Mrs. Kim's father, and I wanted to do it *now.*

I decided to hell with what time it was.

TWO

THE MARK WARMED on my back, anticipating my thoughts. I sensed every twist and curve of the pattern, as if some invisible companion traced his fingers across its surface. The pressure was light, warm, familiar. I breathed shallowly and opened myself to the sensation. The caress sank deeper than my skin, to brush parts of me nothing else had ever touched.

I flushed, and my breathing became rapid as I pulled the Mark into me. It pushed against me, and I responded by taking a step forward.

The room around me blurred and dimmed, as if suddenly I was seeing a thousand different overlapping tattoo parlors, all slightly different. I focused on the wall in front of me as I placed my foot down, allowing the Mark's touch to withdraw almost as quickly as it had come. It left an unfulfilled ache behind itself as it pulled away.

I stood in the same room, yet not the same. The lights were off, and the sun was lower in the sky so that the dawn light reached deeper into the tattoo parlor. On the wall I faced, the rosy light shone on a Buddha seated in a lotus blossom floating above a woman's navel.

There was no sign of the tribal pattern that echoed my own Mark, and its absence was near confirmation of the sense I had connecting me to Mrs. Kim's father.

I glanced around until I saw a clock mounted on the wall. It read 6:45, a little over three hours before Jacob would drive us up to meet Mrs. Kim here. Yet I knew that if I waited here those three hours I wouldn't see myself arrive. Jacob might show up and meet Mrs. Kim, but I wouldn't be his partner and *that* Jacob wouldn't even know who I was.

I stood in the past, but it was a past where I didn't exist.

It was also a past where I could move around without worrying about being observed by Jacob or Mrs. Kim. I knew the front door was locked, but over by where I stood, there was another door. I tried it and made my way past a back office and a bathroom to find a rear exit. It let me out into an alley which was perfect for my purpose.

I checked my own watch and noted I'd been gone less than three minutes.

It was the first thing I learned about the Mark. When I left home and traveled to a place that looked like the past or the future, time itself marched on without me. My Jacob had been talking to Mrs. Kim for three minutes. When I returned home, the same amount of time would have passed for him as it had for me. So if I was going to take care of this, I probably had about fifteen minutes or so before Jacob wondered where the hell I had disappeared to.

Not that I was thinking about that now. I didn't think about what would happen if Jacob noticed me missing, or how I'd explain myself if he did. I was consumed with one thought—finding a version of that gun-wielding punk in the hoodie and the torn jeans.

I let the Mark push me further, inviting its probing touch just enough to flush my skin as I walked down the alley.

The walls of the buildings remained clear, as smaller objects became blurred. Around me, the world had become a video shooting by in fast reverse. At the mouth of the alley, cars and people moved by too fast to be more than a blur. After one step the sun disappeared. After a few more steps I stopped.

A car drove by the mouth of the alley, booming its apocalyptically loud stereo. The sky was ink black beyond the glare of the streetlights, and I could hear people talking out on the street. After the heat of the day, the night air was blessedly cool.

I sucked in a breath and allowed the intimate touch of the Mark to fade. If I had paced myself correctly, I was standing in a place about eight hours earlier than when I started. Close to eleven the previous night.

Before the time stamp on the security camera video.

Soon a guy with a gun would be walking into *Asia FX*.

I checked my own watch and saw I'd been gone a total of eight minutes. Jacob was probably still talking to Mrs. Kim. I walked up to the mouth of the alley and looked to my right. *Asia FX* was open, light leaking from the windows. I started to glance about, looking for a clock to get my bearings. I have a good sense of how far I travel, but not a perfect one.

However, I didn't need it. I saw a guy crossing the street about half a block away: Gray hoodie, jeans with hole on the right knee, crossing toward my side of the street and headed right for *Asia FX*.

I bit my lip. I don't know why it made a difference seeing the guy, but it always did. This wasn't my world, just one of thousands of imperfect copies of the past and future I could travel to. I had no idea how many different times this kid was going to walk into *Asia FX*, or even if it was always going to end with Mrs. Kim's father dead on the floor.

This tragedy could be playing out an endless number of times in unseen worlds. But this was where *I* was, and I *knew* what was about to happen. I knew, because the Mark always steered me toward what I was looking for. In the world next door, this kid might decide to knock over the liquor store or the payday loan place; in this one, the one I came to, he would walk into *Asia FX*.

I started walking nonchalantly down the sidewalk, toward him, past the darkened payday loan place. He came from the other direction and stared into the liquor store, hand drifting toward his pocket.

But the door jingled, and he quickly stepped away. As he continued walking toward me, a guy who looked underage walked out of the liquor store carrying a 24-pack of Bud Light.

The guy with the hoodie stopped in front of *Asia FX,* and I knew he was looking at a single elderly man sitting behind a case of jewelry and a cash register. Completely unaware of me, the guy stared into the tattoo parlor.

He had close-cropped black hair and the edges of a gang tattoo crawling up from his neck. He couldn't be more than eighteen, and the patchy attempt at a mustache made him look younger. *Local kid*, I thought, *and not particularly bright.*

His eyes narrowed, and I could almost hear the switch click as he made his decision. He threw the hood of his sweater up over his head and shoved his hand into a suspiciously bulky pocket. He took a step toward the door, toward his destiny of pumping three bullets into the chest of a 74-year-old man.

But even if this act was going to be echoed before and after, countless times in countless other realities, *here* it was going to be different.

Before his left hand reached the inner door, his right still buried clumsily in his pocket, I had my own gun out.

"*Freeze! Police!*" I yelled.

I had played out this scenario many, many times. When I first started using the Mark like this, as a cop, I had intended to simply watch each crime as it played out, ID the suspect, and follow to determine where any evidence was stashed. That worked fairly well with breaking and entering, car theft, vandalism, and other relatively petty crap. But with my first murder I discovered I couldn't go back and just watch some asshole kill someone.

And it wasn't like I was going to change the future I came from.

When I confront a creep before he does the deed, it can play out one of two ways. Some of the time my target hears "Freeze" and plays dumb and compliant—after all, I reached them *before* they did something illegal.

Most of the time, though, the perp is either too hyped on

adrenaline—or less natural substances—to make that fine a distinction, or they've come across my path already having several good reasons to avoid the cops.

This guy fell into the latter camp. He turned and ran.

I chased after him. He probably was sure he was going to outrun me. The teenagers usually think that. But the sort of guy who holds up a tattoo parlor is generally not the type of person with the discipline to run a couple of miles a day. The guy ran flat out and was panting before I had even hit my stride.

Sprinters only win a timed event.

He dodged into an alley, and when I turned the corner, he was five feet up a rusty chain-link fence. He was quick, but the chase was over. I gave myself a second to aim and repeated the warning, "*Freeze!*"

He didn't listen, and he placed his hand on the top of the fence.

I don't think he expected me to shoot.

I fired my Jericho 941 and put a 9mm round into his left hand as he was pulling himself up. His arm spasmed, and he lost his grip, falling backward. As the gunshot's echoes faded, I caught the trailing syllable of an obscenity. Then he hit the concrete with a thud.

He was still for a moment, stunned, as I walked up to him. Cursing as he was, I saw he was pretty lucky. My shot had hit him in the finger. He'd never flip off anyone again, but he'd retain full use of the hand otherwise.

I kept my gun braced, my aim squarely on his skull. Had he made a move for his pocket, it would have been the last thing he did. Fortunately for him, he grabbed his bloody left hand and started screaming. "You shot me. You bitch! You shot me!"

He was on his back, head pointed in my direction. I stood above him and squatted so I was holding the barrel of the Jericho about an inch above the bridge of his nose. "It's far away from the heart. You'll live."

"I didn't fucking do anything."

"I know," I told him. "That was the point. You were *going* to walk into there and pull out that .45 in your pocket. Whatever you intended to do, it was going to end badly, and you were going to put three shots into the guy behind the counter."

His eyes bugged out at me even as he said, "You don't know what the fuck you're talking about. . . ."

"Yeah, that's why you ran. But this is your lucky day because you're not going to have to live with that old man's murder on your conscience. Of all possible worlds where you made that bad decision, and no one tried to stop you, *here* you get a reprieve. You get a choice now. Do you turn around whatever disaster your life is, or do you end with a 9mm slug in your brain?" I pressed the barrel into the bridge of his nose. "Frankly, I don't care which."

"What kind of cop are you?"

"You ever see *Dirty Harry*?"

He just stared at me, bug-eyed. Probably not a movie buff.

"Are you going to do exactly what I say now?"

"Yes, just don't—"

"Then take the gun out slowly and set it on the ground. You even think about pointing it at me, you're never going to think anything else."

He reached down into his pocket, took it out by the barrel, and set it on the ground next to him.

"Shove it over there," I said.

He pushed it, hard, and the weapon skidded across the concrete, coming to a stop by the base of a dumpster.

He looked up at me, and I couldn't bring myself to feel bad for the fear I saw in his eyes.

"Now your wallet."

"What?"

"You want to continue breathing, you'll take your wallet and toss it over with the gun."

"You're mugging me?"

"I can take it off your corpse easy enough," I started tightening my finger, and I swear he may have pissed his pants.

"Wait," he shouted and scrambled to pull his wallet out of his back pocket. He held it up toward me. "Take it."

I shook my head. "Next to the gun."

He tossed it aside like it was on fire.

I stood up, watching him. Two red arcs marked the bridge of his nose where I had pressed the barrel of the Jericho.

"Now what?" he asked me.

"Get up."

He rolled over, pushing himself upright with one hand, clutching his wounded hand to his stomach. He stood a little unsteadily, facing me. I cocked my head back toward the entrance of the alley. "Get out of here."

"What?"

"Move it." He stood, staring at me in disbelief, and I pointed the Jericho at his chest. "Five. Four. Three."

"What are you—"

"Two."

He finally ran, past me and out the alley.

In the distance, I heard the sound of sirens getting nearer. I holstered my gun and pulled on a pair of latex gloves to retrieve the guy's .45 and his wallet.

Fifteen minutes. Jacob would be wondering by now.

HIS driver's license gave me a name for the suspect, Roscoe Kendal. The license I pocketed, the rest of the wallet went into the dumpster. All I would need now was some probable cause to check up on "my" Roscoe Kendal, the guy who went through with the murder. There was a good chance that if we did, we'd find something from the scene.

The gun was more of a problem. I couldn't just drop it in a dumpster for some random kid to find. And I'd be kind of obvious lugging the huge gun around back to the station. I needed to put it somewhere safe, where I could retrieve it after work.

I decided that it made the most sense stashing it back in *Asia FX*. It was going to be closed and locked up for a while. I walked back to when I had the back door propped open, and let myself back in. Then I slipped into the bathroom and took the last step back home.

I knew "home" because I could feel it, a familiar comfort like my body sliding into my own bed. Even the touch of my Mark relaxed, brushing against me slightly as if only the lightest touch was needed for me to slide back where I belonged.

I also knew "home" because I heard Jacob calling, "Dana."

I cursed. I had taken too long. I looked around for a hiding place for the hand-cannon I had brought back with me and glanced at the acoustical ceiling tiles. Climbing up on the toilet seat, I pushed one of the tiles out of the way. I was just putting the gun up in the ceiling when the door to the bathroom opened.

Damn, should have locked it.

"Dana? What are you doing?"

I froze, precariously standing on the toilet seat, one latex-gloved hand holding up the ceiling tile, the other gripping the barrel of a very large handgun. I slowly pulled the gun out from the opening.

"Holy crap," Jacob said, "You got an evidence bag for that?"

From behind him, I heard Mrs. Kim ask, "Detective Hightower, is everything all right?"

"Yes, I found her."

I stepped down from the toilet, still holding the gun by the barrel. My heart pounded, and I barely heard as Jacob asked me how I found the gun. I babbled something about seeing one of the ceiling tiles askew.

"Didn't you hear me calling for you?"

"I was too preoccupied with what I was doing," I said, which wasn't really a lie.

THE gun went into evidence, so the lab guys could lift fingerprints and do ballistics tests to tie it to the murder. I spent the rest of the day thinking of "Roscoe Kendal" and how I had just completely screwed the case against him. I had planted evidence, however inadvertently. All because my emotions ran away with me, and I didn't give myself the time . . . in the many varied senses of the term.

It was a joke. *I* was a joke.

I got hit with just one case that struck too close to home, and I had pretty much abandoned any pretense of being a cop. Dad must be real proud of me right now.

Worse, I had allowed Jacob to book the gun into evidence. I had been given a chance to own up to everything, and I hadn't been able to say anything. Not that I could admit to it in a way that didn't make me sound insane. If we caught up with Kendal now, and with him the *real* murder weapon, there'd be no sane way to explain it. No possible explanation I could come up with would adequately account for the two guns.

By keeping quiet, I was just delaying the inevitable. No one might realize it yet, but my secret was blown. Things would fall apart as soon as they found Kendal.

I'm sorry, Dad . . . I fucked up.

I sat at my desk, the day's report barely started on the monitor. I took out my badge and stared at it.

Ever since Mom's funeral, I had been interrogating myself, asking why I never told her about the Mark. As guilty as I was about failing Dad that way, I had just been just a teenager then. When he had been shot, I'd had only two months to mentally process what the Mark had done to me. I had been still questioning my sanity at the time.

At first, I hadn't told Mom because I didn't want to admit to that guilt—that I'd kept the nature of the Mark from Dad. And mixed in with the secrecy was the awful suspicion that I could have prevented his death. If I had just gone to a possible future to see what might have happened . . .

Over time, those adolescent fears gave way to a more mature guilt. I continued to hide this thing, not because of the thing itself, but because I didn't want to admit that I'd been hiding anything.

And since I'd become a cop, there was another reason I didn't tell

Mom, or anyone else. I was a fraud. I was playacting at being a cop. For all my stellar conviction rate, when I was confronting suspects away from any possible consequences, I was no better than a vigilante. I had cut so many corners off my job, there was nothing left.

There had been no reason to go after Kendal when I did. I'd only jumped when I did because I'd become too emotionally involved. I hadn't thought about what I was doing. I hadn't acted like a cop.

Not *Dirty Harry*, more *Death Wish*.

I couldn't help thinking that both my parents would be appalled at what I was doing. I could see this all confirming some secret fear they must have had, that there was something not quite right about their adopted daughter.

Staring at my badge, I muttered, "*Why?*"

"Why what?" Jacob's voice interrupted my thoughts, and his hand came into view placing a Styrofoam cup of steaming black coffee on my desk, next to the keyboard where I wasn't typing my report. I turned around, and it felt surreal seeing his face unmoved by the tide of emotion I felt. It was silly, but my own angst felt so deep I almost expected people to join in simply due to my proximity.

I looked up and smiled because it was a relief to think maybe he was having a good day. "Why am I a cop?" I said.

A bit of a cloud crossed his face. It was obviously not an answer he expected. I froze, because it wasn't quite the answer *I* had expected. I didn't realize how close my thoughts were to the surface.

Not only did I not have a clear answer for my own question, I wasn't even sure what I wanted from Jacob. Did I want him to validate what I was doing? Condemn it? I forced myself to pick up the coffee and take a sip, tasting the bitter dregs of a pot that had been bubbling away since morning. It fit my mood perfectly.

Jacob hadn't lost his puzzled expression. "What's gotten into you?" he asked as he slid into the chair next to my desk. The concern in his voice tugged at something inside me.

While we were effectively peers on the force, I had always looked up to him, admired him. He was a good cop without the benefit of the crutch I used. And any time he expressed concern for me, I became uncomfortably aware of how handsome he was—which, of course, made everything worse.

I looked down into the black depths of my coffee and saw a tiny lost version of myself staring back up at me. *Tell him!*

The thought was so sudden and violent that it made me wince. There was no reason left *not* to tell him. We'd find Kendal soon enough, if not from the prints on the gun, then simply because the kid was too dim to avoid being arrested for something.

"Dana?"

I'd never even discussed my family with him. No personal details had ever crossed my lips. I never even talked about music I liked. I just didn't let people get that close.

I couldn't.

I looked back up at him. I should be able to tell him if I could have told anyone. We'd been partners for three years.

"I should tell you something," the words left my mouth, and my heart raced.

"What?"

The Styrofoam cup began to slide in my suddenly damp palms. I set the cup on the desk and tried to force down the panic. My brain was hammered, not just with the thoughts of my carefully-structured life crumbling around me but with the thought of how Jacob would react to my fraud. What I was trying to tell him, it would give him every reason to hate me.

I couldn't deal with that, not on top of everything else.

"I—" I realized I was starting to cry.

"What's the matter?" he asked me, reaching out across the desk to touch my hand. His touch moved me inside, almost as if the Mark was trying to push me. I felt weak and realized I couldn't do it. I couldn't admit I'd been lying to him ever since we'd met.

After a moment, I said, "I don't know if I have the temperament to keep doing this." Backing away from the precipice, the panic receded, replaced by a less urgent, but much deeper, shame.

He squeezed my hand. "Kind of late in the game to have second thoughts about your career choice, isn't it?"

Much too late.

"A woman's prerogative to change her mind." I tried to force some lightness into my voice, but even to my ears it sounded insincere and bitchy. I did not want to be having this conversation.

We sat there in silence for a long time before he said, "You know, talking about it with someone might help."

"I know." *I can't.*

"But you aren't going to, are you?"

I took my hand away and turned away from him. Not telling was almost as painful as the attempt to. "I don't think so."

"Your choice." Something in his voice sounded hurt, but it might have been my imagination. I had never been as good at reading people as he was.

"Just do me a favor," he told me. "Don't quit without giving me a chance to talk you out of it."

"Sure." I didn't even know if I was lying to him anymore.

THREE

I BLASTED THE stereo in my Charger all the way home, letting my iPhone shuffle through every metal/industrial track I owned—as if the heavy guitars and hoarse vocals could drown out my self-destructive train of thought.

Ever since my nonconversation with Jacob, I'd been fantasizing about running away. I could disappear before Kendal's inevitable arrest. The Mark had bequeathed me the ability to walk into other times; there was no reason I couldn't just not come back. I could step a few minutes fore or aft of where I was right now, and I would stand in a place almost identical, except for the absence of myself, somewhere where I had no history of lies to stalk me.

But my fantasy based itself on a false premise. Whatever life I established somewhere else would inevitably be founded upon another lie. I would still face the same question. Do I tell the people I care for about this Mark? Do I avoid the question by not caring for anyone? And what happens when I care for someone in spite of myself?

I parked in the garage of my townhouse and killed the engine, cutting off Trent Reznor mid-lyric.

"Why?" I whispered into the silence.

I hated it. I hated the secrecy I couldn't bring myself to end. I hated what the secrecy had done to me. I hated the fact that I was doing this to myself. I hated being alone.

Through my childhood, I never had a great record connecting with other people. After Dad died, I had stopped trying. Everyone who had shown up at Mom's calling hours had been *her* friends, I hadn't even told my coworkers at the department about the funeral. Jacob was probably the closest thing I had to a friend, and I'd been keeping him at arm's length for three years. I don't think he even knew where I lived.

The fact all of this was self-inflicted didn't help.

I walked into the kitchen and threw my keys on the empty counter and stared at the place I called home.

I prided myself on keeping everything neat and organized: modern furniture, unbroken pastel walls, solid-color curtains, neat bookshelves, and an entertainment center safely hidden behind smoked glass.

It wasn't so much that I found the order comforting. Looking at it right now, it seemed as if I had never thought that deeply about it.

It wasn't anything like the house where I had grown up, and it was certainly nothing like my mom's condo. I had spent several days packing up Mom's life. She'd had pictures everywhere, porcelain figurines, paperbacks scattered on every open surface, plants, and a trio of cats that I had fortunately found homes for. It had always been busy, crowded, cluttered, and had always made me feel a bit claustrophobic.

The only thing I had saved from her place was a yellowing banker's box that had my name scrawled on the side. I'd only had the nerve to glance into it once. One look at the pictures of child me and a sheaf of adoption papers made me slam the box shut. It sat in my bedroom closet now. At some point I'd have the stomach to go through the contents.

Thinking about my mom's cluttered condo now, my own home seemed askew in comparison—fake, as if the place had been staged for a real-estate showing.

I felt as if I had already stepped sideways into a universe where I didn't exist.

I walked into the living room and sat down on the edge of an oversized armchair. I took out my badge, and after giving it a long glance, I tossed it onto the glass coffee table.

I didn't know what to do. For years I had myself convinced that I had found my role in life, a reason for the Mark I was afflicted with, a purpose for myself. Suddenly, it seemed that there wasn't much of myself in my purpose. I felt that there wasn't much of myself, period. The rest of my life, my pretense of being a cop, was all as fake as this living room: calculated, staged, empty, soulless.

Who the hell was I, if I wasn't the façade I'd built for Jacob and everyone else? If that fell apart, was there anything left? Did it matter? Who was I doing this for?

I bit my lip and wondered if I had been doing this as much for Mom as I had for Dad. In the hospital, one of the last things she had said to me was how proud she'd been.

She said that, and I had stayed quiet. . . .

I couldn't just quit, could I?

I had been nearly seventeen when I had first inadvertently used the Mark.

It wasn't the first time I had *felt* it. I had become familiar with the phantom fingers that traced the patterns on my back, mostly when I was still and quiet in my bed at night. I kept quiet about it because it was just another weirdness about me when I tried so hard to be normal. The Mark was something I didn't talk about, even then.

At some point in my adolescence, I realized that, for all their attempts to identify the Mark, find out who had drawn it on my skin, there was nothing my adoptive parents could tell me about it. Without that explanation, I simply wanted to ignore it, pretend that it didn't exist.

If I had been more open, they might have noticed another sign that it was no ordinary tattoo, if it was a tattoo at all.

The Mark grew with me.

At seventeen, the Mark covered the same portion of my back as it had when I was six, and it was just as ebon dark. It hadn't distorted, or faded, the way a normal tattoo would have. It had branched and grown in complexity to cover the new space, almost as if it was a living thing.

And it touched me like a living thing.

I kept it secret. I hid it under my clothes and tried to push away its touch. I only really felt it when I was in my bed, and my control slipped close to sleep.

And, in the shower a week before my seventeenth birthday, my control had slipped in a particularly spectacular fashion. I had spent a very late night studying and had gotten up for school without nearly enough sleep. I got in the shower yawning, and the warm water lulled me into the half-sleep that allowed the Mark to touch me without resistance.

As if annoyed at being ignored, the invisible fingers brushing the edges of the Mark became hands shoving me forward. Startled awake, I took a step. The world around me became hazy, and the feeling of water hitting my skin vanished.

I stumbled to my hands and knees in a bone-dry shower. I almost cried out, but embarrassment made me hold my tongue.

I bit my lip and pulled my knees up, so I sat on the floor of the shower, my damp skin breaking into gooseflesh. I didn't know why the shower had shut off, and it took me a while to collect myself enough to stand up and turn the water back on.

I was feeling almost normal again when I heard my father's voice over the shower. "Who's there?"

I thought he'd left for work.

"Just me, Dad," I called out.

The door to the bathroom burst open.

"*Dad?*" I screamed, backing into the corner of the shower.

The shower curtain pulled aside, and my dad was standing there with a gun in his hand. His eyes went wide as he stared at me. "Who are you? And what are you doing in my house?"

I covered myself and tried to shrink into the tile behind me. "Dad? You're scaring me."

He lowered the gun and shook his head. I wanted to think this was all some sort of nasty joke, but looking into his face I only saw surprise . . . and possibly pity.

This isn't happening. This isn't happening. This isn't happening.

He holstered his gun and grabbed a towel off the rack as he turned off the shower. Suddenly, I could hear myself sobbing.

"I know you're scared," he said as he handed me the towel. "But you need to tell me who you are."

I stared at him. *Stop looking at me. It isn't right. I'm your daughter. . . .*

As if he could read my thoughts, he turned to look out the door, still holding the towel out to me. I grabbed it and wrapped myself. My hands shook, and I was still crying. I was so shaken and upset by my dad's actions that I didn't realize that the towel I wrapped myself in was not the soft fuzzy one that I had hung up when I took my shower.

"Where are your clothes?" he asked me.

"Over . . ." My voice trailed off because my robe wasn't hanging where it should have been. My slippers were gone. But what made my breath catch in my throat was the wallpaper. Two years ago we had rented a steamer and I had spent a Sunday afternoon helping my dad strip the wallpaper from the bathroom. By the end of the day, both of us were covered with melted glue and little pieces of lime-green paper.

"What's happening?" I asked the lime-green walls. The wall mutely told me that day had never happened.

Dad sucked in a breath. "You're confused," he said. He turned around now that I had covered myself with a towel. "Do you remember what happened before you got into the shower? Did you take anything, drink anything?"

"You're scaring me, Dad."

When I called him that, it looked as if I had hit him. "Will you come with me?" he said gently, holding out his hand. "I'll call and get you some help."

"Why don't you know me? Why is the wallpaper still up?"

"Don't be frightened. I know things seem strange right now, but we're going to get you some help and we'll get things back to normal for you."

I took his hand, because as strange as he was acting, I still trusted him. He took me down the hall to my room, but it wasn't my room. The walls were painted a different color, and the furniture was different, more generic. The bed was made, and a set of towels were folded neatly on an unfamiliar dresser. A small clock radio sat on one end table by the bed. It screamed guest room.

I stared at the clock. According to it, I had spent five hours in the shower, it was nearly noon.

No, it says PM. . . .

It was also dark outside. Not near noon. Near midnight.

"Here," he said. "You can stay here. My wife has some old things in the bottom drawer." He pointed at the dresser. "Something might fit you."

I stared at him.

"I'm going to call and get you some help. Don't worry, you'll be safe here."

He closed the door behind him, and I stood in the room that was no longer mine and began to shake. I heard him make the call to 911 for an ambulance, telling them about a tattooed teenage girl breaking into his house, naked and disoriented.

He doesn't know me.

I was never here.

The most horrifying feeling I ever had was, right then, being briefly convinced that my entire life up to that point had been some drug-induced hallucination.

Maybe this is the hallucination.

I closed my eyes and desperately prayed that it was, and that when I opened my eyes, my room would be as I remembered it.

Nothing happened.

Almost nothing.

I felt ghostly fingers trail the Mark on my back. Almost as if they urged me forward. I opened my eyes and took a step, and the room briefly blurred, and the lights went out.

"What?" I whispered. I had the sense that something had happened, but I had no idea what. I reached over and flipped the light switch back on.

"Must have brushed against it?" I said, even though I'd been standing three feet from the wall. I strained to listen to what my dad was saying to 911, but I no longer heard him say anything.

I was going crazy. That was the only explanation I could think of. My parents had adopted a feral child so disturbed and wild that I barely remembered who she was—who I was. What if that dead-eyed child from the old pictures was coming back? What if she'd never left?

"No."

I heard a car rolling into the driveway. The ambulance must be here. I ran to the window and looked out.

It wasn't the ambulance.

Instead, pulling into the driveway was the same Buick Century my dad had been driving forever. Then the door opened, and my dad stepped out.

He looked up, staring at the window. His eyes widened when he saw me.

I stumbled back from the window.

What's happening?

I heard him throwing open the door, and I knew that I was about to relive the conversation I had just had with him, and he would call 911 about the confused teenager breaking into his house. Maybe next time it would be Mom.

Maybe I'd died, and my hell would be forever having my parents forget who I was.

Even through blurred tears, I noticed the clock on the nightstand. It said quarter after eleven.

That wasn't right, it was just reading ten to twelve.

I knew I hadn't been in the shower seventeen hours.

That was the first time I understood what the Mark could do, though I didn't quite believe it. Questioning my own sanity seemed more plausible.

But as I heard my dad running up the steps, I tested this new crazy idea. I willed the Mark's fingers to touch me, and I took a step forward.

The lights went out again, and I no longer heard Dad running upstairs. The clock now read 10:55.

I didn't understand what was happening, but I now had a path back home, to the room, and the life, that I remembered. I faced the clock, and willed the Mark to push me, and with each step the numbers shot backward.

In five more steps the clock was gone, and my room was back. And from down the hall, I heard the shower running.

I sat in the chair in my living room, thinking about my dad, and the version of him that had found me that first time in the shower. *My* dad, the Michael Rohan who had raised me from a feral six-year-old into a nearly normal adolescent, had been shot only two months after my first brush with the Mark's power.

His death was what pushed me to actually experiment with what the Mark could do. That first time had scared me so badly that I had avoided even thinking about it, much less using it. When Mom told me that he had been shot—I was no longer afraid of being trapped in some world where I had never existed.

But I couldn't save him. No matter how many pasts I went to, how many Michael Rohans I could warn, none of them were my dad. I'd come back to my home, and my Michael Rohan, the man who had raised me, was still dead.

It was a uniquely cruel form of time travel.

I stared at the badge on the coffee table. I still felt a near-crippling guilt; still felt I should have been able to do something.

I wondered if I would ever manage to pay my dues for that.

FOUR

IT TOOK A couple of weeks, but my life pretended to settle back into normalcy. My misstep with the Kendal case was a constant pressure in the back of my mind, but that's where it stayed. My extracurricular investigations, I kept to my own time. I tried to act as if nothing had happened.

But Jacob knew something was wrong.

Sixteen days after we left *Asia FX*, he finally asked, "Are you ever going to talk to me about what's the matter?"

We were downtown, eating lunch on the patio of a small Middle Eastern restaurant. The summer heat had broken, and the slight breeze made me comfortable in long sleeves again. I looked up from my falafel and felt everything seize up inside me. I wanted to tell him. I opened my mouth, but nothing came out.

He reached out to touch my hand, and inside I shuddered. "You haven't been yourself since the funeral," he said. "It hit you hard, didn't it?"

I closed my mouth and felt a shameful wave of relief. Very quietly, I told him, "It did. It still does." I was telling him the truth, but it felt like a lie.

Everything felt like a lie lately.

"You know I'm here for you, right?"

Why did he have to be so damn noble? I urged him silently, *If you want to make things easier for me, couldn't you just be a bit of an asshole?*

I reached over and put my hand on top of his, squeezing. "I know. I'm just not very good at this."

"Good at what?"

Expressing emotions. Dealing with people. Knowing what to say. "Accepting sympathy," I said.

"I'm sorry if I'm being too personal."

"No. You're not." I stared down at my falafel. "I'm just too . . ."

I lapsed into silence that felt as if it lasted hours, even though it probably only took him a few seconds to prompt, "Too what?"

"You don't have any idea what a mess I am."

"Name me a cop who isn't."

I raised my head, looking into his eyes, and I squeezed his hand again. "You," I told him.

"Thanks," he said quietly.

"I—" Words were catching in my mouth again. Holding his gaze flustered me, so I turned away. I pulled my hands back and tried again, "I'll be all right."

"I'm sure you will be, Dana. But you don't have to bear everything yourself just because you can."

I stood up, ignoring the remains of my falafel. "We should get back to work."

Anyone else probably would have pushed me, or at least would have noted my abrupt change in subject. Jacob knew me too well to do that. We drove back to the station in silence. Four or five times, I found myself *almost* saying something. I would glance at his profile and bite the inside of my lip, trying to come up with a way to start talking about the real problem.

How could I do it without it coming across as either a betrayal or an insane delusion?

Even during the short drive back, it was painfully obvious that I was avoiding talking to him. It made me feel even worse. Jacob didn't deserve that. I could imagine him wondering what he had done to piss me off. As we pulled into the parking garage, I managed to finally say something.

"It's me," I said, the words coming out in a panic as the car slid into the garage. I was suddenly very afraid that the drive would be done completely in silence, and I had an irrational fear that, if that happened, something irrevocable would happen to my relationship with Jacob.

He glanced over at me and asked, "What is you?"

"I don't want you to think I'm angry at you, anything like that." I sucked in a breath. "I appreciate that you care about what's going on with me. If I'm going to talk about this— If I talked to anyone—you would be—but I don't know how. I don't know if I can. There are things I don't—can't—talk about. It's not your fault. You didn't do something wrong. I'm not angry. Not at you. I'm such a mess."

Jacob pulled into a parking spot and looked at me, "That might be the longest non-work-related speech you've ever made to me."

"I don't want you to think it was something you did."

"I am touching a nerve, though, aren't I?"

I didn't have an answer for that.

FOR over two weeks I'd been waiting for the other shoe to drop. This was the day it did.

For the past two weeks I'd spent some time every day, behind my desk, looking through various criminal databases for recent arrests. I had to work them myself because for most of the cases on my desk, I had knowledge—names, addresses, license plate numbers—the source of which I couldn't explain. I was looking for Roscoe Kendal without much hope, since the identity on the driver's license I had seemed to be fictitious. The address didn't exist, and the name wasn't attached to any priors I could find.

Today I found him.

Kendal had been picked up for possession yesterday in Lindale after running a stop sign. Looking at the small mug shot on his on-line booking sheet, I knew it was the guy. He even seemed to be wearing the same hoodie.

Lindale still had him in custody.

I could have ignored it. He was in another jurisdiction, and without any obvious connections to the *Asia FX* robbery, he'd just go through for the possession bust and probably do some time. Letting it go would ensure that my mistake planting the gun would probably never be uncovered. They may have lifted Kendal's prints from the gun. I hadn't checked, but unless they had a suspect with whom to compare them to, they'd just stay in a file somewhere. Life wasn't CSI.

But if I left it like that, it would deny Mrs. Kim and her father any sort of justice or closure, just to cover my own screwup.

So I called Lindale. While I waited to be connected to the arresting officer, I stared at Kendal's face on the screen, wondering if the Kendal I had shot had managed to turn his life around in his world that wasn't quite mine, or if some sort of felonious destiny led him to be busted for possession in his own version of Lindale.

Someone on the other end of the line interrupted my thoughts, and I said, reflexively, "Detective Rohan, CPD."

"How can I help you?" The voice carried a hint of irritation, as if I hadn't quite answered his question.

I cleared my throat and continued. "This is a long shot, but I'm looking at a mug shot of a guy you arrested for possession about 3:30 yesterday afternoon. Roscoe Kendal?"

"Uh-huh. File's still on my desk."

"Well, looking at him, he could be a guy we have on video robbing a tattoo parlor two weeks ago. Killed the proprietor."

"You don't say." I heard a rustle of paper. "Did your guy make off with anything aside from cash?"

"A whole display case worth of costume jewelry."

The guy busted out laughing. After a moment, he said, "Detective

Rohan, this must be your lucky day. We were wondering what this guy was doing with a dozen nipple rings in a sandwich bag. Do you have someone who can identify the jewelry?"

I gave him the contact information for Mrs. Kim. Then I had him send copies of the guy's prints up to our lab. Even if the gun was eventually poisoned as evidence, they had a few prints from the display case. That, and the video, should be more than enough to seal the deal on the guy.

I hung up the phone, feeling a small weight lift. Whatever my mistake cost me, Mrs. Kim would still see her father's murderer put away.

"Dana?"

I turned to face the voice behind me. Jacob looked a little more concerned than usual. I smiled and tried to project an aura of mission accomplished. "I think we just found the guy from the *Asia FX* robbery."

"The tattoo place?"

"Guy was picked up on a traffic stop in Lindale with six ounces of weed and a dozen nipple rings."

"I hope he wasn't wearing all of them."

I was relieved enough to actually laugh at that. As I closed up what I was doing on the computer, I asked, "What's up?"

"We need to see Royce."

My hands only paused briefly when he mentioned Captain Royce's name. I had the ugly premonition that my relief had been premature. "What about?"

"Someone we're supposed to meet."

THE "someone" turned out to be Jessica Whedon, a lawyer from the "Office of Civil Rights Enforcement" in the Justice Department. Captain Royce made the introduction and then informed us that we were to cooperate fully with Ms. Whedon's investigation in a tone that suggested that we might have been inclined to do otherwise.

She was a brunette nearly a head shorter than me, short enough that there probably weren't many law enforcement jobs open to her. Most police departments, the FBI, and badge-bearing segments of the Justice Department would bar her for being barely over five feet tall.

Very deliberately, Jacob asked her, "What are you investigating?"

"My office does biannual reporting on law enforcement trends for the top twenty-five urban areas in the US. Statistically, your department is a significant outlier, and I'm here to develop background information to explain those statistics."

She smiled when she spoke, and her voice had the fluid cadence of a talk show host or a politician. Her face broadcast earnest warmth as genuine as the Yule Log they put on TV every Christmas. I felt an instant, almost visceral, dislike for the woman. It was only half due to the fact that I had some suspicion what those outlier statistics might consist of.

I didn't trust myself to speak, but Jacob asked the question for me. "What statistics?"

"The typical metrics we track. Convictions versus arrests versus the general crime rate over time and allocated over various demographic groups. Your arrest record, particularly for violent crime, is impressive, and when combined with the rate of conviction, it happens to be rather astounding."

"We just try and do our job, Ms. Whedon," Jacob said.

"And in the past seven years, you've done it exceptionally well." The insincere smile broadened a bit. "I hope my research will help benefit other departments. You're obviously doing something right here."

"We appreciate that, Ms. Whedon." Captain Royce beamed a smile that trumped Whedon's for pure hypocrisy. "My people are at your disposal. Now, if you could excuse us, I need to talk to Detectives Hightower and Rohan about a few things."

"Certainly." As she walked past us, she said, "Thank you very much for your cooperation."

The door was barely closed behind her when Jacob looked at our boss and said, in an even monotone, "With all due respect, sir. What the fuck is this about?"

Captain Royce frowned.

I finally managed to find my voice. "Sir, is someone accusing us of something?"

Captain Royce walked around the desk and settled roughly into his chair. He picked up a manila folder on his desk and said, "'There are lies, damn lies, and statistics.' Mark Twain." He opened the folder and pulled out a page that looked like a printout from someone's PowerPoint presentation. "To someone who hasn't been working in this department the past seven years, our arrest and conviction record is unusually good."

"Does the Justice Department routinely send out their lawyers to give people gold stars?" Jacob did not sound impressed.

"And the Office of Civil Rights Enforcement?" I added.

"A large proportion of the arrests and convictions are of minorities," Captain Royce said.

Jacob sighed. "They do realize the demographics of our jurisdiction?"

Captain Royce shrugged. "Someone in the Justice Department wanted an investigation. It's a pain in the ass, but I'm in no position to say no. That decision is above all our pay grades. You'll give her anything she needs, and she's going to go back to Washington with a glowing report on the exemplary operation we run here. Right?"

"Yes, sir," Jacob said.

"And," the Captain added, "If there's anything you think should be brought to my attention about our 'exemplary' record, now would be a good time to mention it."

The room became quiet and still, the only sound the soft buzz of a fluorescent light fixture above us. I felt cornered. Captain Royce looked at me, and for a moment I was convinced he had figured it all out; he knew what I was doing, how I had manipulated investigations, evidence— Then he looked at Jacob, and I realized I was being paranoid.

"Nothing?" he asked Jacob.

I said quietly, "Nothing that isn't in the paperwork we fill out every day." The lie came too easy.

"Good," the Captain said. "Keep it that way. I don't like surprises."

BEFORE I went home for the day, I received a message from the Lindale Police department. Mr. Kendal had confessed to the *Asia FX* robbery. I should have been happy, but I found myself wishing they had found the other gun.

FIVE

I WENT THROUGH the next several days feeling as if I was in a room without any exit, one that kept getting smaller and smaller. I slept poorly, and I began to have odd sensations from the Mark. At seemingly random times, I would feel a new pressure, as if an unseen hand was *almost* touching the lines on my back.

The sensation was not familiar, as if these unseen fingers belonged to someone—or something—different from the hands that pushed me through the fabric of time. The first time I felt it, I was in the car with Jacob, and I clutched the dashboard in a panic. I thought I might be using the Mark involuntarily, and I had a sudden nightmare of pushing myself into a world where this car wasn't, to tumble face-first into the speeding concrete below me—

"Dana? Are you all right?" He slowed the car and started pulling to the side of the road. I was hyperventilating, and my face was suddenly slick with sweat, but the world around me remained unchanged.

It took me a few moments before I could answer him. "I think I'm okay."

"Are you sure? You don't look good. Should we go to an emergency room?"

"No." I unclenched my hands from the dashboard. The sensation along the Mark was already fading, and the pounding of my heart was returning to normal.

The car was stopped by the curb now. He put it in park and turned to me, then reached out and placed a hand on my shoulder. I felt the pressure of his thumb against a swirl of the Mark through the fabric of my blouse. I thought the touch should freak me out, but after what I had just felt, it was reassuring. "What's the matter?" he asked.

I looked away, because I couldn't tell him the truth. Not the whole truth, anyway. "I think I just had a panic attack."

"I think I know what this is."

For a brief fearful moment I thought he really might know, even though there was no real way he could. "What?"

"You never took any time off when your mom died."

"No, I don't think so."

"You've been pushing yourself nonstop. You haven't taken time to breathe, much less grieve."

"I . . ." I trailed off. He had planted the seed, and now I wondered if my mental state could be manifesting in how I perceived my Mark. "I'm fine now, really." I tried to give him a confident smile, even though I felt like a wreck inside.

Whether or not he was right about the panic attack, he was right about one thing. I hadn't stopped to grieve.

Jacob let go of my shoulder and drove the car back onto the road. He glanced over at me and said, "If you need anything . . ."

"I'm fine now," I said, as if repetition could make it true.

OF course, it wasn't true.

Periodically, the Mark continued to give me these new sensations, and I was able to keep from reacting as severely to them. Tied up with it was the grief I was avoiding. Every day, something would hit me, and it would sink in that my family was gone. I'd feel a crushing loneliness that brought silent tears and almost made me reach for Jacob.

But it stayed "almost."

On top of everything else I felt, the seemingly random reactions of the Mark reminded me how little I actually knew about it—where it came from, what it *was*. If my mental state could suddenly start causing it to behave differently without any warning, my entire life was less stable than I had thought it was.

It took a few more days for me to nerve up and test that I still had some sort of control. Late evening, in the confines of my own townhouse, I pushed myself through layers of time just to reassure myself that, despite the new sensations, the Mark behaved as it always had. I still felt its fingers push me through different worlds, the same invisible companion touching me.

But in the world where my house was empty of any occupants, I felt the strange new sensation again, more intensely and more obviously different than the familiar touch of my Mark. It was a shock, like having a stranger walk in on something very private. I ran from it, pushing my way home and locking myself in my bedroom as if someone had been chasing me.

The Mark felt a part of me, but this was something else. It was as if a stranger was groping for me, their hands not quite touching my body.

That night I didn't sleep.

OF course, Whedon eventually asked for a ride-along.

It was the longest day of my police career, riding along with the Justice Department lawyer in the back seat, on my third day with barely two hours' sleep. To say I wasn't at my best was an understatement. Every question she'd ask, however innocuous, sounded like a potential accusation.

Ridiculously enough, the worst episode was when she asked about my car. I had driven some Charger police squads when I was just starting out as a cop, and I had fallen in love with the vehicle. Three years ago, to celebrate making detective, I had bought my own

Charger SRT8, with a 425 horsepower 6.1-liter Hemi. With custom rims and paint job, it ran over forty thousand dollars. I had paid cash.

When she asked, perhaps reasonably, how a cop on my salary could buy something like that for cash, I snapped a little.

"What are you trying to say?" My voice was brittle and too loud.

"It's just unusual—" she said.

"So fucking what?"

"Dana?" Jacob sounded startled at my outburst. "Maybe you should—"

"Should what?" I glared over my shoulder at the woman in the back seat. "I know. I should cooperate. You know what, I've *been* cooperating. And you know what? This little bitch is so disappointed that she hasn't found something wrong in the department that she's decided to dig into my personal life."

"I think you should calm down, Detective Rohan."

"Why?" I snapped. "I gave my life to this job. My reward is to get questioned because I do it too well? I should sit back and take it? I should just lie back and say, sure you can look all over my bank accounts and taxes and investments over the past five years—hell, the past ten years—just so I can prove to you I *earned* that fucking car?"

"Detective Rohan, I think you're out of line."

"I'm not the only one," I said. I turned around and sank back into the passenger seat.

THE sad thing was I had chosen to blow up about something that was completely defensible. Even with a subpoena and an auditor, no one would find anything untoward about my finances, no income streams that lacked explanation. I had never used my Mark to steal, even though it would have been laughably easy to do it.

I just used my abilities to pick good investments. A newspaper from next week was more valuable than a key to a jewelry store, even if it wasn't 100% accurate after said week came and went. The futures from which I got information were close enough that it wasn't a problem to multiply my cop's salary to afford my car and my townhouse. I had the capital gains taxes to prove it.

The car was really my only indulgence, and when Whedon questioned it, it felt as if she was questioning my identity. In a sense, she was. My car certainly received more attention from me than the sterile place I supposedly made my home. I think I'd spent more time picking out the after-market stereo in my car than I had all the furniture on my first floor combined.

When I got into my midnight-blue Charger, I settled more comfortably into the driver's seat than I sat in the chair in my living room. I told myself that it was all a bunch of psychoanalytical bullshit. I was stressed. I was tired. I was still trying to grieve. The woman had just gotten on my last nerve.

I didn't play any music and drove home to the rumble of the 6.1-liter Hemi. I shouldn't have to justify myself. It was Whedon who was turning her investigation into a fishing expedition. I just wished Jacob hadn't been present. I just wished—

The Mark hit me then, and it was a measure of my self-control that I didn't slam the Charger to a screeching halt. I slowed gently and pulled over to the curb before shifting into park. My arms had broken into gooseflesh as the sensation of strange hands almost touching me ran up and down the length of my back.

I looked behind me, briefly convinced that I had been chauffeuring a cliché serial killer in the back seat and he was about to grab my neck. Of course, there wasn't anyone hiding behind me. I stared into the empty back seat, then glanced up to look out the rear window at the empty street behind me. The sun had gone down, the sky had purpled to a point between dusk and full night, and the streetlights were just now coming on. It was far enough past rush hour that the street was empty of traffic.

Despite the weird feelings from my Mark, I scolded myself for being paranoid. Whatever the sensations meant, I had been having them off and on for a few days and there had been no sign that the unfamiliar almost-touch was connected to anything outside my own screwed-up mind. I sighed and turned around.

A face appeared at my driver's side window. The only reason I didn't scream out in surprise was because my body had decided to stop breathing at exactly the same time. The only noise that came from me was a long, ragged wheeze, as if someone had kicked me hard in the gut.

He had to be homeless. He was cadaverously thin, and his hair was a shoulder-length halo of tangled gray that wrapped his face so that it was impossible to determine where the hair ended and the beard began. His eyes were sunken, so in the glare from the streetlight his face was nearly a skull. It would have been generous to call his clothes rags.

He was pale enough to be a ghost, but he clearly wasn't, since he stood close enough to the door for his breath to fog the window.

My hand reached for the door lock even though it was already locked. I stopped and placed my hand on the door handle. I sucked in a breath, composing myself even as my Mark decided to bring another unfamiliar hand to almost touch me.

I looked into the old man's face and asked in reasonable cop-to-unhinged-civilian tones, "Can I help you, sir?"

He responded by slapping both his hands on the window so hard that I feared the glass might break. Then he started screaming things in a language that wasn't English, spraying flecks of saliva across the window.

I leaned back as he screamed, the closed window a poor protector of my personal space. He seemed completely insane and could have been babbling complete gibberish. I couldn't even guess what language it was, if it was any language. But the more he railed, the more it felt familiar, the more it felt as if I should understand him.

For a moment, I thought I did. A phrase crossed his lips, and I was certain I knew the meaning behind it.

"Wealcan has fallen! They'll come for you! The shadows are coming!"

My eyes widened, and I said to the man, "Please, sir, calm down."

He shook his head and redoubled his babbling, so I lost the thread connecting meaning to his words. He was so distressed, he could have been speaking English and have been just as unintelligible. He was pounding on the window with his fists now. He wanted in, and every rational impulse said: *bad idea*. A homeless schizophrenic was having a psychotic break in front of me, and despite the tantalizing thought that I might have understood part of what he had said, I was keeping a barrier between me and him.

I had just pulled out my cell phone to call 911, when he abruptly shut up and stopped pounding the window. He turned toward the front of the car, and the shadows moved on his face as he raised his head. I could see his eyes then, colored a blue so light they were almost gray. I saw the last of the violent emotion drain from them—I still couldn't tell if it had been anger or panic—leaving a quiet melancholy in its wake.

There was something familiar in those eyes I had never seen before. And in the deepest part of my soul I felt I needed to know this man, understand who he was, what he meant. I needed to know why his tragically sad gaze was familiar, and why I could understand some of what he said when I knew no language other than English.

I opened the door before I saw what he was looking at. It was a mistake. The sudden feeling that I knew this man, or that I *should* know this man, had overwhelmed my situational awareness. He was walking toward the front of the car as I stepped out and said, "Sir? Please. Wait. Who are you?"

I stood next to the door and realized that things were seriously wrong. My Mark ached with two unfamiliar presences, one of which—I now thought—was old, strong, and bore a strange familiarity. Something in my thoughts that split-second associated that sensation with the old man standing with his back to me. The other one was cold, slow, and heavy. Alien. Coming closer . . .

There was something approaching us from down the street, a lumbering shadow between the pools of light cast by the streetlights. It was man-shaped, but larger, with thicker limbs. When it stepped into the light, I first thought I was seeing someone dressed in some sort of medieval plate mail, down to the long sword he carried in his right hand.

But as the armor moved, and streetlights reflected off the etched steel and polished brass, I heard more than just the clanking of padded metal armor. I heard the clicking of gears and the whine of some sort of engine. In the joints I saw hoses and mechanical bits that did not belong in old plate mail. Along the segmented plates of armor, I could see screws and bolts.

This armor came from a machine shop, not a blacksmiths'.

"What the hell?" I said.

In front of me, I heard the old man utter a syllable whose meaning was completely clear to me.

"No."

I was already back in cop mode, I edged out from behind the civilian as I brought out the Jericho. I held the weapon down and ready, trigger finger along the barrel as I called out, "You, in the armor! I'm the police. You need to drop the weapon and stop moving, *now!*"

Its mechanical approach didn't stop, and for a moment I wondered if there was actually a human being inside. My gun rose a bit, the barrel aimed more or less between the armor's knees and groin. The figure was still ten yards away and moving slowly, so my finger didn't wrap the trigger just yet. "Stop moving and drop the weapon!"

It hesitated and slowly turned its helmet in my direction. I realized that its focus had been completely on the old man. As the helmet moved, I saw the streetlight shine into slits in the face and I caught what might have been the glint of a human eye. I raised my voice, both to impress the life-and-death seriousness of the situation, and because the dude inside the armor could not have the best hearing wrapped up in a cocoon of clanking and hissing metal.

"*Now!* Put the sword on the ground and step away from—"

I hadn't forgotten about the old man, I had made a point of moving laterally toward the center of the street to keep him out of the potential line of fire. I kept him in my peripheral awareness as I focused on the main threat, but I was one person, and I had no warning that he might be as potentially dangerous as the guy with the sword. I caught his movement out of the corner of my eye, running toward the armor.

I had a split-second to act, but my only two options were shoot, or not to shoot. The old man had armed himself with a chunk of asphalt from the side of the road and was raising it up.

If the guy had come at me, or had a more effective weapon, or headed toward a guy who wasn't wrapped in metal armor, I would have shot. As it was, the futility of the attack was obvious even in the moment I had to react.

"Stop moving!" I yelled at him, suspecting he didn't understand my words. "Stop and drop the—"

The air resonated with a massive clang as the old man brought the black chunk of asphalt down on the armor, striking the joint between the helmet and the left shoulder. My gun rose, and my finger found the trigger as the armored guy responded with a swing impossibly fast for something that looked so heavy.

The long sword caught the old man across the midsection so hard that the man's feet left the ground. I fired at the armor's center of mass, the gunshot deafening. A spark of a ricochet bloomed in the right side of the armor's torso, under the sword arm that was still swinging.

The old man fell to the ground, slamming into a light pole. The sword glistened red now.

I fired again, and another spark bloomed on the lower half of the armor's breastplate.

Damn hollow-points! They were SOP for police firearms because the bullet fragmented on impact, throwing all the force into the target. Not only did it stop the guy you were shooting at a lot more effectively, but there's no blow through the body where the bullet keeps going and kills some bystander fifty feet away.

Problem was, they're crap against body armor—and with what this dude was wearing, I was going to have a problem.

He moved toward the old man, and I took the dangerous step of aiming at the helmet where I had a better chance of doing some damage.

Another step and the man in the armor disappeared.

He didn't slip into shadow, or run, or hide behind something. He moved forward and ceased to exist. And when the man—armor, bloody sword, and all—vanished from under the center of a streetlight's glare, I felt something that I could almost call an alien inverse of what I felt when the Mark pushed me through time.

Did he just do what I . . .

I ran to the old man, holstering the gun and pulling my cell phone back out. He was crumpled, unconscious at the base of a streetlight. His lower body was already scarlet, and he lay in a dark pool that was spreading underneath him. I had some thought of trying to render first aid, but the wound was the width of his abdomen, and I could see viscera already pushing out.

Still, I tried to help him as I gave directions to the 911 operator. While I did what I could to keep the man's insides inside, I realized the odd sensations from my Mark were fading away. I was not shocked when the paramedics showed up and told me that the old man was beyond help, and there wasn't anything I could have done.

I wasn't even shocked when they lifted his corpse onto the gurney and, under the ragged shirt and smears of blood, I saw the swirling pattern of another Mark across the old man's back.

SIX

I DID NOT permit myself to react for at least an hour after the event. I tried to keep myself under some semblance of control as the paramedics took the old man's corpse. And when the cops questioned me, I told as much of the truth I thought I could get away with. I was so sick of deception that I probably told them way more than I should have.

I described the killer, some nut with a long sword and armor, and I added that it was "possibly home-made" so that I didn't sound completely crazy. I gave them a more-or-less accurate blow-by-blow of what happened, including the two shots I fired. When they asked me what I hit, I told them I'd probably missed the shot. Again, to make the story sound more plausible. Also, no disappearing. In my statement, the suspect ran off while I chose to try and render first aid to the victim.

I had to give a version of that statement twice, first for the original officers responding, then to a couple of detectives who were probably from Internal Affairs. There's always an IA investigation when an officer discharges a weapon. I wouldn't be allowed back on the street until IA came to a conclusion about the righteousness of the shoot. I didn't know how long it was going to be, but I was probably looking at the rest of the week at least.

I leaned my head back in the seat of my Charger, waiting for the latest detective to return, and I thought that at least there would be no more ride-alongs with Ms. Whedon.

It was a self-destructive thought, because I suddenly began wondering what the lawyer was going to make of my off-duty weapon discharge. It seemed almost certain that the woman would make it into something sinister, especially after my earlier outburst.

One of the detectives came back with a clipboard and a plastic evidence bag. I was nodding even before the man said, "We need to take your gun for evidence."

I took it out, pulled out the magazine, and unchambered the last round. Gun, magazine, and lone bullet all went into the bag. He examined it once it was in the bag. "That isn't standard issue, is it?"

"No, it's not the department's gun. It's mine."

He held it up to the streetlight and read, "Israeli Military Industries?"

"Jericho 941. I prefer the way it handles."

He slid the clipboard toward me while he hefted my gun. "Light," he said.

I grunted agreement while filling out a description of my weapon for the chain of evidence, signing and dating the form. I gave it back to him, "I got one with a polymer frame."

"Like a Glock?"

"Like a Glock with a safety." Now I got to wonder what the lawyer was going to make of the fact that I preferred to carry my own weapon rather than a department-issue one.

He took the paperwork and the Jericho, leaving me a receipt. I felt exposed without the gun. He said, "I think we're done here."

You, maybe, I thought.

"Don't beat yourself up over it," the detective added.

"Pardon?"

"Missing the guy," he told me.

"Thanks."

I rolled up the window and drove home.

I pulled into the garage, allowed the door to slide down behind me, and finally allowed myself to react. Or, more accurately, I lost the ability to hold in my reaction. The moment I let go of the steering wheel, my hands began shaking. I stared at them as if they belonged to someone else, and even as the front of my mind was asking, *What's the matter with me?* my vision was blurring.

I still saw the old man pounding on my window. I still heard him talking to me in a language I shouldn't be able to understand. Saw him attack the armored figure. Saw him cut down. I still felt his viscera sliding under my shaking hands as life drained from his body.

And, with it, I saw my mother resting in a coffin, her face a livid mask that spoke more of the mortician's art than it did of anything living.

Have I cried for her yet?

The question slammed me like a sledgehammer to my gut, and the self-imposed restraints to my emotions crumbled at the impact. I bent over the steering wheel, sobbing so violently that I made no real sound. I just drew in spastic violent breaths that stabbed my lungs and made my whole body tremble. Tears burned my cheeks, running down my neck to dampen my collar. I slammed my fists into my thighs like a six-year-old having a tantrum, hard enough that I was dimly aware I was bruising myself.

I didn't think. For a time that could have been minutes, could have been hours, my entire awareness was consumed completely by a white-hot flare of grief that burned through everything else in my brain. I screamed at the universe that had taken everything from me; sometimes I screamed words, and sometimes it was an inarticulate wail, and sometimes it was words in a language I didn't remember. I was probably lucky that I was muffled by being inside the car and inside the garage, or my neighbors probably would have called 911.

When I came back to myself, I was draped across the wheel, sucking in deep breaths. My throat hurt, my eyes burned, and my nose was running. I felt a deep ache in the tops of my legs.

I pushed myself into a sitting position and composed myself before I got out of the car. Once inside my house, I walked into the bathroom to wash all the traces of my breakdown off my face.

After violently scrubbing myself with a washcloth, I looked up and asked my memory of the old man, "Who are you?"

I could have been asking the reflection staring back at me from the bathroom mirror. The red-rimmed eyes, the wild hair, the flushed cheeks, the painful frown that was almost a sneer—I could easily see the feral child my parents had adopted.

"Who am I?" I asked myself.

I turned away from the mirror quickly, telling myself, "I'm Dana Rohan. I'm a cop. And I am going to find out what the hell is going on."

I returned to the scene at three that morning.

I wore a new holster carrying a 9mm Beretta that I'd retired five years ago. The gun was heavier than I was used to, but it shared the same ammunition as the Jericho—and the weight on my hip was a comfort against the onrushing weirdness.

The Mark had been quiescent since shortly after the armored swordsman had vanished in front of me. I now suspected what those alien sensations had meant, and I had returned to the scene of the murder to confirm part of my suspicions.

I stepped out of my parked car into a dead street in a dead city. This late at night, especially in the middle of the week, the life of the city retreated to small burning embers scattered at random. A few fast food joints, a gas station here or there, a few bars close to residential areas . . . those were the places where lights burned and people still moved. Here, close to downtown, everything was dark and closed.

I rested my fingers on the fender of my car and told myself what I needed to do would only take a few moments, especially since I was pretty sure what I would find.

I stepped away from my car and walked into the shadows hugging a closed storefront. Cloaked in the shadow of the doorway, no one looking on, I pulled the Mark into myself, asking its invisible fingers to press against me and push forward. One step and my car disappeared, leaving the street empty.

I walked forward to the base of the streetlight where the old man had bled to death. I remembered the feeling of slick flesh moving uncomfortably under my hand as I had attempted the impossible task of stopping the bleeding.

No trace of blood here, in a world whose clocks ran fifteen or twenty minutes behind my own.

I didn't expect any.

Now, removed from the world where I lived, I was less concerned with being observed. Anyone here who saw a grim blonde woman vanish would never connect it back to me or the life I had built within my own world. I sucked in a breath and allowed the Mark to push me further.

I walked around the base of the lamppost, the Mark pushing me through worlds with a shuddering pulselike intensity, the universe a stop-motion fantasy around me, more ephemeral than real.

I stopped when I knew I walked the threshold across a world that now overlapped the time when I had met the old man. Inside, the glow of the Mark's touch faded, like a second pulse gradually growing fainter. I stood, observing.

This world matched the early evening I remembered, the streetlights having just come on, the sky purple with only the barest hint of fading daylight.

And, unlike every other time I had done this, I saw no sign of the crime I was investigating. It gave me a chill far beyond the receding afterglow of using the Mark. I had stood in all manner of alternate pasts before, and while I knew they were not the pasts I knew—I wasn't in them, after all—I had always been able to walk toward a past where some version of what I sought was taking place.

Here, I didn't have anything: no assailant, no victim.

If they were like me, with their own Mark, it made sense. If they were like me, they would be unique among the various pasts and futures I walked to. Perhaps it was that uniqueness that allowed us to walk between them.

The man in the armor had vanished into some other world, moved beyond my ability to sense his presence.

That was what I had been feeling with my Mark, wasn't it? Invisible alien fingers almost touching, a feeling I had never sensed before—it was the presence of those others. Other Marks.

When I walked home through the veil of worlds, I wondered if either of them had sensed my Mark. Could that have been why the old man had been pounding on my window?

I stood by my car and shuddered a minute, thinking my own Mark might be touching other Marks, leading them to me. I froze, concentrating on the sensations from my Mark, trying to feel the presence of any others.

At the moment, I felt nothing.

Maybe if the armored man was too far away for me to sense, he was too far away to sense me. I didn't know if that was good or bad. He hadn't seemed anything but hostile, but he was also the only living person I knew of who was somehow like me.

I came home after four, and I slept, but not well. I had nightmares of shadows chasing me, chasing my family, and they all spoke a language I shouldn't understand.

SEVEN

I SPENT THE day sleepwalking through my job, tied to my desk composing reports, answering e-mail, and nursing a headache induced by sleep deprivation. I only talked to Jacob long enough to explain what was going on with me and IA, and not to expect me to do anything beyond paperwork until they finished their investigation.

That caused a glance at Whedon, who was standing back and waiting for us to finish our conversation. He sighed and whispered to me, "Almost makes me wish I had to shoot someone."

"You can handle one lawyer."

"I'm sure I can, but if I do, I think it would get me arrested."

Even though I felt like crap, I couldn't help smiling. "It's justified force, self-defense."

"Yeah, but is it ever a good idea to piss off a lawyer?"

My smile went away as I thought of my outburst yesterday. "I guess I'll find out."

He squeezed my shoulder and tried to be reassuring. "It will all work out, Dana."

I watched him walk away. He had a self-assured stride that

reminded me of a panther. *A panther that has no idea what he's talking about.*

AFTER an interview with Internal Affairs officers, I was officially put on administrative leave. The IA officers were refreshingly free of bullshit, which was a relief after days of dealing with Whedon. They didn't think I'd be on leave for more than 48 hours, given the facts of the case. However, they also didn't want me doing any more paperwork since, technically, that was still working.

At three in the afternoon, I had nothing left to do. I wasn't ready to go home, so I went to the gym. When I walked in, I had the room pretty much to myself. There was one other guy, someone I didn't know, a curly-haired kid who looked barely out of high school. He was on the weight machine, doing bench presses. I noticed him glance at me when I came in, but I was in no mood to talk, so I went to the opposite side of the room to the treadmills.

I warmed up slowly, but soon I was going full out. I found the rhythm of it comforting, pumping my legs, my lungs, my heart. It allowed me to switch off my brain for a while. One of the reasons I felt like crap most of the day wasn't just the lack of sleep, but the fact I'd slept in too late to do my morning run. My body was used to two miles a day, and it became cranky if it didn't get it.

The kid moved to various stations on the weight machine, and he took longer than he needed to set the weights on the leg press—looking at me while he did so.

It was almost amusing watching his attempt at being so self-consciously macho.

I tweaked the controls to angle the treadmill up. If I was going to run inside, I might as well take advantage of it for the workout. My normal run was mostly on the flat, without any significant hills. Here, I had the chance to run up a twenty-degree grade. I attacked it almost as a response to the kid, who was doing leg reps with something like two hundred pounds.

I think he might have done fifteen.

The readout treadmill told me I had reached my second mile, and I decided to do another mile up the grade. I pushed myself up a nonexistent mountain as the kid stopped his weight training and looked at me without even trying to hide the fact he was looking at me.

He seemed to want to say something, and I wondered why. I wasn't the greatest looker even when I cleaned myself up. Right now? I was pushing myself, wearing a gray sweat suit that was practically soaked black with perspiration, and random strands of hair had come loose from my ponytail to stick to the side of my face. I could catch a glimpse of myself reflected in the windows on the other side of the weight machine. I looked as if I had just climbed out after falling into a swimming pool.

I wished I could follow up my workout with a swim, but I had yet to find a swimsuit that completely covered the Mark.

The kid never said what was on his mind. He left without talking to me. I didn't know if I was disappointed or relieved.

The treadmill beeped at me; my last mile was done. I lowered the grade and gradually slowed my pace for another quarter mile to cool down before stopping.

I had moved on to punching the crap out of the heavy bag, pretending it was Whedon, when Jacob entered the gym.

I didn't notice him enter until he said, "Aren't you hot in that getup?"

I dropped my fists and stepped back from the heavy bag. Jacob stood in the doorway, watching me. In his hand was a manila folder. I shrugged and said, "So?" I walked to a chair where I'd thrown a towel and a bottle of water. I wiped the sweat off my face and said, "You know I'm off duty until IA dots all their 'I's and crosses all their 'T's?"

"I know."

I threw the towel down and picked up the water.

He continued. "They're probably being more anal than usual with our little Justice Department lawyer running around. It's not like you hit anything."

The way he said it, I knew it was a bit of gentle ribbing. I couldn't even bring myself to smile. I *had* hit something.

"I brought you this," he said. "It's a copy of the file on your John Doe from last night. You were asking for it, weren't you?"

I had. Not that I had mentioned it to Jacob. I had asked the guys in charge of the investigation. "Thank you," I said quietly.

"Why did you want to see this?"

"Are you serious? I had a man die in front of me—" My voice caught and turned into a pained whisper. "He came to me. I tried to stop the bleeding."

"Dana?"

"My hands were inside him. . . ." My voice trailed off and I was panicked that I might start crying again, but somehow I held that back.

"Dana, are you okay?"

I was quiet for several seconds before I said flatly, "No."

"What's going on with you?"

"Do they have a picture of the victim in that file?"

He nodded.

"His back?"

"Yeah. He's got an elaborate tattoo, a full back piece—"

I turned away from him and began sucking in deep breaths. I had been alone for too long, and I had no idea if I was strong enough to do what I was thinking of doing.

"Dana?"

"Shh, give me a moment." I think I was shaking a little bit. I still had no real way to articulate what was wrong. *Everything* was wrong. Ever since Mom died, I had felt as if all my carefully arranged life had begun sliding into something I didn't know, something I couldn't control. Not only was I torn up from losing the last family I ever had, I was aching over the loss of this complete stranger who shared my Mark. A stranger . . .

I wasn't reacting as if he was a stranger. I felt as if he was family. The Mark on him, like mine—what if he was a lost connection to my "real" family. Was that really what I was thinking? The idea hit me almost as hard as my mom's death.

I felt alone, abandoned—and I'd done all I could to push away the one person who cared. Why couldn't I talk to Jacob?

I didn't understand myself anymore, if I ever had.

"Dana?" he repeated quietly.

I held my hand up without turning around. He said nothing more. If I did not start telling him what was happening, who would I tell? Everything that happened lately told me that the life I was pretending to live existed on borrowed time. Was I going to wait until it collapsed around me and just slipped away?

Didn't he deserve something before that happened, some sort of explanation?

If things were going to fall apart, wouldn't it be better if it was on my own terms?

I bit my lip and said, "Jacob? I don't show anyone this."

"What?"

I sucked in a breath. Not everything, not all at once, but I could start. I grabbed the zipper on my top and yanked it down before I had a chance to reconsider. Then I shrugged out of the soaked top of my sweat suit, allowing it to fall down and drop to my waist. From there up, all I wore was a black sports bra. I heard him suck in a breath.

Despite the bra, I felt as naked as I had when I'd been discovered in the shower by a Michael Rohan who had not been my father. I felt his gaze tracing my Mark, my secret scars, as if he was looking into the most intimate part of my life. As if, with the swirls of the Mark, he could see the way it rooted inside me, the way it made me feel.

I could feel a flush burn across the breadth of my exposed skin, its surface going from chilled to burning in a wave of something that was almost shame.

A small, terrified part of my mind screamed, *What are you doing?*

My answering thought was only half-convinced. *If I don't start trusting someone, I will always be alone.*

After an eternity feeling his gaze on my back, Jacob said, "That is amazing work."

You have no idea how amazing. I pulled the top of my sweat suit back on. The damp fabric now felt frigid against my skin. I turned around to study his face, looking for signs of some sort of reaction. I don't know what I was expecting, if I was expecting anything.

I think I saw puzzlement.

"You can see why I work out dressed like this."

"Yes." Then he shook his head. "No."

"What do you mean?"

"It's such an elaborate back piece. Why . . ." He trailed off, studying my face. I realized he didn't know how to go on. He didn't want to upset me, but I had opened the door to so many questions that he would have never dared ask me before.

I asked for him. "Why would I get such a dramatic tattoo, only to spend all my life hiding it from people?"

"Yes."

"Because I didn't put it there."

Jacob looked at me, puzzled for a moment, then his expression darkened. "Someone did that against your will? What happened?"

I opened my mouth and stopped. I was suddenly paralyzed again, unable to reveal my secrets. What was the matter with me? I had exposed myself to Jacob; he had seen the heart of my mystery, and he was still here. . . .

He was still here.

I realized that, on some level, I had expected that seeing the Mark on my back would drive him away. I had expected him to react cruelly, like the children who mocked me in grade school or the teachers who thought my markings were disruptive. I could still hear the chanting, half the words I didn't know because I had still been learning English. *Tramp, ho, slut . . .*

I could deal with mockery. I didn't know what to do with concern.

"Dana?"

"It is a long story," I said. I turned away from him again. "Damn, that's a weak cliché."

"I have time."

"I—"

"Why don't you tell me over dinner? You can talk as long as you want."

"You're asking me out?" I said in slow disbelief.

I looked across at him and saw no trace of mockery in his face. In fact, the lines of his face softened just enough to make him look vulnerable. His smile wasn't forced, but it was tentative, almost as if the words represented a risk on a par with revealing the Mark. "You look like you need to sit down and have something to eat."

As bad as I was at understanding people on a personal level, I knew then that I could hurt him badly by withdrawing again. "I . . . Thank you."

"Over dinner, say as much as you need to," he said. "All of it, none of it. I see how hard it is for you."

"I need to go shower," I turned to face the locker rooms because I didn't want him to see my eyes tear up. "I'll meet you downstairs; I'll follow your car."

"I'll see you in a few minutes."

"Yeah." *Thank you.*

EVEN though I was the only one in the women's locker room, the way I moved in that environment was second nature. I stripped with my back to a wall, and a large towel was over my shoulders before I stepped away from the corner of the room. I stood under the showerhead farthest from the entrance, by the tile wall. Again, my back faced the wall as if I was expecting an attack.

It was how I survived gym in high school. Somehow, I had

managed to eke through the minimum PE requirement without drawing attention to my back—though I think the Mark was smaller then. It had been years since I had worn only a T-shirt in public.

When I shut off the shower, the towel went over my shoulders again.

I was still alone in the locker room. Exiting the shower, I passed a full-length mirror. I stopped a moment, glancing at myself. My oversized towel covered everything, which was why I had bought it. I saw nothing of the Mark in my reflection.

Something made me unwrap the towel. I dropped it like I had dropped my top in front of Jacob, shrugging it off my shoulders so that it dropped in a deep arc between my elbows, sagging to just between my hips, revealing everything from my shoulders down to the small of my back.

I stared at myself, turning away from the mirror. I could see about half of the Mark crawling across my skin, thick black lines emerging from a twisted spiral heart six inches above the small of my back to embrace shoulders and hips without ever crossing themselves, branching and rebranching to echo the whole mazelike pattern in repeatedly smaller scales; like a black, leafless vine growing across my skin, twisting into elaborate spirals.

It resembled a tribal tattoo, and it also resembled a Celtic spiral pattern, and it resembled neither. It could have been a representation of the tree of life if the tree did not distinguish between roots and crown or the spaces in between.

In the end, the Mark resembled nothing so much as itself, which is why I knew the old man was somehow connected to me. His Mark was the only thing I had ever seen that bore the same style as my own Mark.

I thought I heard a noise and quickly pulled the towel back around myself. I stood a moment, heart racing, but I was still alone.

I went back to my locker to get dressed.

EIGHT

IT WAS STRANGE, going out to dinner with Jacob. I don't know why it felt so alien. It was something people did all the time without thinking about it, like driving a car or brushing one's teeth or using an ATM machine. Just because it wasn't something I ever do . . .

Of course, that's why it felt strange. I didn't socialize with people. For all I tried to act normal, I really wasn't normal. If I was really honest with myself, I had to admit that the Mark was only part of it. It might not even be the largest part.

Jacob was more accommodating than I had the right to expect. He didn't push me to talk about anything, when I trailed off into silence, he just fell into the almost-scripted pattern of small talk about work that filled every lunch hour we'd spent together over three years. Nothing personal, nothing threatening . . .

It was wrong for the setting. He had led me to a steak house down in the Flats, all low lighting and wood paneling. Lunch was paper plates, plastic silverware, and condiments that came in a little foil packet. Here, a fresh cut flower sat in a bud vase on our table, and the menu didn't even have prices printed on it. It might have been his favorite restaurant, but if it was, I didn't think he could afford to eat here very often.

While we ate our salads, he was quietly deconstructing Jessica Whedon's attempts to unearth some sort of racial bias on his part over the course of an otherwise pointless conversation with her. I finally said, quietly, "I'm sorry."

He placed down his fork. "For what?"

"For not knowing how to do this."

"You're fine."

"No."

Silence filled the air, growing almost solid, like a wall between us. I knew I had built the wall with all the things I had never said.

I was the only one who could break it.

"There are a lot of things I've never told you," I finally said.

"But things you want to tell me now?"

"Yes. No. I don't know, really. These aren't things I talk about. Ever. I think I need to talk to someone, and you're the only one I have to talk to—and it is asking way too much of you."

"Dana, you didn't force me to come here. I'm here because I want to help."

I forced a weak smile. "And I can't help thinking it's only because you don't know what it is you're dealing with."

He shrugged and said, "There's only one way to find out."

He was right.

I had a choice. I could talk to him and risk driving him away for good, or I could return to the silence and know I'd never have him as more than a coworker.

"There's a lot," I said finally.

"Whatever you think you need to tell me."

I think I need to tell you everything. And I don't know if I can.

The waiter, with impeccable timing, came with our entrees, and I had a blessed moment to reflect on what I was going to do, what I was going to tell him. And more importantly, what I *wasn't* going to tell him.

I couldn't tell him everything. Not all at once.

When the waiter was gone, I told Jacob, "I was adopted."

Jacob nodded slowly. I could read in his expression that he read a good part of the significance I had placed in the word. More than was in the flat statement.

"My dad, Michael Rohan, was a uniform working down in the Flats. Twenty-two years ago he found a naked six-year-old girl, rooting in trash bins for food. She was filthy, feral, violent, and didn't speak any language anyone could identify. She was identified only by a large abstract tattoo on her back."

"You?" Jacob asked. "That happened to you? What happened?"

"I don't know. No one does. I don't have many coherent memories from before the point I started learning English. The doctors all agreed I suffered some sort of trauma, but no one could get any details from me. I don't even remember my dad finding me, or what I was doing on the street."

"Nothing?"

"My real memories start around seven or eight. When I think of my parents, my family, the only image I have is Mom and Dad, the people who adopted me."

"Your birth parents?"

"No clue. Dad started fostering me shortly after he found me. I'm not even sure how long it was before they legally adopted me."

Jacob nodded.

There was something about his expression that worried me. "What is it?"

"Just my cop brain engaging inappropriately."

"Tell me what you're thinking."

"Just the type of investigation that would have caused. Hard to believe that there weren't any clues to your identity."

I nodded. "I know. It's hard to believe myself."

"Are you sure they found nothing?"

I said, "Yes." But Jacob had just put the itch of something into my brain. Yes, Dad had told me the story, on several occasions. But he was talking to a nine- or ten-year-old. By the time I was a teenager, it was not a subject I had wanted to talk about. Then I wanted to be normal, and my past wasn't normal.

Everything I knew about my origins came from a story told to a child. What had Dad omitted? What didn't I remember? Suddenly, another part of my life felt as if it was crumbling.

"Dana? Is everything okay?"

"Huh?" I realized I had stopped talking.

"I hit a nerve again, didn't I?"

"No, it's not you." I forced myself to go on, talking about what I did remember.

I told him about the Mark, at least how it affected me growing up.

It had been the strangest thing about the girl Michael Rohan had found. A six-year-old with a tattoo was unusual, and alarming, by itself. Such marks were usually something homemade inflicted by stoned teenage parents with a sewing needle and ink from a ballpoint pen.

My Mark was nothing so crude. Even at six, it covered my back fully, a strange interwoven pattern drawn in curving ebon strokes.

For an artist to do something like that would require the skill of someone like the late proprietor of *Asia FX* over the course of weeks, if not months. I told Jacob of my few memories of Dad taking me to places like that, showing my back to the men who worked there. I told Jacob how my own Mark seemed to frighten and fascinate them.

"You've had it for so long," Jacob asked, "how is it not distorted or faded? What I saw looked . . ."

"Freshly inked?"

"I don't think I've ever seen a piece that dark."

I sucked in a breath. "It's not a normal tattoo," I said. "It may not even be a tattoo. Over the years, it's grown."

His expression told me I had reached the edge of his credulity. We weren't going to talk about what the Mark really was, or what it did. Not tonight.

But there were enough other things to tell him.

I told him how isolated I was in school, how I tried to hide my difference, and how I grew into being an almost normal teenager. Then I told him how I decided to become a cop.

"It was because I lost my dad. Because of the stupid and pointless way he was shot."

"What happened?"

"A month after my seventeenth birthday, he was called to a domestic. A bad one. The husband was high on meth, the wife had a skull fracture, and their three-year-old had a broken arm and was unconscious."

"Christ, what a mess."

I nodded, frowning, remembering. "My dad tried to control the situation, and he was preoccupied with subduing the husband while his partner removed the child from the scene for the paramedics. No one noticed the wife grab a gun. She didn't mean to hurt my dad, but it was a .44. Two of the shots passed right through her husband and into my dad's chest. One clipped his aorta. Her husband had three more holes in him, and he outlived my dad by about twenty minutes."

"I'm sorry."

I didn't explain to him the nature of the guilt I still felt over that. I could have gone to some future, seen some version of those events, and I could have warned my dad. I had grown up enough to know intellectually that my guilt made no sense, with or without the Mark, but I'd yet to come up with a way to explain that to myself so it sunk in.

"When I lost my mom, I lost all the family I'd ever known. No grandparents left. Dad was an only child. . . ."

"Your mom?"

I snorted. "An aunt, I suppose. Mom's sister—but I've never seen her. Apparently, when they adopted me, Mom's sister objected. She decided that Dad was somehow manipulating her sister into taking care of a damaged child. Mom did not take it well. Her sister didn't even show up at the funeral. They were so estranged that I don't even know what the woman looks like or where to find her if I wanted to."

"You don't want to?"

"The woman wants no part of me. The feeling's mutual. I don't have a family anymore."

When I said it, I felt the itch Jacob had planted in my brain earlier. Could Dad have known something more about where I'd come from? What was in that box in my bedroom closet? The one with my name on it, the one I was almost frightened to look into.

"You're pondering something," Jacob said.

"Just some old papers I have, pictures and stuff from Mom's condo." I changed the subject as if I was still afraid of the box and what it contained. "You understand now why I'm interested in John Doe? You saw the picture in his file?"

"Yes."

"You saw how he was marked, and how I am marked?"

Jacob nodded slowly. "You have some connection to that man?"

"I don't know. I think so. He didn't speak English, yet he ran up to my car and babbled things at me as if I was supposed to understand him. As if he knew me."

"I can see how that would be distressing—"

"Jacob, I think I *did* understand him. He wasn't speaking any language I know of. But I understood part of it."

He leaned back and looked at me. I didn't know if the look was critical or sympathetic. In the depths of whatever he was thinking, most of the emotional cues in his expression seemed to fade, as if he wasn't quite here anymore. I had an urge to reach across the table and grab his arm, pull him back into the present, back to me.

When he spoke, I realized that he hadn't left me. He had just left the restaurant. "Dana, do you know what language you spoke when you were a child? Before you learned English?"

"No. Dad told me that the doctors, at some point, had decided that I had invented my own language. Apparently, it's been known to happen."

"But you think this John Doe spoke the same language?"

"Unless I imagined I understood what he said."

"What do you think he said?"

"'Wealcan has fallen. They'll come for you. The shadows are coming.' That's what I remember."

"Wealcan?"

"I don't know. It might be a word I didn't understand, but it feels like a name."

"Can you say it in the original language?"

I had to think hard, as if I was pulling long unused switches in my brain. However, I could still see the old man at my window, still hear his words, and I was able to slowly pull it out, syllable by syllable.

He listened, and finally said, "It sounds like a language to me, though I have no clue which one. Maybe Germanic?"

"I don't know what to do," I said quietly.

"Of course you do," Jacob snapped. It was such a sudden change in tone that I stared at him as if he had just slapped me. He almost glared, and his expression was hard.

"W-what?" I suddenly felt very small and weak and perilously close to breaking down. After all, I had exposed myself in front of Jacob; his disapproval and his scorn would be devastating.

"Dana, you know exactly what to do. You've been doing it all your professional life. You're a cop, and one of the best detectives we've got. Act like it."

All I could do was stare.

"You have twice as much to go on as your dad did, and you have the luxury of being on paid leave. Follow up on what you do know. Write down that phrase so you don't forget it. With that and a translation you should have no problem tracking down the language. You have the tattoo on you and John Doe, so you know it's not unique—there have to be other people out there with the same mark."

I nodded. Jacob didn't yet know the difficulty of researching others with the Mark, but he was right about the language, and right in that I had much more to work with than my dad ever had.

What's in the box?

"You're right," I told him. I wasn't just agreeing with him. I was grateful for having someone who knew that I needed a kick in the pants to get over the hump of self-pity that was threatening to paralyze me. I didn't tell him how much I needed to hear what he had just said—and how suddenly afraid I was.

The idea I might push him away had become more terrifying the more I opened up. I had thought that once I started talking to him, it would be over. Either he would accept me, or he wouldn't. But it wasn't like that. The more I said, the closer I felt myself coming to some unspecified line that, if crossed, would spell the end of anything between me and Jacob.

And I was beginning to think that there was more between us than I'd allowed myself to think, which made the threat that much worse.

I had gone this far; it was enough for now. I couldn't push it any farther. I couldn't ask him to believe that the Mark made me much more an alien than I had told him already.

Not tonight, not when I had already pushed myself—pushed both of us—this far.

So I let the subject trail off, and Jacob let it go. We spent the rest of dinner talking about things that were much less disturbing. I asked him about his life, his family, what he did with his time off. And by the time we had finished eating, I realized that this had turned into an actual date.

I hadn't been on a date with anyone since high school.

We spent much longer at the table than our meals justified. When we finally left the restaurant, we walked out to the parking lot. I took a step toward my own car, and Jacob reached out and took my hand. I froze.

"Dana?"

I turned around and looked at him. There was something sad, almost melancholy, in his expression.

"What is it?"

"I don't want to put you in a difficult position."

"Huh?"

"I see how uncomfortable you are with this."

"It's not that."

"We work together. I don't want to make that difficult for you."

I saw the concern in his face, and something melted inside of me. I took a step in front of him and placed my hand on his cheek. His skin was warm and just slightly rough from a day's worth of stubble. I felt the contact almost as deep as the Mark touched me.

"Dana, I really—"

"Shhh." I bent forward and kissed him lightly on the lips. Just a brush, but enough to set my pulse accelerating and make his eyes noticeably widen.

I stepped back and told him, "Thank you."

Then I turned around and walked to my car. He didn't stop me, which was good, because I didn't know what the hell I'd just done.

NINE

ONCE I GOT home, I pulled the yellowed banker's box out of the closet and brought it down to the glass coffee table in my living room. I stared at it for several minutes before I gathered the nerve to take off the lid. The top layer was just like I remembered—a few pictures and my adoption papers. I reached in and pulled out the adoption papers, a thick sheaf of legal-sized pages held together with a binder clip. I flipped through the pages and saw the important date.

According to the state of Ohio, Mom and Dad officially became Mom and Dad when I was thirteen years old. Or when we assume I was thirteen. We didn't really know my real birthday, did we? There were more court papers in the bundle: a declaration making me a ward of the state; Mom and Dad officially becoming my guardians; my official name change from a Jane Doe.

It was all exceedingly dry legal paperwork, none of which should have made me tear up. Still, I found myself wiping my eyes. I scanned through it, finding nothing unexpected. All of it I knew about, at least subliminally. The only thing that felt unexpected was how long it took before my parents actually fostered me, and before they could go from fostering to adoption. I was institutionalized for over a year before they took me in. I barely remembered that.

Under the legal paperwork and some more family pictures was a thick manila envelope. I pulled out a stack of medical paperwork from twenty years ago, from that period of institutionalization. Physically I seemed to be okay, but mentally my keepers had me all over the map. I saw diagnoses of autism, borderline personality disorder, schizotypal personality disorder, PTSD—apparently, I was prone to emotional and angry outbursts. It didn't help that I spoke an unknown language. After I started to learn English, the doctors added psychogenic amnesia to my long list of problems, trauma of some sort left me unable to communicate the most basic facts about who I was or where I came from. I don't know why, but it made me uneasy that my lack of self-knowledge went back that far.

Under the medical records was a sealed envelope with my name written on it in my dad's handwriting.

"A letter?" I whispered. "Dad?"

My hands shook a little as I used a house key as a letter opener. I pulled out several pages of folded notebook paper. I unfolded the pages and saw the words, "To my dearest Dana:"

I almost dropped the pages when I read that. My dad had been gone nearly a decade. It was almost too much to be holding a letter from him to me. I glanced at a date scrawled in the corner and saw that it was written five years before he died.

I blinked my eyes clear and read.

TO my dearest Dana:

Yesterday your adoption was made official. You don't even know. I wanted to mark the event with a cake and a party. Your mother—who is now officially your mother—vetoed that idea. She pointed out that you already call us Mom and Dad, and that you have a deep need for us to be a "normal" family. And, in the end, it was only a legal formality. You are already our daughter, aren't you?

Besides, ever since you started going to school, drawing attention to your origins has upset you. I'm no longer certain exactly how much of your past you're still aware of. I still remember the last time I talked about finding you. You were eight or nine and asked me quietly, "Please don't talk about that, Daddy."

I saw how much it hurt you to talk about it, so I stopped.

I'm writing you this in case you ever decide you want to know your past and I'm not around for you to ask. If it still hurts, I urge you to put this letter away without reading further. Hurting you is the last thing I want to do.

If you do want to know, I should warn you that I don't know everything. I should also warn you that some parts of this story—according to the doctors—are responsible for traumatizing you and causing you to repress your memories. But if you want to know, I believe you have a right to this story.

If you're still reading, I want you to know that we love you, and nothing in here changes that.

"OH, crap," I whispered to myself. My hand may have shaken a little as I turned the page over. It seemed forever before I could force myself to read again. After a deep breath I read on and felt some relief at seeing the familiar story in my dad's handwriting. How he saw a dirty, naked, tattooed six-year-old rooting in a dumpster behind a bar. There was more detail than the story I knew: how I ran and screamed in another language; how he had to call for backup to corner me; how I bit and clawed at the officers trying to catch me; how the EMTs ended up sedating me.

That was the story I knew.

Then I read a detail that started knocking the world askew.

ONCE they had you sedated, I followed you to the hospital. I think I may have been protective of you even then. But at the hospital they found it wasn't dirt that covered you. It was dried blood. And it wasn't yours.

I read that paragraph three times. Each time I did, something tightened in my gut, a long-forgotten panic. Devoid of context, it was just *there*, as if it had been waiting patiently for me.

The next few paragraphs talked about my hospitalization, and how there was nothing physically wrong with me. I barely read them, rushing ahead to find some answer, some reason for the blood. Half of me was afraid that there'd be no reason, that it would be just one more unsolved mystery about my origin. The other half of me was afraid that I *would* find the reason.

THAT morning they tasked a bunch of us to canvass the neighborhood where I found you. The blood was a really strong indication that there was a crime scene somewhere in the area, and even if you weren't hysterical and sedated, you didn't have the English to tell us where.

I wasn't the one who found it, but I read the reports.

There was an apartment in a building two blocks away. A man and a woman involved in a double homicide.

I stared at the page describing the crime scene for several minutes before individual words started making sense. Something that might have been a memory started intruding, along with the ancient panic. It was just the briefest sensation of clutching at someone much bigger than me, someone wet, someone unmoving.

I forced myself to think like a cop and read it, ignoring the stirring panic in my gut.

The apartment was the scene of a bloody knife fight, or knife versus sword fight. The woman had died from a gut wound, the man from a slice across the throat. The woman had a butcher knife, the man had a long sword. The weirdness didn't stop there. While there wasn't anything remarkable about the way the woman was dressed, the man was dressed as if he was headed toward a renfaire or a seriously hardcore SCA event. He was clothed for the eleventh century from his pointed helmet, to his leather armor, to his woolen undergarments.

Another weirdness was, from the wound on the man's neck, the woman attacked from behind. Given how badly she was hacked apart, it was also apparent that she attacked first and suffered the guy's wrath until he bled out.

I knew instantly that the man had been going after me, not the woman. He had been raising his sword toward me, and she had come from behind and, in desperation, carved into his throat between jaw and gorget.

I had to stop reading again.

When I resumed, I was not surprised to find out that the autopsies revealed that both of them bore "tattoos" similar to my own. Or that blood tests suggested that the woman was most likely my biological mother. The man, surprisingly enough, appeared unrelated to me.

The cop theory, and the one my Dad subscribed to, was that I had been born into some sort of cult; one that my biological mother was trying to leave. It explained the common tattoos, the weirdly dressed assailant, and the fact no one had any IDs or paper trail. Even the apartment had been rented for cash using a stolen identity.

"They killed my mother," I whispered.

I had no idea who "they" were.

I reread my dad's letter several times over the next few days, trying to tease one more thread of sense out of it. On its own, it didn't give me any more insight. It just left me with even more questions about John Doe, his relation to the people in that apartment, his relation to me.

The simple theory was that John Doe was my biological father and the armored figure that killed him was related to the anachronistically dressed assailant in my mother's apartment. That made some sort of sense. But it made too many assumptions.

Fortunately, thanks to Jacob's prodding, I had another lead to follow.

WEALCAN *has fallen. They'll come for you. The shadows are coming.*

No matter what my origins, or the origin of the old man, I had a lead on the language he spoke.

That *we* spoke.

It took me two more nights on the computer, playing with various translations of the syllables that formed the phrase I believed I understood. And, when my search paid off, I couldn't quite believe it.

"Old English?" I whispered at the glowing screen.

My search had been harder than normal, largely because my transliteration of the words didn't use symbols that the language needed. At first, I thought that the similarity of meaning I found was a coincidence, until I found a YouTube video of a professor from the UK doing a dramatic reading of *Beowulf.* The accent was horrid, and the words sounded wrong, but after three stanzas, something clicked in my brain, and I understood.

I whispered along with the video, "*Weox under wolcnum weorðmyndum þah, oð þæt him æghwylc ymbsittendra ofer hronrade hyran scolde, gomban gyldan; þæt wæs god cyning* . . ."

How far was I from the world I came from?

THE morning after I made my discovery, I ran for a couple of miles as if it was any other day. And instead of listening to industrial or speed-metal on my iPod, I had a free audiobook of *Beowulf* spoken by a reader who seemed to have much better enunciation than the professor on YouTube. I listened as I ran, letting the words sink in despite the unpleasant accent. I had been listening to it repeatedly, and with each iteration more words made sense—it was like listening to an unfamiliar song, and only understanding the lyrics on the third go-round.

By the time I jogged back up the steps to my townhouse, the sun had risen above the horizon, and half the sky was the blocky gray of an oncoming storm. When I went in to the shower, I heard thunder.

In the shower, I kept imagining the lines from *Beowulf*, and I realized that in my head, I was no longer translating the terms into their English equivalents. There were just the words, and with them the imagery.

Who am I?

Who was he?

Was John Doe my father? My grandfather?

Something caught in my chest. I had probably watched another family member, another parent, die in front of me. And not for the first time. The idea filled me with emotions that were ugly, dark, and violent—grief that was indistinguishable from rage.

When I turned off the shower, I had to stand for a few moments and just breathe.

My family—my biological family—should mean nothing to me. I had no clear memories of them, no connection with them since . . .

Since they killed my mother.

Why would someone reappear, years later? Why do that to me? What was the point of putting me through this?

Why did he attack the man in the armor?

"Was he afraid he would attack me?" I whispered.

Was it a repeat of the scene in my biological mother's apartment? The anachronistic assailant coming after me, and my family giving their lives to protect me?

No, the armored figure left after the old man was mortally wounded. It couldn't have been after me.

All of this—the man dead in eleventh-century dress, the armored figure that killed John Doe, the stanzas in Old English filling my head—all of it spoke to a universe much wider and stranger that I had ever suspected, Mark or not.

What kind of future or past had John Doe's killer come from? Certainly nowhere in the slightly imperfect copies of home I ventured into. And nowhere in those worlds I knew would a child learn to speak Old English.

How far would I have to walk to find people dressed like the man who killed my birth mother?

After my shower, I stood in front of the full-length mirror in the bedroom, studying the Mark in a way I hadn't done since I was a teenager. The Mark had always been there, and I had taken it for granted. I had assumed that what little I knew was somehow the whole of what was to be known.

The more I looked at it, the more I realized that I had been hiding from it, from the unknown it represented. I had focused myself on what it did, not what it was or where it came from—and I had done so to the point where I had started thinking of it as an abstraction, not a physical object drawn across my skin. As if the dark lines on my skin were some sort of representation of the thing, like a name or a map or a shadow, but not the thing itself.

Staring at the Mark in the mirror, it would not allow itself to be denied like that. The lines of it held my skin with tendrils of the darkest black I had ever seen, a black that destroyed whatever light shone upon it. What minimal highlights I saw was light reflected from moisture on my skin.

When I brushed the surface of the Mark, the skin beneath felt no different to my fingers—though the Mark itself responded to the touch in a way that made me catch my breath.

No tattoo this.

It had also grown since I was a teenager, since I last gave myself such an exam. I had known then that the Mark was no static impression on my skin. It had grown with me, filling my back without stretching or distorting. But I was about the same height now that I was when I was seventeen, and the Mark had *still* grown. It had not only pushed the edges of itself up toward my neck and shoulders, and down to cover the curve under the small of my back, it had also increased in detail and complexity. I remembered the main design of the thing, but the spirals and curves had grown and branched to fill most of my skin with its unbroken pattern, repeated at many scales, some details drawn in tiny lines no thicker than a hair.

Next to the mirror, I had tacked up the photo of John Doe that showed the pattern across his back. While the style of the thing was the same, I could see that his Mark was different, even with the small scale of the photo.

Maybe it's like a fingerprint.

Something about the idea made me uneasy. I stared into the dense branching of the Mark on my skin and had the sense I was looking at something living—

My thoughts were cut short by a pounding on the door.

TEN

WHO?

I glanced through the open doorway at the clock on my nightstand. It was 7:45 in the morning. Who would be pounding on my door at this hour?

The pounding repeated, and I heard a muffled voice call out, "Dana!"

Jacob?

I grabbed a bathrobe and covered myself, running to the front door in bare feet. The knocking was insistent, and he sounded distressed. I tied my robe shut and checked myself over before reaching for the doorknob.

I only hesitated a moment as I realized that I was going to let someone into my home. The feeling of dread was so sudden and intense that, had it been anyone else on my threshold, I might not have opened the door.

But it was Jacob, so I turned the knob.

As soon as the door was unlatched, the door pushed open, and Jacob stormed in.

"Dana! What the hell are you trying to pull?"

I could suddenly see why his voice sounded so distressed. He was angry. No. He was *furious.* His face was flushed and pulled into a grimace that seemed painful.

I took a step back and asked, quietly, "What's the matter?"

"What's the *matter?*" He stormed into my home, every muscle tense, as if he wanted to hit something and was growing more and more frustrated when a target refused to present itself. "*You know damn well what's the matter!*"

In his hand, I now saw he held a large evidence bag. I didn't need a clear view of the blocky item it contained to realize what was inside it.

The other shoe had finally dropped.

I closed the door and followed Jacob into my sparse, sterile living room. A few nights ago, I was wondering what he would make of it when I finally invited him inside. Now he was here, and I don't think he saw a damn thing.

He dropped the evidence bag on the empty coffee table. It hit the surface with the sound of a door slamming shut. Behind that door I saw myself and Jacob, the way things were before.

We were both silent for a few moments as we stared at the bag and the gun it contained. It laid between us, a solid manifestation of all the secrets I'd been keeping.

"You know what that is?"

I nodded. "It's a .45 automatic belonging to Roscoe Kendal."

"But not the one I saw you hiding in *Asia FX.*"

I looked up at him, and the betrayal in his face was too painful to look at. I turned away.

"Damn it, Dana. Is this why our arrest record is drawing the attention of the Justice Department? How much tainted evidence are you responsible for?"

"It was an accident—"

"An accident? *An accident!* How the fuck do you plant a murder weapon by accident?"

I shook my head, unable to speak for a moment.

"No, Dana, I don't care how screwed up your life was. You don't get to shut down on me now."

"I'm not shutting down," I whispered.

"I deserve some sort of explanation. I can't get my head around what you did. Not only can't I believe you're dirty, I can't figure out how you pulled this off. I mean, Kendal confessed. And in his apartment is the exact same cheap half-plastic Hi-Point 45ACP model you 'found' at the crime scene. You're damn lucky that he did confess, or someone might have gone and cataloged this and realized that we have two guns, same model, same brand of ammo, *same fucking serial number.* How the hell did you fake that?"

"It wasn't fake."

"The hell you say? What were you doing, planting a duplicate of his gun?"

I turned on him. "I wasn't planting it! No one was ever supposed to find *that* gun! I screwed up!" He backed up, and I realized that I had never raised my voice to him before. I grabbed his jacket to stop his retreat.

"Dana, what the hell's going on?"

"The gun—it's real, but it doesn't belong here. I was pressed for time, trying to put it somewhere safe until I could dispose of it."

"Dana? You aren't making sense."

I didn't care. "I shouldn't have tried to track him down while you were standing there. It was stupid. The damn tattoo place reminded me too much— She had lost her dad just like— My mom gone— And I was able to do it right then. I didn't want to wait. Stupid!"

"Do what, Dana?" There might have been a touch of fear in his voice.

I stood there in front of him, knowing that everything I might say would sound insane. I was already raving. My hands were balled up in his jacket, and I could see in his eyes that the Dana he saw now was not the same Dana he knew.

The Dana he knew didn't really exist.

"Do what?"

"This," I told him as I pushed us both forward.

I had never tried taking someone with me when I used the Mark. I was so torn up with conflicting emotions that I didn't much care. I had been hesitant and reflective showing him the Mark, but shoving him was an impulse that caught me up in it before I had even thought about what it was I was doing.

I gasped when I felt the invisible hand of my Mark touch me, pushing me with a force stronger than I'd experienced before. I felt the pressure moving me and Jacob from the top of my spine all the way down, forceful enough that I felt as if I should topple over. But the touch of the Mark wasn't pushing me in a spatial direction.

I suddenly realized what I was doing.

I stopped moving, and the room around us plunged into the darkness of a sudden night. The lights were out in my living room; but it wasn't my living room anymore. In the Venetian-slashed light from the streetlight outside I could see the blocky forms of an overstuffed sectional couch facing a huge entertainment center that was a couple of decades out of fashion. Massed on the shelves of the entertainment center, transfixed by long knives of light, ranks of porcelain clown figurines stared at us.

His voice almost broke as he yelled, "*What the hell did you just do?*"

I knew from my own experience that the change in time of day could be much more disorienting than the sudden change in the surroundings. Jacob stepped back and nearly fell over an end table that hadn't been there before. A tall lamp fell over with a crash. His back was to the window, so I couldn't see his expression in his silhouette.

"What the hell did you do?"

A light came on behind me, by the stairs up to the bedroom, and I saw his face. His eyes widened as he saw my changed living room in all its clown-infected glory. Above, an old woman's voice called down to us. "I have a gun!"

Jacob repeated himself, but his voice was little more than a hoarse whisper, as if he couldn't take in enough air to form the words. "*What did you do?*"

Above us, the clown lady said, "I'm calling 911!"

I grabbed for Jacob again, and he tried to avoid my touch. But I was quicker than he was. My hands made contact with his chest, and I pushed both of us just a step and a half, and this time I paid attention to the shifting environment around us as versions of my living room flashed in and out of existence around us.

I felt the press of the Mark against both of us. I had him in a half grapple, half embrace, and my robe had come partly open against him. My cheek touched his as I pushed him away from the clown lady's house.

I stopped pushing in another room only an hour removed from the clown lady, but this one was empty, unoccupied except for a small folding table.

Jacob tripped and fell backward across the table, scattering business cards stamped with logos from a half dozen realty companies. He landed flat on the table, and the front legs buckled under him, sliding him back toward me to land sitting on the floor, facing me.

I pulled my robe shut.

There were no lights on here, but no Venetian blinds covered the window, so the streetlamp illuminated the whole empty room. Enough that I could see his face in the reflected light.

"Are you all right?" I asked him. My legs felt a little rubbery after using the Mark.

He laughed without much humor. "You're kidding, right?" He pushed himself up with a grunt. "What did you do? Drug me?"

"No, I wouldn't do that."

"How do I know what you won't do?" He looked around the room. "I give up, where are we?"

"My house," I said quietly.

"Bullshit."

I gestured toward the streetlight. "Look outside. You'll see the same street."

He stared at me, and almost reluctantly walked over to the window and looked outside. He stared at the street, shaking his head. "What kind of trick are you pulling?" He turned around and faced me. There was anger in his face, and my heart sank because I was certain then that I had lost him.

"No trick."

"So you took me to a neighboring townhouse. The floor plans—"

"Jacob, that isn't it."

"What is it, then?"

"We're in the same place. It's a different *time*."

"A different time?"

Of course, he wouldn't believe me. It was insane. How long did it take me to understand what was happening when I used the Mark? "We're in my living room, about fourteen hours after we started, in a world where it's vacant."

"Dana, that's insane."

I know. This is why I never told you, or anyone. . . .

I was so wrapped up in thinking of a way to make him understand what had happened that I barely paid attention to the sensation of a ghost hand almost touching my Mark. How could I make him understand? How did I first understand?

"You have your cell phone?" I asked him.

"Yes . . ." He said it very slowly, as if he was trying to talk down an armed psychopath, not a woman he'd known for three years.

"Do you have a land line at home?"

"Yes."

"Call yourself."

"Dana?"

"Please, I'm trying to get you to understand."

He stepped away from the window and shook his head. "Okay, I'll humor you."

He walked past me and dialed a number on his cell phone. He stood there listening to the phone ring for what seemed like several minutes. This was probably going to turn out to be a bad idea. The Jacob that lived in this world was probably not home, or would let the call go into voice mail, or had a different phone number.

I became aware that I was feeling phantom hands hovering over my Mark. The almost-touch was familiar. It was the same feeling I had felt when facing the armored man who killed John Doe.

"Hello?" Jacob said finally. "Who is this?" His voice had a tone of accusation to it.

The touch was growing stronger. It was coming.

"I don't care what time it is. Who am I talking to?" Jacob's expression was turning from shock to anger. "Who are you? Why did Dana put you up to this?"

I started turning around, trying to figure out where the sensation was coming from. I didn't pay any more attention to Jacob's conversation, I felt as if the thing would arrive any moment.

"Jacob—"

He looked up at me and snapped, "What the hell are you—"

"Something's coming," I whispered.

ELEVEN

HE LOWERED THE cell phone and glared at me. At the same time there was a distortion of the air behind him. The light from the streetlight outside rippled in the air as something solid twisted into existence behind him, falling forward through a dimension I couldn't name.

I grabbed Jacob, shoving my left hand into his jacket to grab the gun in his shoulder holster. He shouted, "Hey," as I pushed him to the side, away from between me and the already coalesced image. The gun slid out into my hand as he fell, and I took a step back, bringing the weapon up to brace my shot two-handed.

In the confined space of the living room, the mechanical armor seemed much bigger than it had outside—even though I had seen the old man next to it and knew that it was half again as big as he had been, and he had not been a small man.

I had Jacob's gun braced and pointed at the thing's faceplate, and long habit made me yell, "*Freeze!*"

It took a step with the whirr of gears and a hiss of steam, its sword half-raised preparing to strike at me or Jacob. A sound came from inside it, and before I realized it was language—a heavy accent saying, "Do not—" my finger was closing the trigger.

Like before, I was firing police hollow-points at serious metal armor, but this time I was at close range, almost close enough for the muzzle flash to touch the thing's faceplate. The armored skull snapped back, but the sword continued to rise.

I wasn't used to Jacob's gun, which was heavier and had a worse kick than my Jericho, and my next shot clipped the joint in the thing's right shoulder. It wasn't where I was aiming, but it was a lucky shot, sparking off the joint and releasing a jet of steam.

I had to scramble back as it moved forward, raising the sword. I no longer had time to brace, I just started pumping .45 ACP rounds into the armor's upper body as I backed into the kitchen. It made a wild swing with the sword, the arm trembling slightly, and I dodged deeper into the kitchen as the sword came down on the stove. It hit with enough force that the glass cooktop shattered, sending black shards everywhere in the kitchen. It caved in the oven and bent the door in half.

I did not want to think about the force behind that blow.

I fired again, another wild shot that clipped its left hip, releasing more steam and dripping black fluid. It ignored the damage as it tried to free its weapon from the stove. I took the moment of its distraction to brace and aim, since, back to the refrigerator, I had no retreat left. I was about to place another group of rounds into its face when I saw Jacob clear the doorway behind the thing.

"Jacob, no! Take cover!"

While I was focused on Jacob, the thing pulled its sword free with an inhuman heave that tore the remains of the stove free from the wall and sent it rolling down the kitchen aisle at me. I had nowhere to dodge as the side of the stove slammed into me. Jacob's gun went flying as the breath was knocked out of me.

It only had to take one step to be on the other side of the stove from me. I tried to push the stove away, and it moved just a quarter inch before slamming into a pair of armored legs. My arms vibrated with the effort of pushing against the stove, but it wasn't going anywhere.

The air was hazy from the steam venting from the armor's shoulder and hip. Backlit by the streetlight outside, it looked like the black knight from some medieval fairy tale. The thing's sword came down to point at my neck. Again, the voice came from inside the armor, with a heavy Russian accent, "You will now surrender and return with me."

As it spoke, Jacob darted in behind it, ducking into the space where the stove used to be. He grabbed something and shoved it into the armor's left hip, where steam and fluids were leaking.

A bright blue spark arced from the armor with a sound something like fabric tearing and smelling of burning tinfoil. An incomprehensible monosyllable gurgled from inside as every joint in the armor went rigid. The sword fell from its grasp, and it fell backward into the kitchen aisleway, landing on its back, arm still outstretched.

Jacob held the black and smoldering end of the stove's power cord in his hand, still plugged into the 220 line in the wall behind where the stove had been. He stared down at the frozen armor as if he didn't quite see it.

I vaulted over the stove, now that there wasn't a sword in my way. My thighs were bruised, but I'd managed to avoid getting badly hurt. I tried to be careful landing, but it was dark, and I still managed to get a few painful cuts on my bare feet landing on the fragments of the stovetop.

The first thing I did was scoop up Jacob's gun and hand it to him. "You need to reload," I told him.

He looked up from the armor and said, "What the hell is that thing?"

"I don't know."

"What do you mean you don't know?"

"I mean I don't have a fucking clue! Take the damn gun!"

He took the weapon from me, and I bent down to look at my armored adversary. The metal was peppered with dents where bullets had struck it. The joints were no longer venting steam, just oil and other fluids, pooling into a slippery mess on the floor.

The armor looked less medieval and more industrial the closer I examined it. If anything, the engraving seemed Victorian to me, the segmented plates held on by bolts and screws. After a moment of thinking what the occupant could reach to remove the helmet in an emergency, I found two bolts with wide wing-shaped tops just forward of the shoulders. I twisted both of them, and they moved freely with the ease of something that had been meticulously machined.

The helmet clam-shelled open under its own hydraulic impulse once I released the screws dogging it shut. Inside, an unconscious young man faced me, a nasty black knot on his left temple. I reached down and felt along his neck, and I was relieved to find the pulse steady and strong. He was breathing well, too, despite a trickle of blood coming from a nose that looked freshly broken.

"Let the EMTs do that," Jacob said.

"If I do, he'll just disappear again."

Who are you?

The man inside the armor was handsome, in his mid-twenties at the oldest. His face was pale where it was unbruised, and he had a Scandinavian look to him, with close-cropped hair that was blonder than mine.

"What are you talking about?" Jacob asked. The way he held the gun now, he could have been covering me rather than the man in the armor. "Disappear *again?*"

I found another set of screws that had been nestled underneath the lower edge of the helmet. I released those, and I was able to lift the chest plate off.

I heard sirens in the distance.

I looked up from the man in the armor. "Jacob, this is the guy who killed my John Doe. After that, he did what I just did with you, stepped into some other time, some other world."

I reached down and undid the padded leather straps that held the guy in the armor. Then I reached under his armpits and lifted him to a sitting position, so much dead weight. His arms came free of the armor, but his legs were held tight.

"Dana, you expect me to believe—"

"Look!" I snapped at him, and I yanked the guy's linen shirt up over the small of his back. Of course, I'd never seen him before, but I was almost certain of what was there. I was right. It wasn't as elaborate as my Mark, but the black swirls were etched in his skin as they were on mine, visible even in the dim indirect light from the streetlamp outside.

The sirens were a lot closer now.

"Help me!" I pleaded with Jacob. "This guy is the best clue I have to where I came from. To what is happening. Who I am."

He stared at me, still holding the gun.

"Please?"

He holstered the gun, knelt down, and started undoing a couple more screws I had missed at waist-level on the armor. He lifted the groin plate off and undid a couple more straps holding the guy's upper thighs in place. Once he did that, I was able to strain backward and slide the unconscious man completely out of the armor.

I heard the sirens whoop, and I heard tires screech to a halt outside.

Jacob saw me struggling with the guy and said, "Oh, hell." He holstered the gun and got on the other side of the unconscious man, helping me lift. As we hefted him upright, I belatedly realized that the belt on my robe had been torn free during the fight. When I'd vaulted the stove, I had probably given Jacob a full frontal.

I had to resist the urge to reach down and cover myself. The guy on my shoulders was big, muscular, and even with Jacob's help, I barely had him under control. I didn't want to risk dropping him.

"Forward." I told Jacob.

"Dana—"

"Now!" I said as I heard the front door splintering open.

He took a step with me, and I pushed with the Mark as hard as I could manage.

TWELVE

THE MARK DUG its phantom fingers into my body and practically threw me forward. We stumbled back into the familiar confines of my apartment, and I practically fell to my knees on trembling legs. I was used to the feelings the Mark gave me, but this was different.

"Are you all right?" he asked.

"I'm fine," I told him. I turned away from Jacob and concentrated on the unconscious man we were carrying. We needed to get him somewhere and keep him there. I headed toward the doors to the basement.

Jacob held on to the guy and didn't move. "Where are you going?"

"We need to set him down."

"We should call an ambulance."

"His pulse and breathing are steady, and I'm not letting him disappear before I can talk to him." I yanked the man's arm in frustration and felt most of his weight fall on my shoulders. I grunted. "If I have to do it myself—"

"Damn it, Dana," he said, taking a step forward to take up the guy's weight again. "You know this is kidnapping, right?"

Jacob followed me down the stairs, cursing the whole while.

We had to go down the stairs single file, and in my rush to get sword boy restrained, I'd taken the lead down. Even with Jacob's help, I still bore more than my share of this guy's weight. The whole length of the unconscious man's body leaned into me. I could feel how well-muscled his thighs, shoulders, and chest were.

At the bottom of the stairs, his weight shifted, and I had to turn into him to catch him before he fell and dragged Jacob onto the concrete floor with him.

For a moment I had him in my arms. His limp body pressed into the skin bared by my unbelted robe. His shirt had ridden up, and with him slouched forward, I felt his skin touch mine, just below my navel.

I gasped, barely able to breathe. I started to collapse backward, my knees buckling. With the skin-to-skin contact, I felt something—

Jacob pulled him away from me, taking all the man's weight. I heard the unconscious man groan as I took several unsteady steps back, pulling my robe closed. What the hell was it I had just felt?

Jacob had him supported under the arms, and he took him down the last step himself. As he did, the man's linen shirt fell back down, but not before I saw a sliver of black branching across an exposed hip.

I had touched his Mark.

It had touched me back.

In some sense, it still did. I'd felt his presence, like fingertips too close to my Mark, when he had moved through worlds around me. That had been powerful, impossible to ignore. Here, now, I still felt it, very slightly, easy to miss but still very much present.

"Dana," Jacob grunted, "what are you planning to do with him?"

I had Jacob drag him into the semi-finished part of the basement and sit him down on the carpet, leaning against one of the metal pillars supporting the floor above. Jacob looked up from our unconscious prisoner, who was continuing to groan. "Dana, what do you think you're doing?"

"Improvising," I told him. "You have your handcuffs?"

"What?"

"This guy can do what I just did. If he gets to walk away under his own power, I'll lose the chance to talk to him."

Jacob stared at the unconscious man while he took out a pair of cuffs and handed them to me. "If this guy is really the man who killed your John Doe, we should bring him in. Whatever fantasy world he came from, he's still a murderer."

"And keep him in custody for how long?" I cuffed the guy's arms around the pillar behind him.

"This is kidnapping, false imprisonment, and God knows what else."

I stood up and stared at him. "You think I don't know that? You think I'm enjoying this? I've spent years trying to keep this part of my life from leaking into the rest of it."

Jacob stared at me, and the disapproval I saw was like a slap in the face. "You have a pretty funny way of doing that."

How could I answer that? He was right. All I had ever done was *pretend* that the life I lived wasn't completely founded on my use of the Mark, and Jacob had just thrown my self-deception back in my face.

I was still only wearing an unbelted robe.

"Can you watch our friend while I get dressed?"

"You can't just imprison a suspect in your basement."

I sighed. "Jacob, you've seen what I'm dealing with. If you want to call the station and pick this guy up, fine. You want to grab him and drive him in yourself, fine. You want to arrest me for kidnapping, whatever, fine. But if you're going to do something, please just do it now, before you're an accessory." I started up the stairs. "And whatever you do, I'm still getting dressed."

I maintained some measure of dignity ascending the basement stairs, but once I was out of Jacob's sight, I practically ran to my bedroom and slammed the door behind me.

I wasn't ready, not for any of this. I didn't want to have to deal with my unanswered questions all at once. I didn't want to have to deal with the collapse of the life I had built. I didn't want to have to deal with Jacob's disapproving looks.

I had a strong desire to just walk away, from Jacob, from the man cuffed in my basement, from all the messes I had made.

Fortunately, that fantasy about running away wasn't nearly as powerful as the ones I had entertained in the past, before I'd seen other people like me. The need to discover who they were, and possibly my real family, outweighed any momentary desire to escape by an order of magnitude.

I pulled on clothes without thinking deeply about it and found myself dressing as if I was going into work—black slacks and a gray blouse that hid all of the Mark. I looked at myself in the mirror and suddenly felt a wave of resentment and shame hit me all at once.

The Mark was part of me, yet I spent my whole life hiding it. Not one item of clothing I owned was sleeveless or backless, or even low cut enough to expose anything below the nape of my neck. I didn't own one pair of low-cut jeans, and I didn't even have a white T-shirt or a light-colored blouse that might allow some of the Mark to show through.

I began to realize that I had much less of a handle on the woman looking back at me in the mirror than I thought I did.

"What are you waiting for?" I whispered to my reflection when I realized I was stalling my return to the basement.

I left the bedroom not knowing what possibility frightened me more. The idea Jacob might have turned me in. Or the idea he hadn't.

HE hadn't.

I descended the stairs, and I saw Jacob sitting on an old folding chair. His cell phone was in his hand, but he held it in his lap, as if he had forgotten he had gotten it out. He faced my prisoner, staring at the man.

I paused on the stairs, looking at him. Even sitting down, he seemed more in charge than I felt. Most of the confusion and outright distress I had seen in him during our side trip to the world next door was absent now. He watched the prisoner with an almost dispassionate calm, one I recognized. When our job put us in front of an unstable or belligerent person, he was able to deploy the face of reason and, more often than not, talk someone down. Or at least edge that person away from a dangerous confrontation.

I didn't know if I should be grateful for the return of his professional cool. I didn't want to do battle with him over this. Over anything, really. But, after all I had said, after all the secrets I had stripped away, after exposing myself to him more than any other person—after all that—a part of me felt a sudden sense of loss at the prospect of him retreating behind a professional façade.

I almost preferred the anger, the frustration, and the disapproval. I found myself thinking that at least those meant he was still emotionally engaged in our relationship, in me. Intellectually, I found the thought appalling, as if I was starting to take on the thinking process of a battered woman. And *that* thought was patently ridiculous because Jacob and I weren't in a relationship, and he certainly wasn't abusive in any sense.

Besides, his anger was pretty much justified.

And that thought was also the common rationale of an abuse victim. And, again, my dismay at my own thoughts was ridiculous. I wasn't in any sense abused.

But was I so empty inside that I could accept that kind of relationship?

He turned around and looked up at me. "Dana?"

I was suddenly terrified of him. Not Jacob the person, but Jacob the abstraction swimming in my mind. He had no idea what kind of power he could wield over me. And neither did I.

I decided that on balance I was relieved he had taken on a more distant, professional demeanor.

"How is he doing?"

"His pulse and breathing are fine. He doesn't have any ID on him."

I walked down and stared at my prisoner so I didn't have to face Jacob. I told myself it was a good thing that Jacob had found out about everything this way, better that he was distant from all this, for both our sakes. I had pretty much stopped being a cop, and I suspected that talking to this man was not going to push me back in that direction.

I knelt next to my prisoner. He breathed steady, and his color was good. He didn't have any obvious injury other than a bloody nose and a dark bruise by his temple. He was handsome in a ruthlessly Aryan way. He could have been a model for a Nazi propaganda poster.

"Who did you call?" I asked.

"No one, yet," Jacob said. "If this guy showed any distress, I would have called 911, but he seems fine."

"He should," I said. "This asshole is faking unconsciousness." I grabbed the guy's slack jaw and turned his head to face me. "Aren't you?"

His eyes shot open, almost startlingly blue. He stared at me with a disconcerting intensity and whispered, "*Vi oplatitye dlya etogo.*"

Jacob said, "Sounds like Russian to me."

He'd been positively chatty when he'd been swinging his sword, so I snapped, "English."

Apparently, Jacob hadn't heard him. He began to say, "Maybe he doesn't speak—"

My prisoner interrupted him. "I speak English well enough."

THIRTEEN

"WHO ARE YOU?" I asked, trying to keep the sound of desperation from leaking into my voice. "What are you doing here?"

"I am Ivan Roskov, Sergeant of the Imperial White Guard, and I am here because a rogue Walker has the insolence to chain me to a post."

I didn't like the arrogant way the guy was looking at me, so I stood up. "I'm going to call you Ivan, then." It was a cheap psychological trick, looming over him like that, but after being party to a semi-nude gun-slash-sword fight, I think I'd drained my reserves of subtlety.

"Do not think you can defy the Emperor's Law. Release me now and there may be cause for mercy." *Who the hell is the Emperor?* Whoever it was, it didn't sound good. "You must know no rogue can hide forever, even in the Chaos."

Wealcan has fallen! They'll come for you! The shadows are coming!

"Is that what you're doing in my world?" I asked. I was reviewing the events in my mind, remembering the old man pounding on my window, remembering the specter of Ivan's anachronistic armor emerging from the shadows. I felt something grow cold in me, the same deep anger I'd felt the first time I'd slipped in time to witness my first attempted murder, when I had stared into the eyes of a perp ten minutes before he would have put a bullet into an old woman's brain.

Difference: Ivan had already done the deed.

"Is it?" I repeated.

"Your world?" There was a mocking tone in Ivan's voice which was just the wrong attitude to take with me now. I reached down with both hands and grabbed the front of his shirt and pulled him so his arms were taut against the pole and his ass left the floor. I held him like that, staring into his eyes, my arms trembling with fury.

"*My* world," I said, feeling the strangest sense of protectiveness for the world where I had grown up. Wherever I had come from, this *was* my world. "I saw you kill a man."

Ivan glared at me, unmoved. "The man was a fugitive from the Emperor's justice. What of it?"

At this point it was clear I wasn't dealing with the kind of perp I'd spent most of my adult life intimidating. He wasn't some kid who wasn't smart enough to understand the consequences of his actions, or some low-grade sociopath who was just narcissistic enough to cave once someone threatened the only thing he cared about— himself. I understood that, but at this point I didn't care.

"Who. Was. He?" I strained and heard his shirt tearing.

He got his feet beneath him and pushed himself upright against the pole. Even though I still had a death grip on his shirt, he was looking down at me from about five inches of height advantage. "He was a fugitive from the Empire. Anything else does not matter."

I wasn't going to let some arrogant prick try and intimidate me. I slammed him back into the pole hard enough that I heard his skull clang against the metal. "It matters to me!"

I felt a hand on my shoulder and heard Jacob's reasonable talk-down-the suspect voice, "Dana, ease up."

That pissed me off even more, but I did take a step back, letting go of Ivan's shirt. I took a deep breath and told myself that I wasn't going to get anywhere treating this guy like a wannabe gangbanger.

I tried to emulate Jacob's reasonable tone. "You're going to tell me who he was and why you killed him."

"Who are you to dictate to me?"

To hell with it.

I balled my fist and let him have it full in the face. It wasn't like punching the heavy bag. I felt my first knuckle split against his cheekbone. But I heard his skull clang against the pillar again, and I felt myself grinning at his shocked expression. "I'm the woman who's going to beat you to a bloody pulp."

"What the hell are you doing?" Jacob's voice had lost the professional tone, and he sounded almost as shocked as Ivan looked.

"Demonstrating who's in charge," I said.

Ivan looked past me and said, "Take charge of your woman, sir. An assault on me is an assault on the Emperor."

I buried my fist in his solar plexus. He gasped. It was a dirty move, without him able to defend himself, but I found myself grinning so hard my cheeks ached.

"Funny thing," I told him. "I don't see your Emperor around anywhere."

He sucked in a breath. Before he could say anything, I leveled another punch above his kidney. His linen shirt was smeared with blood from my split knuckle, but I didn't much care. I wasn't even feeling it. I just kept seeing that old man against the lamppost, his gut sliced open.

I raised my fist again and Jacob grabbed me. "Stop it!" He pulled my arm back, spinning me away from Ivan. I was so focused that he needed to use more force than he probably intended. I felt the shoulder of my blouse tear.

I almost brought my other hand up to hit Jacob, but I stopped myself. "Let me go."

"Not until you get a grip. What are you going to do, kill him?"

"If I have to." I was deadly serious.

He let my arm go and took a step back. "I thought I knew you."

"Maybe you were wrong." I swung my arm back to point at Ivan. "But this bastard murdered a man in cold blood in front of me."

"I am no murderer."

I spun around to face him, the torn sleeve of my blouse falling to my wrist. "The fuck you say?" He almost seemed as shocked at my f-bomb as he'd been when I punched him in the face. "You're saying some other sword-wielding psychopath in steam-powered armor killed the man lying in my morgue?"

"The man attacked me."

"With a chunk of *asphalt*. You were in armor that could handle a .45 slug in the head. He was essentially unarmed, and you cut him nearly in half. That's murder in my book, and in any court in this country you'd be damn lucky to plead voluntary manslaughter."

"That was not my intent, my Lady."

"You're swinging a sword about, and—" I stopped, because I realized that Ivan's demeanor had changed completely. *My Lady?* I didn't know what to do with that. Instead, I asked, "What was your intent?"

"To return the man to the Emperor's justice. He escaped, killing seven men in the process. What you saw was my failure. I did not expect the man to attack me, and I reacted before I had opportunity to think."

I sighed, pulling the torn sleeve off my arm. The plausibility of what Ivan said was enough to temper my anger. If anything, my John Doe shared culpability in his own death by rushing an armed man so stupidly.

"So who was he?"

"I have no name. He was simply a fugitive. I tracked him through the Chaos, until I caught up with him here."

Jacob finally joined in the questioning. "If he was a prisoner, what was his crime?"

Ivan glanced at Jacob, then at me. He hesitated for a moment before saying, "He was not a prisoner. He entered the Emperor's demesne without accepting the Emperor's authority. He was a guest, who returned hospitality with bloodshed."

"And who is this Emperor?" Jacob asked.

I swallowed a little bit of irritation at Jacob stepping in like that. I had wanted to be at least a little less forthcoming about what we didn't know, at least until I had a better idea of who this guy was and what he was doing here.

Of course, I probably should have mentioned that to Jacob, who sounded now like he was just questioning a suspect back at the station.

"His Imperial Majesty, Napoleon V, by the Grace of God and the will of the Nation, Emperor of Europe, Protector of the Americas, and Sovereign of a Thousand Worlds."

I wasn't any great student of history, but I remembered enough from high school to know that a Napoleon V was two more Napoleons than was standard issue. That, and the fact that Ivan spoke with a Russian accent, suggested that wherever he came from, "Waterloo" had a different connotation.

"Sovereign of a Thousand Worlds" carried a whole other series of connotations, though. Enough that I decided to abandon any plans to be cagey, especially since this guy seemed to be more cooperative now. I asked him exactly what that bit about the "Thousand Worlds" meant.

"The Emperor is also a Prince, my Lady. His presence stabilizes the Chaos around the Empire. Those worlds that abut his own are also part of his demesne."

"Of course, they are," Jacob said in the way one humors small children and dementia patients.

It took me a moment to respond because the implications of what Ivan was saying were still sinking in. To run an Empire across the boundaries between worlds, that would require an army.

"This Empire of yours," I asked, "it has many people like you and the old man?" *Like me?*

He narrowed his eyes at me as if he didn't understand the question.

I pulled up his shirt and said, "Marked like him, like you." I poked his back where the swirling pattern covered his skin. I really should have known better after almost stumbling down the steps when his Mark touched me before. I was too caught up in the moment to realize what I was doing until after I'd done it.

Touching it, I felt a wrench in my insides as an unfamiliar hand pulled itself across my insides where only my own Mark had ever touched me. I quickly yanked my finger away, trying not to look as if I had just been burned. In a single moment I felt like I'd known Ivan Roskov more intimately than I had known anyone, and I felt weak from the knowledge.

Ivan stared at me with wide eyes.

Oh, God. Please do not tell me that the feeling was mutual.

"*Bozhe, pomogi mne*," he whispered.

"If your Emperor claims territory beyond his own world, he must have an army of men like you to enforce his rule—"

"He claims fealty from all the Walkers who reside in his domain," Ivan said. "In return for administering his rule, they are spared the dangers to be found in the midst of the Chaos. Travelers through his demesne must accede to his rule."

I nodded, not quite believing. After being so long unique, an outsider in a world where I didn't quite fit, it was beyond any expectations to think that there was somewhere where I might be normal, where I wouldn't have to hide what I was . . . even if it was ruled by a French despot.

Jacob asked him, "What dangers? What Chaos?"

Ivan looked at Jacob and said, "Who is this man? He is not—"

"Just answer his questions," I said.

He answered, and he did it with enough condescension that I could tell that wherever he came from, it was common knowledge. However, it was beyond my experience with the Mark.

Ivan explained that the sea of worlds that Walkers could move between was not stable. Universes floated and moved like foam on a storm-wracked ocean, they appeared and disappeared, merged and split apart. Weak Walkers caught out in the Chaos could find themselves forever lost, never able to find a world they had left, and in the worst of it, could find the world shifting around them as the universes remade themselves. It was why he had been armed with a sword rather than a firearm. Any gun was a poor weapon in the Chaos, where reality might only be stable within arm's reach. Shooting someone accurately at any distance, with a gun, an arrow, or a thrown rock, was impossible in such an environment.

Even a Walker with a strong bloodline, like Ivan and those serving the Emperor's White Guard, required years of training to navigate the Chaos with any certainty—and even then, it was an effort.

Only those born of a Prince's bloodline could natively walk through the Chaos unscathed. A Prince could move through the Chaos as quickly as he could through the isle of stability that was the Empire.

No rogue can hide forever, even in the Chaos. . . .

"Are we in that Chaos now?" I asked. If whole universes—past, present, and future—formed and dissolved in the Chaos, could anyone within them really know?

"I apologize for implying such, my Lady. I traveled long in the Chaos tracking my quarry, and I did not know I had entered a new domain."

Okay, what?

Jacob asked, "What domain?" while at the same time I asked, "So the man you killed was one of these Princes?"

Ivan answered my question. "He moved confidently through the deepest parts of the Chaos where I could barely follow. He belonged to a Prince's bloodline, child or sibling if he was not one himself."

"What domain?" Jacob asked again.

"You do not know?"

"Humor me," he said.

"I was not certain until I felt her touch, but this realm belongs to your Lady."

I opened my mouth, but nothing came out.

"And I truly beg her forgiveness for my trespasses."

JACOB followed me upstairs and, after shutting the door on the basement, said, "Give me one good reason not to think that guy's a schizophrenic with paranoid delusions."

I stopped on the stairs up to the bedroom and told him, "Steam-powered armor."

"Okay, then give me a good reason to believe *I'm* not a schizophrenic with paranoid delusions."

"You're saner than I am."

"Right now that's no real comfort."

"What are you going to do?" I asked. "Are you going to turn me in?"

Jacob sighed. "I should, I really should. The games you've been playing are the primary reason we have a Justice Department lawyer breathing down our necks."

"I'm sorry."

"Why didn't you at least try to explain some of this before it got to this point?"

"I—" I turned away from him because my eyes had started to burn. "I don't have an answer for you."

I felt his hand on my exposed shoulder and I had conflicting urges: one to collapse into his arms, the other to run away up the stairs to my bedroom and slam the door. I compromised and stood on the stairs, facing away from him.

"You don't trust me?" he asked.

Do I trust anyone?

"I—" I sucked in a breath and closed my eyes.

"Dana?"

"I do trust you," I whispered. *More than I trust myself.*

"Then why didn't you—"

"I never even told my mother." I shrugged out from under his hand and looked back over my shoulder at him. "You should go. I'm on leave, but you still have a job."

"And a lawyer to babysit."

I turned to go up the stairs.

"Promise me something?" he asked.

"What?" I asked without turning around.

"No more beating on that guy, whoever he is."

I paused a long time because I didn't want to make a promise I might not keep.

"Dana?"

"I promise," I told him.

FOURTEEN

WHEN I CHANGED my blouse, I noticed that in tearing the sleeve, the side seam on the blouse had split as well, leaving the back of my blouse flapping behind me. Ivan would have gotten a chance to see a good part of my Mark.

Right about the time his attitude changed.

"Don't trust him," I told myself. I don't know why I needed the admonition. He had killed the one person alive who could tell me about my past and where I'd come from. I knew that for no other reason than I shared a language with the dead man.

I pulled on another blouse, blue this time, and told myself that if Ivan was going to ask this Lady's forgiveness, I was going to make him earn it. I stopped in the kitchen to pour myself some coffee and walked down to find out more about the world this guy came from.

I sat down in the folding chair that Jacob left and warmed my hands on the mug in my hands. It was high summer outside, but down here I felt chilled. Ivan's anachronistic presence felt more disturbing to me as time went on. I was used to confining my weirdness elsewhere; I had compartmentalized the Mark socially, psychologically, and physically. Ivan's presence was as much a symptom of my world crumbling as my serial confessions to Jacob.

He had sat down at the base of the pillar, hands still cuffed behind him, knees drawn up, face downcast. His hair was light enough that I could see some bruises darkening beneath his hair.

I sipped the coffee and said, "You're rather quiet."

"I am awaiting leave to speak, my Lady."

"Uh-huh." I sipped more coffee. I was going to milk this guy's deference for all it was worth. Even if it was some sort of act, even if he lied through his teeth, I was getting more information from him than I had gotten during years of experimentation. "Tell me more about the man you killed."

As forthcoming as Ivan was, there seemed little more that he could tell me. John Doe had crossed into the Emperor's domain, intentionally or unintentionally. He was initially treated as an emissary, clearly being of a powerful bloodline, but the man had violently rejected the overtures of diplomacy—a rejection that left bodies scattered all over the place.

Ivan didn't have any information about where the man came from or what he might have told the Emperor's diplomats and scholars before escaping. It wasn't his place to know. I didn't press it since I knew what that was like. Ivan was in some sense, a cop. And if I had to hunt down someone lost by DHS or the FBI, probably no one would deign to give me the transcripts of their interviews, no matter how helpful that would be.

However, Ivan's description, if it could be trusted—big "if"—suggested that John Doe had been as disheveled and agitated when he crossed into the Emperor's world as he'd been when he'd entered mine.

His brief period as a "guest" of the Empire was ended by the carelessness of one of the Emperor's doctors.

"The man was a university professor schooled in dead languages, not a soldier or a trained interrogator. He assumed the man was restrained and docile." Ivan snorted and added, "And the man was English."

John Doe, on the other hand, was both highly agitated and apparently quite skilled at hand-to-hand combat. He managed to kill the careless Englishman and two others before getting his hand on a weapon and escaping into the neighboring countryside. He would kill four more before escaping back into Chaos.

Ivan tracked him, and even with the aid of his armor—which allowed him to move at a running pace tirelessly—he could only follow his quarry because of the "straightness" of his path. John Doe was uninterested in evading his pursuit, simply in traveling as far and as fast to his destination as he could.

Ivan caught up with him only because John Doe had stopped when he had reached my world.

While Ivan described finding the man as he pounded on my car window, I learned two things.

The first thing I learned was that Ivan called it the Mark, too. I didn't realize the incongruity until long after he had used the term. The thing on my back had always had that name—but only in my own mind. I don't know if I had ever even spoken its name aloud before today. I had always assumed that I had named it myself in some forgotten part of my childhood. There was an old itch in my brain that started me thinking that it was not an invention, but a memory.

The second thing that became apparent, if it wasn't clear before, was the fact that John Doe's appearance was far from random. The man had come explicitly to contact me. He had made a straight line from Ivan's Empire to my world, and as soon as he reached here, he stopped fleeing.

He had come for me.

I set down the coffee on the floor next to my chair and leaned forward, looking down at my prisoner. It had been a couple of hours since I had cuffed him to the post, and I realized I couldn't keep him there forever. The guy was going to have to, at a minimum, eat and use the bathroom.

But I also knew that one step and he could be gone.

I wondered how the Emperor handled that sort of thing. *Why would John Doe have to kill anyone to escape? One step and he'd be away from them all . . . What am I missing?*

"You attacked me, why? And why come back and do it, and not when I first saw you?"

He bowed his head. "At first, I did not know you for what you are."

"You can track one man from your world to mine, and though you were right next to me you didn't know?"

"Sensing another Mark is complicated. It requires a moderately powerful Walker to do so at all. Even then, most can only sense a Mark in use, a Walker moving between worlds, or their kinsmen. . . ." He trailed off as he seemed to realize something. "The old man was your kinsman, wasn't he?"

In my head I had been hedging my bets, thinking in "mights" and "possiblys," but when Ivan asked me that question, I answered definitively, "Yes."

"That explains how he found you. Someone with a Mark that strong would be able to sense their own blood even when it was Stationary. He was coming for you."

That was probably a correct assessment, though I felt uncomfortable with the flat statement of it. "Why did *you* come after me?"

He sighed. "After I confronted you and him, I retreated to regain my strength for the long trek back, and I planned to possibly recover his body. Then I felt a Mark like his move through Chaos, but briefly, gone before I was able to follow."

I nodded. That was me walking back to try and find a nonexistent crime scene. "You thought I was him."

"I had to assume the fugitive still lived and could move into Chaos at any time. So I stayed and waited."

"Until I used my Mark again."

"Yes."

"And you attacked me because?"

"My Lady, you started shooting."

I started to object, but when I replayed the event in my mind I wondered if that drawn sword could have been in a defensive posture?

He had taken a step and started to say something, then I started firing.

"What will you do with me?" he asked.

"I don't know," I said. I honestly didn't. I wasn't thinking more than an hour ahead of myself. "Keep talking, and I might figure it out."

For another half hour I quizzed him about generalities, how the worlds beyond my little patch of reality seemed to work. He confirmed my suspicion that all Walkers—those with the Mark—were indeed unique in all the flux of possibility that filled the Chaos: past, present, and future. He said that not only was the presence of a Walker the only thing that could stabilize the shifting sands within the Chaos—for a Prince that was even more so—but the Walker, in some sense, influenced the shape of the world around them.

Not only did they lend a permanence to an impermanent universe, they affected the form it took—and the stronger the Walker, the more conscious the direction that form could take.

That was a little too much existential baggage for me. It was bad enough that Ivan was calling me a Prince—or maybe that should be Princess—and placing me at the head of some trans-universal hierarchy. He also was suggesting that the windows of alternate pasts and futures I walked between existed because of me and what I wanted, or what I expected to find. . . .

Worse, it answered a question I had always had, but had been too timid to articulate:

How could the pasts and futures I visit be so similar to my own when I do not exist in any of them? The world where I stopped Roscoe Kendal from murdering the proprietor of *Asia FX* was exactly my own—the same city, same storefronts, same weather, same newspapers, same history—all without over two decades of my existence.

Every time I thought about that question too deeply, it led to questions about the meaning of my own existence. If fate could so blithely steamroll ahead, unchanged down to the smallest detail regardless of my presence in the world . . .

Could there be any better definition of manifest meaninglessness? How could I conclude anything I did actually mattered?

Ivan presented a reality that was so much in opposition to that deeply-held fear that I couldn't fully process the implications.

I didn't have a chance to.

Talking with Ivan, I began to feel as if I was being watched, as if someone just out of sight was here, reaching for me. I turned around in the chair and saw no one just as I began to realize that it was the Mark.

I still felt Ivan's presence with the Mark, but now there was something else. Ivan was a relaxed masculine hand resting against my shoulder blade. The something else was different—jerky, nervous, and somehow *wrong*—soft and slimy as if the unseen flesh was rotten.

I asked Ivan, "Do you feel anything?"

"What?"

Something's coming . . .

I stood up, knocking over the coffee that sat on the floor. I reached for my gun and realized that the holster was still upstairs in my bedroom. "I'll be back," I told Ivan as I ran up the stairs.

The invisible hand kept groping for my Mark, as if death itself was reaching for me. My heart raced as I ran upstairs and retrieved the Beretta.

In my bedroom I held the gun in a ready position as I spun around, looking for anything sneaking up on me. Nothing.

But I shuddered as I felt long spastic fingers brush my Mark with the cold touch of something dead. I edged back down the stairs sideways, my back to the wall so I could keep an eye both upstairs and down. My house was unnaturally quiet, the only sounds the creak of the treads on the stairs as they took my weight. The whole downstairs was painted with muted sunlight streaming through the windows. Even the motes in the air seemed frozen, waiting for something to happen.

Then I heard Ivan yell something in Russian, and I ran.

FIFTEEN

I REACHED THE basement door as it swung slowly closed. I threw it open and ran down the steps. Someone was down here with Ivan. Halfway down the stairs, I heard Ivan's stream of Russian invective cut short by a choked, gurgling sound.

I brought the Beretta up into firing position as I descended enough to get a view of the basement where Ivan was cuffed. A dark figure was bent over Ivan, arms extended, hands clutching his throat.

My finger left the side of the barrel and found the trigger as I yelled, "*Police! Step away from him now!*"

The figure made no move to stop strangling Ivan, so I stepped to the side, taking Ivan out of the line of fire. I repeated, "*Let him go, now!*"

It was as if I wasn't even here. I had no choice, and I fired. I was trying for the center of mass, but the figure was crouched to throttle Ivan, and I had to aim higher than I wanted to keep Ivan out of the shot. The bullet struck the attacker in the left shoulder.

That got his attention. He let go of Ivan, leaving him gasping and choking. Ivan's attacker turned around to face me, giving me my first good look at him.

He looked like his touch on my Mark felt, pale as a corpse. Somehow, up to now, I had been too focused to realize that the guy was naked to the waist.

"Oh, fuck," I whispered.

The guy had a Mark, of a sort. It covered his torso in broad, violent curves that slashed deep into his flesh. The lines of the Mark were edged in ragged flesh as if the black lines were constricting, embedding themselves. The blackness seemed to writhe within the channels of the open wounds it had carved.

Whatever substance formed this man's Mark seemed in the process of consuming him. His eyes looked at me with the same writhing blackness, and the wound I had put in his shoulder didn't bleed, and in the bottom of that crater I saw more of the blackness oozing.

It charged at me, and I fired the Beretta again. The thing blurred as I fired, and I could feel the cadaverous hand plucking the threads of my Mark like a harp as it moved though the space between this world and the next. It flashed in and out of existence so fast that my eyes weren't convinced it had ever gone, but my bullet had passed through the space where it had been, never touching it.

I fired two more times, quickly. It was close enough that both shots should have buried themselves in the creature's chest. But it still blurred as it moved, and the bullets passed through it as if it was a ghost.

As it grabbed for me, I tried the same thing, stepping into a world where this thing wasn't. I found myself in a darkened basement, a semi-mirror of my own, and a cold-fleshed hand grabbed the wrist on my gun hand.

It was here, too?

I could smell the wound I had put in its shoulder. It stank like rotting meat.

It was strong, too strong for me to overpower it. When I tried to free my gun hand, its response was to grab my neck with its other hand and slam me into a wall. Somehow, I managed to keep hold of my gun as my skull bounced off the cinderblock.

I dug the fingers of my left hand into its throat, trying to push the thing off me, but I couldn't make it budge. It appeared to have the pain reaction of someone cranked up on PCP—and I was already feeling faint from the pressure it was putting on the blood supply to my brain.

Even if it can't feel the bullet wound . . .

I took my free hand away from my ineffective attempt to strangle it back and concentrated all I had into an open hand strike at the wound in its left shoulder. Even though that arm still had an iron grip on my gun hand, when I hit it, I could feel the movement of bones the bullet had already broken.

This thing might have defective pain receptors, but that didn't help maintain its mechanical integrity. I could feel the pressure ease on my wrist, and I gave another strike to its shoulder joint, and even though I didn't have the best angle, I could feel the socket give way.

I yanked my gun hand loose and brought the barrel of my Beretta up under the thing's chin.

I didn't have to fire. When it blurred itself to avoid my shot, its hand left my throat, giving me the chance to dodge for the stairs.

I didn't have to look behind me to know it followed me. I could feel the phantom cadaver hands of its Mark tugging at the threads of my own.

What was this thing?

Who? I forced myself to think. Whatever I faced was human. Single-mindedly murderous, but still human. It—*he*—was lucid enough to dodge bullets and try to disarm me.

I ran out of someone else's living room, and he was still chasing me. I saw people on the sidewalk and pushed the Mark as I ran until the sky was midnight dark and the streets were empty. Whatever was happening, I didn't want anyone else caught in the crossfire.

He still followed me, but he lagged. I had an advantage on a straight run, and I could probably lose him. But that would leave him to return his attention to Ivan.

I spun around and faced him. "Who are you? What do you want?"

It was a dim hope to engage this guy in dialogue. He had the same sort of disconnected expression that you see on the seriously schizophrenic and the seriously medicated, and it wasn't just the solid black eyes. He might shift through worlds after me, but the reality he looked out at was not the same one I was living in.

I braced my gun at him as he ran down the center of the empty street toward me. I had gained a hundred yards on him, and he was rushing me. I yelled at him, "*Stop!*" but he paid no attention.

I risked a shot to try and stop his advance, but he blurred, and the shot passed though where he should have been. No reasoning with him, and he was going to close on me in moments.

How had I managed to shoot him in the shoulder?

He had been throttling Ivan, and he hadn't been paying attention to my attack. He had a single-minded focus on his target.

That gave me an idea, and I ran off to stay out of reach. I ran down the right lane of the empty street and an idea started brewing. A dangerous one.

If I had an accomplice, they could probably take this guy out while he was focused on me, blindsiding him the way I had while he was focused on Ivan. Unfortunately, I didn't have access to any allies. Not intentional ones anyway.

Once I had a decent lead on him, I spun around, letting the Mark push me toward morning. Like before, he kept pace with me, and I felt cadaver hands hook into the pattern of my Mark as if I was dragging them along. Then I saw a blurred shadow of what I wanted, and I stopped moving through worlds.

Fifty feet in front of me, he stopped shifting as well—materializing directly in front of a UPS truck approaching from behind. The truck was so close to him already that I didn't hear the brakes begin screeching until after it slammed into him.

The impact threw the guy forward, face into the asphalt and rolling. The UPS truck skidded to a stop just short of driving over the guy where he had rolled to a stop in the street.

I did not need to walk up and examine the mush the guy's skull had become to know that he hadn't survived the impact. I'd felt the dead hands leave my Mark the instant his head had kissed the pavement.

THERE was a strong impulse for me not to flee the scene of the accident. I had done a lot of extra-legal crap in neighboring universes, but never anything that got anyone killed. Even if the guy was psychotic and trying to kill me, what was left of the cop in me objected to me leaving the corpse without any explanation for the locals.

But I left.

This guy was dead, but Ivan was still chained up in my basement. And I had no idea if my late assailant was after me or him. When I returned home, I saw no sign of any more intruders. I descended into the basement, and I was relieved to see Ivan alive and moving, even if he appeared to be trying to work his hands free of the cuffs.

"What the hell was that?" I asked him.

He looked up. "*Gde ten?*"

"What?"

"Where is the Shadow?"

"Shadow? You mean the man who was attacking you?"

The shadows are coming . . .

"No man." He shook his head. "No man."

"He looked like a man to me."

"No. It is an evil born out of the boiling Chaos—" Looking at him, I could see the strain of his effort to retain his composure. He muttered something else in Russian and quietly added, "I never thought I'd see one, have it *touch* me." He looked up and asked, "They are supposed to be impossible to strike or evade. How did you escape from it?"

"I let him chase me in front of a truck. He's dead. Now what was he? What does it mean, he was a Shadow?"

"Have you no legends of them?"

"I've been out of touch."

"I don't know how much of what I know is true. I just know the tales I've heard about them. That they aren't quite alive anymore, that they exist more between the worlds than in them, that they cannot be felled by normal weapons, that they're what is left of Walkers who wandered too far into the Chaos." Ivan swallowed. "What I saw of that thing, I know that part about weapons is true. I saw you fire on it and saw the bullets pass through—"

"When he was focused on me," I said. "A surprise attack could injure him. I shot his shoulder."

"That is comforting," Ivan said. "To know that this was not a ghost or some vengeful spirit."

I didn't know if I was ready to go that far. The past twelve hours had rapidly expanded my threshold for weirdness.

The shadows are coming . . .

"Another legend I know is true now," Ivan said. "They give no warning. They move through worlds, and you cannot sense them. A normal Walker— I would have sensed them approach, like you. I knew as you left and as you returned. That thing, I felt nothing until its hand was on my throat."

He was wrong, though. I had felt the Shadow touch my Mark before it had shown up. Ivan should have realized that, since I had run to retrieve my gun. He was probably thinking more of what the Shadow had done than what I had been doing.

I thought about correcting him, but as I started to talk, a more important question occurred to me. "Why did it attack you, Ivan?"

"Why? That is the nature of Shadows. They prey on those who walk between worlds, who stray too far into Chaos."

"But if these things are from Chaos, what was it doing here? You said that we were not in the Chaos."

"No. It isn't . . ." Ivan looked even more disturbed. "It shouldn't have been here, no more than they should wander the Empire."

"And why would it come to attack you?" I frowned, not liking the thoughts I was having.

"These things prey on the Walkers they encounter; it's their nature to feed on us, consume our flesh—"

"But why you? Why would the first time I've ever seen such a thing be right after you show up chasing one of my family?"

"My Lady, I know nothing of—"

"Bullshit!" I barely had control of my anger now. "There's no way this is a coincidence. You brought that thing here intentionally, or it followed you."

Ivan shook his head. "No, I didn't . . ."

Something clicked in my brain. What if the Shadow wasn't following *Ivan?* Who else could he have followed?

The Shadows are coming . . .

Plural.

I pulled out my cell phone and started dialing Jacob. "Tell me," I asked Ivan, "do these Shadows care if their meal is dead?"

"I've heard stories of them desecrating graves."

"Of course, you have—"

"Hello?" Jacob's voice was staticky and curt, like I caught him in the middle of something.

"Jacob, it's Dana! We may have a problem with John Doe's body."

More static and unidentifiable noises on the line.

"Jacob?"

"Sorry," Jacob said. "bzzt—d connect—bzzt—an't talk."

"Jacob, this is imp—"

"—bzzt—ck later. Th—bzzt—stage situ—bzzt—morgue."

The line went dead. I tried calling back, and I was dumped right into voice mail.

"Crap. Jacob, Ivan was attacked by something called a Shadow, they're murderous and possibly cannibalistic. Think *Dawn of the Dead*. They might go after John Doe's body. Keep away from them, whatever they're doing, and keep—"

The mailbox ran out of time and beeped at me. Jacob was about to engage these Shadows; it would be a hard to believe coincidence that a sudden hostage situation at the morgue *wouldn't* involve them converging on John Doe's body. And I was the only one even marginally equipped to handle them.

I also couldn't leave Ivan here to be picked off by any stragglers. I looked at him and said, "You're coming with me."

SIXTEEN

I WENT BEHIND Ivan to help him to his feet. Then I put him in an armlock before unlocking the cuff on his left wrist. He didn't fight me. I was grateful. If there had been a choice between subduing him and catching up with Jacob when my partner was in trouble, I would have let Ivan escape.

And that would have truly pissed me off.

I stepped him away from the pillar and snapped the cuff back on his left wrist. He looked at me—hands cuffed behind him—and asked, "Is that truly necessary?"

"Call it an incentive to keep you near the key. Come on."

I grabbed his bicep and walked him upstairs and to the garage. I felt his Mark whenever I touched him now, skin or clothes, a strong hand barely stroking my back. I think it had been there before, a subtle sensation that I was now hyperaware of after feeling the charge that had slammed me the two times I had directly touched his Mark.

In the garage, I shoved him into the passenger seat of my Charger and peeled out to race to the county morgue. Ivan was silent as I drove. I tried Jacob's cell twice and twice I was dumped into voice mail.

I felt a mass of conflicting emotions, a knotted ball that was hard for me to distinguish between where the panic over Jacob's situation ended and my anger at Ivan began. I had forgotten the anger for a time, even though I'd been carrying it ever since I'd pulled this guy out of his armor.

He was your kinsman, wasn't he?

John Doe wasn't just some cryptic link to my past. The more I thought about it, the more I felt convinced he was my family by blood, and he'd been slaughtered before I knew the most basic things about him.

Of all the feelings knotted up in my gut—grief, embarrassment, irritation, fear, anger—anger won. My knuckles whitened on the wheel, but before I could act on the building rage, I pulled up to the morgue.

I had other priorities now.

The scene at the county morgue was worse than I expected.

A dozen patrol cars, flashers going, crowded the parking lot. I could see police cars on the street along the other entrances and blocking off traffic on the cross streets. I saw two ambulances idling down the street, safe from any immediate crossfire.

"Shit," I whispered.

I pulled the Charger into the lot, and a young uniformed cop waved me off frantically as he started approaching. I stopped, lowered the driver's side window and had my badge out before he reached me.

The guy saw the badge and pointed me toward the row of patrol cars blocking the parking lot. Uniformed cops surrounded the building, guns drawn; as I parked, I could see a line of people race from one of the exits, escorted by more cops in riot gear.

"This is a mess," I whispered.

"My Lady—"

"Quiet!" I snapped at him, holding up my hand. I still had an untapped reservoir of anger, and I didn't want his voice stoking it while I had other issues to deal with. I tried Jacob's cell again, but it still dropped into voice mail.

I put the phone away and looked at Ivan. "You stay here. I don't want to have to explain your cuffs or your pirate clothing."

Before Ivan could respond, I had gotten out of the car. It was the last thing I wanted, leaving him unsupervised in my car. I would have felt better giving him free rein in my townhouse, where there wasn't anything I really cared about.

But I had no choice. Couldn't drag him into a firefight and couldn't leave him to be food for some wandering Shadow back home.

I ran up and flashed my badge at the nearest uniform and asked him what the situation was. He confirmed my worst fears. There were an unidentified number of terrorists in the building, everyone not involved in evacuating people was sitting tight waiting for SWAT and the hostage negotiation team, and Jacob was in there along with Ms. Whedon from the Justice Department.

There were fifty yards of no-man's-land between the police line and the building, so I couldn't just walk up to the building.

At least not across *this* parking lot.

Once I stopped talking to the cop, everyone stopped paying attention to me. A van was on the curb behind the line of police. I walked away from everyone, hanging my badge around my neck, and stepped behind the van and let the Mark push me once I was out of view.

I stepped out from the other side, and all the police were gone.

I ran across the parking lot, startling people on their lunch break who had no idea that there was a hostage crisis in this same building one universe over. I reached the entrance where, in another world, cops in riot gear were evacuating panicked civilians. I pushed through the doors and ran into a reception area, and two security guards started converging on me.

I stepped forward with a nudge from my Mark and slid back into my own world like slipping into a well-used chair. I had stepped away from the doorways because I didn't want to get tangled up with the escaping civilians, and—badge or no badge—I didn't want to step out into SWAT view drawing a gun.

However, in the time I'd been elsewhere, the evacuation out of this lobby had been completed. I saw the shadow of police flanking the entryway, waiting for orders to converge.

I realized that I was seriously off-script here, jumping into the middle of this.

But I *knew* it wasn't a normal hostage situation. I had started feeling it as I crossed the parking lot, but I felt it now full force—dead hands groping me. I shuddered at the cold touch, it was as if a corpse—multiple corpses—were trying to rape me and couldn't manage the coordination to actually consummate the act. I tried to imagine the touch was something else, just a breeze, but my brain wouldn't cooperate with the interpretation.

I stepped into an empty corridor and, back to a wall, I lowered my gun and took out my cell phone. I called Jacob again. It rang, but Jacob didn't answer.

Deeper in the building, I thought I heard something.

When Jacob's voice mail finally answered, I hung up. I dialed him again, lowering the phone from my ear. Somewhere deeper in the building I heard the strains of Ted Nugent's *Dog Eat Dog* start up again, ending when I hung up again. I kept dialing his number, stalking down the corridors toward his ringtone.

I had the uncomfortable sensation of approaching something evil in the empty building. What my Mark felt was vile, and I wished for Ivan's inability to sense these Shadows.

As I closed on the source of the ringtone, I started passing signs of the Shadows' arrival, or the occupants' retreat: an overturned water cooler, a microwave hanging open, a busted window on an office door. I reached an intersection in the corridor. On one wall was a bloody handprint, and in the area where the three corridors met, a copy machine made unpleasant mechanical noises, a bullet hole marring its side.

Oh, hell, Jacob.

I ducked around the corner. The corridor facing the copy machine was empty. It was short, the only exit a large pair of swinging doors marked "Authorized Personnel Only" and "Caution, Automatic

Door." The white walls were marred by a few streaks of blood, and another gunshot had darkened one of the fluorescent fixtures, dusting the linoleum with glass and broken plastic.

In the middle of the floor, in front of the doors, lay Jacob's cell phone wailing about overturned cop cars in Ted Nugent's voice.

I hung up.

A big button was on the wall about three feet away from the doors. I braced my gun at the doorway and hit the button with my hip. The doors swung inward, revealing a continuing corridor toward the morgue proper. They stopped moving when they hit a body.

I gasped a moment, thinking it was Jacob, but as the doors closed again, I could see the security guard's uniform. Blood smeared on the linoleum as the door swung itself shut.

I hit the button again and moved forward as the doors opened, slipping past the dead guard as I covered the hallway and swung around to make sure no one was concealed behind the half-opened doors.

The hall was empty, but the floor was covered with bloody footprints from a half dozen people, some with bare feet. A few sets seemed to appear and disappear at random as the owner moved forward.

I followed the footprints, hugging the wall and holding my Beretta ready. I passed two more bullet holes in the wall before I reached the doors to the room where the footprints led.

The footprints led right to the door and through. The surface of the door was smeared with bloody handprints, and I could hear muffled wet noises beyond them.

I pushed on the door, and it didn't want to budge.

Locked?

The Shadow I had seen seemed too narrowly focused to lock doors behind himself. That was just one guy, though; others might be less monster-of-the-week.

Or Jacob could have tried to barricade himself inside.

I pushed my Mark and stepped forward to face another door. I expected it to be free of bloody handprints, but it was as smeared as the one I had left. Behind me, I heard someone say, "What the hell?"

I glanced behind me and saw the twin of the dead security guard. He was bent over a pair of lab techs who were sitting on the floor, one holding a compress to his head. The guard looked at me with wide eyes, and I could tell he had just seen me appear out of nowhere.

At my feet were more bloody footprints.

The Shadows had been here for the same reason I'd come, to get around the blocked door.

As the guard reached for a sidearm, I pushed my way inside, shoving the Mark as I went, feeling invisible corpse hands pulling and tugging as if they were trying to flay the Mark from my skin. I stumbled inside the room, feeling violated.

I brought the gun up to cover the room, and it took me a moment before my brain had fully processed the image in front of me. John Doe's body sprawled half on and half off a stainless steel table. A bright overhead light carved everything into visceral clarity. The corpse had been rolled facedown so the upper torso hung over the edge of the table. I could see into the shadowed cavern opened by the massive Y-incision of an unfinished autopsy.

Nothing was left of the Mark on his back, nothing of the skin bearing the Mark. Under the harsh fluorescent light glistened raw muscle and the exposed nubs of his spine.

My gorge rose, half from the sight of the mutilated corpse, and half from the sensation I felt from being so close to six Shadows. The three nearest me, at the head of the autopsy table, responded to my presence by turning toward me.

I started firing.

My first shot got one who was still bent over John Doe's corpse; the 9mm slug slammed into the side of his skull, and he slumped across his unfinished meal, sliding to the ground. That was the last of my luck. The first gunshot alerted even the most oblivious of them, and the four following shots passed through their shifting bodies as if they were ghosts.

"Dana!" I heard Jacob's voice from deeper in the room, where he had braced himself behind a cart carrying surgical tools and tissue samples. Ms. Whedon was trying to fade into a corner behind him, apparently unhurt.

The Shadows converged on me as I backed up. No time to coordinate anything. I yelled, "I'm going to lead them away—"

I wanted to shift back with my Mark, but I couldn't do it scrambling backward, and I couldn't turn my back on these things. The bastards were too damn quick. I barely got the sentence out when the first leaped on top of me, grabbing at my gun hand. I got one shot off, grazing the guy's hip, but it didn't faze him.

Like the last one to attack me, this one was cadaverously thin, but way stronger than he appeared. He wore a shirt, but it was ragged and unwashed and splattered with fresh blood, as was his face.

He slammed me against the wall as the other four crowded around, looking for an opening. I tried to scream something at Jacob about going for the door while these things were distracted, but I was choked off by a hand clutching my throat and my field of view was filled by a crazed woman's face, all anorexic lines centered on a pair of eyes that were as completely black as the Mark on my skin. Her breath smelled of carrion, her teeth were rotting, and there were shreds of something unmentionable caught between them. I swear her jaw dislocated as she opened it, bending her face toward my shoulder.

I struggled against the hands holding me down, tensing for the feel of her teeth in my flesh. A red flash came out of nowhere, and a metal cylinder slammed into the side of her head. She stumbled away from me, the side of her face leaking a mixture of blood and black fluid, revealing Jacob raising a fire extinguisher up to bring it down on the arm holding my gun hand.

I didn't spare any thought for where his gun had gone as I heard bone crunch under his improvised bludgeon. I just wrenched my gun hand free and leveled it at the face of another one who was holding me down. My finger tightened, but the Shadow vanished before I fired. They understood how vulnerable they were while they were in the process of grappling with their victim.

I was suddenly free as the Shadows dissolved around me.

Jacob spun around in a circle, brandishing the fire extinguisher, "Fuck!" he yelled. "What are those things? Where did they go?"

"Ivan called them Shadows," I gasped, staring at the half-skinned corpse. I still felt dead hands perversely stroking my Mark. "They haven't gone far."

"They're part of—" Jacob was interrupted by Whedon, who had spent the time pulling away the barricade in front of the doors.

"Come on," she said. "Let's get out of here!"

SEVENTEEN

I TOOK UP the rear as we ran through the building, feeling the touch of the Shadows reaching for me all the time. I asked Jacob where his gun was as we ran.

"One of those things appeared behind me and grabbed it out of my hand."

I didn't want to hear about ambushes. It was bad enough to feel them around me without seeing them, I didn't want to add onto that the idea that they might be engaging in some sort of strategy.

We turned the corner, and I saw the light from the parking lot though the doorway up ahead. Just then, the feeling from my Mark became nearly intolerable. The sense of the Shadows around me intensified to the point where I probably couldn't tell if they flayed my back right then like they had John Doe.

"*Run!*" I called out.

Something appeared and grabbed for me, and I spun around, firing a shot into a gaping, blood-smeared face. I didn't wait to see the effect on my attacker. I pushed my Mark going forward, away from the Shadows, taking three steps through a hallway filled with startled people innocent of the cat-and-mouse game I played with the Shadows. When I reached the wall of the corridor, I turned around and took a step back.

I'd never used the Mark like this before, but the tactic was effective. I had stepped through a line of eight or nine converging Shadows. I was behind them now. Jacob and Whedon were running for the doors pursued by a trio of the Shadows, and one of them was just about to grab Whedon. I raised my gun, braced it two-handed, and took the extra seconds to aim because I knew I was only getting one shot.

It touched Whedon, and I fired, striking the Shadow dead center between the shoulder blades. It crumpled as it was hit, just like anyone else would have.

He . . .

It . . .

The remaining Shadows converged on me, and I pushed with the Mark and stepped toward them. The Shadows disappeared, and I ran toward the door past confused civilians who were still trying to make sense of the woman who had suddenly appeared in their midst. Halfway to the exit, I discovered the flaw in my tactic.

The Shadows were better at it.

I ran, and directly in front of me the remaining two Shadows who had been pursuing Jacob and Whedon suddenly blurred into existence. Someone here screamed as I plowed into the suddenly corporeal Shadows. The collision was too quick for me to use my Mark to slip by them. I felt a hand take an iron grip on my arm, twist, and I was slamming into the floor. I tried to turn, but I only managed to get on my side, my gun arm pinned under me as one Shadow fell to its knees, straddling my torso as the other yanked my Beretta out of my hand.

I'd been thinking of them as impersonal monsters so much that I think that I was surprised when the Shadow with my gun pointed it at an approaching security guard.

"*No!*" I screamed, but it fired, striking the guard in the chest.

I struggled under the weight of the one on top of me. But

it—*she*—had me pinned to the ground under her thighs, and I couldn't get the leverage to dislodge her.

This Shadow still looked human. She looked about nineteen, and her gauntness wasn't nearly as severe, and her hair wasn't as matted. She wore a black concert T-shirt for a band I'd never heard of, and mostly intact blue jeans. The only signs she was abnormal were the solid black of her eyes and the edges of unhealed wounds pulsing black revealed when her T-shirt rode up.

I struggled, and she grabbed the lower half of my face in a viselike grip. She said nothing, just shaking her head as, out of my view, I heard more screams and gunshots. She brushed the hair from my face with a free hand, licked her lips with a black tongue, and smiled.

The hunger I saw in her face made me shudder.

I could feel the other Shadows drawing closer even if I couldn't see them.

At least Jacob and Whedon had got away. . . .

Then, as the teenage Shadow on top of me bent down, a pair of arms dropped over her head. I saw a flash of chrome, her head pulled back, and her weight was suddenly off me.

I pushed myself upright and saw Ivan.

He had the chain of his handcuffs around the Shadow's throat, and as she struggled, he spun around with her to face the Shadow with the gun. The last two shots slammed into the Shadow Ivan was holding up. The Shadow with my gun threw it aside once it was empty, and Ivan dropped his shield. He turned toward me, and his eyes widened as he yelled something imperative in Russian.

I didn't need a translator. We both ran out the door with something more than ten Shadows following us.

"*Shit!*" I cried out as we ran into the parking lot. Even with the gunshots, things had happened too quickly for the parking lot to empty of people. At the far end ahead of us were half a dozen people exiting cars, returning from their lunch hour, and just now realizing that something bad was happening.

I didn't want to lead the Shadows into another mass of civilians.

They might be coming after us, but they had shown no reluctance to kill anyone who came between them and their target.

I grabbed Ivan's arm and pushed with my Mark as we ran. Around us the light and most of the cars dissolved as overcast day became a rain-swept night. I risked a glance behind me as we ran across the rain-slick asphalt. I saw the Shadows appear behind us, flashing into existence one at a time.

I led Ivan out of the parking lot, the Shadows less than a hundred feet away. On the night-empty street, I pushed forward with my Mark again as I ran. This time I could feel Ivan pushing as well, a strong comforting hand that brushed aside the corpselike fingers grasping for me.

The world around us became an indistinct blur, the sky melting into a blue-gray that pulsed in time with my heart. The traffic on the road became shimmering walls flanking the double yellow line, walls made of fluid metal and glass. Even the buildings around us became less substantial, as if they verged on the edge of unreality.

I pushed myself harder with the Mark than I had ever tried before. Ivan's phantom hand on my back urged me forward, past the point where I would have normally fallen back. My breath burned in my throat, but even though I ran full out, my body had begun to acclimate itself. My muscles were used to this; it was the Mark that ached with new use—and as I forced the Mark through the wall, I felt a burst of endorphins that gave me a runner's high like I had never felt before. I wasn't running anymore, I felt as if I was flying, dragging Ivan behind me.

My body throbbed with the new contact, the fear pushed aside, feeding into the new sensations, sharpening it in a way I'd never done on my own. Ivan's presence, the danger, it all fed into a throbbing rush with every running step, every ragged breath, every step through the surreal landscape around us.

Around us, the world itself began to lose its physical character, as if a fog began to warp everything in a featureless white mist until even the asphalt I ran on became indistinct under my feet. If anything, the dissolving of the world around me enhanced the feeling that I flew through the barriers between worlds. My legs felt very far away, and Ivan became a negligible weight on my arm. My Mark throbbed with a new sense of power; the touch I felt was now completely my own. *Its* own. The touch I felt now overwhelmed my entire body, no longer only hands. I felt as if I was in contact with something so much larger than myself that with the touch of one phantom finger it could lift me into the sky.

For a brief moment of physical near-ecstasy I forgot about Ivan, John Doe, Jacob, Shadows, and everything else outside of what I felt at that moment. As I flew through a white nonworld unlike anything I had ever seen before, even sound became washed out to the point where all I heard was my own breathing.

A small faraway voice screamed, "*Stop!*"

That cut through everything, and I let go.

Pain and exhaustion slammed into me like the UPS truck had slammed into the Shadow. I sucked in gasping breaths as my legs buckled under my trembling body. I barely perceived it as Ivan fell, his arm slipping from my fingers, the touch of his Mark fading from my own as he dissolved into the white mist around me.

"No!" I yelled in an agonized gasp as I pitched forward into a road of broken asphalt. I forced myself back to my feet, even as my body shook with the painful aftershocks of my exertion. I turned around to find Ivan, but the street behind me was empty of everything but the occasional weed. Above me, the gray sky was pregnant with snow, and my breath fogged. The buildings around me—the ones that still stood—were little more than empty shells. The area here was more far gone than the worst parts of East Cleveland, and what was truly disturbing was the lack of graffiti or plywood. Everything here appeared completely abandoned by even destructive human contact.

The only sound here was the screaming of a million crows that perched on every horizontal surface like a black rot in the surface of reality itself.

I felt no touch from the Shadows, and I barely felt Ivan. And I could feel my sense of his presence getting weaker. As if he was moving away. Why would he try to escape when he had come in to save me from the Shadows?

I stared at the black shells of buildings around me and remembered what he had said about Chaos, about worlds being fluid and not having fixed relations to each other.

He wasn't moving away from me; where he *was* was moving away from me. And *fast.*

Around me, the plague of crows burst into flight with an apocalyptic burst of wings.

I ached and felt as if the most sensitive parts of my body had just been scooped out with a melon baller. The last thing I wanted right now was to feel the Mark's touch. But I had no choice.

I pushed my Mark with a gasp and moved off toward what I felt of Ivan. It may have only been a second between losing my grip on him and when I'd stopped, but it took an agonizing three-minute run though the whiteness to catch up with him again.

I found him in an unfamiliar city park. The grass was well kept, and the trees were turning bright red. He leaned against a pedestal and above him loomed a rearing equestrian statue that looked to be, of all people, Dennis Kucinich.

He turned around and looked at me as I came up to him.

His face was flushed, and he was out of breath. "I'm slowing you down."

Parts of me still trembled and it took me a moment before I could catch my own breath enough to talk. "We outran them," I said.

I pulled out the keys with a shaking hand and unlocked the handcuffs from his wrists.

He looked around the park. "How can you know that?"

"I don't feel them anymore."

"What?" he said. "Everything I know about them says that you can't ever sense them coming."

"You're saying you know everything about them?"

He rubbed his wrists and shook his head.

"Like where the hell they came from?" I said, my voice becoming harsher. I was rediscovering the anger I had been feeling earlier, helped along by the massive aches I felt now that I had stopped running.

"I don't know."

I grabbed his shirt, "Why should I believe you? You killed the only real family I've ever found. You broke in on me waving a sword and came pretty damn close to killing me. And you show up and suddenly the ground is thick with extras from a George Romero movie." I shoved him against the base of the statue. "You owe me some explanations."

"My Lady, I came to help you even when I still bore your shackles on my wrists!"

"You can start by explaining why you did that."

He *had* saved my life from these things, and that tempered my anger, but only a bit. I still thought it was a good fifty-fifty chance that these things showing up were his fault.

"Because I serve my Emperor."

"You better start getting more specific."

He stared into my eyes and almost seemed ready to strike me. I might have wanted him to; a physical confrontation was more straightforward and easier to understand. I had known Ivan less than twenty-four hours, and already our relationship was way more complicated than I wanted it to be. I wanted to push things back to the place where it was only attack and defend.

"Well?"

"I told you. I wish to bring you back to my Emperor's court."

"Told me?" I remembered this morning, which already felt as if it had been years ago, when Ivan had me pinned behind a stove and had leveled his sword against me, *"You will now surrender and return with me."*

"You expect me to surrender to you? *Now?*"

He shook his head. "No. But if you came voluntarily, as a guest, it could . . . ease what I must face on my return."

"I should not only let you go, but go *with* you to make things *easier*? Are you insane?"

"Not only have I failed in my charge to recapture the escapee, I've lost the badge of my office, my weapon, my armor—these are capital offenses."

"You expect my tears?"

"I expect your curiosity."

I let go of his shirt and took a step back. I had fallen into the predictability of the argument, prodding him along as I prodded myself along. But what he said shook my confidence.

He straightened himself, regaining something of a dignified military bearing. "You want to know about the man I was charged to recapture. I do not have those answers, but the Emperor's advisers do. You are clearly a Prince. The way you glide through Chaos tells me as much. But your ignorance tells me that you've had no training, or exposure to the worlds beyond your own."

I was sure at some point I had tried to play things close to the vest, but I suddenly had the feeling that I had told Ivan more about myself than he had told me.

"You are a sovereign, even in your ignorance, and no right is granted me to compel you to perform my bidding. However, should you allow me to escort you to my Emperor's demesne, you would have the status granted any ruler who comes in the spirit of diplomacy, and I suspect you would find answers to many of your questions."

I slowly nodded. "And this would be a coup for you that might mitigate anything else you got screwed up."

"As you say."

I shook my head, wondering if it was possible for things to be even more complicated than they already were. "We need to go back home and see what kind of damage those Shadows are responsible for."

EIGHTEEN

I SENSED RELUCTANCE from Ivan though he didn't voice it. He was giving me a lot more deference than I was comfortable with, and I got the feeling that it was more than he was comfortable with as well. I wasn't the type of woman who was cut out for nobility—at the very least I suspected that I was pushing the envelope of whatever respect Ivan felt duty-bound to give me.

I could see he didn't want to return. I almost didn't want to myself. My body still ached from the effort of running, from what I felt from the Mark.

Ivan followed me as I pushed back toward home, and I didn't have to pull him along. As we returned, I got my first good look at Chaos.

While I'd run, it had been a featureless white blur. At a more sedate pace, I could see why. At home, passing through worlds past or future, the vast majority of the landscape had some constancy. People, cars, and the odd bit of trash would blur from one world to the next, but the streets and buildings, lampposts and fire hydrants, those remained stable, giving a solid backdrop when I used my Mark.

This far away from my home, the universe lost that constancy. There was no longer a solid backdrop to my movement. Buildings and trees flitted in and out of existence, and even the road under my feet mutated with each step, crumbling and uncrumbling, changing from asphalt to concrete to brick to gravel to disappearing entirely.

And, as I used the Mark, I *felt* the instability around me. Before, I had been overwhelmed by the rush to escape, and then the euphoria of fully unleashing the Mark for possibly the first time. Now, as I moved slowly through universe after universe, I could feel more subtle feedback from the Mark. If walking through the worlds familiar to me was like walking down a wide concrete highway, out here it felt as if I walked across free-floating chunks of ice moving across invisible rapids.

Also, more than ever, I felt a direction to my motion—beyond us walking forward. I always felt that the Mark's push was in some other dimension, beyond the three I could point to. Out here now I was more aware of my motion in that invisible dimension because I could feel other movements in directions perpendicular to the Mark's, and, somehow, it felt as if there were more than two other axes of motion involved. Like walking into a headwind, I had to shift my movement with the Mark to compensate and keep going where I wanted.

I began to understand how people could become lost in this. Now that I was aware of what my Mark felt, I could feel that if I simply stopped in one of these worlds, I would keep "moving" farther away from my home. It reignited one of my first visceral fears about the Mark, that I could use it and never find my way back.

I picked up the pace.

IT took over an hour to make it back home. Partly because the relative motion meant we moved away much faster than we could return, partly because Ivan couldn't move through the worlds as fast as I could. I probably could have grabbed him and pulled him along like I had during the escape from the Shadows, but I didn't want to come that close to feeling his Mark again. It was already an uncomfortable warm presence between my shoulders, more distracting now that the Shadows were not touching me.

As we came back to my world, the buildings around us became more stable and eventually solidified. The ground seemed to firm up beneath my feet, and muscles I hadn't known had been tensed started to relax. I may have even sighed in relief.

I stopped using the Mark once I could feel I was back on familiar ground. We weren't quite back where we started, but I needed to regroup a bit. The road and the buildings were familiar as we walked along a nighttime street toward a Rapid Transit stop about a block east of the county morgue.

I rolled my shoulders against an ache deep in my Mark, though the ache I felt was in places that didn't seem to exist in the same spaces the rest of me did.

"Have you ever walked in Chaos before?" Ivan asked after several long moments of silence.

"No," I told him. "It's tiring."

Ivan shook his head. "My Lady, without the additional speed granted by my armor, it would have taken me days to navigate what you just blithely strolled through. And if my attention faltered . . ." He trailed off.

Now that I knew he had an ulterior motive, I had decided to take any of his deference with a grain of salt. He had some reason to exaggerate my distinctiveness, both to ingratiate himself to me and to play up my importance to his Emperor.

Cynicism was one cop thing I did right.

I walked up to a newspaper machine to see how close I actually was to home. I think I gasped when I saw the date.

"Are you all right?"

I turned to him and said, "1986?"

"I don't understand?"

"I never . . ." I shook my head. I'd never gone more than a month or two away from home. But I didn't even know any more if my idea of time held any real meaning. If I thought of the places I went as other worlds, it seemed natural to think of them as being five minutes, ten minutes, an hour, away in past or future. . . .

"There's more than one direction," I said to myself.

"My Lady?"

"I felt movement in more than one direction out there." All my life I'd only walked in one dimension, back and forward, past and future. It began to dawn on me how far beyond my prior experience we had gone. My side trip through Chaos had displaced me thirty years from the world I knew.

The *worlds* I knew.

How densely packed were these universes? If I went five minutes ahead from this "now," would I find another 1986? Five seconds? A fifth of a second?

"Are you all right?" Ivan asked me.

"No." I looked away at a world three decades removed from my own. "There's too much. Can there really be an infinite number of worlds out there? How can anyone not become lost in this?"

"It is not Chaos here."

"How do you know that?" He was right, though; I felt the stability of the world around me, so unlike the fragile reality I had just experienced.

"Because it is of your realm."

"How? If I've never been to this world before, this 1986?"

"You're here now."

"What does that have to do with anything?"

"It is the nature of a Prince. To remain anywhere for long, even somewhere boiled up from Chaos, is to grant it permanence. We are close enough to the heart of your domain that just your act of stopping here was enough to solidify this place."

To Ivan, it was the presence of a Walker that made a place real to begin with, and it required a powerful Walker—a Prince—to lend that reality any sort of persistence. If I understood his elaborate description—and at this point that was a big "if"—then my world, my home, would be a large cluster of very similar places, all marked by my extended presence at some time or another. Their form would be dictated by a combination of my desire—since I had used the Mark to push me toward what I wanted—and by their proximity to the more "solid" world I lived in.

One of the side effects of this "solidity" would be to make these worlds more "there" for other Walkers. Once within the fuzzy boundaries of my influence, other Walkers, even Princes, would find themselves limited to moving along the paths I had already trod.

The way he talked about it made me uncomfortable, as if this version of 1986 and all the people in it only existed because I had decided to stop here at random. And, according to Ivan, without a Walker's presence periodically, this 1986 would eventually dissolve back into the Chaos from which it came.

What about the people who live here? I wondered. Was all of this beyond their perception? Did they exist before this place came out of Ivan's Chaos? What about when it returned?

"When you say a place returns to Chaos, does that mean it ceases to exist, or does it just mean we can no longer reach it?"

"What is the difference?"

I could move quicker this close to home; there was little, if any, feeling of the world shifting under my feet. It actually made things more uncomfortable for me. Without the constant slipping and maneuvering to take my attention, I found myself focusing on Ivan's presence. Feeling his touch on my own Mark was too intimate and there was nothing I could do about it. It wasn't as if he had control over how I perceived his own mark.

At least I doubted he did.

We finally reached the morgue—my morgue—close to two hours after the Shadows' attack. The police blockades were gone, and the parking lot held only about four police cars. I also saw two local news crew vans and a couple of ambulances.

My Charger sat by the curb, still where I had parked it.

It beeped welcomingly at me as I pressed the unlock button on my keychain. "Okay," I told Ivan, "I need to sort things out here. After I make sure Jacob's all right and has things under control, I'll take you home and pack."

"You will come back to the Empire with me?"

I nodded. "Yes."

Half of me was screaming *bad idea,* but the other half told me that I had little choice. Even if I disregarded the need I felt to understand where I'd come from, who my birth family was, and what existed out there past the Chaos, the existence of the Shadows made those questions much less academic. I couldn't ignore everything John Doe and Ivan had brought to my doorstep. Not when those things could return and wreak havoc.

Like it or not, trust him or not, Ivan was the only solid living connection I had to anyone who might be able to tell me anything. Not just about my own origin, but—at this point more important—what the Shadows were and why they were attacking here and now.

I opened the passenger door and waved Ivan in. I had planned to make him wait while I hunted down Jacob, but my partner saved me the trouble. I heard him call "Dana," before Ivan had even taken a step toward the passenger seat.

We turned to see Jacob and Ms. Whedon from the Justice Department walking across the parking lot toward us. Jacob looked a little rumpled, but Ms. Whedon looked like she'd been through hell. She was as white as a sheet, and she gave me a stare that was half-accusing, half-terrified.

It dawned on me that she had seen me use the Mark, possibly more than once. They both had. After all I had been through in the past two hours, after nearly being killed, it wasn't until now that I finally felt full-blown panic.

Facing death and a multi-universe-spanning existential crisis didn't affect me nearly as intensely as seeing the carefully crafted fiction of my life crumbling within Ms. Whedon's expression.

"Where did you go?" Jacob asked me. He drew up short and looked at Ivan. "And what are you doing with him?"

"We came to an understanding," I told him.

Whedon walked up to me. "I would like an explanation, Detective Rohan."

I'm sure you would.

"Who were those . . ." Whedon asked. "*What* were they?"

I sighed. This was a mess several orders of magnitude beyond what I'd been expecting when my secret finally unraveled.

"We have another dead body in there," Jacob added. "One you shot."

I shook my head. It was becoming too much. "Look, can we do this somewhere else? It's a long story, and I don't know how—"

I was shocked when Whedon pushed by me and slipped into the open door and took the passenger seat. She looked up at me, "We can have the conversation wherever you want, but we're having it now."

I felt the urge to grab her and tell her to get the hell out of my car, but I restrained myself. Instead, I opened the back door and told Jacob and Ivan to get in.

I slammed both doors and, as I walked around my car, I had another impulse—to push with my Mark and just abandon everything. I could escape to 1986 and start over—leave my Charger, Jacob, and everything.

I'm just going to talk to them. It won't change anything, it's all done already.

I pulled open the door and slid into the driver's seat.

As I pulled away from the curb, Whedon asked, "Where are we going?"

"I don't know." And I didn't. I originally intended to go to my house, but I wasn't going to do that with Whedon tagging along. It had been hard enough letting Jacob into that part of my life.

I drove toward downtown. I could drop Whedon back at the station when this was over with.

"Tell me what happened," she said. There was a different character to her voice, as if this wasn't the same woman who'd come to harass us from the Justice Department. Her voice was steady, but very far away, as if she wasn't completely in the car with us.

I glanced across at her. She stared intently out the windshield, at the late afternoon traffic down Chagrin Boulevard. Her skin was still a colorless shade of near-terror, and her body language was so tense that I wouldn't have been surprised if she just spontaneously began screaming.

I looked back where I was driving, suddenly surprised to discover how petty my irritation with her actually was. Had been. She had been in the right. I had been going around the rules of police procedure to produce the statistics that brought her here. I just wasn't bending the rules in the way she had expected.

After what she had just been through, she deserved an explanation.

"I can explain," I told her, "but it's a little hard to believe."

"Harder than teleporting zombie cannibals?"

NINETEEN

THE DRIVE TO the station was way too short for me to tell the whole story as I knew it. So when I got downtown, I got on I-71 south, toward the airport. The more I spoke, the more words came out, way beyond the thumbnail cosmology that Ivan had granted me—and I was thankful he didn't interrupt—but I confessed to her about how I had used my Mark to become a trans-universal vigilante. I even started talking about my childhood, and how I could never talk to my parents—my adoptive parents—about this.

The only thing that stopped my manic confessional was the touch of a corpselike hand along my Mark.

Oh, shit.

"What's the matter?" Whedon asked me.

"They're here," I whispered.

"Who's here?" Jacob said from behind me.

We had just exited the freeway, and I was driving past the airport on the surface streets, intending to turn around at a gas station ahead. But the corpselike touches multiplied, and the traffic ahead of us was slowing to a stop.

"Who's here?" Whedon asked, a slightly more intense note to her voice than had been in Jacob's.

I slowed the Charger as I rolled toward a sea of brake lights. I saw signs of a commotion up ahead, a possible accident. Then I saw figures moving between the cars, running in our direction.

I slammed on the brakes with a screech and—not having the space to turn around—shifted the Charger into reverse and backed up, accelerating across the double yellow line. Horns blared at me as a small horde of Shadows ran toward my car, weaving through the ranks of stopped traffic.

Whedon gripped the dash and stared at the Shadows with widening eyes. "My God."

I spun the car around in a move that I'd only ever attempted in an offensive driving course where the other traffic was a rank of orange cones. The rear fishtailed with a screech of burning rubber and the nose of the Charger pivoted to point back toward the freeway. Cars blared horns and swerved to miss us—but the northbound lanes had much lighter traffic than the Shadow-clogged southbound ones.

I floored it back toward the on-ramp for I-480. As the Charger flew up the on ramp I yelled, "How did they—"

I never finished the question. A wrecked Ford F150 on its side blocked both lanes of the on ramp. I could just see Shadows emerging from behind the wreck.

"Fuck!"

I slammed on the brakes and did something I'd never done behind the wheel of a car.

As the Charger sped up the ramp toward the underside of the pickup truck, I pushed with my Mark.

A panic reaction—the jolt rammed through my body hit before I had any time to consider what I was doing.

The world around the on ramp went blurry, and the Charger flew through the space where the wrecked pickup had been. The sky went dark and, when I'd stopped pushing, a nighttime rain sheeted down across the windshield. I brought the Charger to a skidding stop in the breakdown lane of a near-deserted I-480.

I gasped, body shaken from the sudden effort. This time it was more than the touch of the Mark, it was a deep visceral fear over what I had attempted. I'd never tried using the Mark from a moving vehicle because, if it worked at all without me moving under my own power, I'd always suspected I would have appeared in the next universe three feet above the road, flying through the air at sixty-five miles per hour, leaving a runaway vehicle behind me. My heart pounded, and I clutched the wheel in a death grip because my body was not convinced that hadn't happened.

Whedon hyperventilated next to me, gasping, "What. Was. That?"

"I . . ." I trailed off. Everything was still sinking in. As the panic receded, I realized that in the few moments I had pushed the Mark, I had gone farther through worlds in a shorter time than I had even during my panicked run into Chaos. It was as if, for a brief moment, I had become the Charger, racing down the road.

"I can do that?" I finished.

From the back seat, Ivan said, "A truly powerful Prince can lead an army into—"

"*What was that?*" The level tone in Whedon's voice had cracked completely, the hysteria breaking through in full force. I turned toward her. Not only had her skin become pale and waxy, she had broken out into a sweat. In the sudden darkness, she looked nearly as corpselike as one of the Shadows.

"It's what I was telling you." I tried to put a calm, commanding tone into my voice, even though the magnitude of what I'd just done was freaking me out as well. "I moved us into another—"

"Why does it hurt?" Her voice was breathless, and her eyes were wide. She looked at me as if I was one of the Shadows about to attack her.

"Hurt? What's the matter?" I glanced back at Ivan, but in the shadowed back seat I couldn't read his expression and he didn't volunteer anything that might explain what her reaction might mean.

She grabbed her arm and turned away from me. "Take me back," she whispered.

"Your arm?" Jacob asked from the back seat. He leaned over and said, "You're injured?"

"I-it's nothing." She shook her head.

I reached over and put a hand on her shoulder. She winced. "If you're hurt, you need us to take a look at—"

She screamed as a figure slammed itself against the passenger window.

"*Shit!*" The empty lanes of I-480 were suddenly clogged with converging Shadows. My initial panic, followed by worry over Whedon, had distracted me from the fact that the feeling of the Shadows along my Mark had not gone completely away. I floored the Charger at a cluster of three of them, but they blurred out of existence as my car passed through them.

"Ivan! How do I get rid of these things?"

"I don't know!"

I rushed down a rainy stretch of I-480, leaving the Shadows behind by the shoulder, but the feeling of the Shadows on my Mark was not receding. *Crap, did one of them grab onto my car?*

Ahead, in the westbound lanes, I saw a pair of headlights approaching. They were about a mile away and rushing forward. A moment later, I could also see the yellow lights framing the silhouette of a semi with a double trailer going way too fast for this weather. I was pushing the Charger at nearly ninety myself, so it came up on the left a second or two after I had noticed it.

I wasn't completely surprised at what happened because I could feel the Shadows' grip on my Mark intensify.

When the semi was barely two hundred yards away from us, it swerved into the median with enough momentum to half destroy the concrete barrier, and half climb over it. The cab kept moving into our lanes, dragging a trailer that started disintegrating and rolling toward us at the same time.

I skidded to avoid the wreck of the semi tumbling toward us, and if

I hadn't already primed myself to push again with the Mark, we would have been chewed up like a bicycle thrown into the path of a combine.

My windshield filled with a cascade of tumbling metal that almost kissed the front bumper when it blurred out of existence. I floored the Charger and pushed with my Mark as hard as I could, away from the touch of the Shadows. The world blurred around me, gripped quickly by the white fog of Chaos. I strained hard, everything inside me gripped by the effort, a pulsing throb in me, pulled forward in a nearly unstoppable cascade.

I barely heard Whedon screaming.

I drove the Charger, pushing the speedometer toward ninety, pushing myself until I was pulled as tight as a piano wire. My entire body vibrated with the power of the Mark slamming into me, the pressure cascading through me with such intensity that it took me several seconds to realize that the vibrations I felt were resonating through the whole car. I slowed the car down, forcing my awareness outside myself and the throbbing pressure of my Mark.

The shaking got worse, and I slowed to just under ten miles an hour. I felt no more touches from the Shadows, so I released myself from the Mark and fell back into the world with a gasping shudder as the aftershocks from my effort wracked my body. I held the wheel in a white-knuckled grip as the Charger rolled to a stop in front of the blade of a large bulldozer. I gritted my teeth to keep from groaning.

The rain and the Shadows were long gone, and daylight streamed down from a cloudless blue sky.

Whedon sobbed next to me.

"Are you all right?" Jacob asked.

"N-No," Whedon said. "It hurts."

I barely felt in control of myself enough to release the wheel and say, "Show me where you're hurt."

She looked worse in the daylight. In addition to the sweat and the white skin, she was shivering. Whatever was wrong, she had all the appearance of someone going into shock. I'd already decided she needed to go to the hospital before she rolled up her sleeve.

"Oh, God," Jacob groaned. I didn't know if he was reacting to the sight, or the smell.

On Whedon's left forearm, just short of the elbow, was a bite mark. Two crescent marks where the individual teeth could be just made out. The wound seemed to have eroded the flesh around it, the edges of the wound a blood-tinted white, the depths of it an impenetrable featureless black that stank of rotting meat.

That would have been bad enough, but black threads traced up and down from the wound, etching the flesh from beneath, and in a few cases erupted through the surface of the skin so the flesh pulled back from a slash of black carved into the skin.

Like the pattern carved into the flesh of the Shadows.

Someone pounded on the driver's side window and I almost jumped out of my own skin. Fortunately, I felt no touch from the Shadows, and when I turned to face the window, I saw a face that bore a reassuringly human expression.

Even so, the guy looked pissed.

I rolled down the window, letting in the guy's speech mid-sentence. "—the fuck you think you're doing. This area's restricted, ain't even a goddamn road here yet. You wanna wreck your shiny new car, or you just trying to get yourself killed?"

The man was in his late forties, early fifties, wearing mud-spattered overalls and a hard hat. Those could have marked him as a foreman anywhere. However, I couldn't help but stare at his anachronistic hair style. A pair of almost comically long sideburns emerged from under the scuffed yellow of his hard hat. That, combined with the porn mustache, made it hard to take the guy seriously.

"Sorry," I told him, "wrong turn."

"You fucking kidding me? Are you stoned? We haven't built the goddamned on ramp yet."

"Just tell us how to get off the—"

"Fuck that, sister. You staying right there until the cops show to lock up your hippie ass. I'm fucking tired of—"

I think I muttered, "Sorry" as I shifted the Charger into reverse.

It wasn't an off-road vehicle, and it threw up a sheet of mud and gravel as the rear wheels tried to get a grip on the ground beneath us. It splattered Mr. Porn-stache chest-high as the Charger lurched backward. I didn't use my Mark again. My body was crying *enough*, and I had plenty to concentrate on, just keeping control of the Charger.

More construction crew ran toward us from behind the bulldozer, jumping down from other earth-moving equipment ahead of us.

Luckily the proto-road was mostly clear behind us—even if it was mostly compacted earth slashing across the landscape. I kept the Charger going backward, craning my neck behind me to navigate.

I drove that way until we were out of sight of the construction crew, because I didn't want to bog my car down trying to turn around. I backed until I passed a muddy track that was an obvious construction entrance. I went slowly forward down the trail, avoiding the worst ruts, and passed a white trailer, several parked items of Caterpillar equipment, and stacks of rebar, and stopped in front of a closed chain-link gate. Beyond the fence was a residential neighborhood across the street.

Whedon groaned next to me.

"Don't worry," I told her. "We'll get you to a hospital." I looked behind me at Jacob. "Can you open that?"

"Yeah." He stepped out and ran to the gate.

In the rearview mirror, I saw the door open on the trailer and three people got out. They all wore hard hats, but theirs were white. Instead of overalls, the one in the lead wore a gray suit and tie. That guy carried a bricklike walkie-talkie.

I felt a hand on my arm, and I turned to look at Whedon. I could see pleading in her eyes. "Please, d-don't do that again."

"Do what?"

"You drove away from those things. When you do, it hurts. It's eating into me."

She was talking about me using the Mark.

Did I do this to her?

I looked into the back and asked Ivan, "Do you know what's happening to her?"

He shook his head. "Before this day, I had never even seen a Shadow."

"Don't your legends tell of how to treat a wound by them?"

"No. In the legend, no one survives contact with them."

"So who's left to record the legend?"

Ivan didn't respond.

The trio from the trailer had converged on Jacob, and I returned my attention forward. I found myself bracing to run the gate, but it was the adrenaline speaking. I took a few deep breaths and told myself that the concern right now was getting Whedon to a hospital, and there wasn't any reason that the construction crew wouldn't call an ambulance—even if we were stoned trespassing hippies. It took an effort, but I unclenched my fingers from the steering wheel as I watched Jacob talking to the trio of men.

He gestured at the car a few times, and eventually he showed them his badge. Whatever he told them, it was effective. The guy in the suit started talking on his walkie-talkie and walking back to the trailer. The others went and started opening the gate for us.

Jacob walked back to the car and got back into the seat behind Whedon. "Okay, we're good to go."

I started rolling forward, through the gate. "What did you tell them?"

"Police investigation of an exotic car smuggling ring."

"What?"

"You realize the weirdest thing about us is that you're driving a 2016 Dodge Charger? They started building 480 in the 1970s."

"The 70s?" I said, half-disbelieving even though I was recently in 1986. But I only had to drive half a block before the cars made it obvious what era we were in. VW Beetles, first-generation Datsuns, Plymouth muscle cars, and Oldsmobile land yachts. As I drove through the neighborhood bisected by the interstate construction, people with scary 70s hair turned to watch us pass.

I was getting the kind of looks one would expect driving a Lamborghini through Parma Heights. *Exotic car, check.*

"Okay," I said, "we need to find a hospital."

TWENTY

I PULLED THE Charger into the parking lot outside of St. Vincent's Charity Hospital circa 1975. I didn't like taking Whedon to a hospital that was over thirty years out of date, but if my pulling her along with the Mark was worsening things for her, I had no choice. My only consolation was that these doctors would have just as much experience with this as a more contemporary team.

She started to become delirious when we walked her into the emergency room. When the admission nurse saw her wound, they immediately took her back into the trauma room. Jacob managed to use his badge to get us back where we could keep an eye on her as they started the exam.

The three of us stood back by one wall as they placed her on a gurney. Whedon was saying, again and again, "It hurts . . ." One of the nurses drew a hypodermic of something as one of the orderlies held her shoulders down. The doctor told her that they were just going to make her a little sleepy so they could see what was going on.

The nurse rolled up her sleeve and injected something in her good arm. Once she did, the doctor and another nurse started cutting away the shirt around the wound. Whedon's left sleeve fell to the ground by the doctor's feet, the material spotted with black and flecks of blood.

The doctor's face grew pale as he said, "Oh, God."

I never before heard a doctor say those words in that tone of voice. I hoped I never would again. What I could see of Whedon's arm through the crowd of emergency staff confirmed my worst imaginings. The threads of black hadn't stopped their growth, and everywhere they grew, the skin had split open in a new wound filled with black. It had grown as far as her shoulder.

"Gangrene," the doctor said, though I'm sure I heard a note of uncertainty in his voice. "Have them prep the OR for emergency surgery."

Whedon groaned on the table. The doctor leaned over. "Relax, we're going to have to remove the infected tissue." Then he stood up and looked at one of the nurses. "She's not fully sedated, give her another 5ccs of—"

He was interrupted by a crash as a stainless steel tray fell from a cart next to him, scattering instruments across the floor, including the hypodermic the nurse was using. One of the orderlies cursed, scrambling back, and a stand with an IV bag fell noisily onto another cart with heart monitoring equipment.

Jacob stepped forward. "What the hell?"

Everyone was backing away from the gurney, and Whedon was sitting upright, waving a scalpel. One of the orderlies cradled his arm, his scrubs splattered with his own blood.

Her hand shook as she pointed the scalpel at the doctor. "I need to go home now." Her voice slurred, probably from the sedation. She wobbled a bit as she sat up, and the blouse she had worn fell off her left shoulder where the doctor had removed the sleeve and slit the material to the collar. It revealed a lacy satin bra that seemed so unlike the businesslike pain in the ass Whedon had been. It also revealed the perverse Mark that ate its spidery pattern into her arm, and up across her shoulder.

The doctor got points from me for sliding in front of the nurse and the wounded orderly to face Whedon. "Put that down," he said, "You're sick and not thinking clearly."

Whedon slid off the edge of the gurney and stood, swaying back and forth. "I'm going home."

Jacob cursed, and I saw his hand reaching for an empty shoulder holster. I held out an arm in front of him and stepped forward. "Jessica?"

The IV stand leaned up against one of the carts, still attached to Whedon's scalpel-wielding arm. When she took an unsteady step forward, she pulled it crashing forward before the tube finally pulled free of the needle taped in her arm.

She squinted in my direction. "D-detective Rohan?"

I swallowed when I saw her eyes. I could see spreading patches of black, as if someone had put drops of India ink to bleed across the sclera. "Listen to the doctor."

The doctor said, "You have a bad infection, and it's spreading. We need to treat it before—"

"Bullshit!" She swiped with the scalpel so aggressively that the doctor stumbled back, almost knocking over the nurse behind him.

I took a couple of steps forward. It wasn't close to ideal, but she was unsteady enough that I was pretty sure that I could get control of her arm before she managed to do me any real harm with the scalpel. I kept my hands low, spread, and open as I said, "We're trying to help you."

"You don't even know what's happening to me!" Her voice and her posture steadied, as if anger increased her lucidity. She pointed the scalpel at the doctor. "You're not cutting my arm off."

I felt the touch of a Shadow on my Mark.

I didn't want to believe what was happening, and for a fraction of a second as I moved to grab her arm, I'd convinced myself that I was feeling the approach of another ambush.

As I moved, she took a step toward the doctor, and disappeared. At the same time I felt the cold hand of a Shadow slide across my Mark.

A cold, small, feminine hand.

"No, damn it!" I said to the air as I pushed my own Mark to follow her. The hospital room blurred as the more ephemeral contents disappeared. I caught a glimpse of her as our movements through Chaos were briefly in sync. I called out to her, "Jessica! Stop! You don't know where you're—"

Her visible presence was long gone before the sentence was finished. I ran through the slowly mutating corridors of the hospital, now only following the feeling of her Shadow hand on my Mark. I raced outside to a parking lot that was eerily empty as I ran through layers of potential worlds where only the surface of the asphalt and the lampposts held any congruency beneath a pulsing gray-blue sky that bore no sun, moon, or clouds.

I ran across the parking lot, moving deeper into Chaos from our temporary 1970s haven, and the lampposts dissolved into fog with the hospital, and the ground became unstable, mutable, fluid. I felt her, but she had run full-tilt into this Chaos, and her touch on my Mark was fading . . . faded . . .

Gone.

I could feel the wild motion of the Chaos around me, and I had instinctively run along the most stable route. Whedon hadn't. Again I had the feeling of running across ice floes floating on a raging rapid. Problem was, while I was dancing on top of the ice, she dove straight into the water.

I stopped, and a world resolved from the fog around me.

I stood on a street of weed-shot brick between ranks of burnt-out Victorian housing. The cold here made my breath fog. A rusted-out Model T squatted tireless on the road in front of me. Through the weeds on one side of the road, I saw a flash of bone—the skull of some large animal staring at me.

Below the blood-red sky, the entire world was silent.

I tried to sense Jessica Whedon's presence, but I felt nothing. Alone. Cold.

Too close, I heard a canine growl, then multiple ones. The weeds rustled around the overgrown road, and through the underbrush I saw flashes of black-silver fur, the glint of an eye, and the curl of a wolf's muzzle.

Time to go.

Like my travel before, escaping the Shadows, it took me four times as long to return as it took me to leave. But I could return. It seemed that I had a sense of direction in Chaos that prevented me from losing myself.

What happened to her?

I don't know why I should think that question. She was clearly joining the ranks of the Shadows. The Mark scarring her body ate into her skin like the other Shadows, and she been granted the same ability to move through worlds that I shared with the Shadows. . . .

But why didn't she share the same homicidal tendencies that drove the ones chasing me and Ivan . . . or John Doe?

Maybe it's progressive, like some sort of zombie dementia.

That couldn't be quite right either. The Shadows that had stalked me and Ivan were homicidal, but they were also functional. They set elaborate ambushes, used firearms effectively, and had hijacked a semitrailer. They were far from mindless, more like an enraged mob than shambling hordes.

That wasn't quite right either. The Shadows were far from being a directionless mob. They were focused quite tightly on a few definitive targets. If it was just a predatory mindset, sensing our Marks like a shark smelling blood in the water, they should have dispersed the first time we escaped them, losing themselves back into the ocean of Chaos to hunt their next meal. I told Ivan that these things showing up now was no coincidence, and the more I thought, the less random it appeared.

To engineer the almost successful ambush at the airport, they had to track us, and somehow coordinate the convergence of two or three separate groups toward the exit by the airport. That's not trivial for *police* to do with full radio communication and a helicopter.

Someone, somewhere, had to be coordinating their attack.

I don't know why, but I had a strong and unfounded fear that I would return and neither Jacob nor Ivan would be there. However, as soon as I walked across the parking lot where my familiar blue Charger, coated in mud-spray, sat between a VW microbus and a lime-green Pinto, I saw Jacob and Ivan waiting for me, huddled by the emergency entrance.

Jacob saw me first and ran toward me. "Dana, are you all right?"

"Yes."

"Whedon—"

"She's gone."

The color drained from his face. "Dead?"

"No, just *gone*. I couldn't follow her. She got lost in the Chaos."

Ivan walked toward us, and Jacob edged away from him and lowered his voice. "Dana, what you do—what he does—it's *contagious?*"

I sighed, and even though it was a perfectly reasonable concern, I felt no urge to rein in my irritation. "I'm not going to bite you, Jacob."

Ivan stopped before me and said, bowing his head slightly, "My Lady, are you going to accompany me back to the Empire?"

"Hold on," Jacob said. "What?"

Ivan ignored him, and his voice took on a grave tone. "I must return as soon as I can, with or without you."

"I thought you couldn't return empty-handed."

"I'll face severe discipline, yes. But I must report the activity by the Shadows, and what happened to your friend. I know of nothing that explains her transformation. She was just another of the Stationary before the attack, wasn't she?"

"Stationary?"

He cursed something in Russian and clarified by looking askance at Jacob. "Like him."

"Wait a moment here," Jacob said.

"No," I said. "She didn't have the Mark."

"I must report that Shadows exist so close to the Empire and can multiply their numbers. I've delayed returning too long already. Will you accompany me?"

Jacob looked at both of us. Then, before I could answer, he took my arm. "Can you give us a moment in private?"

I let him take me a few steps away from Ivan so he could whisper, "Are you seriously considering going back with that guy?"

"Yes."

"The same guy you had handcuffed in your basement six hours ago?"

"Yes."

"Do you trust him?"

"No."

He sighed.

"What do you want from me, Jacob? You've seen what I'm dealing with. Ivan comes from a place where people deal with this as a matter of course. Not to mention the fact that if I don't go with him, a mob of Shadows might follow me home."

"They could be following *him*."

"You think it's a better idea I risk that, and lose what chance I have at learning about—"

"Indoor voice, Dana," he whispered.

I realized my volume had been ratcheting up with my frustration. "Damn it, I don't know what else to do."

"I know."

"I won't strand you in the '70s, though. We'll swing back home so I can drop you off back where you belong."

He touched my hand. "No."

"What?" My voice started rising again.

"You aren't going to leave me to wonder what happened to you. You go, I'll go."

"What? No. This isn't your fight."

"Partners, remember?"

"This isn't a police investigation."

"Way I see it. I'm keeping an eye on a suspect in an unsolved homicide." He nodded back at Ivan.

I froze, unable to talk. The fact was I *wanted* him with me. I had aired all my dirty laundry in front of him, and he was still around. I did not want to let that go.

And I felt like a selfish bitch for not trying harder to talk him out of it.

"You don't know what you're getting yourself into," I said, my token effort to give him one last out.

"And you do? You're just going to follow this guy home and say, 'Take me to your leader?' "

"Unless a better option presents itself." I looked up at the dark sky. The air was chill, and my breath fogged a little. I felt very tired and hugged myself. I wanted to go home, put some old Metallica on full blast, and pretend that nothing existed beyond the walls of my house.

I turned around and walked up to Ivan. "How do we get there?"

TWENTY-ONE

THE LAST THING I wanted to do was use my Mark again, but I also did not want this opportunity to slip away, no matter how ragged I felt inside. I felt bone-tired, but it wasn't really physical. According to the clock on the dash, it was only three in the afternoon, despite the setting of the sun here in 1970-something.

My fatigue was psychic and spiritual. I felt myself shaking, vibrating like a piano wire, and if anything so much as brushed against me, I felt an involuntary shudder. Every nerve felt overstimulated to the point I couldn't really distinguish pleasure from pain, or from simply incidental contact.

I needed my bed . . . or a long soak in my bathtub with my eyes closed.

Instead, I drove slowly out of 1970s Cleveland while Ivan rode shotgun and explained what he wanted us to do.

According to Ivan, my car was necessary to return to the Empire in any reasonable time. It served the same purpose his armor had, pushing the occupant through worlds faster than anyone could walk. The weight might slow me down, but the speed at which it covered ground more than made up for it.

Ivan said that it was only due to his armor and the fact that his quarry had taken a "straight" route through Chaos to my world, that Ivan had been able to keep up with John Doe.

He believed that driven by a Prince—driven by me—my Charger could traverse the worlds between here and the Empire as quickly as it could cover the ground between here and where we were going. Perhaps faster.

"The ground between here—"

"We need to go to the North American capital, Washington."

Of course, we did.

I looked at the clock again, and if it had been a normal drive he was talking about, it wouldn't be horribly out of the question. Seven hours, give or take. I licked my lips and thought about the last few excursions into Chaos.

Could I do that again, for that long?

Muscles inside me shuddered with anticipation just thinking about it. I drove out of Cleveland and onto the freeway. I glanced at the gas gauge and sighed, "One side trip first."

"What? Why?" Jacob asked.

"We can't get to DC on a quarter tank."

"Oh," Jacob said. "Why don't you stop here?"

I shook my head. "Leaded gas is not a good idea for the catalytic converter, and I don't think the Sohio station there would take twenty-first century plastic."

"You have a point there."

I pushed the Charger back toward home, but only briefly. I did not want to return too close to the Shadows. Less than a half minute pushing with my Mark found us back in a familiar 1986. Jacob looked at the boxy cars with rectangular headlights and said, "I don't think a station here will take your plastic either."

I nodded. "But if memory serves, we're in an era before all self-serve pumps were prepay."

I pulled off of the interstate and filled the tank at a Shell station. It was unleaded and not prepay. It was only 90 cents a gallon, but

I still felt guilty for stealing the gas. I wondered why, since I'd done a hell of a lot of more legally questionable things as a cop. Up to now, I'd only been concerned about legal niceties in my "home" world.

I wondered if I was reacting against Ivan's solipsism—as if, after hearing about universes appearing and disappearing throughout Chaos, I wanted them to be more real.

However I felt, I was committed once I started pumping. I had no way to pay at a 1986 gas station. Even my folding money would look fake in this decade.

The attendant ran out cursing when I drove away, but a nudge from the Mark and he and the Shell station were gone.

I needed a rest, and we were close to the Pennsylvania border before I felt prepared to try using my Mark again. When I told Ivan I was ready, he asked, "Can you follow my direction?"

I felt his hand on the small of my back, but it wasn't his hand, and it wasn't really my back that felt it. He looked at me, and I could tell he had no clue exactly *how* he was touching me.

Without the distraction of needing to flee for my life or the unpleasant touch of the Shadows groping me, I was fully aware of the sense of his Mark brushing me ever so lightly with a masculine touch that elicited goosebumps and little shivers on my skin.

I bit my lip and forced myself to stare at the road ahead of us. My knuckles cracked as I gripped the wheel.

"Yes," I said. What I thought was: *seven hours*?

I steeled myself as I pushed forward with the Mark. Again, I opened up with everything I had in me, and the motion of the Charger seemed to pull me even farther, faster. Ivan's touch came along with me, embracing me, guiding me, as I felt my Mark pulling me deep into a bottomless well inside myself.

Along with Ivan's guiding touch stroking me, with my senses heightened to bursting, I could feel the world around me, as if it embraced me, too. I could sense the way worlds slid by, obeying their own motion through dimensions I could feel but couldn't visualize.

I had the general sense of where Ivan pushed me, just as the geographic direction I needed to go was generally due southeast. But there was the immediate feel of Chaos sliding by me and the Charger, I no longer seemed to be stepping across the ice floating on the rapids, I was surfing the crashing water, submerged in the current, with infinite streams of probability washing across my skin in frighteningly intimate waves.

I had control though, like a surfer, I could sense and find paths through the shifting Chaos I could drive an 8-cylinder muscle car through. When I concentrated on sliding through the worlds where I wanted to go, I held onto the reality of a solid roadway under the Charger's tires. Above us, the sky became a pulsing blue-gray twilight while everything fell away around us into the white mists of Chaos.

But the road remained solid, the one thread of reality knitting together all the worlds we passed through. My confidence rose. As I trembled inside, I gripped the wheel so tight I felt part of the car. I felt the hardness of the road as clearly as I felt Ivan's touch on my Mark.

The speedometer hit ninety and stayed there.

The prolonged drive kept pushing me. Over time, the excitement evolved into discomfort, then began to blossom into pain.

I had never done this to myself—driven the Mark so hard, so long. As tightly as I held the wheel, I could feel muscles shuddering, and the Mark itself felt scoured raw, and while the surface of my skin felt like a raw open nerve, I couldn't flinch away from the Mark's touch. My breath came staccato through clenched teeth, and my eyes watered, and all I wanted was to let go.

If I didn't, I was afraid I'd have no choice about it. "We have to stop."

I let the indeterminate Chaos around the car collapse into something real and pulled the Charger to the side of a shady macadam country road. I held on until the car came to a complete stop, then I let all the internal barriers go, and everything that had built up crashed over me in an uncontrolled flood. I folded over the wheel and groaned, every muscle in my body shaking as it all hit me.

I was dimly aware of Jacob's voice asking if I was all right.

Yeah, sure, I'm fine.

I trembled as if I had just suffered a seizure. I pushed myself up from the wheel and said, "I need a break." I didn't look at my passengers. I fumbled with the seatbelt, opened the door, and stepped out.

I had no idea where we were. The road was a tar-bound gravel slash through the woods on either side. The trees were full and green, the afternoon sun shining through the leaves. I walked out, about fifty feet into the trees, and my legs felt so weak that I had to lean against the trunks to keep from toppling over.

I stood in the middle of the trees and looked up, staring at the sky through the leaves. I felt empty, as if someone had drilled a hole in my life and drained away everything that made me *me*. I should have been feeling the loss of my old life, fear of the Shadows, some sort of excitement at finally learning something about my Mark. Instead, I was just very tired.

Jacob's voice came from behind me. "Dana?"

I lowered my head and stared at the mulch under my feet.

"Are you all right?" he asked.

I shook my head. "I can't do that for so long."

"Does it hurt you?"

I couldn't help but laugh. "I'll be all right. I just need a break."

"I can see that."

I licked my lips. "I'm sorry for that display."

"Don't be." We stood in silence for several moments when he added, "I don't know exactly how this stuff works, but Ivan says we're already close to the Empire here."

I turned around. "What? How long was I driving?"

"An hour, give or take."

I shook my head. "Even at the speed I was driving . . . It's at least six hours to DC."

Jacob shook his head. "I told you, I don't really understand how this works, but apparently this . . ." He waved his hand as if he was having trouble with the word. "'Universe?'" I could hear the quotes he put around the word. "He says it's something like halfway or two thirds closer to the Empire. I think you impressed him."

Made an impression, at least.

Jacob glanced back to the car. My Charger shone blue through the splatters of mud. At that moment I wouldn't like anything better than to be back at my townhouse with a garden hose, some rags, and a Sunday afternoon with nothing more urgent to do than make it shine.

"Anyway," Jacob said, "We can spend a few hours driving—normal driving—until we get closer to DC. If you're not up to it, I could drive."

"No one else is driving my car," I told him as I walked back to my Charger.

AS onerous and exhausting as my explosive drive through the universes between the 1975 where we lost Whedon, and wherever here was, I actually found driving at a normal pace, without recourse to the Mark, relaxing. My body had finally run out of adrenaline, and now that there seemed no immediate threat to life, limb, or sanity, I felt as if every muscle in my body was slowly unconstricting.

The Charger's Hemi purred even though I had almost literally driven it through hell. The tires crunched across the archaic country road at a more sedate thirty-five. I slowed, because now that the world was static around me, the road wove around, went up and down hills, and I didn't want to drive any faster than I could see. I couldn't imagine the levels of pissed I would reach if I'd driven my car into another *universe* only to hit a deer.

Beyond that, it was pretty country to drive through. I rolled down the windows to let in the fresh air and fished out my iPhone and put it on the cradle and hit shuffle. The first band to come on was Slipknot.

Ivan gave me a horrified look and said, "What is that?"

"Just some traveling music," I told him. I think I was smiling for the first time today.

He muttered something in Russian, but I left the music on. The tortured vocals were a perfect match for my day. And it was my car, damn it.

We rolled by farms, and I saw pastures with horses or cows. In the distance I saw bearded men with broad hats, black pants, and light blue shirts tending the land. We'd passed the third farm, when I realized that I hadn't seen any modern farm machinery at all.

I wondered if we were driving around some version of the nineteenth century. As we continued southeast, I passed three or four horse-drawn buggies that would have been familiar to anyone who'd passed through Amish country, though these were lacking the orange reflective triangles on the back. And, almost disastrously, they were driven by horses that seemed unfamiliar with automotive traffic. The first buggy we came to, despite my pulling over as far as I could, caused the horse to spook, roll eyes, and rear, and almost manage to spin around in its harness. Fortunately, the driver was able to gain control, whipping the animal and shouting German harsher than the Korn lyrics growling through my speaker system.

With the next two, I pulled over and stopped. And both times, my Charger received evil stares. I don't know if they reacted to my vehicle, my clothing, the music leaking from the car, or just the fact that I was a woman driving two men around.

I couldn't have been more out of place if I tried.

It was another hour before I saw any signs. I drove through miles of more farmland until I came to a T-intersection with two signs, one pointing right to East Palestine, the other pointing left toward Beaver Falls. The road was paved, rather than tar-bound gravel. Since I was pointed south, I took a left toward Beaver Falls.

Less than a mile down the blacktop I got the first real indication of how different this world was from my own. It was a large sign in black, yellow, and red. The text was bilingual in English and German. The English portion read: "Warning! You are leaving the Amish Zone!"

I slowed as I approached the sign until I came to a complete stop.

"Tell me that is *not* a swastika," I muttered.

Neither Jacob nor Ivan obliged me.

Below the scare text on the sign was a little graphic emblem for some federal agency or other. It was circular and featured an eagle prominently in a seal a little too detailed to be contemporary but streamlined enough to be post Art Deco. The eagle bore a shield that was familiar enough in the federal iconography, at least the lower portion with the vertical stripes. The upper portion, though, instead of a collection of stars, bore a circular badge with the Nazi symbol on it.

I'd always seen the Department of the Interior as a relatively innocuous federal agency. But with that kind of seal, it took on some really ominous overtones.

"I guess World War II went a little differently here," Jacob said.

"World War II?" Ivan said.

I looked at him and said, "World War II? Nazis? Hitler? Germany—"

Ivan just gave me a blank look.

"—and I guess you never had a World War I." *Not by that name, anyway.*

Despite my reservations, I started the Charger again and began driving down the blacktop away from the Amish reservation. The small road fed into another road, and I finally saw other vehicle traffic. Until I merged, I could still pretend that I was driving in some remote corner of the Pennsylvania I knew.

Even with light traffic, I couldn't pretend anymore. If anything, my Charger was more out of place along this stretch of highway than it had been in the midst of the Amish. The four-lane highway was the province of truck after truck, and all of them seemed to have been built in the forties at the latest. The diesel-belching cabs pulled trailers of every description—and not one trailer gave any hint of its contents. Like railroad cars, there were only logos for freight lines and cryptic serial numbers. I didn't realize how much a part of the normal roadway landscape the ads on the side of semitrailers actually were, until they were gone.

Even though the trucks were all different makes and models, and the trailers were various colors, the fact that the sides were mostly blank gave everything an ominously uniform mechanistic feel.

At least the road was in decent shape, so I could make good time weaving past the trucks. The signage was strange looking, but it directed me toward the Pennsylvania Autobahn, where I got to safely open up the Hemi and make up the time I lost driving around the Amish.

Along the Autobahn were billboards showing images that wouldn't have been out of place in any totalitarian state of the twentieth century. Idealized workers labored in the soil, or in the factory, or in the office. Slogans hovered over the heroic portraits, things like "The right to earn enough" and "The right to a decent home" and "The right to a good education," and—disturbingly when I thought about it—each bore the legend beneath them: *Out of Many, One: The National Progressive Party USA.*

"So we lost the war?" I whispered as we passed one of the billboards where smiling white women happily tended a massive hunk of textile machinery that was busy weaving a recognizable American flag.

"I don't think so," Jacob said as we passed it.

"It *looks* like we lost."

"Not the war," Jacob said. "The Germans, for all their military buildup, couldn't crack England, or push very far into Russia. There would be no way they could take the US by force—with an ocean in the way."

"There are *swastikas* on our road signs."

"By *force*," Jacob said. "Before the war there were plenty of folks who thought the Fascists and the Nazis had good ideas how to handle the economy. Look at these signs—those aren't Nazi slogans. They're lifted from FDR's Second Bill of Rights."

Ivan shook his head. "These details do not matter."

"It doesn't matter that *Nazis* won?" I snapped.

"This is just one world that's solidified out of boiling Chaos. It will vanish back into Chaos when we leave."

I couldn't wrap my head around that. "Hundreds of millions of people are under some totalitarian regime, and it doesn't matter?"

"They're Stationary," Ivan said, as if that could explain his disinterest.

I wanted to believe that he just wasn't aware of the particular evil Nazism was. He was from an Empire that grew out of the Napoleonic era, far removed from the genocidal impulses of the twentieth century.

But he Walked through worlds like this. That was his job. He was just as likely to have seen things *worse* than the history of my own universe.

I was about to argue that the people trapped in this world were just as important as the people in my world or in the Empire, when the sound of a siren cut through our conversation.

TWENTY-TWO

"WHAT ARE YOU doing?" Ivan asked.

I hadn't even realized that I was in the process of pulling over until he said something. Reflex, I guess. However, something in his tone irritated me. "That's a cop," I said. "I'm pulling over like a good little citizen."

"You can push the car—"

I cut him off. "When I'm ready, Ivan. I've had enough of jumping into your Chaos without any preparation."

"Is this a good idea?" Jacob asked. "We don't know anything about this place."

I pulled the Charger to a stop beneath a billboard that showed heroic portraits from the branches of the military—though the Air Force seemed conspicuously absent. Below the soldier, sailor, and marine were smaller, more human-sized portraits of a policeman, a fireman, and a doctor. "Security abroad. Security at home," went the motto on this billboard.

Jacob, I already know too much about this place.

The police car behind us was black and white, with a dome light on top the size of a bowling ball. It looked like a Ford from the 1950s, though it was a 50s where automotive design had sanded off all the frills and unnecessary details. The side panels were smooth metal, and any little flourishes or chrome accents were gone, until it was little more than a functional brick.

It made sense in a police car, but after seeing all those trucks, I thought that the design I saw probably went beyond just police cars.

The police car pulled up behind me, giant flasher going, and the driver got out. He started walking slowly up toward us on the driver's side. The uniform he wore resembled a paramilitary outfit from South Africa circa 1965 more than it did the Pennsylvania Highway Patrol circa 1950-something. All of it black. Black fabric, black leather, shiny black boots, black sunglasses clipped to his breast pocket, and matte black grip for a machine pistol sticking out of the holster on his hip.

Ivan turned and started at the approaching cop and started muttering unpleasant Russian.

I flexed my hands on the wheel. The engine still purred as I watched the officer walk up behind the Charger. He was giving my car the once-over, I could see the kind of combination of confusion and wariness that you never want to see on the face of someone with a gun. His hand went to his holster.

Great.

"Dana," Jacob said.

"It's okay," I whispered.

The cop straightened up and started to walk up along the driver's side. I eased my foot off the brake and allowed the Charger to roll quietly forward at idle speed. As the cop jumped back, drawing his weapon, I gave a small push with my Mark, and he vanished. It was a short jolt, a less than gentle friction against a part of myself already rubbed raw.

I rolled to a stop again, under a nighttime sky of stars and a full moon. The highway still sprawled empty alongside us, but I noticed the billboard was gone.

Also gone was the tension I'd felt rising in the car. I could hear Jacob exhale slowly, as if he'd been holding his breath.

I looked over at Ivan and said, "I pulled over because I didn't want to do that at 70 miles per hour. I'm *still* feeling the effort from before."

"Apologies, my Lady."

"Yeah," I said, "accepted."

I pulled out onto the road again.

THE universe hopping had completely destroyed my sense of time. I felt as if I had been awake for days. I checked my watch, and it was only about fourteen hours since I had woken up this morning. Less than a day since Jacob had stormed into my apartment and everything started disintegrating around me.

The Mark throbbed on my back, a raw pulse reminding me that I had never used it so hard, or for so long.

I'd even lost track of how long I'd been driving. It had been long enough. "We need to stop," I said, "I need some sleep."

Jacob yawned. "You want me to spot you at the wheel?"

"Still trying to drive my car, huh?"

"No," Ivan said.

I looked at him and said, "That's presumptuous. This is my car."

"And you need to drive in the event we must avoid some danger."

Yeah—

"I guess you have a point," Jacob said. "I guess you can't drive it like she does, can you?"

It was a not so subtle dig against Ivan, and from his expression, Ivan felt it. Whatever deference he gave me due to status, he was still someone who resented being outperformed by a woman.

This was not going to go well.

"We are all going to stop and get some rest. I think we've put more than enough distance between us and the Shadows."

Ivan frowned. "We will not be safe until we're back in the Empire."

"And I'm not chancing putting my car in a ditch."

"So," Jacob asked, "you're going to start looking for a Day's Inn?"

Yeah, there was that. I could pull the Charger over somewhere, but as much as I loved my car, I wasn't up to sleeping in it. Also, where I was driving now was only a few steps removed from the Fascist police state we'd been pulled over in. Not the place to just randomly find a place to crash for the night.

Nighttime Pennsylvania slid by us, dark and somewhat ominous.

I was going to need to push the Mark again, at least a little. The realization made me wince inside. I still felt as if I had ravaged myself.

But we needed a safe place to hole up for at least eight hours.

I pushed the Charger into Chaos again. As the universe boiled apart around me, I felt a twinge quite aside from the effort of using my Mark. As a billboard for the National Progressive Party USA swirled away into an inconstant pattern of light and shadow that might have been a billboard, or a lamppost, or a tree, or a road sign, I couldn't help thinking about the cop I had left by the side of the road.

Did he boil away like the sign as Ivan suggested? Did he just cease to exist? Did his whole history, birth, awkward adolescence, service in the military in a bizarro version of World War II, his stint in the police academy, marriage, birth of his kids—did all of that just disappear along with billions of other unique individuals just because I was no longer focused on them?

I couldn't think like that; it was madness. If Ivan truly believed that's what happened, he almost had to believe that those people, those billions, were meaningless. *Stationary.* I couldn't accept that idea. It meant that Mom and Dad—even Jacob—were just some meaningless side effect of the Mark. Ivan was wrong because he had to be.

The bouncing of the Charger's suspension brought my attention back to the Chaos surrounding us. I struggled to get my grip back around the roadway. Jacob or Ivan had become alarmed and had started talking excitedly. I ignored them to focus on the trembling breathless effort of the Mark pushing against me, against the car.

I couldn't keep this up.

I tried to grope around the seething randomness, feeling for something concrete, like the road beneath us. I tried to pull us toward somewhere safe, where we could rest. When I touched something within the swirling twilight, I pushed the Charger out of Chaos and into another world of blazing noontime light and broken asphalt.

I let the car roll to a stop and gasped with the effort. A painful spasm slammed into me, and I was surprised it didn't leave me bleeding.

No more of this, I thought. *No more.*

I looked up from the wheel and looked down the road. The road itself was gravel and ill-maintained, with crumbling shoulders, massive potholes holding brown pools of water, and weeds invading from the edges. Tall grasses waved in the wind on either side of us, and beyond the tops I could make out the roofline of a barn to our left.

I started the car rolling again, slowly on the broken roadway. We passed a battered sign half-fallen into the weeds by the roadside. Through the sun-faded paint and rust I could make out "State Line 15 Miles."

"If my sense of direction holds," I told my passengers. "We're almost at the Maryland border."

"Dana?" Jacob sounded worried.

"What?"

"You don't sound well. Are you okay?"

You're kidding, right? I sucked in a breath and put on a brave front, more for Ivan than Jacob. I think if it'd just been Jacob with me, I might have let my guard slip. A little. But, instead, I pasted on a smile, said, "Everything's fine," and gritted my teeth. I tried to ignore the throbbing from parts of me that really never should throb.

Wherever we were, it looked abandoned, which was fine with me. I followed the broken road until I saw the remains of a decaying split-rail fence being reclaimed by the tall weeds at the side of the road. I kept my eyes open until I pulled up to the wreckage of a gate. The driveway was close to invisible from the overgrowth, but it was there. I pulled to a stop in front of it and looked back at the other two. "Help me move the gate," I told them.

They were a set of wooden gates that had gone gray and warped. The two halves had been chained shut at one time, but while the chain had fused to itself, the gate to the left had so weakened that pulling on the chain caused a section of wood to disintegrate. That gate was more rotted than its twin, but it also had sunk in and buried itself in the ground, making it immobile.

We worked on the other side, spending nearly twenty minutes forcing it open. In the end, the hinges refused to give, but the post—weakened with dry rot—decided to snap free at the base, sending all of us into a ditch by the side of what had once been a broad gravel driveway.

I checked the ground for foreign objects, picking up a few long nails and tossing them aside. I pulled the Charger up, through the gate, and then about another ten feet into the weeds. Then I jumped out and locked it up.

"What?" both Jacob and Ivan began to say.

"I want it off the road." I waved ahead, along the overgrown gravel drive. "And since I can't see the driveway, I'm not driving it any farther than this. I'm not getting us stranded with a flat tire."

"Now what?" Jacob asked.

"Should be a farmhouse up this driveway, and given the state of the property, I think it's unoccupied." I turned to find my way along the long, overgrown gravel driveway, I trusted the guys to follow me. More accurately, I was so burned out that I was preoccupied with finding a place to rest a while. If there was no immediate danger, they both could lie down in the weeds for all I cared.

The drive was covered with waist-high grass, which still separated it from the old pastures where the growth had reached chest-level. It had obviously been years since anything had grazed here. I walked up a hill and when I crested it, I could see the remains of the farm over the weeds.

I saw acres that were still recognizable as long-abandoned cornfields, I could see stalks poking up out of weeds, still following hints of the original field's geometry. Closer, nestled in the weeds at the edge of the field, I saw the skeletal hulk of an ancient tractor listing toward the corn as if it had unfinished business.

The barn stood, sun-bleached and swaybacked, between the cornfield and the farmhouse. Parts of the walls had fallen away so that, in places, I saw the sun shining all the way through it.

The house seemed much more solidly built. Sun had blasted the old Victorian building until all the colors had turned variants of bone gray, and some of the gingerbread trim and about half the shingles had fallen away. But the walls were straight, and most of the windows still reflected a glassy stare at me.

I had asked my Mark for a safe place to rest, without any people. I wondered if I could really trust that.

Lord, what choice do I have?

I was too tired to try and push through to find someplace less haunted-housey. I walked down through the weeds toward the empty house. I heard Ivan and Jacob following behind me. Jacob wondered aloud what happened to the place.

I shrugged. I didn't much care, even if it was kind of eerie. It was even more so when I thought that the main road had seemed just as abandoned. It didn't much matter; whatever happened to this place had happened a long time ago.

I got an idea how long ago when I tripped over a wood plank shoved in the ground. It brought me up short and looked down at it. The wood was weathered, untreated gray, and carved in the face were the words: Abigail Miller, b. 1910 d. 1919.

I stared and found my mind returning to my mother. I bit my lip and knelt down to straighten the grave marker. As I did, Jacob said, "There're more."

There were more. Seven markers for the Miller family, ages ranging from infant to just seventy years old. From the dates carved in the boards, three generations had all died between 1918 and 1919. I touched Abigail's marker, from the dates, Abigail had lived at least long enough to see her grandmother and two of her siblings go.

Good lord, what would that be like? I'd just buried my mom, and

I still hurt from how my dad died—I couldn't imagine watching an entire family wiped out in such a short time. I couldn't imagine being the one left to dig the graves.

"Flu," Jacob said.

I looked up and asked, "What?"

"The Spanish Flu hit around then, the end of World War I."

I turned back to the house and shuddered. "Is it safe, then?"

"It looks like it's been a decade or two," Jacob said.

I nodded, only half convinced. I wondered how often people like me and Ivan, travelers with a Mark, spread a disease to a population that had never been exposed to it? How many times had a population been devastated by some virus that had come out of nowhere?

I straightened up and looked back over the abandoned farm. The tractor was the only sign of the twentieth century here, and I realized its skeletal appearance was less decay than it was obsolete design. I also now noticed the absence of any telephone poles or wires, nor was there any sign there had ever been exterior lighting on house or barn.

The jet lag and general disorientation hit me full force. Not only did I know that this place had a much different history than the world I was familiar with, I had no real idea where in that history we stood. Back on the freeway, I felt as if we'd been in some version of the fifties after a very different World War II. Where we stood now? I didn't know other than 1919, the latest year on the grave markers, had come and gone. I had no idea how long ago, though. Ten years? Twenty? Thirty?

"Dana?"

Jacob's voice shocked me awake. I had closed my eyes and had been nodding off while I was standing there. I glanced up at the hard blue sky and said, "Let's find a place to rest."

TWENTY-THREE

THE FARMHOUSE FELT like a corpse that had dried and mummified into an empty husk. Wood furniture had turned gray and showed long splits where the wood had dried and shrunk. The padded couch in the living room had gone gray with dust, and some animal had long ago made a nest in its innards, cannibalizing it from the inside. Guano and old feathers coated the flat surfaces in the kitchen where the windows had lost their glass.

I'd been afraid that we'd find the last Miller in one of the rooms, but whoever had dug the last grave had not stuck around to greet us. The only dead things in the house were mice and birds.

The beds, of course, were hopeless. Not that I liked the idea of sleeping in a dead guy's bed even if it wasn't a literal rat's nest or covered with bird droppings.

Fortunately, Jacob found a cedar chest that had seemed proof against bugs and mice and managed to pull out two large quilts that were only slightly musty. He tossed one to Ivan and told him to find a spot to rest. He gave the other one to me. "You, especially. Get some sleep."

The quilt felt dry and smelled of dust and cedar so strongly it made me want to sneeze. I glanced into the chest, and there wasn't anything left inside. "What about you?"

"I'll be fine."

"It's a big quilt," I said somewhat lamely. We stared at each other for a long time as if we were both struggling to admit what I had just offered. I remembered Ivan with some embarrassment and looked over toward him, but he had already stepped out of the room.

I looked back at Jacob and unnecessarily elaborated, "We can share."

"Are you sure you're all right with that?"

I turned around so he couldn't see my expression. "Come on and let's find a spot where we can lie down."

THAT spot turned out to be on the Victorian's wraparound porch, which turned out to offer the cleanest surface to spread out the quilt. Ivan had beat us to it and was already dozing, wrapped in a bundle to the right of the stairs leading up to the porch.

I found a spot by the corner of the house where the floor of the porch didn't seem too springy, kicked branches and other debris away with my foot, and spread the quilt on the cleared surface. As it settled down, I felt a twinge when I realized that this was a handmade quilt with an elaborate wedding ring design. Back home, something like this would fetch over a grand.

I realized I was so tired my mind was wandering. I knelt and spread myself out on one side of the quilt. Every muscle in my body suddenly realized I had stopped moving and decided to melt. Even the Mark seemed to ache from fatigue and weigh me down. I don't think I could have gotten back up if I wanted to.

I heard Jacob grunt, lying down next to me. He didn't touch me, but I felt his presence, and something made me roll over slightly, so I ended with my head leaning against his shoulder.

"You okay?" he asked me.

"Uh-huh," I answered, already half asleep.

"Why are we trusting Ivan?"

I opened my eyes. "Jacob?"

"You know nothing about him, and you're letting him lead you into God-knows-what."

I sighed, reached over, and placed a hand on his chest. "I need to know," I said. "And I don't trust him, really. I trust you."

"Then does this make sense?"

Very weakly, I shook my head "no" and closed my eyes.

JACOB had a point. I had seen Ivan kill someone, and the only information I had about what was going on came from him. The deference he showed could easily be an elaborate act to get me . . .

Get me to do what?

Do exactly what we were doing.

Deep down, I knew I was being played. I had been a cop too long to take Ivan at face value. It was obvious he was working some sort of angle. It was worse because even if I knew so for certain, I would still end up going with him. I didn't have a choice. I couldn't ignore the connection to my Mark, what it was, what it made me.

Worse, I was certain that Ivan understood that about me. I hadn't been too good at keeping that secret. It was obvious exactly how easily I could be manipulated about this.

I fell asleep wondering if there was any way out.

I dreamed of a tall cold building of stone and wood. Everything seemed huge, tapestries and furniture built for giants. The air smelled of smoke. I hid from the smoke and the noise and sobbed to myself. I wasn't sure exactly what had happened, but I knew it had been bad. My nightshirt was scarlet with blood that wasn't mine. I hugged myself, curled in a corner, rocking back and forth on my knees behind a tall chest, half behind a heavy tapestry that showed a man with a crown and a sword.

The door to the room burst in, letting in the sound of men screaming and the crackling roar of something burning. A huge man burst into the room calling out an unfamiliar name, "Llewellyn! Llewellyn!"

I saw the man's face before he saw mine, and it was craggy and handsome and black with soot except where tears had drawn tracks across his cheeks. I knew the man—both my terrified dream-self, and the me that was somewhere aware I was dreaming.

The huge man spinning desperately in the room was the same man who had appeared to pound on my window, who had been cut down by Ivan. My dream-self knew him but couldn't bring herself to move or acknowledge his presence. I stayed where I was, rocking back and forth, as if nothing I did could change anything.

The man drew the tapestry aside and found me. "I'll take you to safety." He spoke in Old English. "To your mother."

I didn't respond to him or even look directly at him. I kept rocking back and forth. It was a dream, and I was going to wake up. Part of me knew that was true, but some other part of me realized that for the small girl huddling behind the tapestry it hadn't been.

The small dream girl said one thing as the man gathered her up.

"Where's Papa?"

To my horror, as soon as I realized that I perceived an actual memory, the vision started falling apart. The scene was a phantom image that I could only see out of the periphery of my vision. When I focused on it with my full lucid attention, the part that was memory consumed itself. I stood in place of the blood-covered child, dressed like I had just come from work, holding my IMI Jericho 941 in my right hand as if I was just about to take down some suspect. The old man had vanished, to be replaced by my mom on a hospital bed.

The stone room had transformed itself into a hospital room; the only holdovers from the memory were the hanging tapestries, the smell of smoke, and the distant sounds of men fighting.

I walked up to the side of the bed and said, "I'm sorry."

Mom looked up at me. "You know I'm not your real mother."

"I know."

"You were adopted."

"I know."

"Maybe you should talk to her." Mom raised a finger and pointed.

I turned around and saw another woman, covered in blood, collapsed in the corner. The hospital room was gone, replaced by a cheap apartment. The dream girl had returned, hugging the woman as she died.

I knelt next to them, asking, "What happened?"

The dying woman coughed blood and said, "They killed your father." She pointed at the anachronistically dressed corpse on the floor of the apartment. "He tried to kill you."

"Who are they?" I asked.

"Your brothers . . ."

. . .I woke up. I whispered a curse in frustration as I tried to grab the threads of the dream and fix them in my memory before wakefulness burned them all away. It was frustratingly elusive, the elements of clarity seemed irrelevant, while the parts that seemed important were shrouded if not completely gone.

Some of it, at least, I was certain was a real memory, something that happened to me.

I opened my eyes to the night-shrouded porch and whispered, "Llewellyn."

Jacob stirred next to me and said, "What?"

"Nothing," I whispered. "Go back to sleep."

"Too late," he said. "I'm awake. What did you say?"

"Llewellyn," I repeated.

Beyond the porch, night had come to cover the world in a silver-blue blanket. I saw the bottom edge of a fat moon just peaking under the eaves.

"Llewellyn?" Jacob said. "Should I know that name?"

"Maybe. I think it's me."

"You remember something?"

"I don't know." The farther I got from the dream, the less certain I was that it meant anything.

"I think I like you as Dana."

"Am I?"

"A memory doesn't change who you are." I felt his hand find mine and squeeze. I wanted to believe him. I wanted to believe that knowing the answer to the questions that had plagued me my whole life would not change who I was.

But that was wrong.

I had defined a large chunk of myself around the fact that I didn't know these things. If I uncovered that knowledge, whatever the truth might be, the knowing couldn't help but change everything I was.

Instead of following up that line of thought, I changed the subject. "So you're a history buff?"

"Hmm?"

"FDR's Second Bill of Rights? The Spanish Flu? You've been a font of trivia—"

"The Spanish Flu wasn't exactly trivia."

I elbowed him. "You know what I mean."

"I grew up with it," he said. "My dad is a history professor at Kent State."

"Really? You never mentioned that before."

"Dana, we've never talked about anything personal."

I sighed. "I'm sorry about that."

"Don't be. I figured out a long time ago that there was something there you didn't want to deal with."

I sat up. "You were right."

He sat up next to me, reached out, and hugged my shoulders. I leaned into him. It was nice, resting my head against his shoulder. I reached up and squeezed his hand. This was something I had never had, never allowed myself.

I didn't realize I was crying until Jacob reached over and brushed the tears from my cheek.

I could feel the blood rushing to my cheeks, and I felt hot, even in the chill night air. I bit my lip and hugged myself. I was too embarrassed and flustered to say anything coherent, and it made me feel even worse about how I had treated Jacob, shut him out pretty much since I'd met him. I wanted this, but I had no idea how to do it.

His hand was still touching my face, and he gently turned me to face him. I felt as if I was burning away inside, and I couldn't form the words to explain myself. All I could come up with was, "I'm sorry."

I felt so incredibly lame.

"I understand," Jacob said. But I was pretty sure he didn't have any idea.

He caressed my cheek and then, without any warning, he kissed me.

At least, to the self-obsessed, self-involved woman he held, it came without warning. I was too wrapped up in my own regrets and my own discomfort to pick up on what he was thinking, even though we had just slept next to each other.

I felt him hesitate, and I realized that when his lips touched mine, I had frozen like the little girl I had just dreamed about. I willed myself to move again, placing my arms around his shoulders, leaning into him as if I was falling. I let my lips move to feel his own, and I let my lips part and felt the tip of his tongue find the gap. My own tongue, with a mind of its own, darted out to caress his. At the touch, my skin flushed so hot I felt as if my clothes might catch fire.

He hugged me to him, and I fell forward, pressing against him with the entire length of my body. I wanted him, and it scared me.

I felt his arms embrace me, his hands caress me. My blouse pulled free from the waistband of my slacks, and his hand touched the naked skin on the small of my back. I shuddered. Then his fingers brushed the Mark, and everything inside me vibrated on the verge of snapping.

I raised my head from the kiss and said, gently, "Stop."

"What's the matter?" There was an edge of fear in his expression that silently asked if he had done something wrong. It made me want to cry.

I touched his face. I didn't want to hurt him. That was the last thing I ever wanted.

"Dana?"

Damn it, I was crying again. I rolled off him and tried to compose myself. "It's not you . . ." I realized what a trite cliché it was, and the words choked themselves off.

I heard him sit up, then he placed a hand on my shoulder. "I'm sorry, I didn't mean—"

"Don't apologize!" I snapped at him. "You're fine. You're wonderful. I'm the one who's all fucked up."

"Are you going to be—"

"I'm a virgin," I told him.

"—all right? What?"

"I said, 'I'm a virgin,' Jacob."

"Really?"

I turned around to look him in the face and said, "With what you know about me, that surprises you? You realize that was the first time I even kissed someone like that?"

"No, I didn't." He let his hand fall from my shoulder, and I had an urge to grab it and hold it in place. I still really wanted the contact, to be close to him. But I let it fall. To do anything else would be really unfair to him.

"It really isn't anything about you. I'm just not ready for that. Not here."

"Yeah," he said quietly. "I probably should buy you dinner first."

I reached out and squeezed his hand. "Too much has happened. I just need to get my head together." I let go. "I never really had a boyfriend before."

"So I'm your boyfriend?"

I leaned forward and kissed him again, lightly on the lips. Then I told him, "If you can deal with all my baggage, then yeah, you are."

TWENTY-FOUR

IT WASN'T UNTIL we got up to continue our road trip that I realized I had completely forgotten about Ivan. That gave me another reason to be glad I hadn't gone any farther than I had with Jacob. If my first time had been interrupted by a third party, I could imagine being put off the idea for life.

It was worse because, when Ivan "directed" me with his Mark, it was as if he was touching me more intimately than Jacob had attempted. In some sense, my body felt as if I'd already lost my virginity to Ivan. That was something I was never going to let either of them know.

I took the Charger back out onto the broken road and pushed us all back in the direction of Ivan's Empire. It was easier to do this time, the Chaos tugged at me like Jacob had, but the sensations were less raw. The Mark stroked me, egged on by Ivan, but it was less breathless, less jangling nerves.

Which meant that something else had to go wrong.

"Dana?" Jacob said.

"What?"

"Your gas light came on."

I glanced down, and the Charger's fuel gauge was on empty, and the fuel warning light was glowing at me. I cursed. I tried never to let the tank go below halfway.

Then again, I was on my third state without a fuel stop. What was I expecting? "Okay, we have to stop for gas."

Like I had with the farmhouse, I tried to reach out into the Chaos around us to find something that felt like a gas station. As I did, I began to realize that my Charger, much as I loved it, was not the greatest vehicle for time travel. It would only be useful this side of the turn of the twentieth century. Even then it confined us to major roadways.

I began to appreciate Ivan's steam-driven armor.

I steered the Charger, more with the Mark than the wheel, and let the gray twilight around us coalesce into a paved country road running between acres of farmland. The road signs said we were headed south on National Pike Road and Spoolsville was ten miles farther along. It was about midday, overcast, and, like the world we'd just left, I saw no sign of other traffic.

I saw the obvious destination, a large circular sign hung on a pole advertising Davis*Quality*Gasoline in a garish early twentieth century font that was reminiscent of a blue Coca Cola logo. I pulled into the lot in front of a little Tudor-style cottage that had a single blue-painted gas pump out front. At least that was what I thought it was, it was cylindrical, and had a hose hung up next to it, but it was topped by a giant cylindrical glass tank with graduated hash marks on it.

That looks real safe, I thought.

I honked the horn.

"What are you doing?" Jacob asked.

"This doesn't look like a self-serve kind of place," I said.

"Aren't we a little out of place for a Depression-era gas station?"

"Yeah," I said. "But I'd rather try explaining ourselves to the proprietor than surprise him by stealing his gas."

"She's being wise," Ivan said.

I honked again. Nothing.

I'd been worried about swiping gas and being confronted by a shotgun-wielding proprietor. Now the emptiness was getting to me. There'd been no traffic on the road with us, and now there was no sign of life at Davis*Quality*Gasoline.

"More Spanish Flu?" I wondered aloud at the emptiness.

"Maybe it's Sunday," Jacob answered.

I chuckled and shut off the engine. The latter was probably—given the infinite possibilities the Chaos implied—a lot more likely. A one in seven chance, in fact. "Okay, why don't you see if you can get that pump working, I'll go inside and see if I can find anyone."

"Okay," Jacob said.

I glanced at the antique gas pump and added, "And be careful. I have a nineteen-gallon tank, and that thing probably doesn't have an auto shutoff." I closed the door and had to force myself to walk away from my car while Jacob got out to fuel it. I had the OCD urge to stand by and make sure he didn't overflow the tank.

I was inordinately proud of myself for not turning around to check on him as I walked up to the little Tudor building. The door was glass, and looked in on a dark interior, so I guessed the Sunday hypothesis was right. I expected the door to be locked.

It wasn't.

I pulled it open, and some little bells chimed above my head. The air inside seemed still, stale, and empty. All my cop instincts started telling me something was wrong. It was the feeling you got walking into a 7-Eleven right after some punk's just shanked the cashier and run for it. I reached for my gun and realized that it was in the hands of some Shadow in an alternate universe somewhere.

I cursed under my breath and scanned the room.

"Is there anyone here?" I called out. The bells on the door had announced me, so there wasn't a need for stealth.

No answer.

There wasn't much here, just half-bare shelves with candy and cigarettes and automotive odds and ends. I noticed that, above the cigarettes, a small cardboard sign told me how many ration coupons I needed to purchase them.

Back by the counter, a heavy cash register that looked that it came from the prior century squatted like a pagan altar. On the back of the register a neat hand-lettered sign read, "US Currency Only." The drawer hung open and empty.

It *was* a robbery.

I edged up on the counter, expecting to see the cashier crumpled in a bloody heap beneath the empty cash drawer. I leaned over to look, and nothing was behind the counter but an upturned stool and a newspaper dropped carelessly on the floor.

The paper blared a headline, "ARMISTICE TALKS FAIL." The date was June 7th, 1919. I don't know why, but the date on a random newspaper gave me more of a sense of dislocation than anything else I'd gone through since I started this road trip of the damned. Even driving along a post-Fascist Pennsylvania Turnpike complete with propaganda billboards didn't hit me in the same way. Maybe because at the time I had been too exhausted for it to really sink in.

I was almost a century from home. More, if I took into account that the world I was in was not the same 1919 that history textbooks back home recorded. At the very least, I seem to remember the armistice talks for World War I succeeding.

I bent to look at the text under the headline. I had only just read half a sentence about "Southern forces massing for a new offensive," when I heard buzzing outside. Over it, I heard Jacob's voice. "What the hell?"

I ran back outside to see Jacob bent over the side of my Charger, dispensing amber liquid from the baroque glass dispenser. He faced across the street, toward a cornfield. Above the field buzzed a biplane, disconcertingly low.

Crop duster?

The plane aimed right at us. I saw a flash from the nose, and a streak of the parking lot exploded in dust and gravel. I'd seen enough war movies to jump aside before I realized what was happening. I didn't hear the gunfire until the bullets tore apart the glass door and the façade of the little Tudor gas station.

"*Shit!*" Jacob yelled.

I yelled back, "I'm fine. *Get in the car!*"

I scrambled back to my feet. The biplane buzzed above the gas station so low that it seemed I could reach up and touch the landing gear. It banked around for another pass at us. I ran as it turned, and by the time I reached the driver's side of the Charger, it had already looped around back toward the cornfield.

It passed in front of me, barely fifteen feet above the trees next to the gas station. I could see canvas pulled taut over the airframe. I could see the wicked black tubes of the machine guns on the nose. I could see a gray-clad pilot, head hidden under helmet and goggles. I saw three starless American flags stenciled on the side under the cockpit and I could almost read a name.

And, on the tail and wing I saw a circular emblem painted with the battle flag of the Confederacy.

A Confederate biplane?

I remembered the newspaper. "Southern forces massing for renewed offensive."

I yanked the door open and slid into the driver's seat. I started the engine before the door had closed. The plane had looped back around the cornfield for another strafing run.

Jacob must have seen the plane's markings, because he yelled up at the approaching plane, "What the hell, Johnny Reb? *We're not a military target!*"

I shifted into drive just as I started to hear the delayed hammer blows of the machine guns. I let off the brake and pushed the Mark as the car rolled forward. The driver's side door slammed shut on a suddenly silent twilight. I smelled smoke and glanced back at the gas station twelve hours removed from the one we had just vacated.

This one had burned. Nothing remained of the little Tudor cottage except a pile of rubble and a few blackened timbers pointing upward, like spears giving the *coup de grace* to a charred corpse. In place of the gas pump was a crater in the asphalt that was less a sign of explosion, then the scene of some intense melting.

Ivan looked at the scene and said, “This is a military target.”

“What?” Jacob said.

“Logistics and resupply—any fuel depot in wartime is a legitimate target.”

I heard realization in Jacob’s voice. “Oh.”

I checked the rearview mirror and saw the gas cap still open. I shifted into park and got out to close it. I tuned out Jacob and Ivan as I stepped out. I’m no shrinking violet, but while they were doing some sort of male bonding about military tactics, I was starting to get the shakes from having someone try to kill me just because I was in the wrong place at the wrong time.

Good lord, was this actually somewhere where the Civil War lasted another half-century? Or, maybe, the Confederacy wasn’t defeated. Maybe in this world the Civil War ended in a truce, or a stalemate, or maybe came to some sort of accommodation. The biplane might belong to renewed hostilities, someone wanting a rematch.

My hands shook when I placed the dangling gas cap back on and closed the door on it.

Was I standing in a world where there were still slaveholders around? It was a chilling thought, made more surreal by the thought that where I stood here in this version of 1919, I was closer to the Civil War than I had been to World War II when I stood in my own world.

I heard thunder in the distance, and it dawned on me that the sky was still clear. It wasn’t thunder I heard. “War zone,” I whispered, “bad plan.”

I ran back and got in the driver’s seat and quickly drove us back into Chaos—which, by comparison, seemed a lot less threatening now.

TWENTY-FIVE

"*OH, FUCK!*" I shouted at the dash. My voice had a bit of breathy vibrato caused by the Mark caressing my insides raw as the gray twilight Chaos roiled outside the car. My frustration fought its way out through the layers of building tension and physical sensation as I allowed Ivan to guide me.

"What's the matter?" Jacob's voice had an edge of concern that sounded barely in check.

"The 'check engine' light," I half gasped, half snapped in frustration.

"What? What does that mean?"

"That must have been leaded gas we filled up with." *You're a guy*, I thought, *you should know this stuff.*

"I thought they didn't start using leaded gas until the 20s."

"Yeah," I said, "and the Civil War ended in 1865."

"Point taken," he said. "Are we going to break down?"

I sighed. "No. But it means I probably just fucked up the catalytic converter."

"Oh, that's all?" The relief in his voice pissed me off.

"That's all? You know what it costs to replace one? Over a grand, damn it! I can't afford this crap."

"Dana, after the last day or so, does it seem that important?"

"It's my car." Even as I said it, I knew how crazy it sounded. But, well, it was my *car.* But it was looking less and less practical as a mode of travel between universes.

Ivan interrupted my automotive angst to tell us, "We've reached the Empire."

I drove out of Chaos, and the Charger pounced onto a concrete highway like a captive cheetah finally being released back on the savanna. Six arrow-straight lanes worth of freedom, and I think I could hear the Hemi almost sigh in relief.

I patted the wheel and thought, *Sorry about the bad gas.*

After all the travel through Chaos, I was getting a feel for relative dates. I guessed that we had landed about a decade farther away from home than the universe of the risen South, and I asked Ivan what year it was here.

"1908," he responded.

Right on the money.

The highway paralleled a set of train tracks as it headed east. Dawn shaded the sky ahead of us in reds and yellows, and we passed the first road sign proclaiming Ten Miles to Imperial District, in English, French, and Russian.

Imperial District, aka the District of Columbia.

Jacob leaned forward from the back seat and asked, "So how does the Napoleonic Empire gain a foothold in North America?"

"I should ask of you, how could it not? The old United States destroys itself in civil war and asks the Franco-Russian alliance for aid. The Empire saved this nation."

"I guess Napoleon's invasion of Russia ended differently," Jacob said.

Ivan laughed.

"What?" Jacob asked.

"There was no need to invade. Marriage is so much simpler."

The history of Ivan's world diverged from my own somewhere in the first decade of the nineteenth century where the Napoleonic Wars didn't take the bad turn in Russia that my Napoleon had suffered—here there was no Waterloo, no Elba, no disintegration of French domination in Europe. Instead, there had been a tense stalemate that ended with the joining of the Imperial families of Russia and France. When the US started breaking apart here, and things went bad for the Union, the North pleaded for intervention by the Empire.

It worked, since the Empire was the most powerful nation on the planet. It was also expansionist as all hell, and once it had troops on the ground, the "assistance" quickly managed to reunify the country—under the Empire's flag. For half a century, the Empire had been peaceful, since no one was really interested in pissing it off.

I listened with half an ear because the scene I drove into was even farther removed from me than the world with the Johnny Reb biplane. The highway was arrow-straight through the Maryland countryside, the kind of road that was more an expression of power than logistical necessity. Every wrinkle of the ground was smoothed or filled so that the road never wavered from level. The surface was unmarked, but I kept to the right, by the train tracks, to avoid other traffic.

And, as the dawn light grew, I began to see other traffic, much of it horse-drawn. There were self-propelled things as well, but they seemed too ornate for me to call them cars. They puttered along on spidery-thin wheels, and the passengers sat in plush lounges nestled in cabins as elaborately decorated and as fragile as a Fabergé egg.

I wondered at the lack of anything but horse-drawn cargo until a train approached on the tracks next to us. I heard it whistle and glanced in the rearview mirror and saw the massive engine bearing down on us. On the nose was a massive shield, with a painted golden double-headed eagle on a midnight-blue field. It clutched thunderbolts in its talons.

Then the engine shot by us. The engine itself was at least fifty feet long and loomed over the Charger as if it was a toy. The drive wheels were easily half again as tall as my car. The rest of it screamed by the highway in an endless chain, a great moving wall of elaborately painted passenger cars and somewhat more dull cargo containers.

I passed a sign announcing that the Imperial District was five miles ahead, and the farmland next to the highway gave way to long aisles of trees flanking the highway. Something floated in the sky above us and Jacob asked Ivan incredulously, "Is that a zeppelin?"

Ivan looked where Jacob pointed and said, "What? Do you mean the airship?"

"Yeah . . ."

"So, what's a zeppelin?"

"An airship designed by a German engineer."

"Then that is probably not a zeppelin."

THE traffic became more congested as we approached a sign announcing the border of the Imperial District in elaborate cursive English, French, and Russian. Our fellow travelers gave the Charger odd looks, but nothing as bad as the Amish in Fascist Pennsylvania had given us. Still, the road was crowded with slower moving traffic, and I had to ease back and go less than twenty-five for fear of running over a horse-drawn fruit cart.

We'd barely crossed the border into the district proper, when the traffic ahead of us began pulling aside. At first, I had a hope they were pulling apart to let us through, until I saw past the traffic ahead, someone bearing a banner with the golden double eagle on it. The bearer was the one causing the traffic to part, more efficiently than a police siren, and probably for the same reason.

The carriage in front of us pulled over to the side of the road so I had a clear view. A dozen horsemen galloped down the road toward us, the point man bearing a lance on which the banner fluttered ahead of them. The rest of the men behind him seemed more practically armed, with swords and rifles. Their uniforms consisted of tall black boots, scarlet trousers, navy jackets with brass buttons, elaborate braids, and insignia. A few of the riders, the ones with swords, wore white gloves and elaborate plumed hats. The riflemen had bare hands and wore plainer caps that reminded me of movies about the Foreign Legion.

I pulled the Charger over and asked Ivan, "So is that our welcoming committee?"

He nodded and said, "Let me go out and talk to them." He left the car before I had a chance to say anything to him.

"I don't like this," Jacob said quietly.

"I know."

Ivan spread his hands and walked up next to the front of my car on the passenger side as the cavalry surrounded us. He shuffled his feet as the horseman with the nicest hat called out in Russian-accented English, "Everyone must exit the carriage now."

I frowned when Ivan started talking back in Russian. "Okay," I whispered, "he's hiding something." I put my foot on the brake and shifted out of park. It had worked with the Fascist cop and the strafing biplane. I'd just let the car roll forward and push slightly with the Mark and we'd be somewhere else where the Franco-Russian police weren't.

I lifted my foot off the brake and pushed with the Mark. Nothing happened except a distracting shudder. "What?"

"The bastard shoved something under your front tire!" Jacob undid his belt and reached for his gun—which still wasn't there.

"Jacob," I said, "They're the cops here."

My foot moved to the gas, but I hesitated. They had leveled rifles at the car, and if I didn't goose the car into motion with the first try, we'd be dead. If it was only me in the car, I might have risked it. Then walls of horse flesh clopped into place immediately ahead and behind the car.

I really wish I'd thought about reverse before they'd done that.

I shifted back into park and cut the engine. The Charger shut down with a few barks from the exhaust to remind me that I had fed it bad gas. Then I made sure to keep my hands on the steering wheel. The lead horseman repeated, "Out of the carriage. Now."

I opened the door and stepped out. Free of the confinement of the vehicle I had a moment of freedom where I could have run into a neighboring universe, but I didn't want to abandon Jacob. Then a horseman dismounted and took my arm firmly in a gloved hand and the point was moot. Jacob followed suit, shooting me a dark look. Ivan wasn't looking at us at all.

What did I expect? I thought. *I saw the bastard kill someone.*

Ivan faced a trio of the mounted police himself. He still spoke Russian, so I had no clue what he was saying.

"Was it *all* lies, Ivan?"

I thought I might have seen him flinch. But I suspect that any sign of guilt or regret might have been wishful thinking on my part. Some part of me wanted to believe that he was explaining things to the guards and it was a misunderstanding.

Then someone snapped a black metal band on my wrist. The metal was cold, heavy, and felt like cast iron. It clicked shut on my wrist with a dense mechanical click. It not only weighed down my arm, but I could feel it weigh down my Mark.

Oh, crap! What the hell is this?

It wasn't a handcuff or a manacle, the ring of metal was not connected to anything else. If it wasn't so thick and heavy, it could have been a piece of jewelry. I stared at it, feeling it weigh me down as the man holding me let me go. I glanced over at Jacob and saw they had snapped a similar band on his wrist. He looked at it, but he just seemed puzzled about the thing. From the way he moved his arm, I could tell he didn't feel the same weight on his that I did with mine.

I looked up at the officer who had held my arm and asked, "What is this?"

The officer glanced at Ivan and looked uncomfortable. He stood at attention and said. "Any Walker coming without leave into the Empire's domain must be restrained. I apologize, but it is the law, my Lady."

"My Lady," again.

I felt the iron band with my opposite hand and thought of the way the officer said "restrained." I didn't like it, and I didn't like the weight I felt in my Mark. I took a step toward the officer, pushing myself with the Mark—and I almost doubled over in pain. It was like I tried to run without realizing that my wrist was chained to something massive and immobile. I felt a wrenching force tying me to Ivan's world, so heavy that my movement with the Mark ended before it began.

Ivan turned to look at me as if he had sensed the effort.

I glared at him and balled my hand into a fist. The sudden rage I felt was horrifying in its intensity. I'd gone through all of this because of the Mark. I was able to take risks—even so far as coming here—because in the back of my mind there was nothing I could get into that I couldn't walk away from.

Idiot! Ivan had even told me that this was possible. He didn't explain it or go into detail, but there was the fact he said that the Emperor had held the dead old man a prisoner. *Why did I never ask* how *they could imprison him?*

If they'd been aware of Walkers for any length of time, of course they'd develop some sort of countermeasures. I felt stupid and helpless as it sank in that getting out of this was not going to be nearly as easy as getting into it.

THEY loaded me and Jacob into the back of a wagon with barred windows. We were the only passengers in the back as it rolled forward, continuing into the Imperial District.

Jacob leaned forward once the doors closed on us. "Okay, you followed Ivan to his Empire. You can get us out of here now."

I stared at my hands, balled into fists on my knees, so I didn't have to meet his eyes. I whispered, "No."

"What?"

"The bracelets," I said. "I can't move with them. It's like it chains me in place."

He felt the band on his own wrist. "This? How can it keep you from doing your thing? You were driving that Charger of yours—"

"I don't know!" I snapped, much more harshly than I intended. "I don't even know how the Mark works; how should I know what can stop it?" My vision blurred. My eyes and my cheeks burned. "Oh, God, Jacob, I'm sorry. I'm sorry. You shouldn't even be here."

"Dana? It's not—"

"You told me not to trust him. I didn't. But I followed him anyway. I was so damn sure I knew what I was doing. If we got into trouble, I could . . . Damn it, they have you, they have me, they even have my damn car."

Jacob chuckled.

"What's funny?"

"I actually got billing above your car."

I frowned. "I'm serious."

"I know. But you can't blame yourself for me being here. I came freely, and you can't even say I didn't know what I was getting into. I pretty much saw firsthand before we reached this point."

I bit my lip and turned away from him.

"What's the matter?"

What isn't? "I just was thinking about Whedon," I said.

"That wasn't your fault either."

"I know, but it's hard not to blame myself for it."

TWENTY-SIX

I DON'T KNOW what I expected to see when they let us out of the carriage. Whatever it was, I didn't see it. Instead, we stepped out onto the Mall in a Washington DC that was recognizable and completely alien at the same time. The Mall and the reflecting pool were the same, but the Capitol was different; the dome wasn't white but gilded so that it shone like a golden egg under the morning sun. Other details of the neoclassical building had been gilded as well, pickings of gold against a building that I always remembered as pure white. It was as if someone had spent a great deal of thought into picking one architectural detail that could symbolize the distinction between a constitutional republic and an empire.

If that wasn't enough to drive the point home, the larger-than-life equestrian statue between the Capitol steps and the Mall itself was there to proclaim the Empire's sovereignty. Even at a distance I could see the unmistakable hat and cloak that had defined Napoleon I in so many paintings. His mount faced the reflecting pool, both hooves raised, and Napoleon held a sword aloft as if directing a charge at the Washington Monument.

Then there was the Washington Monument itself.

The monument itself was as I remembered it, at least as I remembered pictures of it—a white-clad obelisk without the gratuitous gilding that had been added to the Capitol. We were close enough that I didn't really understand what had changed until I heard Jacob whisper, "Holy crap."

I looked at him, and he was looking up at the monument. I followed his gaze and sucked in a breath. They had led us out facing the Capitol, so my first impressions had been of the changes on that end of the Mall. The shadows over the Mall I had unconsciously interpreted as cloud cover. It wasn't.

The sky wasn't overcast at all. Above the Mall was a massive airship, nose moored to the tip of the Washington Monument. The length of it pointed back toward the Capitol. From where we stood, it might have been easily as long as the monument was tall. The Empire's crest was painted on its side, the image probably a hundred feet wide, large enough so individual feathers on the double-headed eagle were easily discerned from the ground.

The massive airship bore a large resemblance to pictures of airships I'd seen from the 1930s; the basic shape was a long cigar with large control surfaces on the tail bearing smaller versions of the Imperial crest. But there were differences. First, I saw no sign of any sort of gondola below the main ship. The underside was completely smooth. Also, for some reason, the thing had wings. Broad stubby wings stuck out along its length at various heights.

"What does an airship need with wings?" I asked no one in particular. "I thought they didn't work like that?"

"They aren't wings," Jacob said. "Look at what's attached to them."

I did and realized that what I had originally taken to be little underslung propellers like I'd seen in more conventional aircraft were airplanes themselves. A dozen biplanes were slung under the airship's "wings." The behemoth was a flying aircraft carrier.

"I think Nazi Germany was experimenting with that idea before the Hindenburg."

"Isn't that a little advanced for 1908?"

Jacob shrugged. "Not by much, they had planes like that in the First World War, 1915 or so. And I think Zeppelin patented his first airship designs in the 1890s."

"You really are a history buff."

While we were surrounded by armed guards, they kept a respectful distance and didn't try to manhandle either of us. An officer came for us after about ten minutes; the same one who had called me, "my Lady." I recognized his hat.

"If you both would follow me?" he said. He bowed slightly.

Jacob looked at me, pointedly waiting to follow my lead. We were surrounded by armed guards, so it wasn't as if I wasn't going to follow instructions. Polite or not, we were certainly prisoners.

I decided to push my luck, a little. I stood as straight as possible and held out my wrist with the iron bracelet on it. "What about this?"

"I apologize, my Lady," he said, a hint of tension in his voice. "It is necessary."

Well, if they were going to pretend that I was some form of aristocracy, I might as well act the part. "Is this how your Empire treats all its guests?"

"Those that arrive unannounced. Again, my apologies. Please, come with me." The officer was very polite, almost deferential, but we were still surrounded by a lot of armed men who, I suspect, would be considerably less polite if they had to be.

Still, since I seemed to be getting some response, I folded my arms, "What about my car?"

"Your . . . car?" He spoke the words as if he wasn't sure what I was talking about.

"My vehicle? Automobile?"

"Oh, the carriage."

"What did you do with it?"

"It's safely under the Emperor's protection. It will be returned once you leave the Emperor's demesne. Such artifacts are not permitted here outside the control of the Emperor."

"Of course not."

"Now, my Lady, we must go. They are waiting for us."

I sensed that I'd reached the limits of stalling, and I followed him, silently hoping that whoever had the job of moving my Charger could figure out a stick shift. If I was lucky, Ivan had been paying attention when I was driving.

The officer led us across the Mall, toward the Washington Monument, under the tethered airship. The thing was even more imposing when it was directly overhead. And it quickly became obvious that the airship was, in fact, our destination. We entered the monument, and walked back through unfinished-looking hallways, into a massive and cranky-looking elevator.

The majority of our escort stayed on the ground, while the officer and one token rifleman accompanied us on the shaky ascent as the machine took us six hundred feet up to the tip of the monument. I stood as close to the center of the elevator as I could. There were no walls or doors. The iron framework was wide open, so I could see cables, wheels, and gears above us, and the stone and brick of the shaft sliding by us with agonizing slowness. I could understand how some people got claustrophobic on elevators, but the openness felt much worse to me. My palms became sweaty, and I was very aware of the beating of my heart.

Heights had always gotten to me a bit. It worsened after I had become aware of my Mark. The more I had used it, even in the limited fashion I had, the more I'd grown aware of the dangers of any temporary perch above the ground. My first big mistake using the Mark was in high school. I'd slipped into a parked school bus to hide my disappearance and used my Mark to Walk to a point where the school bus wasn't parked there anymore.

I'd fallen four feet into the asphalt and twisted my right ankle badly. When I finally made it back home, hours later, I had to go to the ER and I was on crutches for a couple of weeks.

So, while having access to the Mark made me a little reckless about some risky situations, it also made me a little more afraid of being too far off the ground. Just knowing that a step to the side with my Mark could send me tumbling six hundred feet down the elevator shaft made me tense up even though the band on the wrist prevented me from doing any such thing.

The elevator came to a stop facing a small room that had windows looking out at blue sky all around us—except directly in front. Ahead of us, a large doorway stood open, flanked by a pair of windows that were blocked by shadowy gray, flat and featureless. Two guards flanked the doorway, dressed in elaborate uniforms that matched the coloring of our officer's uniform, navy jackets with brass buttons and gold braid, pressed scarlet trousers with black piping, boots polished to a mirror shine. They wore peaked caps with the Imperial insignia on them, and even the stocks of their rifles had been polished.

A pair of flags also flanked the doorway and the guards. Even draped on their flagpoles I could see that the one to the guard's right was—again—the gold double-headed eagle on a blue background. The one on the left was more interesting. At first, I saw the red-and-white stripes and thought it was a normal American flag. But there were no stars. Instead, in the upper quarter where the stars would be, on the blue field was a duplicate of the Imperial eagle. I saw what looked to be a banner with some sort of motto above the figure, but I had no time to read it. The guards came to attention at the appearance of our officer, and he ushered us through the door.

The elevator was disconcerting, but what greeted me on the other side of the door induced something close to full-bore panic. I think I only kept moving because my brain froze up so badly that I couldn't even coordinate the motor control to stop.

We walked out onto a catwalk. The air had been still on the ground, but up here the wind whipped against us with a tearing, flapping noise, striking me with the immediate visceral realization that I had walked outside. To the left and right, Imperial DC spread out below us, the ground terrifyingly far away. The sides of the catwalk were walled with some sort of mesh netting, but it didn't seem nearly strong enough. And neither did the cables that slung the catwalk under the airship's nose. To my panicked eyes, they seemed less substantial than the netting.

It seemed to take forever to cross the suspended walkway to the airship itself, though it probably only seemed so in retrospect. The shock of finding myself in the open air so far above the ground took much longer to process than it did to walk across. It was something I was grateful for, because by the time it had sunk in enough for me to think about screaming in terror, we were already inside the airship.

"Wow," Jacob whispered. I was envious of his ability to speak. I was still concentrating on steadying my breathing.

The room the catwalk led into did not belong in anything that wasn't solidly attached to the ground. The oval chamber belonged in a European castle, with its elaborate mosaic floor, the Corinthian pillars lining the walls, the paintings displayed on the walls, and the crystal chandelier suspended from the domed ceiling. The only sign of where we were happened to be the placement and orientation of the windows.

The windows all faced out the front half of the oval room, in the direction we had come. They were each five feet wide and ran from the floor to the start of the domed ceiling twelve feet above us, and they tilted outward between the columns that lined the room's parameter, following the outer skin of the airship, and not the vertical walls of the room. The eight windows dominated the forward third of the room, flanking the entrance, so that looking in that direction felt as if we stood on a huge balcony looking down on Washington DC.

I only glanced that way once. Then I quickly turned and focused my attention on the half of the room that resembled a very expensive hotel, trying not to think about where that room was.

In front of us, at the rearward-facing end of the room, a staircase unfolded upward in curves of faux marble and carved wood. At least I assumed the marble was fake. It seemed to me that real marble would be a weight issue. Along the walls flanking the stairway, I saw dozens more flags. In addition to what I thought of as the Imperial US flag that I had seen back by the entrance, I saw the familiar UK flag with the addition of a shield bearing the gold double eagle in the center.

Before I had a chance to look at more of them, someone cleared his throat. I focused my attention to our right, and saw a couple waiting for us with a posture somewhere between calculated disinterest and military parade rest. The man wore a black tuxedo jacket and a gray-striped cravat under a collar so starched and upright that it seemed as if it could keep his neck clean shaven all on its own. He wore a pair of pince-nez that, with his mustache and round face, made him resemble Teddy Roosevelt. The woman wore a black dress and an apron in a frilly ensemble that was probably several shades too modest for any French maid fantasies Jacob might have had.

Once I had taken notice of them, the man gave a slight bow with such military precision I almost expected his heels to click.

Behind us, our military escort said, "Will you escort the Lady and her Gentleman to their rooms?"

"Yes, sir, General Lafayette."

I glanced at Jacob, and he looked at me with an expression that mirrored my reaction. I wondered if he was surprised at the "General," who'd been our escort, or at being my "Gentleman."

Either way, despite the armed troop that had taken us prisoner, and the bracelets they'd slapped on us, they weren't treating us the way I'd expect for typical prisoners. If I'd rated a general, maybe Ivan had been telling the truth about the whole "Prince" thing.

Teddy and the maid led us up the staircase, through a hallway filled with textured wallpaper, scrollwork, and brass fittings more appropriate to Versailles than an airship. The only sign of the nature of the vessel showed in the doorways and in the way the passage was segmented. I could see, every twenty feet or so, recesses where a bulkhead door waited to divide the hallway. And the doorways off the hall seemed to come not from a palace, but from the submarine in a Jules Verne novel: all metal with a smoky-colored oiled finish that went with the wallpaper and wood scrollwork, the locking wheel and other fittings in gleaming brass.

We stopped in front of one of those anachronistic doors, and I noticed an enameled plaque with cursive black numerals on a white background: "0230." Teddy stepped forward and turned the brass wheel in the center of the door. It spun silently, and I saw long rods slide back from ceiling and floor and from the wall opposite the hinges.

It glided open on a small alcove that opened into a huge chamber beyond.

"Your stateroom, my Lady, with the Emperor's compliments." Teddy indicated the room inside with a minimal hand gesture. I had to suck in a breath once I stepped across into the stateroom proper. It had seemed large from the doorway, but from there I had only seen part of the sitting room. Once past the alcove, I could see the whole sitting room, complete with a Louis XIV settee and a window with navy-and-gold–brocade curtains large enough to cover three king-size beds. On either side, doors led into other rooms; on one side was a lavatory complete with a claw-footed bathtub, on the other was a bedchamber with a four-poster bed with a canopy.

A *canopy* bed. In an *aircraft*.

I'd only flown once, a nerve-wracking experience, and I'd been happy for the extra bag of peanuts.

I walked to the window that dominated the sitting room. It tilted out, but less so than the windows by the gangway entrance. I looked out and saw the White House. It looked pretty much as I remembered it, and it only served to reinforce how weird things seemed. I almost preferred the gilded Capitol Building with its Napoleonic equestrian statue.

I heard a very soft impact behind me, and I spun around. The door had shut, leaving me alone in the room with the maid. "What? Wait a minute. Where are they taking Jacob?"

"Your Gentleman is going to his own rooms, my Lady," the maid said. She had a Germanic accent that worked at cross-purpose to her uniform.

"Of course, he is," I muttered. I suspected Jacob had just become a hostage to my good behavior.

TWENTY-SEVEN

THE MAID'S NAME was Greta. It went with her accent. She was, apparently, my personal servant for the duration of my stay. It took me several tries to get my head around that. Apparently, Ivan's deference to me hadn't been a complete act. The Mark must carry considerable status here if the Emperor loaned me my own minion.

Of course, it was also clear that it meant that I had a pair of the Emperor's eyes in the cabin here with me. I just hoped that Jacob's cage was just as gilded. It would make me feel a little less guilty for involving him.

I talked to Greta about what was going on. She informed me that this wasn't just an airship. It also served as the seat of the Empire itself, sort of a cross between Air Force One and Versailles. The Emperor ruled from this vessel as it made its way from capital to capital. I had the honor of being a personal guest of the Emperor.

Apparently, I was also invited to dinner.

I tried to get more information about Marks, Walkers, Shadows, and the White Guard from Greta, but she was—in Ivan's words—Stationary. All she knew of me or people like me was that we could move outside the world she knew, and that made us either angels or demons, and elevated us beyond normal men, and beyond mundane aristocracy.

Whatever else had happened to twist this world's history away from my own, I realized that the primary divergence wasn't the outcome of the Napoleonic Wars; it was the fact that people like me were known and integrated into the society.

Greta was no historian, so I wasn't sure how accurate her stories were, but according to her, in the first decade of the nineteenth century, when Napoleon I was just starting to consolidate his hegemony with Europe, he divorced his wife Josephine and married Catherine III of Russia.

I knew this daughter of Catherine the Great never existed in my world. Not because I knew anything of Russian history, but because this Catherine bore the Mark of a Prince. It was decades before that fact became widely known, and even longer before it was generally understood that Catherine's Mark meant that she had been an illegitimate product of the notoriously randy Catherine the Great and some otherworldly lover rather than her late husband Peter III. By then, the French Empire had merged with the Russian one, and Napoleon II could claim the throne of the Czars as well as the power of a Prince's Mark.

That all helped explain how Napoleon Bonaparte could spawn a cross-dimensional dynasty. Not only had he consolidated his power without a Russian campaign, but he gained the advantage of Catherine III's abilities.

In Greta's story, it was as if the Hand of God itself had come down to grant the Empire favor. I suspected that there was a century of propaganda behind the sentiment, but I could see how just having one Walker of any sort in the control of a military organization would be hard to fight.

I actually felt a little embarrassed that I had limited my use of the Mark to street-level crime fighting. Then that was followed by the powerful realization that, if I had kids, they would be like me.

Like me.

Marked.

Ivan may have said something along those lines, but I hadn't really thought of that before. That it applied to me.

While I listened to Greta, the airship disengaged from its moorings and began to move out to sea. The White House slid out of view of the window, followed by the rest of the alien DC skyline, to be replaced by the blue-green of the Atlantic Ocean.

They're probably missing me at work, I thought randomly, and the incongruity of it made me giggle slightly.

"Are you all right, my Lady?"

"Oh, I'm just peachy."

Greta stared at me as if she was trying to make sense of the statement.

"I'm fine." I clarified. "I've just been through a lot lately."

Before she could say any more, the door to my cabin opened. I turned around and saw Ivan, flanked by two younger soldiers who stayed back and stood at attention. Ivan himself had cleaned up, shaved, and was wearing a polished dress uniform that looked annoyingly good on him.

I've always had a thing for uniforms; if I was into pop psychology, I'd probably mark it down to unresolved feelings about the loss of my father, but I'm not. I just think most guys tend to look hotter when wearing dress blues, especially when they're built for it, like Ivan.

I think it made me even more pissed at him.

I folded my arms and glared at him. "I bet you're proud of yourself."

"My Lady, I told you I would bring you into the Empire."

"To be taken prisoner?"

"You aren't a prisoner here."

I extended my arm to him, showing the dull-black metallic bracelet. "Then what is this?"

"*Métal Stationnaire,*" he named the thing. "An alloy developed by the Empire's scholars." Ivan reached out and gently took my wrist.

He held my hand in a way that made me uncomfortably aware of the presence of his Mark. It was as if his Mark was gently brushing my own, slipping beneath the weight of the thing on my wrist, as if he was joining me under a heavy lead blanket.

Then he took out an odd-shaped key and slid it into a slot in the side of the bracelet. The metal parted and slid off my wrist. The removal of that weight triggered a wave of vertigo and made me feel as if I was in imminent danger of suddenly floating away. I gripped the hand that held my wrist, just to steady myself. His arm was much steadier than mine; I felt like I hung on to a tree.

He held out the bracelet, and one of his uniformed companions stepped up and took it from him.

Once the *Métal Stationnaire* was no longer in contact with either of us, I felt his Mark full force, as if in some sense the entire length of him pressed into me. I pulled my hand away and watched as he took a deep breath.

Great. He feels it, too?

I found it all rather creepy and folded my arms to avoid touching him again.

"Okay, thanks for getting that off me. But what *is* it? What did it do to me?"

"It does nothing *to* you. It's an alloy that cannot enter Chaos. It is Stationary in all senses. Anything forged of this material cannot be moved from this world. Walking while carrying it would be like trying to pass through a closed door or push your hand through a solid rock."

"They slapped that on me, and I'm not a prisoner?"

Ivan frowned. "I spoke on your behalf, convinced them to present you to the Emperor himself."

"Awfully convenient that you did that all in Russian. How do I know *what* you said to them?"

"They did not shoot you."

I supposed Ivan did have a point. No one had roughed me up or had even been rude to me. I suspect someone going to visit the

President would go through an irritating series of security hoops themselves—especially if they showed up unannounced.

Of course, there was a practical reason they could remove the *Métal Stationnaire* bracelet now. I stood in an airship that, by my last look out the window, had floated up several thousand feet above the Atlantic. One step with my Mark and I'd be in free fall somewhere where this airship *wasn't*.

It was an elegant solution to a problem unique to this Empire. Once you had Walkers who could sidestep into another universe and walk around any security measure, it became very hard to secure any location. You'd have to find a spot that was equally inaccessible from any potential universe. If your palace was mobile and airborne, that would be a pretty big step in that direction.

"So now what?" I asked him.

"I'm here to escort you to the court scholars."

I had a brief hope that my meeting with the "scholars" was an attempt to answer the growing pile of questions about the Mark, about the Empire, about the Shadows, and my family. These would be the people who could tell me about the old man who had tried to talk to me, to warn me.

That was me being naïve.

Ivan took me deep into the airship, away from the rich wallpaper and the elaborate brass fixtures. We descended several decks to a place where corridors were merely functional, and paint merely protected surfaces from corrosion. Near what I thought had to be the bottom of the airship, Ivan led me into a large suite of rooms. The central room looked like I imagined the back rooms of a natural history museum might look. The walls were hidden behind floor-to-ceiling shelves made of dark wood. Books hid behind sliding doors made of heavy glass. Other shelves held boxes and specimen jars, safely behind their own doors. Other walls hosted tall stacks of drawers, one series made of the kind of broad and flat drawers that stored maps or blueprints, another made of drawers with square faces about a foot square.

Everything was identified by white cardboard cards written on with a neat French script I couldn't hope to read. Each card slid neatly into a brass holder on the face of a drawer.

Two men bent over a chart laid down on one of a pair of long tables that dominated the room. They were so similar looking that I could have taken them to be brothers. Both were on the tall and thin side. Both wore long white lab coats over tweed jackets—though the man on the left wore a brown suit jacket underneath, while the man on the right wore a charcoal gray one. Both wore gold wire-frame glasses, and both had mustaches and goatees that drew their already-thin faces to sharp points on their chins. Both had gone gray, but the man on the left retained a small amount of rust-colored hair.

They looked up simultaneously at Ivan's entrance, and Ivan gave them a small bow and introduced me as "Lady Dana Rohan." Then he said, "I present to you Dr. Durand of the *École Polytechnique* and Dr. Lefevre of the *École Normale Supérieure*."

Dr. Durand was the grayer of the two; he looked me up and down as if he was inspecting an unexpected shipment of lab animals. He didn't smile when he said, "Welcome to my laboratory, Lady Rohan." He then turned to Ivan and said, "May I presume that the Emperor wishes an assessment now, despite whatever other work is pending?"

"He needs your report before this evening."

"Of course, he does." He turned to the other man and said, "Dr. Lefevre, would you take care of our guest?" He didn't wait for a response before he bent back over the chart spread on the table before him.

I glanced at the paper that took all his attention. It was a broad sheet, like a blueprint. In the brief glimpse I couldn't make out much detail, but I saw large circles dominated the surface, labeled in neat, tightly-spaced French. The circles varied considerably in size, and their borders ranged from thick bold lines to faint dotted lines that were barely there. The circles were connected by a variety of lines, also labeled in neat French. Embedded in the text I could only understand numbers which seemed to be cryptic dates with extra years, 13/5/1906/1877, 7/8/1907/1855.

After just a glance, the slightly younger Dr. Lefevre said, "Will you come with me, my Lady?"

Unlike his colleague, Dr. Lefevre could manage a smile and did not seem resentful at having his work interrupted. Ivan stayed in the outer room as Dr. Lefevre led me past the long table and through a door in the back that led to a small antechamber the size of an elevator, with three doors. He turned, cranked open the door to the right, and led me into a tile-covered room.

He pulled a knife switch on the wall, and a large lamp flickered to life above us, casing a sterile white glow over the room. The place made me uneasy; the bright light and the white tile reminded me too much of an operating theater. Or a morgue.

"I presume this is your first visit to the Empire, my Lady?"

"Yes."

"Excellent. For all the work we do, our studies are limited by the nature of our subject."

I looked around the room, squinting in the intense light. One wall hid behind a large black panel suspended from a track in the ceiling. On the panel was a white grid made of inch-wide squares. In the bright light, the grid almost seemed to hover in midair, leaping from the matte background. On another wall hung a large chart that showed a branching tree that resembled an NCAA bracket that had crossbred with a spiderweb.

I walked toward the chart to see the detail and asked, "What is it you study?" The title of the chart read, "*Descente de la Marque de Chaos.*"

"We map the shifting sands of Chaos and those gifted ones who traverse them."

The chart had small illustrations at the end of each branch, and in the swirling abstract patterns I could recognize the kinship with my own Mark. Each branch ended with a small drawing of a symmetrical branching pattern of various sizes. Some labeled *petite*, some *grande*, and near the bottom were a collection labeled *Grande Marque de l'Empire*. Those illustrations were elaborate, intricate, and very unlike my own Mark. The Mark of "*l'Empire*" showed a trefoil symmetry and spirals that alternated clockwise and counter-clockwise. In fact, even the simpler *petite* Marks illustrated on the chart didn't share much with my own—or with that of the old man.

It made me suddenly very angry that I had no name for him. He may have been my family, and I could not even say who he was.

I turned around to question the doctor about the old man the Emperor had imprisoned and saw Dr. Lefevre adjusting a tripod that supported a large box of a camera. It pointed at the panel with the grid.

"What are you doing?" I asked.

"To properly account for you in our studies, we need a reference image of your own Mark."

TWENTY-EIGHT

I FELT MY skin get hot. I didn't show people the Mark. I'd only ever shown Jacob, and I still felt uneasy about *that*. This was some strange French guy from an alternate universe. I couldn't strip in front of him. I shook my head, because embarrassment didn't allow me to speak.

"There's no need for modesty, my Lady, you only need to show the area where your Mark is."

"Only that much," I whispered. "Why?" I asked.

"The more Marks we catalog, the greater our knowledge. The better our studies."

"What can you tell from someone's Mark?"

"Many things. The power and control the person has within Chaos, the likelihood of passing the Mark on to children and how powerful those children might be. Family relationships. Where in Chaos the person may have come from—"

Damn.

My heart pounded, my skin burned, and the thought of exposing myself made me want to curl up and die. But this was exactly what

I had come here for. I came to find out about myself, and how could anyone tell me if I kept hiding like I always had.

"Mademoiselle?"

I held up a hand and controlled my breathing. I wasn't hiding anything, I told myself. These people already knew what I was, what I could do. Exposing my Mark here didn't mean anything, not like back home where it made me different—an outcast, a freak.

I couldn't do this.

The hell I can't.

I couldn't let the fear rule me. I'd come too far to back away now. I swallowed my embarrassment and said quietly, "Please, tell me what you see." I shed my jacket and began to unbutton my blouse.

Dr. Lefevre's eyes widened and he said, "Please, only disrobe as far as necessary."

I walked over toward the grid and faced it as I shed my blouse. I did it quickly, so I wouldn't second-guess myself.

I heard a sharp intake of breath from the doctor.

"Tell me about what you see."

"Y-yes, my Lady, but the straps, and the waistband—"

I sighed inwardly, both my bra and my pants covered parts of the Mark. I wanted to run away and hide in one of those wooden cupboards where no one would see me. I sucked in the emotion. I'd committed myself to this.

I undid my pants and dropped them so I stood in my panties. Then, with one hand to my chest, I unhooked my bra and shrugged out of the straps. The doctor said something in French that I didn't really want translated.

"Can you see it all now?" I snapped. It didn't help that I was cold on top of everything else.

"Almost, my Lady."

"What?"

My Mark was even larger than I had thought. It had begun to sneak along the sides of my rib cage, under my arms, and it had descended below the small of my back. For the doctor to get it all on film I had to pull my ponytail, short as it was, over my shoulder, pull the waistband of my panties half down my ass and do a quarter turn and strike a pose like a lewd Statue of Liberty. Then I had to repeat the process with the other arm.

Through it all, I felt a sickening mix of embarrassment and irritation, my skin flushed and breaking out in gooseflesh at the same time. Despite clinging to my underwear, my modesty was in tatters. Because of the Mark, I had never so much as tried on a bikini before.

"Can I get dressed now?" I asked. I pulled up my panties and reattached my bra before he finally said, "Yes."

"So?" I asked as I pulled my blouse back on, covering the Mark.

"Hm?"

"Tell me about the Mark," I said, allowing all the irritation I felt into my voice. The embarrassment, I kept to myself. After going through that, putting myself on display on the off chance he could tell me something about myself, I thought I might strangle him if he held out on me.

"Yes." He didn't look at me as he packed up the plates from the camera. "A *Grande Marque*, the size and detail are exceptional, my Lady. Though I am certain you know that."

"What else are you certain I know, Dr. Lefevre?" Once I had dressed myself, I felt the embarrassment fade if not completely vanish. The confidence crept back into my voice, especially since my cop instincts had picked up on his sudden obvious discomfort. It was more than could be explained by near nudity. Especially since I thought the French would be a lot more blasé about that sort of thing; especially a French scientist whose job, apparently, encompassed taking pictures of people's skin.

"You are not of the Emperor's line," he said quietly. He walked away from the camera and slid the covered negative plates into a cabinet along the wall. "The patterns of your Mark show almost no points of similarity. Any common ancestor must be over six generations gone if one exists at all." He walked up to the *Descente de la Marque* chart, and I noticed he still avoided looking in my direction.

He reached his hand out and started tracing the lines of descent without actually allowing his fingers to touch the surface of the chart.

I noticed that his fingers trembled slightly.

"No," he said quietly. "You are of no family we have managed to study."

"Dr. Lefevre?"

"Hm?"

"Would you look at me?"

He froze, fingers hovering over the portion of the chart with the *Grande Marque de l'Empire*. He balled his hand into a fist and allowed it to drop to his side as he turned to look at me.

"Why are you afraid?" I asked.

"What a silly thing to say." He broke into an insincere smile and spread his hands. "Why would you say such a thing?"

I took a couple of steps forward, and I could see the edge of his smile twitch, and his eyes twitched ever so slightly in the direction of the door.

"Because you're terrified," I said.

He licked his lips and stopped trying to hide his glances toward the door. "You have a powerful Mark, my Lady, as strong as any of the Emperor's line. I've never seen one so large or elaborate. If you aren't the scion of a great dynasty, you must be the foundation of one yourself. Just your presence in Chaos would be enough to define an Empire."

"That scares you?"

He hesitated too long before saying, "Of course, it does."

"No, it doesn't. What else?" I kept my voice firm and level, just like I was back being a cop, and this guy had been pulled over for a traffic stop. He was hiding something, and I didn't know if it was a beer bottle in the foot-well or a body in the trunk.

"I don't know what you mean."

I stared into his eyes and saw real fear there. Something about me had completely unnerved him. "You know exactly what I mean, and you are going to tell me what it is."

He closed his eyes and said, "*La Marque des Ombres*."

"English."

"The Shadows' Mark."

I opened my mouth, closed it, and just stared at him, dumbfounded. Of all the things he could have said, I don't think he could have hit me with anything more unexpected. I couldn't fathom any connection between me, my Mark, and those . . . things. It took me a moment to regain my composure enough to speak, and what came out was little more than a whisper.

"Explain."

"*Ombres*. Shadows. They exist within the Chaos, preying on Walkers who stray too far. They are barely human, and the Marks they bear are abnormal, asymmetrical, scarred. Over a century, only three bodies have ever been retrieved for study, but they show patterns of descent like all those who are Marked."

"I am not one of those Shadows." For some reason, my voice did not carry the conviction I wish I felt.

"No." He agreed with me, and I felt inordinately relieved by that one word.

"But?"

"You share many of their characteristic patterns, in fully developed form. The Shadows have irregular and stunted patterns, your Mark is what they might be if they developed normally."

"You're saying I'm *related* to the Shadows?"

"What I know about the patterns of inheritance tells me that only a generation separates you. Two at most."

I stood very still. The only muscle that moved was behind my jaw. It trembled violently, and I could not will it still. I stood here, in an alien place, a world removed from mine by centuries in a direction I couldn't name, because I wanted to know who I was, where I came from, what it all meant.

I refused to accept the notion that somehow I was related to an army of cannibal monsters.

"I think what you know about the patterns of inheritance is wrong."

He frowned, and I think challenging his expertise managed to override his fear. "My Lady, it is not *wrong*. The best minds of the Empire have studied this subject for nearly a hundred years. Our archives catalog the patterns of thousands of Walkers from a dozen distinct family lines. If you gave me a dozen Marked children, I would be able to identify the parent of each one, and in some cases both. There is no doubt. You share a bloodline with the Shadows."

I took a step back.

"I am sorry, but this is science as pure and exact as geometry. But, perhaps, I should say that the Shadows we've seen share a bloodline with you. Your Mark is unblemished and fully developed. The Shadows, unquestionably, have undergone some form of corruption. Perhaps some form of bastardization or miscegenation."

I did not like the way this was going. Europe did not have a stellar history when it came to dealing with questions of racial purity, and this guy came from a generation that, in my world, laid the groundwork to put the worst part of that history into practice.

"Perhaps some sort of infection," I said quietly.

"What?"

"I saw a woman attacked by these Shadows. Within hours after being bitten, she had become one."

He stared at me as if I had just explained how squirrels were space aliens bent on world domination.

"That is impossible," he said flatly.

"I saw it. I *saw* that twisted Mark eat its way into her flesh."

"I'm afraid you are mistaken. You do not understand how this works. No one could be 'infected' by a Mark, any more than they can be 'infected' with blue eyes, or red hair, or negroid features."

"What I saw—"

The fear was gone, trampled by the academic persona who rushed in to explain to the poor confused woman how the world worked. I got the Cliff Notes version of the germ theory of disease and Mendelian genetics and the difference between the two. If I could have gotten away with it, I would have slugged him.

I wondered if I could have gotten him to listen if I'd been a man.

In any event, the episode demonstrated to me that, when it came to the nature of the Mark, the scholars of the Empire did not know as much as they thought they did—and it left me wondering how the Mark could behave like an inherited trait for some, and like some sort of disease for others.

That led to an uncomfortable thought.

You could pass infections to an unborn child. I knew about HIV and hepatitis, and there were probably many others I hadn't heard of. What if the Mark wasn't genetic, but some sort of disease passed on in the womb? That could explain the different ways it showed up.

Also, when I thought about it, I could understand the doctor's too impassioned denial of the possibility. I'm certain that someone actually studying the subject would have had the same idea, but these scientists worked for an Empire that was based on hereditary power and on the *Grande Marque de l'Empire*.

Suggesting the Mark wasn't an inherent symbol of the bloodline, but some sort of sexually-transmitted fetal infection, would be politically dicey to say the least. It could be very easy for the powers that be to see the idea as undermining the power base of the entire political system.

In any authoritarian regime, the best-case scenario in that situation was loss of position—and I could easily see consequences that could be much worse.

I was still irritated, but I lost the urge to punch Dr. Lefevre.

I decided to stop with the science questions and go into the cop questions. As he walked me to another exam room to take blood and take my vital signs, I interrupted his discourse on nineteenth century genetics and disease theory to ask him if he had ever seen anyone else with patterns that tied to the Shadows.

That got a reaction.

"What do you mean?" He asked the question in a way so obvious that he might just as well have waved his arms and shouted, "Wait while I stall."

"I know about the prisoner who escaped."

"Um." He drew my blood with a glass syringe.

"Tell me about him."

"I can't, my Lady."

"Why not?"

"I have no direct experience of the man you talk about. Those who did are dead."

"But—"

I was interrupted by Dr. Durand storming into the exam room. "Dr. Lefevre? Is there a reason this is taking so long?"

I stood up and said, "I've been asking him some questions."

Dr. Durand ignored me and continued talking to Dr. Lefevre. "We have a report to draft before the end of the day, and I trust you do not want to be cited as the reason for its postponement."

"The assessment is nearly complete—"

"Complete it, then, and get her out of here. The sooner these foreigners are out of my lab, the better."

"Dr. Durand . . ." I started to give him a piece of my mind, but he had stormed out without ever acknowledging my presence. ". . .you are an arrogant prick," I finished lamely, facing the door to the exam room.

"I apologize for Dr. Durand, my Lady."

I turned around and saw Dr. Lefevre holding a tray of implements. I was glad I didn't suffer from any real medical phobias. Otherwise, the tray of gleaming antique examination equipment might have given me the shakes. He set the tray down by the examination table.

"Can we continue?" he asked.

"If you talk about the prisoner."

He sighed, but he nodded.

TWENTY-NINE

THE DOCTOR HAD never seen the prisoner himself. He had seen images of his Mark, and he confirmed the man's relationship to me and to the Shadows. I don't know if I found the confirmation of my initial suspicion reassuring or disturbing now that I had to fit the Shadows into that equation.

Not that I didn't have to fit the Shadows in somewhere. They had come from somewhere, and the fact they showed up on the heels of John Doe strained coincidence. The cop in me knew that they were related. I just didn't want it to be so literal.

Like Ivan, he couldn't give me a name. Unlike Ivan, he could give me at least some reason why he had been a prisoner of the Empire in the first place. Uncle John Doe had walked through the Empire's extended domain, and there were members of the Emperor's White Guard who felt the foreign movement and converged to challenge him.

Such things were routine. Chaos moves, and often new people are brought to the Empire's shores. All that is required of them is an acknowledgment of the Emperor's authority in his domain and a pledge to abide by the laws of the Empire; those laws require that a Walker of any power that crosses his domain be documented by the

Emperor's scholars and appear before the court or the court's representatives.

Uncle John objected to that, violently.

They'd subdued him and brought him back to a holding cell in DC, bound by *Métal Stationnaire*. Apparently, some of the Emperor's scholars on the scene had made the mistake of assuming his bonds made him safe. During his exam, he killed the doctor, overcame a guard, and, freshly armed, he managed to carve his way out of the building and make his way into the wilderness. He was ten miles away by the time he had managed to remove his restraints and escape through Chaos.

I didn't want to side with the Empire—it was authoritarian, autocratic, and subtly racist—but I couldn't quite fault their reaction. Monitoring the border, whatever its nature, was a basic government function, like maintaining the roads. And I doubt even the most utopian democratic republic wouldn't hunt down my John Doe after a similar incident.

It also dawned on me, the way Dr. Lefevre spoke, that there was an additional wrinkle to John Doe's brush with the Empire. The nature of the society here implied a lot about a Mark, and those who bore it. A *Grande Marque* such as mine, or John Doe's, implied some form of aristocracy—the old school kind where the King *was* the State. Ivan called them Princes because their presence stabilized Chaos, creating their own demesne simply by existing.

That meant that anyone with a *Grande Marque* had the potential of being another head of state of some yet unknown empire, and that made John Doe's reaction more puzzling on a number of levels. Especially when Dr. Lefevre's story opened up a question that I hadn't even known was a question—

Where had he been before he crossed the Empire's boundary?

The old man who had died in front of me had borne the signs of an extended captivity: the pale skin, wild hair, scars from being bound, the rags and the filth. . . .

But according to Dr. Lefevre, John Doe had been in the Empire's captivity for less than 72 hours. He had already been escaping from something before he had ever come here.

And whatever he had escaped involved the Shadows.

Cheery thought that.

AFTER Dr. Lefevre was finished giving me the once-over, Ivan escorted me back to my cabin. We walked back in silence. I was too wrapped up in my own thoughts. Finding out about the Shadows and their origins were important; they were an obvious threat, and if I didn't find some way to address them, I suspected they'd keep turning up until I did. But what'd kept me pushing down this road trip from hell was the thought that I might be able to find out who I was, where I came from.

I might find my family.

Now I was looking at the possibility that the two things were the same question, and I really wouldn't like the answers.

I wondered about Ivan's family. Unlike me, I suspected he knew who his people were and how they fit into the universe. Given his Mark, and the way society seemed to work in the Empire, he could probably trace his lineage back to Catherine the Great.

Back in my cabin, Greta was waiting for me. I had to stop in the doorway because the cabin looked as if a fetish lingerie shop had exploded. I saw corsets, stockings, and all manner of things that required boning and an excess of laces, the kind of things that could have been in a dominatrix's closet, if it wasn't for all the frilly lace. Greta stood in the middle of the whirlwind of Victorian undergarments with a smile that seemed almost predatory.

"What's all this?" I asked.

"My lady, you must prepare for dinner with the Emperor."

"Prepare . . . I'm supposed to wear all this?"

Greta chuckled and shook her head. "Not *all* of it, my Lady. I gathered a selection for you to choose from."

I felt a little relief. I looked around and pointed at the least uncomfortable-looking frilly thing draped across the settee. "How about that?"

"Oh, dear. That's a nightgown."

"Oh," I suddenly felt a little overwhelmed. I was about to say I'd go as I was, but "as I was" included a set of clothes that were business casual at best, and now held the aroma of a few days' continuous wear. They'd be ripe even if I hadn't been exerting myself and walking through overgrown farmland. I ran my hand through my hair, and it felt greasy and knotted. I sighed. "I must look like hell."

Greta gestured past all the underwear. "I've drawn you a bath, my Lady."

IT had been ages since I had actually taken a bath. I had a shower and a tub in my master bath at home, but I think I might have used the tub once since I'd moved in. After all the running around, the idea of a long soak was enticing to the point of eroticism.

I stepped into the little washroom off the sitting room, found a brass washtub that was all Greco-Roman bas-reliefs and clawed feet, and stared at the steaming water filling it. Just being that close, feeling the humidity on my skin, made me realize how much I itched.

When was the last shower I'd taken?

The light came from a window, not as large as the one in the sitting room, but large enough that—with the right angle—the tub looked as if it was floating above the clouds.

I wasted no time stripping off my clothes. The idea of clean was suddenly foremost in my thoughts. Things had been so chaotic—or Chaotic—lately that, deep down, I half expected I might not get another chance.

Greta was certainly right about my need to change clothes. Not only was my outfit wrinkled and spattered with mud, when I reached my underclothes, I felt a fresh flush of embarrassment. I had peeled these off for Dr. Lefevre, so he had seen the faint gray streaks of dirt on my skin outlining where they had been. That now felt worse than being nearly naked in front of him. My blush made me itch worse.

I stood at the edge of the steaming tub anticipating a long soak so badly that my muscles ached. I stared into the water, placed my hand on the edge of the tub, and almost jumped out of my skin when I felt someone touch my hand.

I spun and saw Greta standing there, lifting my hand to help steady my entry into the tub. Seeing her there felt like a punch in the gut. In retrospect, I don't think it should have hit me that badly, my modesty had already taken a beating today. But earlier had the pretense of being a medical exam; this was different. I had stripped myself without expecting anyone there to see me. Just like the unknowing version of my dad finding me in the shower.

I squeezed her hand in shock. It must have hurt, but she didn't react. I opened my mouth to say something, but no words came. That was a good thing, because I don't think the first things that might have come to mind would have been particularly helpful.

They gave me a maidservant, it was her job.

I released my death grip on her hand and said, "I'm sorry, you startled me."

"Apologies, my Lady." When she looked at me, I was uncomfortably aware of every inch of exposed skin, especially the Mark. I could feel her gaze on it. Though she hid her expression well, my experience as a cop gave me a good eye for people's faces when they were trying to hide a reaction to something. Her brows barely moved when her eyes shifted toward my back, but the very slight intake of breath I saw her take told me that the Mark made an impression on her.

When her eyes shifted back to my own, I could tell that she had a similar history reading the expressions of aristocrats, and I could see it dawn on her that I had noticed her reaction. We froze in that tableau for the space of several heartbeats, neither of us sure how to acknowledge the discomfort, or even if we should.

It became obvious that I was the one here who had to react, or not.

She was waiting for a reprimand. I just sighed and used her offered hand to help steady myself as I stepped over the tall edge of the tub.

Having a servant help me bathe was the most decadent thing I'd ever experienced. I wasn't in a state of mind to enjoy it. Aside from my backlog of existential questions and the open question of if this was a friendly environment or not, I just felt too vulnerable and exposed. Even if I suppressed that discomfort, having Greta scrub my back made me feel as if I was in the midst of some elaborate act of sexual role-play.

I didn't know if my refusal to dismiss her and take care of things myself was an act of courage on my part, or an act of cowardice. I would have felt more at ease dealing with an armed gangbanger hopped up on meth. At least there I knew what the options were.

I did notice that when she touched the Mark, I felt none of the sensations I'd felt when Ivan had touched mine, or I his. That was a relief. The bath was awkward enough.

When Greta declared me clean, the sky out the window glowed red with a sun just starting to set, the clouds flaming golds and oranges below us. I stood up, flushed from scrubbing and the still warm water, and she helped me out. Then, before I could hunt up a towel for myself, she was rubbing me down with something white and fluffy. It took an act of will not to jump.

She dried my skin and my hair and spritzed me with something that I supposed must have smelled pretty. I was too uncomfortable to bother making an assessment.

When we got to the clothing, it became apparent that for the aristocracy—the women at least—a maidservant wasn't just a luxury, it was a necessity. With the exception of the panties, garters, and the stockings, it appeared that all the clothing from the corset on up required two people to assemble.

I saw where that was going early enough in the process to request a bathroom break while I was still able to accomplish the task unaided. Greta paused just long enough before retreating to let me realize that at least some of the ladies she had served had not requested that kind of privacy.

It was hard for me to get my head around that.

THE clothing overwhelmed me with choices, and after the first few questions from Greta I just told her to dress me in something that fit and went together.

I've never been the frilly dress-up type. I don't know how much of that was my nature, and how much of it was the fact that since my dad died I'd avoided interacting with people much. It meant I never really dressed for anyone but myself, so everything I'd worn had been picked with the idea of comfort, efficiency, and hiding the Mark.

None of those adjectives described how Greta prepared me for dinner with the Emperor.

First was my hair, which rarely got any attention beyond being pulled into a ponytail. Occasionally, I'd let it down, but it almost always pissed me off by flying in my face. Greta combed it out, spritzed some more sweet-smelling stuff on it, and braided it. Then she took the braid and spiraled it on top of my head, locking it in place with a clip adorned with a gold filigree dragonfly with emerald eyes and mother-of-pearl wings with a span as broad as my palm.

The dress itself went on me like a minor construction project. When it was over with, I had a sweeping floor-length skirt of silver, cream, and white that matched the dragonfly wings, accented by gold embroidery with green highlights that glinted in the evening sunlight. The bodice pushed me up, so I now had more boob than I'd ever thought possible, and I was a little grateful that the neckline was only cut low enough to give a hint at my enhanced bust. Of course, there was another brooch with more gold, mother-of-pearl, and emerald, a flower this time, placed to draw attention to the small slice of cleavage the neckline did reveal.

More unnerving than that was the fact that the dress was shoulderless and dipped down the back about an inch farther than it did on my bust. Between that, and having my hair up, my Mark felt more on display than it had when I was naked. The black lines of it now not only stood out on my pale skin, but they practically screamed for attention contrasting against the cream and silver of the gown itself.

I looked like the lead singer in an over-produced music video.

I looked at myself in a gilded mirror, the oval frame alive with cherubs and twisting vines. It wasn't me looking back. I don't know who it was, but it was someone who was definitely not from the same time and place I called home. I reached over my left shoulder and traced the top of the black swirling pattern with my fingertips.

"Is there something to cover my shoulders?"

"My Lady?"

"I'm not comfortable with all this showing."

"You're dining with the Emperor. You wish to hide the mark of your status?"

"I think he knows about it."

Greta appeared puzzled but acquiesced and produced an embroidered wrap that could fit over my shoulders, hiding most of my Mark from view. As she adjusted the material, she said, "It is remarkable."

"What?"

"I've served the Emperor's guests for fifteen years and I've never seen a *Marque* as large and finely detailed as yours."

I knew it was a compliment, but it only made me feel more uncomfortable. I hugged the new wrap around myself and looked in the mirror. It didn't hide the Mark completely, but it did enough so I looked less the punk chick and more the Disney Princess.

"Does the Emperor receive a lot of guests?"

"Like you? Not many. Two or three a year. Cousins mostly. An occasional envoy."

I turned to face her, interested. "Envoys? From where?" I was starting to wonder how many "Empires" there might be out there.

Unlike the kind of empires I was used to thinking about, these had no constraints around physical borders, and the potential territory was—it seemed to me—infinite.

"Many places, most far away even for one who Walks through worlds. Not many women, and aside from the Emperor's family, not many from any civilized race."

I didn't respond to that one because I didn't want to go into a long explanation of what exactly was the problem with that statement. But it let me know that there was a broader world out there. For all I knew right now, the Empire here amounted to a remote backwater. It made me wonder again about where it was "my" people came from. As much as I'd discovered, the only thing I knew for certain about that was that they were not from around here.

I started to ask Greta another question, but I was interrupted by a knocking at the door to my cabin. Ivan had come to escort me to dinner.

THIRTY

IVAN WAS CONSIDERABLY more flamboyant now than the last time I had seen him. He wore a white jacket that showed more gold braid than a bellhop convention. The cuffs and collar were stiff, wide, and scarlet, sporting brass buttons the size of golf balls, bearing the double-headed eagle of the Imperial arms.

He held out his hand for me, but I wasn't about to touch him again. He stood there, hand extended for a long moment.

"Where's Jacob?" I asked him.

I honestly wasn't trying to poke him. After all, I didn't know him nearly well enough to be interacting with him on that level, no matter how much he annoyed me. That didn't explain exactly why I found it gratifying that he barely hid a hurt expression when his hand dropped.

"He will be at dinner."

"And it's your job to escort me?"

"Yes, my Lady." He was subtle about it; only his eyes moved, but to me the way he sized me up was blatant. His gaze flicked up and down, taking in most of the details of Greta's makeover.

"Lead on, then." I've never been haughty or aristocratic. That isn't me. But when you work as a cop, one thing you do learn is how to project an air of command. So I did know how to boss people around, even if I wasn't the one in uniform.

Immediately after I spoke, I got the feeling again that I was needling him. However, the social rank my Mark gave me worked in my favor and Ivan only frowned ever so slightly, turning to face down the corridor. "If you would please accompany me?"

I followed him, ignoring the offer of his arm. Even if I wasn't still pissed at him for leading me into an ambush, I just didn't want to feel his Mark that close to mine.

I wasn't exactly sure of the direction, but I was pretty sure we were going up and forward. The hallways became progressively more elaborate in their decoration. He led us to another grand staircase that, like the entryway that had greeted me to the airship, appeared to be carved marble. This time I had a better look at it, and when I touched the molded banister, I realized the marble was simply a very good faux-finish paint job over a thin metal shell.

Near the head of the stairs were a pair of men who might have been guards, but given their elaborate blue, red, and white uniforms, they might have also just served as more decoration. Between the decorative guards, a massive pair of doors awaited us. They were the first conventional-looking doors I had seen aboard the airship, though I suspected that, like the staircase, their true nature was disguised.

Ivan waited at the head of the stairs for me.

"What now?" I asked him as I caught up. I'd fallen a bit behind him. The elaborate skirts restricted my movement way more than I was comfortable with, especially on the stairs.

"We're waiting for you to be announced."

"To?"

"The other guests."

I began feeling self-conscious. I hadn't thought about other people being involved. I was wrapped in this ridiculous dress and had half my Mark hanging out. I wasn't great with crowds of people in normal circumstances. My mom's calling hours had been brutal, and I'd *known* most of those people.

Way too soon for me, the door opened, and someone was saying something about, "*Dame Dana Rohan de la Marque Grande.*"

I stepped into the doorway because I didn't have much choice.

Beyond was a room that had no place on any sort of aircraft. I faced down the long axis of the room, at least fifty feet. The walls were dominated by tapestries, portraits, and sculpture, and the ceiling arched twenty feet above everything, dangling a half dozen crystal chandeliers from what looked like molded plaster.

Beneath the chandeliers, dominating the parquet floor, was a long mahogany banquet table that could easily seat thirty people. Past the end of the table, four musicians congregated around a harpsichord in front of a vast window that appeared to be looking out the front of the airship and into the night sky.

Of course, once I stepped into the room, all the guests turned to look at me. I could feel my cheeks burn, and that made me feel even more self-conscious. At least, the music didn't screech to a halt to draw attention to my entrance, as it would in some cliché western saloon.

I smiled when I saw Jacob. They'd dressed him "appropriately" as well. They had wrapped him in an Edwardian tuxedo that looked much less silly than I pictured my own outfit. He stood when he saw me enter, followed a bit more formally by the other men at the table.

All gave me looks that ranged from amused to analytical, but Jacob's look was the only one that held any warmth, and his gaze was the only one that didn't make me feel as if I was naked and painted with clown makeup.

Ranks of servants stood at attention, blending into the walls. One of them darted forward ahead of me and drew back an empty chair for me, just short of the head of the table.

To my chagrin, it wasn't anywhere near Jacob. The men were across the table from the women, and while I sat next to the head, Jacob had been seated all the way at the other end. Even though the table was only a third full—a dozen people at most, intimate for the space—that still put him about fifteen feet away from me.

That has to be intentional.

They'd decided to treat me like a peer rather than a prisoner. And that probably meant that they were more likely to be playing at some sort of intrigue. I hadn't heard of any royal court in history that was free from mind games or politics.

That made me wish even more that Jacob was next to me. He was the history buff. Instead, to my annoyance, Ivan got the seat across from me. My only real consolation was the fact that the table was too wide to easily converse with people on the opposite side.

The woman next to me was a sharp-faced brunette in a pastel blue dress. She'd been whispering something in French to the woman next to her, and something about the tone made it sound catty. Once I was seated, she turned and gave me a warm smile that held all the sincerity of a congressman at a parole hearing. She asked me something in French, and I did my best to sound polite, "I'm sorry? I don't speak French."

Her smile became even wider. "Oh, I do apologize. So embarrassing for me that I did not even consider you might be a foreigner." Her eyes lit up as if we were keeping score and she had just won a point.

I should have held my tongue, but the woman was already annoying me. "Technically, if we're still off the coast of Washington, aren't you the foreigner?"

She laughed. "Oh, but it is all *l'Empire,* is it not?" She took a drink without taking her eyes from me. The crow's feet and the few strands of gray made me guess her age at forty plus. It gave her a maturity that made the laughter and the light tone in her voice feel false, calculated. She carefully set down the crystal glass without taking her eyes off me.

"So you are the Emperor's new plaything?"

I wanted to smack her, and I realized that was exactly the reaction this woman was going for. I could see it in her eyes, the desire for a confrontation. There was something primal in the eagerness, and I wouldn't have been surprised if she wasn't even aware of what she was doing. I'd seen plenty of people with that same look; most had more than their share of beers in them and had some psychological need to mouth off to a cop.

When I was a cop, it had been easy enough to deal with. Here, much as I wanted to, I couldn't threaten to cuff her.

I picked up a crystal glass and took a sip of a wine way too dry for my taste, mostly to gather my thoughts. I was never particularly good in social situations, and most of the potential responses running through my head seemed to be inadvisable when I didn't know anything about who I was talking to.

Returning the insincere smile, I set down my glass and said, "You seem to have me at a disadvantage. You know all about me, but I know nothing about you."

"Of course we have not been introduced properly. I am Comte Juliet de Caulaincourt."

Of course, you are. . . .

Juliet was probably aware of the fact that her name without any context told me nothing, and she didn't elaborate for me. I got the uneasy feeling that I was being tested. Conversations ranged around the table, but I could feel the attention of five or six people focused on my interaction with her.

"Do you often dine with the Emperor? Or is this a special occasion?" It was an innocent, inoffensive question, but something about Juliet's attitude had infected my voice. I heard condescension leaking into my voice like an unwanted accent.

"My family has served the Emperor for four generations. But this *is* a special occasion. We honor a guest from the untamed wilds beyond the *Paix de l'Empire*."

"So this is unusual?"

Juliet smiled. "The Emperor has eclectic tastes in his amusements. He has honored Chinese acrobats and trained African monkeys in a similar fashion." She raised a glass toward me. "But the acrobats were not great conversationalists, and the monkeys were not nearly as well groomed."

I racked my brain for a response that wasn't confrontational. It was clearly what she wanted. Thinking about the social politics made my stomach do slow rolls, but I began to think she was trying to sucker me into some sort of outburst. The why of it eluded me, until I realized that if I wasn't here, the seat I occupied would probably belong to her.

Juliet was probably narcissistic enough to resent attention drawn away from her, even by a performing monkey.

"I doubt I am as entertaining as those acrobats."

"That remains to be seen. The monkeys were diverting, at least until they soiled the linens."

I was saved from the agonizing conversation by a short fanfare and the cessation of the chamber music. I turned, and from everyone's reaction it was obvious that the Emperor had arrived.

THIRTY-ONE

AROUND ME I heard the scrape of chair legs on the parquet as everyone stood up—the synchronous sound broken by two late additions as both Jacob and I stood a half-second after everyone else.

The Emperor didn't have anyone announce him, but it was pretty obvious who he was. He wasn't physically imposing; he was a few hairs shorter than Ivan and not nearly as broad. He didn't go overboard on a uniform either. He wore a tuxedo only a bit more refined than the one they'd given Jacob. The only sign of any rank was a medallion he wore in lieu of a tie, with the Imperial crest inlaid with semiprecious stones.

Despite his subdued appearance, he carried a presence larger than he was—as if the room around him distorted to place him at the geometric center wherever he moved. He walked into the hall accompanied by a uniformed man larger than Ivan, and the Emperor's presence was such that the huge bodyguard was barely noticeable.

He stopped next to the massive carved chair at the head of the table and stood in front of me. He had a hairstyle that reminded me somewhat of old pictures of General Armstrong Custer. His sandy brown hair had gone salt-and-pepper gray, leaving his facial hair several shades darker. His expression was friendly, if distant, and he regarded me with the most intense blue eyes I'd ever seen.

He nodded slightly. "You must be the Lady Dana Rohan."

My breath caught when I answered him, not because of his appearance or his bearing, but because of what I felt with my Mark. I had to actually touch Ivan or have him use his Mark next to me in order for me to have much more than a faint sense of it. I felt the Emperor's Mark full force just from him standing close to me. The sensation was something like having a cat unexpectedly rub against me, if that cat was a large Bengal tiger.

"And you are the Emperor."

He smiled at me and nodded absently at the table. In response, everyone took their seat, Jacob a fraction of a second late. The Emperor and I remained standing. Once the clamor from chairs scraping the parquet had subsided, an ominous silence filled the hall. The musicians did not move to play, and all conversation around us had died.

I felt more than ever that I was trapped in some sort of test where the questions were in a language I didn't understand. I had the feeling that, whatever I did, I was going to commit some nasty social transgression with some ugly consequences.

Do I sit? Do I remain standing? Say something more?

I clamped down on the growing panic.

"I'm pleased to finally meet you," I said, gratified that my voice didn't tremble.

"And I am pleased to meet an agreeable traveler." His smile seemed genuine, if distant. "I apologize if the necessities of processing an unexpected guest of your nature were unpleasant." He gestured at my chair. "Please, be seated. We can talk as well over our meal."

I took my seat, and the Emperor paused, surveyed the table, and took a seat in the throne-like chair at the table's head. That was the signal to release the paralysis that had overtaken the hall. The musicians revived themselves, playing something from Mozart, I think—though that might have just been me assuming anything remotely classical was Mozart. The servants that had been stationed against the wall sprang into action, moving plates, filling glasses, carrying food around. Conversation resumed around the table as if it had never paused. I glanced down the table at Jacob, and I was gratified to see him talking with someone. At least most of the people here could speak English.

I had a surreal moment when I realized exactly how mundane that relief was. I was in a wholly bizarre situation, on an airship in another world, and I was worried that my partner might be left out of dinner party conversation.

I turned back to my host. On the plate in front of him sat a small ceramic crock with some sort of pastry crust on it. He took a fork from the arsenal of silverware on the table before him, and gave the flaky top a token poke, lifting a small bit to his mouth. A nod of approval signaled the servant army to mobilize and slide similar crocks in front of everyone else.

I was grateful for the deference to the Emperor, since it gave me a chance to watch him and figure out which fork I needed to pick up. I knew I probably shouldn't start interrogating my host, peppering the local ruler with questions was probably bad form at the very least. And, for all I knew, could be dangerous on more than a social level.

But, as intimidating as the situation was, I told myself that the reason I was here was to find out about myself and my Mark. I wasn't going to discover anything by meekly waiting to be spoken to.

I took in a breath, promising myself that if I took a misstep, I would probably get some sort of pushback before I overstepped what they were willing to tolerate. And I was a foreigner, so they should probably cut me some slack.

It was so much easier questioning someone with a gun.

"So, you've had travelers that weren't so agreeable?"

"Your kinsman in particular," he said.

I noticed that the conversation around me quieted at the words. There was a subtle accusation in his words, one that served as a reminder of how precarious my situation here was. However they decided to treat me right now, I suffered from guilt by association with a man I never even knew.

"I didn't know him."

The Emperor looked at me, as if he was assessing the truth of the statement, or if it mattered. After a moment, he said, "We choose our friends, not our blood. Are you concerned I will hold you liable for his actions?"

Of course, I am. "I'm here because I need to find out who he was."

"Pity then he only left behind a few corpses." The Emperor smiled at me and suddenly things felt a little creepy. "However, if his actions brought you here, perhaps some of that can be forgiven."

I doubted that this evening would ever be displaced as the most uncomfortable dinner conversation of my life. The situation was unnerving as it was, but what could I do when the Emperor started flirting with me? I wasn't the best at dealing with that in normal circumstances, but this time the guy hitting on me was royalty, and currently the most powerful person on the planet. Saying any flavor of no could have serious consequences.

The one bright side of the situation was the fact that he was fairly free in providing information. He confirmed everything I'd already found out. His scholars had placed me in a family of Walkers that was outside any historical contact with the Empire, and my *Grande Marque* put me—in the eyes of the Empire—at the top of that family's hierarchy. As did John Doe's.

My presence here was akin to hosting the member of a royal family from a distant and unknown kingdom. There was great potential in such a relationship.

And I didn't like the connotations of the word "relationship" coming from a man whose ancestor had managed to take over a good part of the world by use of a strategic marriage. He didn't make me feel better when he talked about how the Mark descended parent to child. To have an heir with a *Grande Marque*, both parents must bear the Mark themselves, and the mother's bloodline was always more prominent. It was possible that two parents with Marks could have a child more powerful than either, but like a brown-eyed couple giving birth to a blue-eyed son, it was rare. The outcome was much more certain when both parents had blue eyes.

I had the ill luck of being unusual, and not just by being "agreeable." I was also a woman of the right age, and in the Emperor's own words, a more pleasing presence than five sixths of the *Aristocratie de l'Empire.*

At least, it was clearer why the Comte de Caulaincourt was so catty with me. If the Emperor was currently unmarried, I suspected that every other woman in his court was striving to rectify that in her favor. Anyone just walking—or Walking—into that was carrying a target, regardless of what the rules of status here said about Marks, *Grande* or otherwise.

Understanding it didn't make me feel any better.

Fortunately for my state of mind, the Emperor was the first to depart, after the dessert course and after the servants offered cigars and brandy snifters to the men. To my great relief, Ivan came around to escort me back to my cabin.

Back in the hallway, away from the court, I sighed with relief. "I think I'd almost prefer you lock me up in a cell."

"My Lady?"

"That was agonizing."

"The Emperor clearly favors you."

The defensive way he said it raised some ugly suspicions on my part. "Ivan? Were you trying to set me up?"

"I don't understand what you—"

"You never said your Emperor was looking for someone to shack up with. You weren't bringing me here just to present me as some sort of diplomatic coup."

"You've been in a single place long enough to empower your own realm. One unknown to the Empire—"

"Like he cares."

"Of course, he—"

"And bringing home the Emperor's next consort is probably a bit more praiseworthy than bringing back some random Walker, no matter how they're Marked."

"You don't—"

"Good lord, just be honest. You owe me that for bringing me here."

Ivan walked me down the corridors in silence. After a while he spoke, almost embarrassed. "It did cross my mind that he might favor you."

"What if I don't favor him?"

"He's the *Emperor.*"

"Of course, he is."

"The merging of your bloodlines would create a demesne more powerful than either of yours' alone."

"What are you talking about?"

"The power you have as a Prince is at its height in the area favored by your blood, your family line. That demesne expands the longer Princes of that bloodline inhabit it, stabilizing it. The Emperor's line here is a century deep. Should you and he produce an heir, almost certainly a Prince in his own right, he would wield such power in this demesne, and yours."

"Apparently mine isn't much in comparison—"

"And that of your family line."

"I don't believe I'm listening to this."

"If you've been as isolated as you say you've been, you will need to make alliances."

"You're talking about a lot more than an alliance."

"And you're facing a lot worse once any rival takes an interest in you."

I was about to snap something angry at him, but something about his tone stopped me. He sounded concerned, as if he was actually interested in my welfare. I was probably reading too much into it;

Ivan had plenty of reasons of his own to push me into the arms of the Emperor. I suspected there would be significant rewards for someone who did successful Imperial matchmaking. Probably enough to offset the indignation of the Comte Juliet.

Something about the way he spoke, though, made me think that wasn't his only concern. Possibly not even his primary one.

It didn't help that he was right. The Shadows came from *somewhere*. And I had Dr. Lefevre's testimony that my Mark bore some kinship with the Shadows'. That, along with my John Doe's warning to me before he died . . .

Could the Shadows be from that hypothetical rival that Ivan just suggested?

What I had heard from Dr. Lefevre, Ivan, and the Emperor all described something that amounted to a biological aristocracy—power passed from parent to child like pan-dimensional European royalty. Jacob might be the history buff, but I knew enough to know that such royal families weren't the kind that held cozy reunions.

If somewhere out there was another Empire formed by Princes with a Mark related to mine, and my relation made me as powerful in that demesne as they were, would they see me as a long-lost cousin, niece, or sister? Or would they see me as a threat?

Wealcan has fallen! They'll come for you! The Shadows are coming!

Something burned in my chest, and my eyes became suddenly blurry.

"Are you all right?" Ivan asked.

"I'm fine!" I snapped at him. Because of this train of thought, I was losing my family, the one I'd never had, all over again. Of course, I wasn't all right. I was suddenly irrationally pissed at Ivan for not seeing all the implications the way I saw them. It was unfair, but I was in no mood for fairness.

He had the good sense not to continue the conversation as we returned to my cabin. We went on in silence until we reached my door, where he turned to me and said, "I apologize if this has upset you. I know it is not the Emperor's intent."

Good lord, he sounds as if he's trying to hook me up with his old college roommate.

"He has left you a token of good faith," Ivan told me. "I hope you will consider it."

And now he sounds like some Mafia thug. "Nice car ma'am. Shame if anything happened to it."

He opened the door to my cabin, and I was relieved to see that the explosion of clothing Greta laid out before dinner had returned to wherever it had come from.

A silhouette stood out against the windows, looking over a night-time cloudscape illuminated by a full moon that hung fat over the horizon. He turned around, and I felt something catch in my throat.

I managed to croak, "Jacob?" as the door shut behind me.

THIRTY-TWO

HE LOOKED AT me and smiled. "I don't think I've ever seen you in a dress before."

I might have blushed. "I don't think I've ever seen you in a tux before."

He turned to look back out the window, at the clouds rolling slowly under the night sky. "I don't think I really let everything sink in until now."

I walked up next to him. "Really? You *were* on the same road trip with me?"

He reached out and took my hand and gave it a squeeze. Then he let it go. I found myself reaching to take his hand back, but something about his manner stopped me.

"I know," he said. "I guess I didn't realize what it meant."

"What are you talking about?"

He chuckled and shook his head. "Was it two or three days ago? This Walking business is worse than jet lag."

"Was what two or three days ago?"

"When I barged into your apartment, with the extra gun."

I opened my mouth, then I closed it. In the face of everything that had been happening, it had been easy to forget the life I had. The life I'd half-seriously thought of abandoning. Now that it looked like I might have abandoned it, it felt as if a massive hole had been torn out of myself. It might have been dysfunctional and defined by a self-imposed loneliness, but unlike the anachronistic dress or the Imperial sitting room, it had been *mine.*

And what had I been thinking, dragging Jacob into this? Pulling him out of *his* life. "I'm sorry."

"I think I'm over the whole planted evidence thing, Dana."

"No, I'm sorry for dragging you away from home. I should have thought about what I was doing—"

"I seem to remember making that decision."

"Like you, or Whedon, had any idea what you were getting into." I dropped myself into the settee in a very unladylike fashion. I didn't much care. "Especially her."

"Don't beat yourself up over that. Did you know what was happening?"

"No, but I should have made sure neither of you were injured after that fiasco at the morgue."

He walked around and sat next to me. He sat stiffly, as if the tux was uncomfortable, and stared off toward the door to the cabin. "What's going on here, Dana?"

"Going on where?"

He sighed.

"What?"

"They took us on board at gunpoint, and now we're having dinner with the Emperor?" He turned and looked at me. "Ivan wasn't kidding about all that Prince stuff."

"Apparently not."

"So you're really some sort of royalty?"

I shook my head. "I'm not sure what it means. But my Mark seems to be impressive."

"As impressive as our local Napoleon."

"Well, I don't know about—"

"Dana, people did talk at my end of the table. And I know some French."

"You know some . . ."

"High school and some college, hearing so much of it at once helped it come back."

"What did you hear?"

"That the Emperor should choose his consorts from within the Empire."

I felt my face burn. "That's not what I'm here for."

"That's why they brought you here. I think if you were a guy, you'd get a much different treatment."

"Crap."

"I'm pretty sure that's why I'm here."

"What?"

"To encourage your favor. Remind you that they have me as a hostage."

I didn't have a response for that. Deep down, I felt as if I should have known what I had been getting him into. I didn't know if fate was punishing me for failing to be open about my Mark long before now, or if I was being punished for finally breaking down and revealing it at all. If Jacob was going to be a hostage to my good behavior, it meant that he'd be trapped here as long as I was.

"No," I said quietly. "We have to get out of here."

"What about the Mark? What they know about where you came from?"

I wiped my hands on my skirts and avoided looking at him. "I've learned enough. There are others like me, and other worlds where people have this Mark. They don't know much more about John Doe than we do, other than he was related to me . . . and the Shadows."

"The Shadows?"

I gave Jacob a short version of my examination at the hands of Dr. Lefevre. As I spoke, I became aware of my naked shoulders. I had removed the wrap I'd worn to the dinner. I twisted it in my hands as I became aware of it, but I resisted the ingrained impulse to hide the Mark again.

Jacob didn't seem to notice the gesture, which made me more comfortable with it. I finished my story, untangled my hands from the fabric, and smoothed it across my lap.

"That's . . ." he paused. "I don't know what that is. It doesn't sound good."

"No, it doesn't."

"But if there wasn't any doubt that the Shadows were after John Doe and Ivan, followed them—"

"I don't think they were after John Doe."

"You just said his Mark was tied to the Shadows, and they showed up right after—"

"They were after *me*."

"What?"

"John Doe, whoever he was, passed through the Empire. Instead of paying at least token respect to the guys in control here, and probably being able to move on after dealing with the bureaucracy, he tried to fight his way out from the White Guard. Then, when they had him imprisoned with their magic handcuffs, he actually did manage to escape, killing a couple of people along the way. Why?"

"Outstanding warrant?"

"When he escaped, he wasn't trying to be evasive and escape pursuit. He was a Prince; he should have been able to evade Ivan in the Chaos, the way I was able to evade the Shadows. He didn't. He traveled the multi-universal equivalent of a straight line."

"To you."

"To me."

Jacob muttered under his breath. "Wonderful."

"He was trying to warn me."

"As if you'd know what he was talking about. He probably led those Shadows right toward you."

"Or he knew they were coming."

"Dana, this guy might be related to you, and he might have had this all-powerful Mark of yours, but it doesn't mean he was the sharpest knife in the drawer."

I sighed.

"Why would they be after you?"

"Wealcan has fallen. They'll come for you. The shadows are coming," I quoted.

"What?"

"Why is Emperor Napoleon the Umpteenth interested in me? Why would anyone be interested in me? This damn Mark. And it ties me to a bloodline somewhere, the same one that gave us John Doe and the Shadows. If the Empire here is typical, it ties me to a family, a dynasty, somewhere."

"Wealcan?"

"I think it's a name." I turned to look at him. "If we're talking about the fall of some ruling house somewhere, especially somewhere where they still speak Old English, they might not like having extra family members about. I'm not the history buff here, but I've seen *Richard III*."

"I see what you're saying."

"Am I wrong?"

"No. Given the implausibility of the situation we're already in, what you're saying is all too reasonable. An aristocracy based on a Mark might be even more paranoid about rogue heirs."

"What do you mean?"

"Lines of succession in a normal situation are completely a social construct. Sure, who fathered whom is high on people's mind, but crowns have gone to bastards, cousins, and rabble off the street when enough aristocrats could be convinced to give lip service to legitimacy. Some unknown heir wasn't a threat unless they got support from someone . . . the Mark changes that."

"How do you mean?"

"It has inherent power. It isn't given by a priesthood or a clique of powerful landowners. It can't be denied, or forged, and no one can pretend it doesn't exist. If there's some power struggle in a place that bases its ruling class on this Mark, you'd be a potential rival just by existing."

That wasn't even taking into account what Ivan had said. If someone of my "bloodline" had formed an island of stability in the Chaos out there, my Mark would be at home there as much as it was where I had settled. It wasn't just individuals that founded these demesnes. In fact, logically that would be the exception rather than the rule. If the affinity for a "stable" collection of worlds was passed down like the Mark, it would make sense that families of Princes would eventually settle down and, like here, form some sort of dynasty.

So I wasn't so much a general threat to other Princes, just the ones from my own family.

My hands balled into fists in my lap, and I realized I was shaking.

"Dana?"

"I'm okay." The words came out strained, and my voice sounded anything but okay. I had seen John Doe die in front of me, and ever since I'd been tearing the scab off my past, inflaming the wound of my lost birth family until I'd felt that pain as acutely as I did the loss of my adoptive one. I had known, intuitively, that the attacks by the Shadows were connected to me, to where I had come from, to my family. Somehow, though, I had managed to avoid realizing that it meant that my long-lost family might not want to hear from me; that it meant my real family was actively hostile.

Out there, I had brothers, or uncles, or cousins, and they wanted to *kill* me.

I tried to blink the burning from my eyes. I'd been obsessing about my birth family, and I hadn't been thinking about my real family. The one that actually cared for me.

"Dana?"

"She's dead, Jacob." I sucked in a breath. "She died, and I never told her about . . ." The tears hit like a baseball bat in my gut. The guilt, the loss, the loneliness, all slammed into the wall I'd been using to hold back the grief. My words dissolved into an inarticulate sob, and I buried my face in the wrap I'd used to hide my Mark.

I had nothing left. I had no family, no friends, and what life I had, I'd abandoned in this fruitless search for a family that wanted me dead. I had allowed my mother to die without telling her the most significant part of my life, and I'd poisoned my memories of my father with my narcissistic adolescent guilt—as if his death was all about me, how I was special, and how I had failed him.

I felt Jacob place his arm around my shoulder and it made me sob more. The one friend I had, the one person I'd trusted enough for me to bare my secrets to voluntarily, I'd taken him away from his life, his *world*, to a place he was hostage to my good behavior.

"Fuck." I spat half coherently into my hands.

"I'm here," Jacob whispered.

As my wracking sobs subsided, I said, "You shouldn't be."

"We're partners."

My sides ached from crying, and my hands were a slick mess of tears and the makeup Greta had put on me. I raised my head slightly and sniffed. "This is far beyond your job description."

"You're my friend, too."

I looked at the mess in my hands and winced. I took deep breaths, half afraid that the sobbing jag would return, but I seemed to have gotten it out of my system. All I felt at the moment was a deep ache. I stood up, out from under his arm. His fingers brushed my naked shoulder, and I shuddered slightly.

I wish I wasn't so screwed up right now.

"I need to clean up." I walked over to the lavatory and found a basin where I could wash the smeared makeup from my hands and face.

As I washed, Jacob asked, "What do we do now?"

"Wait until this airship docks somewhere, then I can Walk both of us home."

"What about your car?"

"I don't think that's all that important anymore."

"I don't believe I just heard you say that."

Me neither. I felt a twinge at the loss of my Charger, but it was insignificant even aside from the residual ache from my breakdown. "I can get another car." I found a towel to dry my face and hands. I caught a glimpse of myself in the mirror and saw someone strange staring back. From the neckline down I was still some dainty French aristocrat fresh from the ball. Above that, though, I was some feral wild woman with tribal markings, untamed hair, and bloodshot eyes that looked crazed as much as grieved.

I shuddered when I realized I was looking into the adult face of the damaged child my parents had adopted.

"What about the Emperor?" Jacob asked.

I turned away from the mirror. "What about him?"

"If you're a target of a power struggle somewhere, you could use an ally."

"You can't be suggesting what I think you're suggesting."

"You're telling me you haven't thought about it yourself?"

"No. I haven't." Of course, because of Jacob, I was thinking about it now. It certainly made some sense. If there were people out there Walking around Chaos looking for me, I would be better off surrounded by an army that knew what that involved.

But I wasn't a sixteenth century princess to be bartered around to form some sort of national alliance—even if that alliance was with myself. I might have been pushing my limits lately, but spreading my legs for someone as if I was paying protection money?

"No," I said. "Just no."

Jacob shrugged. "I thought as much, but you'll need to come up with some idea what to do if he doesn't take that as an answer."

"I know. It all just keeps getting more comp—" I gasped as I felt something brush my Mark.

Jacob sprang to his feet. "Dana, what's wrong?"

"*You're kidding me,*" I whispered, almost afraid to breathe. It felt as if dozens of rotting fingers were hovering over the boundaries of my Mark, reaching for me. . . .

He ran to me and grabbed my shoulders. I shuddered when I felt him touch my skin, and this time there was no pleasure in it at all. "What is it?"

I looked in his face and couldn't believe the words, even as I spoke them, "The Shadows. I feel them coming."

THIRTY-THREE

"THAT MAKES NO sense," Jacob said.

"I know! We're thousands of feet in midair over the Atlantic Ocean. The whole point of this airship is to keep people from just Walking in." *Or out*, I thought.

"Are you sure?"

"I can feel them." I shuddered and hugged myself. "I feel them coming."

"Okay, that means the Emperor and his goons can, too, right? They should take care of them."

"Yes." I slowed down, remembering something Ivan said, and the memory gave me a chill beyond the touch of the approaching Shadows.

Oh, crap!

"Jacob?"

"What?"

"When they first showed up, and Ivan told me about them, he said the Shadows were dangerous because you couldn't sense them coming."

"Okay, maybe he's wrong about that—"

"He *didn't* sense them coming."

"He could have just been oblivious."

"Or maybe I can sense them because they're related to me, my Mark."

Jacob stared at me as if he was about to say it was a crazy idea. I could see the point where it dawned on him that the whole concept, everything around us, was crazy.

"Why don't I hear any sort of alarm?" I asked.

Jacob let me go and darted to the door.

"What are you doing?"

"If you're right, we have to raise an alarm, warn the crew, Ivan's people."

Well, duh. That was obvious. I silently thanked Jacob for finding the thread of reason in our situation. I ran to join him at the door just as he started cursing in frustration.

"Apparently, they don't trust you completely," he snapped. "Can't get the blasted door open."

"Great," I looked around at the stateroom for some form of communication. I couldn't find a phone. I saw Jacob look around and say, "There we go."

He went over to one of the inside walls of the room and pulled open a small cabinet door set into the wall. A brass plaque on the door read "*utilisation pour l'aide.*"

Inside was something that could have been an antique-style phone, or intercom, or one of those Victorian medical devices you see in quack museums. He pulled a brass cylinder out of the recess drawing out a thick fabric-covered cable after it. Inside the recess, beneath a brass grille embossed with a floral motif, three large toggle switches were labeled helpfully, "*un*," "*deux*," "*trios.*" Next to those was a large mahogany knob.

Jacob looked at a sign mounted on the inside of the cabinet door. "How to call emergency . . . here . . ." He flipped all the switches on and pulled the knob. A small light above the grille glowed a weak incandescent yellow. A moment later, a second light came on next to it. The grille started crackling, and I heard a voice in distant and slightly irritated French.

Jacob had been holding the brass cylinder to his ear. He lowered it to his mouth and spoke into it. "Hello? Hello?" Nothing happened, and the French voice became more irritated.

"Hello, do you speak English?"

The French speaker gave no sign of hearing. My heart raced as he talked over Jacob's attempts to speak to him. If anything, it felt as if the number of dead fingers tracing the edges of my Mark were increasing. It felt unclean, a corruption spreading beneath my skin, as if their phantom nails were attempting to split the skin and release a corrupt infected version of the Mark like the one carving through the Shadows' skin—scarring my body the way they had Whedon's.

If their presence made me feel like this, I could only shudder at the thought of what Whedon must have felt as this corruption ate away at her.

After about thirty seconds, the voice snapped something derisive, the speaker died, and the second light winked out.

"What?" I suddenly realized that Jacob hadn't been able to communicate at all.

Jacob stared at the device in his hand, then at the grille. "What the hell?"

"What did he say?"

"Something about wasting his time. Pissed off and shouting through a bad connection, I'm lucky I understood anything. I haven't used any French since school."

"Did you use that?" I pointed at the cylinder in his hand. Along the length of it was an elaborate lever that made the whole thing look more like an expensive showerhead than a microphone.

"Crap, I'm an idiot." He grabbed the mahogany knob, pushed it in, and yanked it out again. "Single duplex, an intercom, not a telephone. I need to switch the mic on to talk."

The annoyed French voice came on-line again in a burst of static, and the second light came on. I did manage to catch one word, "*merde.*" This time Jacob worked the lever and repeated, "Hello, can you speak English?" A third light glowed when he spoke and winked out when he released the lever.

"Oui. Yes. What—bzt—going on down—bzt—"

I heard a click as Jacob worked the lever on the mic. "I'm here with Det—*Lady* Dana Rohan. She needs to talk with someone in charge of security on this airship."

A click as Jacob released the lever, "—know what cabin you—bzt—am officer of the night—bzt—can talk to—bzt—cessez de perdre mon—"

Jacob handed me the microphone. It was cold and heavy in my hand, like talking into a lead pipe. I worked the lever. "You need to raise an alarm. I can feel an attack coming. The Shadows."

"—c'est ridicule, you cannot—bzt—serious, my Lady. We are fifteen thous—bzt—feet above—"

I hit the lever again. "Listen, I know where we are. But I'm feeling it now, and I felt it before. I've seen these things before."

"—you wish me to wake—"

I never heard him finish, because the lights in the cabin died, including the little bulbs above the recessed intercom.

"That's not good," Jacob said.

I hadn't even realized that the light fixtures had been electric, with their elaborate cut-glass chimneys. I guess I'd been thinking they were gas if I'd thought about them at all. Then again, open flames on an airship were probably not the best idea.

It took a moment for my eyes to start making out shapes. Fortunately, the moon was full and low in the sky above the clouds outside the window, so we weren't plunged into complete darkness.

Jacob stepped back from the intercom.

I backed up with Jacob into the center of the stateroom. My skin rippled gooseflesh as I felt invisible corpse-fingers reaching for me. Every couple of seconds I had to resist the effort to turn around and stare at the nothing that was stalking me. The more I thought about the sensation, the more aware I was of every detail.

I shuddered.

"What do we do now?" Jacob asked.

"I don't know . . ."

We were trapped in the stateroom, unarmed, with no way to open the door or communicate with the rest of the airship. I was free to Walk to another world, but one step and I would be above the Atlantic Ocean without an airship around me. The thought sent my heart racing.

The Shadows are coming from somewhere.

"Oh, crap."

"What?" I glanced over at Jacob and saw he was staring out the window to the stateroom. I looked out expecting something dire: another airship on a collision course, a massive storm cell, a flying dragon—I didn't see anything. "What do you mean, 'Oh, crap?'"

"The clouds, you can see the light reflected from the airship."

"Yeah, so."

"Running lights, other cabins—this isn't a general power failure."

"Just us?"

"Just us."

If the Shadows were after me in particular, then having our cabin lose power was just stretching coincidence too far.

"Oh, crap," I echoed.

A creak filled the darkened stateroom accompanied by rotting fingers brushing my Mark.

There was only one possible escape. Then, only if my otherworldly sense of direction held, and only if I was right that I had felt a direction to where they had come from. "Jacob, grab me now."

"You can't think—"

"Now!" I yelled as the door to the stateroom creaked open on a half dozen shadowy figures. They started darting toward us before the door was completely open, I saw flashes in the silver moonlight; torn uniforms, scarred skin, wild black eye sockets.

Then Jacob threw his arms around me, I shoved my hand under his jacket and twisted my fingers around his belt as I took a step away in the direction I thought the Shadows had Walked from.

"*Fuck!*" Jacob screamed in the wind as the airship around us disappeared.

THIRTY-FOUR

BITING COLD.

Weightlessness.

Clouds.

Full moon staring down at us, huge, blind, and blinding.

Tumbling headfirst toward clouds a thousand feet below us. A large shadow drifting across the clouds below us.

I pushed myself back as we fell.

We slammed into a bulkhead and tumbled onto a cold steel floor in a maintenance corridor somewhere in the lower decks of the airship. Jacob groaned beneath me. I pushed myself up off him. "Are you all right?"

"Few bruised ribs, I'm okay." He pushed himself up into a sitting position and I watched him wince. "I can't believe you timed that right."

Me neither. "That wasn't my first plan."

"Oh." He grabbed a pipe along the bulkhead wall and pulled himself upright. He reached down to help me off my knees. I let him help me up, even though he looked the worse for the fall. "What were you *trying* to do?"

"The Shadows came from somewhere. I was trying to follow them back."

Jacob grunted and hugged his side. "I think I prefer Plan B. Plan A sounds a lot more like going from the frying pan into the fire."

I looked up and down the corridor. "Which way you think is the best way to find someone to raise an alarm?"

"The signs say engine maintenance this way. Should be people there, or at least another intercom." I followed in the direction he pointed. After going a few dozen feet he asked, "So that wasn't where the Shadows came from?"

I shook my head, "No, I think it was."

"What? Nothing there but air, clouds, and a very long fall."

"And another airship, below us."

"What?"

"They must have come from that airship, but I waited too long to follow them back. It only matched the course of this airship long enough to let the Shadows come across, then it dropped down below our course to avoid someone like me Walking back on board."

"That sort of cuts off their retreat, doesn't it?"

"I don't think whoever's behind this looks at the Shadows as soldiers. More like guided missiles."

"Great. Wonder how long before they strap a bomb to them?"

"Please, don't give them any ideas."

Jacob was built for strength, not for speed, and my primary means of keeping in shape was running a few miles every day. So, all things being equal, I should have easily kept up with him, especially since he was grunting and holding the side of his chest with his injured—hopefully only bruised—ribs.

Things weren't equal. My Disney Princess ball gown was seriously restricting my movement, even after I kicked off the uncomfortable shoes. The skirts tried to tangle my legs and catch on every bit of hardware projecting from the walls. I ended up having to grab the skirts and hike them up like a showgirl just to keep up with Jacob.

We were deep into the corridors, lit only by minimal red-tinted lighting. I had lost much hope of finding anyone down on these decks; there didn't seem to be anyone working down here. But before I decided to tell Jacob to look for a passage back up into the ship, we finally ran into someone.

It was almost literal, as the guy appeared out of a side passage that was nearly invisible from down the corridor. Jacob stopped short so quickly that he almost fell back into me.

The man was tall and almost as broad as the corridor. He was shiny bald and had a full black beard. He wore boots, overalls, and a white shirt marred by streaks of black grease. He carried a massive wrench, a length of steel about five feet long that looked more like a medieval weapon than something you'd find in a machine shop.

"Anschlag! Keine Eintragung! Wer sind Sie?"

"Okay," I said, "That's not French."

Jacob held up his hands and asked, "Do you speak English?"

"Dieses ist nur ein eingeschränkter Bereich, Mechaniker und Technik. Sind Sie verloren?"

"I'd guess that's a no," Jacob said. "*Parlez français?*"

"No high school German?"

The big guy with the wrench looked at Jacob and said, slowly, "*Non laissé. Retournez.*"

"I think we're in a restricted area," Jacob said.

"I don't speak a word and I figured that out."

Jacob grunted and said, "*Avertissez.*" He spoke slowly, his own accent worse than the German mechanic's. "*Nous sommes attaqués. Avertissez.*"

"*Attaqués?*" The mechanic prodded Jacob's chest with the end of the wrench, leaving a big greasy smear on his shirt. I saw Jacob wince and lean over in the direction of his injured side. However, he kept his hands up in an attempt to be nonthreatening.

"No, not us. Why would—Damn—*Pas nous. Pas nous! Ombres.*"

The big man paused, narrowing his eyes at Jacob. "*Ombres?*"

"Yes! *Ombres!* Shadows!"

Big guy looked unconvinced.

"Damn, what's the German word? I've seen enough World War II movies. Shatter, Shatner—"

"*Ombres?*" The guy prodded menacingly with the wrench again.

"*Shatten*!" Jacob said, and the guy froze. "That's the word, *Shatten*."

"Schatten . . . Angreifen?"

"Attaque d'ombres."

He shook his head and said, "*Nein*." But he lowered the wrench. "*Woher würden sie kommen?*"

I looked at Jacob, and he sighed. "No clue."

"*Woher kamen Sie?*"

Jacob looked at the guy and said, "I'm sorry, my command of German is somewhere between *Hogan's Heroes* and *Where Eagles Dare*. Can you get us to someone who knows English?"

The man pointed down the corridor where we'd come from. "*Sie müssen zur—*"

His words were cut off by a shrill klaxon. He froze and looked up as if the body of the airship was about to collapse down on him. Quietly, he said, "*Nein. Dieses geschieht nicht*."

He was frozen for another moment, but then he moved as if one of the Shadows was already chasing him, running back down the corridor toward where he'd come from.

"I guess they figured it out," Jacob raised his voice over the klaxon.

"Yes."

"We should probably lay low and let them handle it."

I'd already resumed our trek down the corridor.

I heard Jacob behind me. "Where are you going?"

"This is going to keep happening."

"What?" He shouted over the klaxon.

I turned around. "Someone is sending these things after me. We can't just let these people handle it!"

"It's not your fault."

"If we don't get the one in charge, whoever's sending them,

whatever these people do about it will be pointless." I resumed running down the corridor.

Jacob caught up with me. "You don't know who's in charge or where they are."

"I don't know who, but I'm pretty sure where." I stopped in front of a cramped-looking staircase spiraling up into the ship. "You saw this thing when we boarded. It has airplanes attached, doesn't it?"

IT was insane, and Jacob spent a great deal of effort trying to talk me out of it. But I didn't see that I had much choice. I'd meant everything I'd said. If someone was targeting me, just relying on the local guards to pick off the Shadows wasn't going to solve the problem. My unknown nemesis had shown little problem in tracking me down, and there was no reason to think they'd stop after this attack.

But I had seen the airship drifting below our position. Whoever had orchestrated this certainly had to be on board. And, if the bad guy was on board, we were still thousands of feet above the Atlantic Ocean, a day's flight from shore; there was nowhere else to go.

I couldn't not take advantage of that.

If the dress didn't kill me first.

If you ever get the chance to ascend a cramped spiral staircase in a full ball gown, I'd suggest taking a pass. The skirts were annoying in the corridor. In the cramped space twisting upward, they became actively hostile, snagging on every third step. By the third deck up, there were enough rips in the skirts themselves that I had to start tearing free the petticoats.

The klaxons had died down after the initial alert, and Jacob said from behind me, "I don't think we'll be able to just walk into that section of the ship."

"We'll worry about that when we get there." *If we get there.*

A couple more decks, and we ran out of staircase. I stepped out into a corridor that was clearly in the residential part of the airship, even if the corridors were less ornate than the ones by my cabin. The walls were paneled and bore a fancy wallpaper design, and the floor was carpeted, but anything more elaborate—art, furnishings, tapestries—was missing. I guessed that we were in a servant's passageway.

Across from the stairs was a white enameled plaque that seemed to show a map of the deck layout. I couldn't make heads or tails of the cursive French legend, so I waved Jacob over, "Can you make sense of this?"

He walked over and started touching parts of the deck map, "Kitchens . . . Lavatory . . . Dining halls A, B, C . . . Cabins . . . More Cabins . . . Electrical Junction . . . Another Lavatory . . . Janitorial . . . Restricted—"

"Where's that?"

Jacob studied the map and pointed down the corridor. "That way, then the second corridor to our left."

I started in that direction. Jacob walked next to me. "'Restricted' is a vague term, are you sure that's what we want?"

"No."

"As long as we have a plan."

We kept going through the empty corridor, the muted klaxons almost sounding like the airship's pulse. Twice, the lights dimmed to a sickly yellow then returned to normal. As we closed on the passage we wanted, the air began to take on the hint of something burning.

"Do you smell a fire?" I asked. I heard the edge of panic in my own voice as visions of the Hindenburg ran through my head.

"Yeah. I hope the fact these guys have control of North America means that they're using helium."

We had just reached the passage to the left when a sharp crack echoed through the corridor. Another, more muffled, report followed.

"Gunshots?" It was less a question on my part than an expression of alarm. Beyond the corner, before another shot tore through the air, I heard scraping, shuffling, and something moaning.

I crouched so my head was much lower than eye level.

"Dana—"

I snuck a half-second peek around the corner and pulled back before a gunman could take a bead on me. Turns out that was the least of my worries. The gunmen had other problems.

"—don't." Jacob finished.

"Shadows," I gasped. "Five or six. Two guards pinned against a door."

"Okay, we should—"

I stood up and started frantically looking around the corridor. "They sense me. Two are headed back toward us."

THIRTY-FIVE

I SAW WHAT I needed, directly across from us on the other side of the cross passage. Without listening to Jacob's objections, I ran across the front of the passage, giving the guards a perfect shot at me had they been so inclined. I heard two shots tear through the corridor, but neither came anywhere near me.

On the other side of the passage opening was an alcove with a sign reading "*urgence du feu*" in bold red letters. Beneath the sign was a roll of canvas hose, a squat brass canister with a triangular handle that must have been some sort of extinguisher, and, hanging on a bracket on the wall, a fire ax.

Just as I reached the alcove, a trio of Shadows emerged into the corridor between me and Jacob. All three turned their inhuman black eyes toward me. They were less ragged than the ones that had converged on me back home; their clothes fresher, less dirty, covering them so I could only see glimpses of their perverted Mark eating into their flesh along their wrists or their neck, or—in one disturbing case—their face.

I grabbed the ax off the wall and dodged to the side as the nearest one lunged at me. I swung the ax clumsily and cracked that one in the back of the head with the flat. He fell into the alcove and slammed his face into the brass fire extinguisher.

The one with the scarred face grabbed me. His Mark had clawed across his jawline, cheek, and temple, eating away flesh badly enough that I should have seen bone, though all that was visible was a glistening black that seemed to sink even deeper.

The touch of it was like falling into an open cistern overflowing with filth. I could almost taste the corruption sliding across my Mark like a swarm of maggots. I probably screamed as I swung the spiked back end of the fire ax up into the Shadow's no-longer human face. It tried to dodge, but it was clumsier than the Shadows that had attacked earlier, and despite my awkward swing, the end of the ax buried itself up under its scarred cheekbone. Its head snapped back, away from the impact, and it let go of its hold on me.

I scrambled back, yanking the ax with me. The Shadow stumbled off to my right, dragging its left leg and arm as if they didn't work anymore. I kept backing up as the third Shadow reached for me—

Just as something heavy and brass came down on its head from behind. It crumpled to the ground in front of Jacob, who held the fire extinguisher cylinder in both hands.

I looked down at the Shadow, then at Jacob, then at the fire extinguisher. "That's becoming a habit."

"Maybe I should start a new martial art."

"Extinguisher-fu?" I asked as I edged back around him. The three Shadows that had come after me were no longer threatening, two unconscious or dead, the third shambling away, leaning against the wall smearing blood and black fluid after itself, and apparently no longer aware of us.

I shifted my grip on the ax as I stepped back into the line of fire. The hallway was littered with four Shadow corpses, and without a rush of attackers between us anymore, the guards leveled their guns at me. I suddenly realized that with my torn-up dress, grease stains, and Mark exposed on my shoulders, I could easily be mistaken for one of the Shadows. I threw the ax aside as if it was on fire and raised my hands, shouting, "I'm not one of them!"

One of them spoke English.

"Who are you? What are you doing here?"

Jacob emerged from behind me and said, "This is Lady Dana Rohan, and we are headed to the hangar deck." The guard had spoken with a Russian accent thicker than Ivan's, and I noticed that Jacob had adopted a slight, but noticeable, French accent when addressing him. Also, despite being as out of place and overwhelmed as I was—more so even, since my Mark gave me at least one point of common ground with the world we were in—Jacob managed to put on an air of confident, almost dismissive, authority. The slight arrogance made the tux he wore fit better.

"Hangar deck is White Guard only," the one guard continued to speak, while the other pointed the barrel of his rifle at the deck between us and them. I glanced down at the Shadows and had the ugly realization that the clothes they wore were more contemporary to this world than my own. I realized why their clothes looked fresher.

The *Shadows* were fresher.

"We understand that," Jacob said with the air of someone explaining to a petulant child why it was not a good idea to eat the furniture polish. "But you might have noticed we are in the middle of a crisis here." He walked over and nonchalantly picked up the fire ax from where I had tossed it. Intellectually, it was a stupid move, grabbing for a weapon while guns were trained on him, but he seemed to be reading the guards right—the guns weren't actually pointed at us anymore, and he moved casually enough that if they'd felt threatened they'd have plenty of time to warn him away from it.

Instead, the guards just watched him as he hefted the ax and leaned it on his shoulder. "The Guard is going to need all the help it can get. The Lady Rohan is a guest of the Emperor precisely because she is a Prince in her own right. She is offering her assistance in the defense of this airship. Will you tell her no?"

Listening to Jacob's faux accent, I began to wonder if gall and Gallic had some etymology in common.

The guards looked at each other, and I could see in their faces that neither of them wanted to take responsibility for answering the questions Jacob posed to them. After a few moments of silent consultation, the one who'd been speaking to us shouldered his weapon, said a few short words in Russian to his comrade, and stepped toward us. "I am Corporal Mikhail Andreyev. I will take you to the next checkpoint; the officers of the Guard can decide what to make of your assistance."

WE followed Mikhail up through a series of decks that were distinctly more functional than ornamental. While we jogged after him, I whispered to Jacob, "Thanks, you didn't need to do that."

"In for a penny, in for a pound."

"Really, I dragged you into something you didn't need to be involved in."

"Dana, I'm not a cop because I like sitting back and watching the bad guys. Not only are these Shadows trying to kill people—you, in particular—but it looks like something really nasty was *done* to them."

"Like Whedon."

"Yeah. If whoever's responsible for that is on that other airship, they need to be taken out."

I really wouldn't have blamed Jacob for not wanting to be involved, but as I thought about it, I realized that if he had, he wouldn't be the Jacob I knew. He was the one with the solid sense of the right thing, much better than I'd ever been. I'd built so much of my life with guilt and secrets and lies that I think I couldn't even perceive right and wrong in the same terms as he did, much less act on it.

It was why the episode with Roscoe Kendal's gun was such a betrayal. It was also why, despite that, he was still here with me. He was the kind of guy who made doing the right thing look easy.

Mikhail led us up several decks above where we started. During the journey upward, it became obvious that it was a few decks above the residential cabins. The stairways became skeletal, and once we passed through a bulkhead door, the walls vanished, and we moved past girders and guy wires as if we climbed through an unfinished office building.

The stairway climbed up between two curving walls made of gray rubberized fabric. At the same time I realized we climbed up between two of the gas cells that held this whole thing aloft, I also realized the smell of smoke was becoming worse. I silently echoed Jacob's hope that it was helium behind those gray walls.

When we reached the checkpoint, no one was there to meet us. We emerged onto a broad catwalk that seemed to bisect the short axis of the airship. Mounted across from us, a small room had been built on top of the catwalk. Through the windows I saw a white wall where clipboards hung, and at least three of the intercom devices were mounted. No one seemed to be inside. When Mikhail saw the door hanging open, he cursed something in Russian and ran to the doorway.

"What—" I didn't finish my question because I took another step and saw what Mikhail had: a single foot, just visible through the half-open doorway.

I heard more probably-obscene Russian, and Mikhail emerged from the room carrying a pistol and a grim expression. He walked up to Jacob and handed the butt of the pistol toward him. "My friend, you have been promoted."

Jacob glanced in my direction, then handed me the ax before taking the gun. I felt a bit of irritation that Mikhail handed the gun to Jacob and not to me, the obviously unarmed person, not that I had any time to express it. As soon as Mikhail handed off the weapon, he was running down the catwalk toward the outer skin of the airship.

Jacob and I followed.

I heard gunshots and the smell of smoke became worse as we headed toward the open door at the end of the catwalk. As we got closer, the temperature dropped until our breath started fogging, and I could hear the sound of wind tearing past the gap in the open door.

The air pressure probably should have slammed the door shut, but it had closed on someone's unmoving leg.

Jacob took cover, flattening against the wall on the open side of the door. Mikhail unslung his rifle to point at the gap. That left me with the job of pulling the door the rest of the way open.

I stood behind it, pulling the door to me, letting in the smell of smoke and the sound of rushing wind. Mikhail stepped forward, sweeping his gun back and forth. Jacob followed, and I took up the rear.

I had to suck in a breath as we stepped around the corpse that blocked the door. The man's back had been torn open, skin and muscle torn ragged until glints of bloody spine and rib were visible through the shredded remains of his uniform.

The White Guard were Walkers like me or John Doe. I had seen what they had done to John Doe's corpse. The corpse could have been Ivan—

The snap of another gunshot brought my attention back to where we were. We stood at one end of a very long, narrow deck that seemed to run nearly all the way along the side of the airship, along the outer skin. The wind and cold came from openings to the outside, the night beyond seemed pitch-black from the lighted deck.

About sixty feet away, I saw a makeshift barricade made of a bulkhead door, a tool bench, a pile of crates, and machine parts. The White Guard had taken refuge behind it, opposite us. Up against the other side of the barricade were over a dozen Shadows, maybe more.

I saw a glimpse of a garish uniform and was relieved to see Ivan's face. Then the Shadows surged toward the barricade, and my view was blocked as someone took a shot and part of a Shadow's head tore away in front of him.

I realized that using the airship didn't stop the invading Shadows, but it still took away their main advantage. Unlike the morgue, these Shadows weren't in a place where they could dodge bullets or "Walk" around blockages like the makeshift barricade.

Unfortunately, there wasn't any such barricade between us and the Shadows, and as soon as we entered, about half of them turned to face us, moving like a pack of hungry dogs just catching a whiff of a rare steak.

Me, I thought as the group broke off from the rear of the attack and started running back toward us. *They're attracted by the Mark.* I realized that, standing behind Jacob and Mikhail, I'd attract these things right through them.

I hefted the ax and ran out from behind Jacob and Mikhail. I ran at an angle toward the outer wall of the airship to avoid putting myself in the line of fire. Jacob shouted some objection, but the Shadows did as I expected, and veered off from their frontal attack to intercept my course. Jacob and Mikhail both picked off stragglers at the rear of the attacking group, and I heard more shots from behind the barricade.

I didn't pay much attention because I was focused on the trio of Shadows leading the group headed at me. Two were dressed like the mechanic who'd challenged me and Jacob belowdecks, and the third was a woman who might have worn a servant's outfit like Greta's, but because it was shredded and crusted in blood and black fluid, it was hard to tell.

Whatever action movies might show to the contrary, a fire-ax is no great hand-to-hand weapon, especially if you're fighting off more than one person. It's heavy, unwieldy, designed for two hands, and—if you're wielding it with effective force—it leaves you completely undefended while attacking.

Fortunately, it wasn't my only form of attack.

The only excuse I had for even attempting the stupid maneuver I was contemplating was the fact I had done it once already and managed not to kill myself.

Once they were almost on me, I spun around and faced them, braced myself, and jumped at them holding the handle of the ax out in front of me with both hands to take the closest one across the throat.

THIRTY-SIX

JUST AS THE wood made contact with the Shadow's Adam's apple, I pushed with my Mark. The airship winked out of existence in a swirl of freezing wind, leaving me and the Shadow suspended above moonlit cloud cover.

This time I was expecting it, and I responded by immediately jerking the ax back toward my body, breaking my contact with the Shadow as I pushed with the Mark again.

I rolled to a stop on the deck behind the advancing Shadows, my mind just beginning to register what might have been a look of surprise on the face of the Shadow I had left falling over the Atlantic Ocean.

The other Shadows turned to face me as I sprang to my feet. The one I had clotheslined into another universe was not among them. I had a brief impulse to reprise my successful attack, but they were now bunched up between me and Jacob and Mikhail. No stragglers I could pick off as they charged me.

I backed away from them, toward the barricade and more Shadows. I heard gunfire which probably thinned their numbers, but I was focused primarily on the ones that were almost on me. I braced my feet on the deck as well as I could, my bare feet sliding on gore, and I shifted my grip on the ax and swung low at the first Shadow to run at me.

I took out the knee on the Shadow's forward leg. Not a mortal wound, but I recovered control of my weapon almost immediately, and it had the necessary effect of halting the Shadow's advance.

The Shadow face-planted in front of me, and I brought the ax up into the hip of the one immediately behind it. Through the handle I felt the blade chew into bone as I knocked the Shadow a step to my right, stumbling into the path of a third Shadow.

I let them collapse into a heap and took another step back.

Something grabbed my shoulder and I belatedly realized I had backed into the Shadows that had remained by the barricade. I spun to face the one grappling with me, bringing the ax up. For a moment I was face-to-face with a nightmare. The malignant Mark on this one had eaten away the upper part of its face, leaving a pair of eye sockets to stare at me. The sockets weren't empty. They were filled with the same black that carved the Mark into its skin.

It opened its mouth and hissed at me, revealing the flesh inside painted with the same blackness.

I brought the ax up into the side of its skull. It was a clumsy underhand swing across the arm it was grabbing me with, but it still hit with a satisfying thud that caused it to let go. Before I recovered control of the ax, I heard a gunshot and the two black sockets in its face turned into a single gaping black hole.

As it collapsed, I could feel the other Shadows closing on me from the sides and behind. I took a step up on an engine block that was part of the makeshift barricade in front of me and pushed myself in an upward leap. I was leaping toward a solid wall made of a bulkhead door, but I pushed with the Mark just as I reached it.

Wind tore at me and I spent a brief quarter second staring down into the cloud cover.

The airship was still there, pacing our course.

I pushed the Mark again and slammed into the deck, rolling to a stop next to a member of the White Guard aiming his rifle through a small gap in the barricade. I pushed myself upright and heard the sound of tearing fabric as the remains of my skirts gave way after catching on a piece of twisted metal poking from the barricade.

I bent to pull free the fabric, and something slammed into my back, tackling me over. I rolled and found myself staring into a woman's face; her eyes were jet black, no whites, as empty as the eye sockets in the last shadow. Her face twisted in a feral snarl that could have easily been as much pain as bloodlust.

I realized that I'd just shown the Shadows how to get past the barricade.

The Shadow-woman squatted on my hips, pinning me as her hands clamped on my throat. Her touch caused paralyzingly ugly sensations to run across my Mark. I didn't have the ax anymore, and I didn't know on what side of the barricade I'd dropped it. As far as I knew, it could be tumbling toward the Atlantic in the next universe over.

But my hands were free.

The Shadow was unnaturally strong, but untrained. She was throttling me, but she had no real idea where to put her hands. If I'd been attacked by someone who'd known what they were doing, I would have already been unconscious.

I locked my hands together in a double fist and brought my arms up between hers to land a solid blow on the bottom of her jaw. The impact snapped her head back, and the wedge of my arms forced her own arms apart enough for me to catch a breath.

She fought against me, trying to put more pressure on my throat, but I already had my arms up between hers. A skilled brawler would have let me go to retreat and regroup, but my Shadow leaned forward to try and keep the pressure on my neck. When she did that, her weight left my hips as she crouched over me, half-squatting, half-standing.

Once I wasn't pinned, I folded my legs and brought both feet up into her groin. It wasn't a damaging kick, but I run every day and can leg press about three times my own weight, so it was easy enough to push her up off the ground. I grabbed her upper arms and flipped her over my head to slam her back on the deck.

I rolled onto my hands and knees while twisting her right arm into a joint lock. She screamed because when I did that, her shoulder dislocated. It gave me pause, and I hesitated, remembering what happened to Whedon. I was fighting a human being, not a monster.

Either way, she had been trying to kill me.

I started to fold her over, pulling her wrist up to her shoulder blades. I had her immobilized, a prisoner we could question once—

A gunshot interrupted my thoughts, and half my Shadow-woman's head erupted on the deck in front of her. She slumped forward, no longer struggling against my grip on her arm. I let go of her wrist and she fell to the side, unmoving.

I spun around to see Ivan holding a pistol, still pointed at where most of the Shadow's head had been.

"What the hell do you think you're doing? *I had her restrained!*"

Ivan turned back to defend the barricade and said, matter-of-factly, "It was a Shadow."

Two other Shadows had discovered the trick to passing through the barrier, but the White Guard defenders made quick work of them. The Shadows were little better than a mob, and like most rioters, they formed a terrifying mass when facing unarmed civilians, but when aimed at an armed and disciplined force, they became much less effective. By the time I had grabbed a length of pipe to rearm myself, the battle had pretty much ended.

All the Shadows were dead. I counted only three defenders among the corpses, all by the door, victims of a surprise attack. About twenty Shadow corpses littered the rest of the deck. To my relief, Jacob and Mikhail were unscathed.

I knew it was Ivan who grabbed my arm, even before he spun me around to face him. I knew his touch, the feel of his Mark brushing close to mine. After the corpse fingers of the Shadows, feeling his touch was almost enough to make me sigh in relief.

"*Vi byezoomniy doorachok!* Are you trying to be killed? *Glupaya zhyenshshina!*" He screamed into my face, quickly evaporating any relief I felt at his touch.

"Take your hand off of me," I said through clenched teeth.

He shook me, instead. "What were you thinking? Running into crossfire—"

"Let go!" With him grabbing me and shaking, the sense of his Mark on mine had become suffocating. My gut filled with a toxic mix of anger and claustrophobia as I grabbed his wrist with my off hand. "*Now!*"

I'm not quite sure what I did. I brought my other hand up to push against his elbow, but at the same time I pushed inside myself. Not the same as letting the Mark push me through to another world, not pushing me, pushing *away* from me.

Ivan yanked his hand away as if I had suddenly burst into flame. "*Chto vi*—What did you do?"

I glared at him because I didn't have an answer. Quietly, I told him, "Don't ever grab me like that."

He nodded, very slightly. "Yes, my Lady."

I began feeling a twinge of guilt. My incandescent rage had banked itself down to a low smolder, and that let me realize that he had just been upset that I'd jumped into a suicidally dangerous situation. Understandable, and even somewhat endearing that he was that concerned for my safety. Given the cultural differences, I'd even give him a pass on being so damn condescending about it.

But I was still furious that he had taken out the Shadow I had restrained. Whatever was going on physically and mentally with the Shadows, they were human beings, and what Ivan had done was little more than murder. I might not have been a respecter of rules, especially when it involved dealing with the bad guys, but that had crossed over any of the lines I had ever come near.

And I don't think he even understood what he had done.

"Are you all right?" Jacob's voice came from the other side of the barrier. I was grateful for the distraction. I called back, "Everyone's fine over here."

I reached up and started pulling furniture from the makeshift barricade to let Jacob past.

Ivan asked me, "What are you doing?"

"Helping them in. Give me a hand here."

He only hesitated a moment, then he got in and pulled aside a bulkhead door that cleared a path so Jacob and Mikhail could squeeze past. Once both were inside, Ivan slid the door back. I saw that the other members of the Guard were busy shoring up the defenses. Ivan saw me look and said, "They will be back. Our orders are to defend the aircraft and prevent them from cutting off our retreat."

I looked down the deck, behind the barricade, and saw large doors in the outer skin. Parked on deck behind the doors were two-seater biplanes, wings folded back like a line of origami cranes. "Those can't be anywhere near as heavy as my Charger."

"What?" Ivan asked.

"We need an airplane."

THIRTY-SEVEN

"YOU NEED *WHAT?*"

I finished stripping off the remains of my skirt. Fortunately, the underwear that Greta had dressed me in was so elaborate that I was probably three layers away from actually impacting my modesty.

"An airplane," I repeated.

"We're holding these for the Emperor and the court. We can't—"

"Ivan, do you know how these things got on board?"

He just stared at me.

"These Shadows are made, not born. Just look at their clothes. They're from here, or a world so close it doesn't matter."

"They're monsters born of Chaos."

"They're human beings. You were there when Whedon got infected. Sick, possibly psychotic, but *human*." I looked to the dead woman that Ivan had shot out of my arms. "They were made, then they were brought here."

"How? Why?"

"How? Another airship. My guess is that someone slipped aboard that ship and did this to the passengers and crew, then flew parallel enough to this airship's course to offload the victims like someone tossing grenades into a foxhole." I looked away from the dead woman, and back at Ivan. "Why? Someone wants me dead."

"You?"

"The John Doe you killed was trying to warn me. Either the person behind the Shadows knew where they were going, or they followed you and John Doe to me. Either way doesn't matter. The one behind the Shadows followed us from my world to here, and right now they're almost certainly in an airship flying in the next universe over." I stepped up to Ivan. "I don't care what your orders are. You are going to give me a weapon and an aircraft, so I can stop this now."

The rest of the White Guard had circled around as I argued with Ivan. I noticed Mikhail took a step back to join the encircling soldiers, leaving me and Jacob as the focus of everyone's attention.

"Our orders are to hold the retreat for the Emperor and the court."

"You're also supposed to fight these things, right?"

The guards ringing us were tense; it felt as if one wrong move could start a volley of gunfire. I was lucky, I think, in that Ivan seemed to be the ranking guy here. Mark or not, I had the feeling that if Ivan wasn't here, I would probably join the Shadows littering the ground.

"You're certain about this?"

"The airship is in the same world I felt them come from."

Ivan narrowed his eyes. "You feel them—"

"Yes, I've always felt them."

Someone in the ranks said something in Russian, and I didn't need to understand the language to know it was a challenge. I saw the barrel of a gun raised, and Ivan snapped back, shouting something else in Russian that didn't sound pleasant. The guard hesitated, but the barrel lowered.

"You can't sense Shadows like normal Walkers," Ivan said. "That's why they're Shadows."

"It's why I knew you were being attacked in my basement."

"That's . . . why are *you* different?"

Fuck it. He'd have to ask that.

Well, if no one had shot me yet, the truth probably wouldn't break their discipline. "Because we share a bloodline," I said.

I didn't realize how much of the ambient noise was because of the guards shuffling around, shifting their weight and whispering among themselves, until all the noise stopped. Suddenly the only sound was the wind.

"You share a bloodline? That isn't possible."

I turned around, showing my naked shoulders, and the upper part of the Mark. "You've seen my Mark, enough of it anyway. Look at it, look at them."

Ivan paused, then he turned and marched off, through the ring of guards which parted for him. He knelt next to the Shadow he had executed and pulled her blouse up so hard that the material tore off her body. Her underwear was less elaborate than mine, and he tore it free as well, exposing her naked back, and the twisted Mark carved into her skin.

It was the first time I had the chance to see the Mark on one of the Shadows while it was still. Before, I always had the sense that their Marks were deformed, asymmetrical, random . . .

That wasn't quite right. It couldn't be, not if Dr. Lefevre could draw a relation to my Mark and the Shadows'. When I told Ivan to check, I had been gambling that the similarities would be perceptible to a layman—like the schematics drawn on the charts in Dr. Lefevre's exam room.

They were.

And the Shadow's Mark wasn't random, or even asymmetrical. What deformed the pattern, and made it appear so random, was that its symmetry did not coincide with the Shadow's body. Exposed, it appeared as if the Mark was a literal shadow, cast upon the Shadow's body at a strange angle. Where my Mark seemed to grow out of a point in the center of my lower back, the dead woman's Mark grew from a black-lipped wound above and in front of her left hip. Not only was the pattern offset to center there, it tilted itself by thirty degrees off vertical, so the center of the Mark slashed across her side and her back from hip to shoulder-blade.

You didn't need to be Dr. Lefevre to see the similarities with the Shadow's Mark exposed. I was familiar enough with my own to see the likeness in the way the crude branches split and spiraled.

Ivan stood up from the corpse. He didn't look happy. He raised his pistol and aimed it at me. "You are one of them."

With a rustling wave, I was suddenly the focus of a dozen weapons pointed in my direction.

The embers of rage that had been banked and cooling suddenly flared up into a full-blown conflagration. Being pissed beyond all reason is the only explanation I had for snapping the way I did.

"You fucking asshole! Did you listen to one goddamn word I said?"

"You're related to—"

"Like that makes me a Shadow? I guess the squiggles on your back make you the Emperor?" I folded my arms because I really wanted to take a swing at someone, and I wasn't pissed enough to do that with all the guns pointed in my direction. "They're trying to kill me, remember?"

Jacob stepped up and placed a hand on my shoulder, "Dana?"

"You want to kill me now, Ivan?"

"Don't antagonize him, Dana."

"Antagonize *him*? I've saved his life at least once, and he's the one pointing a gun at *me*."

"Sort of my point," Jacob whispered.

Just like Jacob to find a solid piece of reality and tether me to it. My anger leaked out as I realized that I was poking an armed man with a rhetorical stick. Not something they recommend in cop school.

I think Jacob was as surprised as I was when he lowered the gun.

"And how were you planning to fly it?" Ivan asked me.

THIRTY-EIGHT

I WAS GLAD to have Ivan back on my side, but I was also irritated that he did have a point. Not only had I never flown an aircraft, I'd only flown *in* an aircraft once—my current airship ride excluded. If I was going to do anything, I needed a pilot.

I glanced over at Jacob, who shook his head—which wasn't very surprising. Even if Jacob, by some miracle, had a pilot's license, I doubt it would have qualified him to fly one of these biplanes.

I turned back toward Ivan and said, "I guess I'm going to have to learn how."

He gave me an "Are you serious?" look, then said, "I'll fly you." One of the guardsmen raised an objection in Russian, but Ivan cut him short.

"You're a pilot?" I asked incredulously.

"No," Ivan said. "However, standard training for the White Guard includes fifteen hours of flight training."

Fifteen hours did not sound like a lot. Jacob must have felt the same way because he touched my arm and asked, "Are you sure about this?"

"It's this, or try not to die as we wait for the Bad Guy to attack from a more accessible location."

Jacob sighed and said, "Here." He held out the gun Mikhail had given him. It was an oversized automatic, bearing some resemblance to a Luger if the Luger had started taking steroids and doing some serious weight training. "I checked the magazine. There are five shots left."

It took me a moment to figure out where the safety was on the thing. Just when I found it and was trying to decide what part of my underwear could be used as a holster, Ivan cleared his throat. I turned around to see him holding out a long coat that must have come from one of the other guards. "You'll need this," he said.

I almost made an asinine remark about not worrying about my modesty when I realized that these biplanes had open-air cockpits and I was naked from cleavage upward. The only reason I wasn't freezing now was because of the adrenaline rush from fighting the Shadows.

I let him put the jacket on me. The thing hung on me like I was a little girl trying on daddy's sports coat. It smelled of gun smoke and a stranger's sweat, and the heavy wool was not meant to rest on naked skin. My shoulders started itching immediately.

But at least it answered the question of where to put Mr. Luger's big brother. The gun went into one of the coat's oversized pockets.

"Come this way," Ivan waved toward the large doors opposite the folded biplanes.

THERE was an elaborate system of tracks and cables in the ceiling, leading from where the folded biplanes were parked and out the skin of the airship above the hangar doors. The cable and pulley system would suspend the folded plane like a cable car from the track above and allow it to roll out the door.

The doors felt large, but objectively they weren't any bigger than the garage door at my townhouse. With the wings folded, and the propeller vertical, the biplanes weren't any wider than my Charger.

Ivan didn't go to one of the parked planes. Instead he walked up to a smaller, human-sized door set next to the big door. He checked a lighted console between the big door and the small one, opened a panel, and threw a pair of knife switches that looked like they belonged in Frankenstein's laboratory.

"This one is fueled and ready," he said. He began turning the wheel on the smaller door.

I looked back at the parked biplanes and said, "What about . . ." I trailed off when I realized that when I had seen the airship from the outside there were biplanes suspended from the sides of the airship already. What I saw parked on the deck here were reserves.

The one Ivan wanted to fly was already outside.

He opened the door, and frigid air started rushing by me. He shouted over the sound of the wind ripping by us. "Come through! I have to close the door!"

I stepped over the threshold and winced as my feet touched the metal ledge on the other side of the door. I'd kicked off my impractical shoes earlier; now I wanted them back. The metal was cold enough to have a layer of frost. I grabbed a wall of mesh netting to keep from falling and found myself looking down along the shadowed length of the airship into the moonlit clouds.

I gasped, and the frigid wind cut at my throat.

Ivan pulled the door shut behind us, and we were alone outside the airship.

"Come on!"

He held on to a cable strung along a gangway that led away from the airship. It was only about twenty or thirty feet long, but that was thirty feet into midair, and from where I cowered, it looked like a mile.

I told myself to get a grip, I had jumped twice now into places where I didn't have so much as a good intention between me and the ground. Of course, both cases lasted less than a second, and I could have the Mark push me back into the relative safety of the airship.

I think my body knew the difference. I could feel terror boiling inside me as I grabbed the guide cable and followed Ivan. It got worse with every step away from the safe confines of the airship. My stomach clenched itself into an acid-soaked ball, trying to squeeze the Emperor's dinner back up my throat.

I pulled myself along the gangway, up next to Ivan, and gulped down the rising gorge when I reached the edge of the protective netting.

The gangway paralleled the track that had led out the main hangar door and under one of the stubby wings that projected from the airship's skin. The track ended here, buried in the wing above me in an impenetrable mass of struts and cables. Cables and pulleys descended from the track above, past the level of the gangway, to suspend one of the biplanes below me.

On either side of the complex system of cables holding the plane dangled a pair of ladders. Each ladder was nothing more than a pair of chains set about a foot apart, with a metal bar joining them every two feet along its length. They swayed slightly in the harsh wind.

So did the plane beneath us.

So did the gangway.

So did my stomach.

And each one moved at a slightly different frequency and amplitude.

I swore, but whatever sour words I managed to say were lost under the sound of the wind.

Ivan didn't have to tell me what to do. It was pretty obvious. The biplane was a two-seater, and the ladders fore and aft were the only way down. Ivan had already grabbed the forward ladder and was climbing down into the pilot's seat.

I reached out for the other ladder, leaning around the edge of the netting one-handed. The metal rung was cold around my fingers, but I held it in a death grip as I let go of the netting with the other. I carefully raised one foot and set it on a lower rung—and the whole ladder swung out with my weight.

"*Fuck!*" I screamed as my other foot left the gangway and I swung back and forth. I shoved my other foot into the ladder so forcefully that the swinging got worse. For a moment everything felt wild and chaotic, the cold metal burning the skin of my hands and feet, my shoulder slamming into the cables supporting one wing of the aircraft. The swaying made me so dizzy that I had to screw my eyes shut to keep my grip.

I think it only lasted a couple of seconds, because the ladder had become mostly still before I heard Ivan yell back up to me, "Are you all right?"

I managed to choke out one word. "Fine!"

I started climbing down, eyes shut and burning with tears, groping downward slowly, one naked foot at a time. It felt like hours before I reached down with one foot and briefly panicked when there was no more ladder to descend. Then I felt my sole brush something, and I looked down.

My left foot was dangling just above the back of the copilot's seat.

I sucked in a frigid breath and lowered myself into the plane. I felt an immense relief when I slipped into the seat and was no longer dangling from the ladder, which wasn't to say I wasn't still dangling. The whole plane was suspended by the track above and swaying just enough to make me aware of the motion.

"Get ready and strap yourself in." Ivan called out to me. I fished around and found a harness attached to the sides of the copilot's chair. I pulled the straps over my shoulders and buckled myself in, and I realized that the restraints were not designed with women in mind. I'm not particularly busty, but I still had the upper part of the evening gown on, along with underwear at least as structurally complex as the shell of this biplane—and both still conspired to extract extra boob from the ether, while the harness attempted to crush them back where they had come from.

"Ready?" Ivan called back.

"Yes," I gasped, forcing myself to breathe against the restraints.

I heard a grinding whirr, and the plane started vibrating. In front of us, I saw the propeller begin turning as the engine noise and the vibration intensified. It kept getting louder, going from lawnmower, to chainsaw, all the way to Rammstein concert. Ivan yelled something at me, but I couldn't hear him over the engine.

The plane was angled about forty-five degrees off the axis of the airship, pointing forward. As the engine revved, the propeller dragged the body of the biplane forward, the cables attaching us to the track above were now angled away from the ship.

There was a severe bounce, and my stomach tried to slam up through my diaphragm as the cables all popped free of the wing above me. The biplane fell at an angle toward the silver-lit clouds, the airship shooting away behind us impossibly fast.

I didn't breathe, staring unblinking, eyes watering in the freezing air slipping by the stubby windscreen. The silver-backed clouds raced up to meet us, and I felt my dinner racing up to join them. Ivan leveled us out before either decided to meet. Once we seemed to be actually flying, he throttled back the engine to buzz saw levels.

"You can take us to the enemy now?" Ivan called back.

I clenched my teeth and closed my watering eyes. I felt battered and abused, every exposed surface of my body burned from the cold and the wind, my insides felt as if they'd gone through a blender. I felt as if I'd have trouble walking five feet, much less to another universe.

"Yes!" I yelled back.

My Mark was still there, and unlike the rest of me, nothing about it felt shaken or abused. In fact, the more ragged the sense of my physical body became, the more solid it seemed. I focused on it, and it seemed more real than the world around me, the cold, the nausea, the stinging wind in my eyes. I could feel the world I was in, and I could feel the worlds around it unfolding like petals of a flower blooming in infinite directions. I felt the neighbor spaces; for a brief moment my sense of direction failed me, and I couldn't find the place the Shadows had come from.

I panicked and opened my eyes. I couldn't lose track of this, not now. Then I focused on the full moon as the nose of the Emperor's airship began to eclipse it.

Seeing that, something clicked in my brain. I had moved relative to the airship, and I had also moved relative to the place where we were going. Suddenly, my sense of the surrounding worlds fell into place and I knew what direction inside myself I had to look.

"Get ready!" I called to Ivan.

I reached out with the Mark and pushed myself, Ivan, and the biplane.

THIRTY-NINE

THE CLOUDS SHIFTED around us, and the shadow of the Emperor's airship vanished from the moon.

"Be careful!" I called out. "If there's another Prince on board, they probably felt us arrive!"

"Where is it?" he shouted back.

I closed my eyes and tried to picture the brief image I had seen. "Below our airship, just barely above the cloud cover."

"Bearing?"

"Same course, direction. Might have just started turning."

Ivan banked the biplane and started ascending toward the clouds that were above us now.

The plane slid into a towering pillar of clouds and the world briefly turned an opaque silvery black. Something large loomed in the shadows.

"Look out!" I yelled.

He was already cursing in Russian as he violently banked to the left and steepened the ascent until we broke out of the top of the clouds. I could feel the biplane flex ominously as it took a turn that it probably wasn't designed to survive. Below us, close enough to touch, the silver-gray skin of an airship slid by.

Ivan leveled out the plane with a sickening lurch as we shot over the airship and past the nose. Ivan still cursed in Russian as he brought the plane around in a slow bank in front of the craft.

It was smaller than the Emperor's airship, but by no means small in absolute terms. It looked as if it still could cover a football field. Our biplane was a buzzing gnat next to it.

Once he had control back, Ivan called back to me. "What now?"

"How close can you get?" I had been planning my jump on board the enemy ship ever since I'd used the Mark to drop several decks on the airship. We could fly over it, and I would just push myself outside of the plane, drop, and push back when I had fallen into where the airship was. Sounded simple. Now that I was flying in the open air, wind slicing my cheeks, it didn't seem nearly as straightforward.

"I don't have that much control," Ivan said. "If I get too close, I might crash into—"

An explosive banging interrupted Ivan. It sounded something like a stuttering thunderclap. I turned to look toward the airship and saw a small cylindrical projection on the side of the gondola rotating slightly, as if it was tracking us.

Two or three meters of flame flashed from a nearly invisible slot in the cylinder, then a moment later I heard the thunderous sound of it firing. "They're shooting at us!"

At least Ivan didn't berate me for stating the obvious. He dove and banked and brought the plane up again in an effort to give the enemy a harder target. The firing didn't stop, as more turrets joined in, the gunfire merging into an apocalyptic roar. I saw a fist-sized hole appear in the wing above me, and I pushed my Mark.

Sunlight washed us in an explosion of silence. The plane shot into blue sky, and in the absence of the gunfire, the buzzing of the engine was almost soothing.

"Are we badly damaged?" I yelled at Ivan as he leveled off the violent maneuvering.

"Engine's fine, but I've lost some maneuverability."

I looked back and saw that part of the tail trailed ribbons of fabric as if it was a well-used cat toy.

"We're lucky," Ivan said. "At that range we should have been dead. I'm not that good a pilot."

"I guess Shadows don't have great aim."

"Or the gunner's inexperienced. Those are probably operated by mechanical relays from the bridge."

"Damn, is there a way to approach that thing that doesn't involve machine guns pointed at us?"

"No. At best, we'll have a few seconds before the gunner orients on us."

I felt my plan falling apart. I'd already started questioning the viability of doing another skydive when we had the option of a leisurely approach. Trying to buzz it at top speed . . . Worse, even if my plan worked, it left Ivan at the mercy of those cannons. He couldn't escape with the whole plane like I just did.

The whole plane.

"Change in plan," I said. "I just need you to fly this thing as straight as possible."

I expected more of an objection from Ivan, but it wasn't the kind of environment that was conducive to an argument. He just shrugged at my plan and said, "I can't land this thing anyway."

"You can't . . ." I yelled back, unsure I'd heard him correctly over the engine.

"Pilot has to have a few hundred hours training before they let him attempt to dock with a moving airship."

"You should have said something!"

"I wasn't sending anyone else to do this."

Crap. If I'd gone with my original plan, I would have left Ivan stranded in a plane he couldn't land . . .

I told myself to stop that train of thought and concentrate on plan B.

As directed, Ivan brought our craft around under the blue sunlit sky and started a line of attack on the way we had come. I pushed. The sun went out, and the moonlit shadow of the enemy airship hovered about two miles ahead of us. The plane shook, fighting its damaged control surfaces, as Ivan turned into the airship's flight path, aiming at the nose of the massive thing. Just as our bumpy course flattened out, I could see flashes from the sides of the gondola. I pushed the Mark again, and sunlight blared down on us. The plane vibrated worse when the universe changed.

"Keep it on course!"

"The air current's different! We dropped a couple hundred feet."

"We can't afford that!"

"I know!"

I pushed again, and the sun winked out. The airship loomed less than a mile ahead and above us. Ivan pulled us up into a climb, throttling the engine until it screamed. "Don't move us again until you have to!"

"The guns!" I yelled. In response, the airship's turrets flashed again, and I heard their staccato thunder almost on top of the flashes.

"Too close!" Ivan yelled over the engine, the screaming wind, and the gunfire. A line of holes tore through the lower wing on my left. The sounds of the airframe protesting were something I felt more than heard. "Wait!" A cherry-red ball of fire erupted on the right side of the engine housing, vomiting oily black smoke. The whole plane shook as the engine's noise screeched into oblivion.

The nose of the airship was just visible beyond the oily black smoke from the engine fire. Our nose was already dropping as the propeller stuttered to a stop, but we were too close to avoid hitting.

"Now!" he yelled as another volley tore through the rear of the biplane, shredding the tail section. I pushed us, and again sunlight washed us, this time in a sudden, complete, silence. We were no longer in an airplane, we sat in a lump of wreckage barely more aerodynamic than my Charger, that had just reached the apex of a ballistic arc that was about to fling us down into the Atlantic.

Before we plummeted twenty thousand feet into the ocean, I pushed again, and everything went completely black. No moon, no clouds, and even the engine fire flickered out. The silence was even more complete than before, not even the sound of wind. I gasped, and it came out as an inhuman squeak.

Then we slammed into the floor. Fabric tore, and metal screeched in protest, I felt air rushing by as the impact threw me against the painfully boob-crushing restraints. Everything crunched to a stop, and I fell against the left side of my cockpit, which now canted at a forty-five–degree angle.

"Ivan? You okay?" My voice sounded like a cartoon mouse. I coughed a few times to clear my throat.

I heard a high-pitched Russian obscenity above the ticking of cooling metal. "Unhurt." He caught his breath and grunted. In a more normal tone he followed with, "Mostly."

I unbuckled myself and looked around. I'd been more successful than I had a right to be. The biplane was lodged in a catwalk between two of the massive gas cells, one of which we had just burst out of.

I could still smell smoke from the burning engine and realized I'd answered Jacob's question, "Hydrogen or helium." Of course, they'd probably lay off the firearms on a hydrogen-filled airship.

I pulled myself out of the wreckage and onto the catwalk that extended between the two neighboring gas cells.

Ivan followed me, looking around at the damage. "We'll be losing altitude. They may have ballast to drop, but they've lost two gas cells."

"Two?"

Ivan pointed away from the massive hole that the biplane had torn out of the one cell. I followed his gesture and saw the nose of the plane next to the canvas skin of the next cell. The propeller had torn a diagonal gash in it the length of my forearm. Not as dramatic, but a hole is a hole, I guess.

I was still finding my feet from the impact, still shaken, when I sensed an almost familiar touch on my Mark, one that wasn't the corrupt sensations that preceded the shadows. Whoever it was I sought, that person was here. I was about to say something when I felt something of more immediate concern; vibrations in the metal of the catwalk. It was followed by the sounds of running feet clanging in the echoless space.

"Ivan—"

I didn't need to warn him, he already had his gun out. "This way," he said with a confidence that didn't reach his eyes.

I followed him along the catwalk down the length of the ship, unsure myself of what direction the running feet came from. At least, we had a fifty percent chance of moving away from them.

Not that we were so lucky.

We only made it a few yards when a trio of rifle-wielding men appeared around a gas cell ahead of us. Ivan practically threw me in a gap between a gas cell and some complicated plumbing, a cramped niche of struts and valves that really wasn't intended to accommodate one person, much less two.

"I'm having doubts about your plan," Ivan said.

So was I. I thought of reprising my earlier maneuvers, Walking to midair and back, dropping us lower in the airship's superstructure. But aside from the dangerousness of the maneuver, Ivan had inadvertently cut off that option by wedging me in this cramped space. I did the next best thing and pulled my Luger-analog out of the pocket of my borrowed greatcoat.

Five shots, three men; those odds weren't too bad.

Unfortunately, that didn't count another trio of men coming from the other direction. With our attention focused on the men down the corridor, we were caught by surprise by another group coming from behind us. We didn't see them until rifle barrels were pointed at our heads and someone was barking in Old English to drop our weapons.

Even though Ivan probably didn't know the language, the meaning was clear enough. He held his hands up, gun dangling from the trigger guard. One of the gruff men snatched it from him. I followed suit, thankful at least that these weren't Shadows. Another hand shot out and grabbed the Luger, shoving it into a wide leather belt.

Our captors were an anachronistic lot, even for Ivan's neck of the woods. They bore rifles that obviously came from the Imperial armory. Otherwise, they appeared out of another century entirely, clad in scale, leather, and fur. They wore hair and beards much longer than Ivan's contemporaries.

Not to mention they spoke a dead language that I, somehow, understood.

One of them held a rifle barrel to my chest as the other two dragged Ivan back out onto the catwalk. By now the three others, all of a similar ilk, had caught up. One of them brought a rifle butt up to the side of Ivan's skull.

The action was abrupt enough to make me forget my position. Almost involuntarily, I lurched forward to intervene. Then something hard collided with my own skull, sending everything into a pain-fuzzed blur.

FORTY

I NEVER LOST consciousness, but for a time I lost awareness of everything except the throbbing in my skull. Not that I had any great options, unarmed and being manhandled by three large men. I don't know how long I was stunned, but I doubt it was very long. When I could focus on my surroundings, not much had changed. We were still in the airship's interior, amid the support struts and the catwalk. Something wrenched my shoulder, and everything snapped fully into focus.

They had bound my wrists with a heavy rope and had hauled me up by a crossbeam between two gas cells so my feet dangled uselessly about six inches above the catwalk. The ache that inspired in my shoulders made me forget my throbbing head.

Well, that was one way to prevent me from Walking anywhere.

I heard someone curse in Russian, and I looked up to see them doing the same thing to Ivan, about twenty feet down the catwalk from me. Behind him, toward the front of the airship, I could still see the shredded remains of the biplane half-blocking the catwalk.

I suppose we were lucky that we hadn't been killed out of hand.

A woman walked onto the catwalk, leading another anachronistic armor-clad man, distinguished from the other six by the elaborate braids in his hair and his fur-lined cloak. As she approached, I couldn't restrain a small gasp, and not just from the eerie familiarity of her Mark as she neared.

Looking at her was like staring at a twisted mirror. She had long blonde hair the same shade as my own, lightened slightly by a hint of gray. Her face bore lines and creases from about fifteen or twenty more years, but the major landmarks—the jawline, the nose, the shape of her cheekbones—were all echoes of my own. All except the eyes, which smoldered green and harbored a darkness I hope had never crossed my own expression.

She strode past Ivan without a glance and spoke as she drew a dagger from her belt. "Why does she still live?" The woman's voice was cold and distant, much calmer than the fury in her eyes seemed to warrant.

The man with the braided hair answered her, "On my orders, my lady."

Her murderous gaze didn't leave me as she said, "You know my purpose is to remove Father's bastards."

"As you wish," he said, "but I thought it wise to give you the choice."

"What alternative do you propose, General?"

"Taking her has cost you many Shadows, forces you need to take the throne."

"You're suggesting she might serve?"

"Look at her Mark, my lady."

The woman lowered her dagger and walked around me as I dangled. The great coat had disappeared while I'd been knocked senseless, and my party dress was so much shredded fabric. The upper part of my back was exposed, and apparently that was enough to satisfy the woman. "More a sibling than I had thought."

"I had thought, my lady, that with so little of the boy's skin remaining—"

"Say no more, General. Fully grown as well. Enough for an army."

"What are you talking about?" I finally said.

"Mind your words, woman!" snapped the man she'd been calling General.

"She speaks the mother tongue," the woman said. She stepped in front of me, a ghost of a smile on her lips that I did not find at all comforting.

"She speaks insolently," responded the General.

The woman waved a hand in a dismissive gesture, as if such a thing was beneath her concern.

"What do you want of me?" I asked.

"Until a moment ago? Simply your death. I spent much to achieve it. Dear Uncle Tobin thought he'd escaped his dungeon as my brother's house fell, but I let him slip through the ranks of my Shadows. I knew the sentimental fool would lead me to you, if you were still reachable."

The name, Tobin, hit my memory like a brick into a clouded window. A flood of disconnected memories bubbled up, all of the old man who had pounded on my car window, decades younger. All the memories came in a jumbled flash, him carrying me on his shoulders, telling me a story at bedtime, leading me on a pony through a field overgrown with wildflowers, him wrapping me in a blanket and slipping out of the cold walls of the castle into a night that evaporated into the boiling gray of Chaos.

The woman smiled evilly. "I see, from your expression, you share our uncle's sentimentality."

Our uncle, she'd said.

More a sibling, she'd said.

"You're my sister?" Even in my current position, the words still blocked a well of emotion.

"We share our father's blood, but do not go so far as to claim that manner of kinship from me. You're just another of his bastards."

"Why are you doing this?"

She shook her head. "So I can claim the throne of House Wealcan. Why else? I will not make Father's mistake of leaving rivals about to threaten me. Even Uncle Ulmar made the same mistake after wresting rule from Father, preferring to imprison his siblings rather than eliminate them."

"Uncle Tobin," I whispered.

"Imprisoned in his nephew's tower for supporting Father over Ulmar. He always claimed, even under torture, that you and your mother were lost to Chaos during his flight. The fact that his assassin never returned from his hunt for you convinced Ulmar. It never convinced me."

Assassin . . . My thoughts turned to the anachronistically dressed body that had been found in my mother's apartment.

I felt torn between grief and rage knowing this was the family I'd been born to, and how poorly it compared to the one that had adopted me. I snapped my next words in a tone that must have displeased the General. "Why don't you just kill me, then?"

"Because I did not know how fully developed the Mark you wore was until now. It is just what we require to create the Shadows we need to take on my brother's defenders."

"Create the Shadows . . ." The thought was appalling enough that my breath caught.

"All we need is a piece of skin with the Mark. Well, with the Mark of Wealcan. Some other Mark and I cannot control the Shadows birthed from it, which makes them worse than useless. As the General has noted, you have much more skin than the boy we've near used up . . ." She trailed off and turned to the General. "Why is the ship listing?"

I'd been largely unaware of it, between my throbbing head and being suspended, but now I realized I was hanging almost fifteen degrees off of true, my feet dangling toward the nose of the airship.

"I know not, my lady."

They don't know how an airship works. My sister and her minions didn't understand that the gas cells kept the ship aloft, so they didn't realize that the damage caused by the biplane would unbalance the whole thing.

That raised the question of who was driving.

"Come, you and your men, to the bridge." She pointed to the man who had shoved my pseudo-Luger into his belt. "You guard the prisoners."

Everyone but the lone guard marched off past Ivan and the biplane wreckage, the tilt on the catwalk now enough to make their steps somewhat clumsy. Our guard slung his rifle over his shoulder and watched them go.

"Ivan," I called to him in English, "are you okay?"

"Conscious," he grumbled.

"No talking!" snapped the guard in Old English. His expression betrayed nerves as much as anger, and it gave me an idea.

"How much time before we hit the ocean?" I shouted at Ivan.

"No idea. Don't know how fast we're descending."

The guard looked from us, one to the other, obviously with no clue what we were saying. "I said, no talking!" he repeated in his language.

"I suppose you're going to make us?" I said in English. "You pathetic little troll," I repeated in Old English, just so he'd focus on me.

He cursed so rapidly and so violently that I could make no sense of the words. One of them might have been "whore." He raised a hand and stomped up the canted catwalk toward me, just as I'd intended.

I work out a lot. In addition to my normal daily runs, I am no stranger to pull-ups. I might not have the upper-body strength of Ivan or Jacob, but I can manage my own weight. I hadn't been dangling long enough for fatigue to set in, so my muscles could respond, albeit painfully.

As the guard charged, I swung my legs up to meet him. He was too surprised to back up, and the way he leaned toward me on the canted deck made it that much easier for me to wrap my legs around his neck. He beat at my thighs, but I locked my ankles together and concentrated on strangling him. By the time he had the presence of mind to draw a dagger from his belt, he was already too weak and too badly positioned to do more than deal some superficial cuts to my legs.

Eventually, he just dangled there.

Out of caution, I held the pressure on for another full minute. Then I dropped him on the catwalk with a clatter, my legs tingling from lack of circulation.

"That's impressive," Ivan called to me in a low voice. "But what's your plan to get us out of our bonds?"

Yes, that was a good question.

Our unconscious guard had a dagger out, but it was on the catwalk. It was ten inches from my dangling feet, and it might as well have been a mile. I looked up and wriggled my hands. The knots were hasty and not very tight, but there was no hope of me pulling my wrist through without any leverage. Some action heroine would be able to swing her legs up on the strut I dangled from, but that was easily a foot or two above my wrists, and I didn't have *that* much upper-body strength.

But that gave me another, more dangerous thought.

I could swing.

I started swinging my legs back and forth until my whole body was tracing an arc.

"What are you doing?" Ivan croaked.

I wondered myself. I knew that all that mattered for the Mark to move me was the motion. If I could do it while jumping to clothesline a Shadow, I could do it here. *Couldn't I*?

I had never done so while attached to something like this. I remembered the sensation of the *Métal Stationnaire*, how it felt as if it chained me to a wall when I tried to Walk with it. So that could be all that would happen, the rope holding me in place. But what if the pull into that unnamable direction was stronger than the rope's hold on me? That was what I counted on. But a nasty part of my mind wondered, *What if the pull is stronger than my wrists*?

No, if the *Métal Stationnaire* didn't yank off a limb when I tried to Walk, neither would this.

I still swung back and forth three more times before I pushed my Mark.

FORTY-ONE

MY SHOULDERS AND wrists burned with such flaring agony that I was barely aware of the sudden cold wind cutting across my whole body. Again I was in midair, my eyes watering as much from the wind as the pain. I barely had the presence of mind to push myself back into the airship.

I slammed ungracefully onto the metal of the catwalk, rolling down the slope a couple of feet until I came to a crumpled moaning stop.

A Russian-accented voice came from far away, "Are you all right?"

"No," I groaned. I blinked my eyes and looked at my wrists. Fortunately, my hands were still attached. But they were covered in blood, and the skin was badly abraded where they had been torn free of the ropes. It took three tries before I got my pained arms to support my weight and push myself up.

No time to recover. My evil sibling would have sensed my use of the Mark. Her people were probably already coming back here. The moment I could get my arms to obey me, I scrambled to the guard's body. I pulled my sort-of-Luger from the man's belt with one hand and retrieved his dagger with the other. Then I ran to Ivan. The ropes suspending him ran over the strut above and down to tie to the railing of the catwalk.

"Get ready to drop," I told Ivan as I started sawing through the rope with the dagger. It didn't go well. The dagger may have been sharp, but it wasn't designed to hack rope apart, and the effort was made worse because the grip from my injured hands was poor and slick with smeared blood. I was barely a third of the way through the rope when I saw movement by the wreckage of the biplane. I dropped prone before I heard the crack of a rifle.

"Shit!"

I dropped the dagger and got my gun up in a two-handed grip in front of me. Flat on the ground made me less of a target, but that wouldn't faze someone who took time to aim, especially since the floor of the catwalk tilted toward the enemy. I fired one of my five shots simply to pin them down and deny them that chance for a moment. The gunshot seemed an order of magnitude louder than the rifle crack.

They hesitated just a fraction too long before returning fire, time for my hands to stop shaking, time for me to aim down the length of the catwalk. The first guy sprang from the alcove of pipes and struts where Ivan had hidden us shortly after the crash. He was using a rifle and had to swing it around to bear on me after leaving his cramped cover. Time enough for me to place a single shot into his center of mass.

The explosive gunshot set the surface of the catwalk ringing under my arms, not that I could hear it because I was already half deafened. My injured wrists stung from the recoil from the massive pistol. The sound had barely faded from my noise-ravaged ears when the next guy tried to shoot me. I saw the muzzle flash, but barely heard the shot. This guy used the biplane for cover, but that meant he was mostly hidden by fabric. I fired a fraction of a second after he did, aiming at a point about five inches below the flash of his rifle. The shot blew through the body of the biplane, and the gunman dropped behind it.

I saw another flash and felt something hot and stinging against my leg. It took a moment for me to zero in on the new shooter, enough time for him to get off another shot that, thankfully, missed. I found him past the biplane, using the stairs downward for cover. He was twice as far from me as either of his fallen comrades. Before he managed a third shot, I fired, striking the catwalk in front of him. He ducked below the level of the catwalk.

Damn!

I only had one shot left; it needed to count. I held my breath and aimed at the small area at the top of the steps he needed to take a shot. I waited and waited.

And waited.

I exhaled. Did I actually get him? I doubted it. My shot had hit the ground maybe three feet in front of him. At best he'd been stung by a sliver of shrapnel. Did he retreat?

Another few breaths, and the airship seemed to shudder beneath me. "What was that?"

I barely heard Ivan through ears that felt packed with cotton. "Ballast."

No more shots came, and I scrambled back, grabbing the dagger and sawing frantically at Ivan's rope. I finally cut through it, and Ivan dropped. He crouched and rolled as if he did this all the time. When he came up, he held his wrists out. I approached with the dagger when I saw movement out of the corner of my eye.

"Down!" I shoved Ivan, and we both collapsed to the deck as a bullet sparked the handrail next to us.

Our friend had circled around to come up behind us at the other end of the catwalk. Like before, he used the stairs for cover, but from that direction, without the wreckage half-blocking the catwalk, he had a much clearer field of fire. Prone, I brought my gun to bear again. My position was even worse now. Given the still tilted airship, the gunman had the high ground. He was also twice as far from us, not a huge amount for the rifle but enough to impact the accuracy of my handgun.

And I only had one shot left.

He'd ducked down the stairs, so I couldn't see him. I did my best to aim, waiting for him to pop up. When he did, I fired. The shot missed him entirely, shredding the edge of a gas cell three feet away from him. I watched helplessly as he levered his rifle in my direction.

I dimly heard the rifle shot, but I saw no flash from his gun. Instead, I saw his head snap back in a fog of red mist. I looked off to my right and saw Ivan. He had managed to get one hand free and had liberated the rifle from the guard's body next to us.

Ivan's voice sounded far away. "By my count, that leaves three, plus the woman."

After we untangled the rope from Ivan's other wrist, we headed up the catwalk toward our last attacker. I was beginning to realize how beat up I was. My wrists burned and throbbed. As the adrenaline ebbed, I could feel the two wounds on my left leg, one slice from our guard's dagger, and one graze either from a rifle shot or wayward shrapnel. I limped now, and my bare foot was slippery with a slick of blood.

We stopped by the body by the stairs and I picked up the dead man's rifle. As I did, the whole airship seemed to shudder around us. "More ballast," Ivan said, his voice a little clearer now that my ears had stopped ringing.

"Can they keep this thing airborne?"

He shook his head. "I doubt it, especially now with all the bullet holes."

"We have to stop her," I said.

"I know."

I swallowed. "I'm sorry for dragging you into my fight."

"It is my fight once they attack the Empire."

I nodded. I still felt guilty, but I didn't want to argue the point. "I don't think any of them know how to fly an airship."

"Someone's flying."

I nodded. "She must have the crew hostage. She was taking her people to the bridge."

"Then we should head to the bridge."

WE climbed down from the catwalk into the stern of the airship. As we made our way down, we passed signs of fighting beyond our own gunfight; bullet holes marred bulkheads, smears of blood covered the walls, and the smell of smoke filled the air. We passed a few corpses that had been left where they had fallen. Two were Shadows that had taken bullets to the head. The remainder appeared to be normal humans who had taken wounds from things more gruesome than gunfire: skinned, disemboweled, dismembered.

The air in the ship stank of blood and smoke, bile and death. The nausea I had felt aboard the biplane returned in more force.

"Where is everyone?" Ivan asked quietly. "There would be many more passengers and crew than this."

I looked at the latest dead body, bisected to spill its entrails across the tilting corridor in front of us. "They're on the Emperor's airship."

"What?"

I knelt by the upper half of the body and pulled the shreds of the dead man's jacket and shirt away from the skin of his back. Above the massive wound and smears of blood, parts of a Mark were visible traced into the skin. "The dead they left. They're all Walkers." I stood up.

"But the other people? This airship carried dozens."

"That's who was attacking you."

"My Lady?"

"The Shadows came from this airship's passengers." I looked up from the corpse and realized that Ivan wouldn't have understood anything my sister had said. "She talked of making Shadows."

"What?"

I described what she had said, and Ivan responded with a horrified expression. "Just using Shadows is abominable enough. Creating them . . ."

I felt a rumble through the floor of the deck, and suddenly the floor tilted against itself, throwing me against one wall and forcing me to step into the gore left by the bisected corpse.

"What's that? Ballast again?"

"Maybe they're venting gas," Ivan said. "Trying to straighten us out."

The floor had flattened out side to side, but it still tilted downward, even more steeply toward the nose of the aircraft. I felt my stomach lurch.

"I don't think so," I said.

Ivan grabbed the wall as the tilt became more pronounced, and my gut felt like I was in an elevator in free-fall. "Why—"

He must have felt the same thing I had, the sense of being torn through the skin of the world and into Chaos.

"The airship?" Ivan whispered incredulously. "She's moving the whole airship?"

"And diving to pick up speed," I said.

We started running toward the bridge.

FORTY-TWO

WE WENT FORWARD along the steeply inclined deck. As we moved, I felt corresponding movement through Chaos like an invisible windstorm blowing across my Mark; like the feeling on your skin when you hold your hand out the window of a moving car, if the car was doing ninety through a hurricane-force ice storm.

The corridors of this airship were more cramped and less ornate than the spaces in the Emperor's. Most of the signage was in Spanish rather than French, and as we made our way past a couple of more corpses, Ivan said something about it being a troop transport out of South America or Cuba.

"How could such an invasion slip by us?"

"It was only a few people . . ."

"Even one person couldn't Walk into the Emperor's demesne unnoted."

"Maybe they didn't."

"What?"

"If another 'Prince' showed up on the Empire's fringes with her retinue, what would be done with them?"

"They would be bound and taken to—" He broke off, cursing in Russian.

"You'd cuff them like you did me, and transport them in an airship so they couldn't just Walk away. Right?"

He continued cursing in Russian. He got it. They had given my sister and her people the same treatment they'd given me. But, unlike me, she had the ability to create Shadows out of otherwise normal people. Somehow, she could infect people with a piece harvested from someone's Mark. Even if she only managed to do so with one or two, having those loose on a cramped ship like this, spreading the infection, could easily overwhelm a crew that wasn't prepared.

Their overwhelming attack worked in our favor. The door leading down to the bridge had been busted open badly enough that it could no longer be dogged shut. We took up positions on opposite sides of the door. We hadn't run into my sister's remaining troops on the way here, so they had to be waiting in ambush.

Ivan stood on the hinge side of the door pointing his weapon along it as he pushed it inward with his foot. A diffuse gray light spilled in from the corridor beyond, washing out the weak electric light from the corridor. For a few moments as the door swung, everything was ominously silent except for a distant thrum of engines.

Then a rifle shot exploded and we were in the midst of a gunfight. For several seconds we exchanged gunfire with them down a short flight of steps that led into what I presume was the bridge. They had similar cover to us, ducking around the doorway into the bridge.

I ran out of ammo first.

The others ran out in quick succession. Then a bearded barbarian was charging up the steps toward us, brandishing a sword. I though briefly of jumping with my Mark past him, as I'd done with the Shadows, but I felt the pressure of the entire airship moving through Chaos and wasn't certain I'd be able to repeat the trick while we were moving in those nameless directions.

Ivan quickly shifted his grip on the rifle and swung it up to parry the attacker's sword. I scrambled back, and without the time or the space to flip my rifle around, I simply thrust it as if I had a bayonet. I aimed for his face, but just grazed the side of his head. I only managed to attract his attention.

But that gave Ivan enough of an opening to bring the butt of his rifle down on the bridge of the man's nose. His face erupted into a flower of blood as he fell back down the stairway, thudding like a sack of concrete and moving with about as much animation.

The door hung open in front of us, and Ivan dove to grab for the sword the man had dropped. As he did, the last of my sister's anachronistic guards stepped out on the foot of the stairway above his fallen general. He was bringing a pistol to bear at Ivan. With only a fraction of a second to act, I screamed and dove at the man, my reservations forgotten. I leaped over Ivan's crouching form. The man drew up the gun to cover me rather than Ivan.

I pushed with the Mark just as he fired. Instead of a gunshot, I only heard the dull gray silence of empty Chaos around me, I pushed back the way I had come immediately. Even so, it felt almost too late, despite my pushing my Mark as hard as I could, it seemed I fell for a full second through Chaos before the airship surrounded me again.

Then I was face-to-face with the guard, less than an inch between us. I had no time to brace before plowing him down, stunning myself as much as I stunned him. My empty rifle sailed somewhere off into the bridge. Before I came completely to my senses, I saw the man next to me, scrambling to sit and bring his pistol up. Ivan ran him through before he got the chance to fire again. The pistol flew from his hand and landed by me, and by then I'd recovered enough sense to grab it.

I scrambled to my feet to face the bridge.

Men in uniform stood in front of various control stations covered with panels of obscure-looking dials, levers, and meters. A large table in the center of the room had been covered with charts that had half slid off in the ongoing descent.

Floor-to-ceiling windows dominated the front of the room,

half-spidered by multiple bullet holes. Beyond them swirled Chaos that wiped away any sense of up or down. Ivan stood up and took a step into the room, holding his bloody sword.

"*Nyepravda*. Something's not right."

Our quarry, my sister, stood before the windows, facing Chaos, ignoring us.

Something tingled my Mark's senses. The sense of so much mass moving through Chaos was overwhelming, but I still felt the sense of something familiar and corrupt underneath it.

Ivan, oblivious, pointed his sword at the blonde robed figure across the bridge from us. "We have you. Free your hostages and return this ship from whence it came."

"Ivan! Those men aren't hostages—"

The crew manning the various stations on the bridge sprang into motion before I completed my sentence. The moment they turned, the ink-black eyes told what they were even if there weren't dark scars carving across their faces. I braced my wrist and fired my newly-acquired pistol at the one leaping at Ivan's back. The shot hit off-center down and to the right of the sternum, but my appropriated weapon had a kick like a Magnum, and the Shadow went down clutching a black-bleeding hole in its abdomen.

I saw Ivan swing his weapon, as another Shadow leaped up in front of me. I couldn't aim, I just fired twice, and the attacker fell back without most of his lower face. But that was enough of a distraction to have two others grab my arms. My gun went tumbling into the bridge as I was dragged to the ground.

As I fell back in the doorway, I heard the sounds of a sword hacking from Ivan's direction. I heard cracking glass, a whistle of wind, and livid curses in Russian. My attackers had me pinned, immobile, but I could lift my head enough to see Ivan silhouetted against one of the huge windows overlooking the roiling Chaos the airship descended through. Cracks webbed the window, emerging from a pair of bullet holes.

Three Shadows leaped on him, slamming into the cracked window.

"No!" I yelled as I saw the window bulge outward with the impact, the spiderweb of cracks multiplying. For a fraction of a second the glass turned opaque—right before it exploded, sending Ivan and the three Shadows tumbling into the Chaos. I stared at where Ivan had stood, eyes wide and burning in the sudden wind from the missing window.

"Ivan!"

No answer, of course.

In the back of my mind, I think I'd always expected to die in the line of duty, like my dad. In a moment of clarity, now that that moment was imminent, I understood that in some sense I *wanted* it all to end like that. For years I'd been chasing after my dad, pushing things, hoping on some level to share his fate.

But not like this. Not torn apart by half-human cannibals.

The Shadows snarled at me and, after a couple of seconds I realized that they weren't tearing into me the way I expected. Then their heads turned away from me, toward an approaching form silhouetted against the broken window.

"You think to challenge me?"

"You didn't give me much choice."

"Yet you bedevil me for no good end." She shook her head. "I had you before, and I have you now." If anything, it was that arrogant, dismissive attitude that infuriated me. I was still trying to process the fact Ivan was gone, and this mockery of family showed little more than irritation over losing her own men. They might as well have been the Shadows she sent to destruction for all she seemed to care. I struggled against the Shadows' grip, but they were large men and the infection they suffered seemed only to increase their strength.

She picked up the pistol I had dropped when the Shadows had overpowered me. "The General gave good council, but the cost is too high." She leveled the gun at me.

"Who are you?" I asked.

"I am Ulrika, daughter of Ulthar, heir to House Wealcan, and I shall not leave you to challenge my power."

"Please, don't."

"Pleading shall not aid you."

"The fact we're sisters means nothing to you?"

"It means you are a threat to my power."

I raged internally. The threat on my life almost didn't matter. What gripped me more than anything was the violence this evil bitch had done to my idea of family. She had taken something I had deeply longed for and perverted it as much as she had perverted these Shadows.

She leveled the gun and pulled the trigger.

Nothing happened. I'd emptied the gun before the Shadows had jumped me. I saw her eyes widen, and felt I had the only opening I was going to get.

I pushed out with my Mark, the way I had with Ivan, shoving my own phantom fists into the mass of rotting fingers reaching for me. The Shadows let me go as if my blows had been physical. Ulrika scrambled back, her composure finally broken. Her expression said she had not expected this.

My sister screamed at them, "Grab her! She's not me! Tear her apart!"

They didn't move to grab me as I struggled to my feet. It was harder now, the angle of the floor steeper. She dropped the empty gun and reached for her belt, I didn't know what she was reaching for, but I wasn't about to let her get it out. I tackled her from a crouch, and we both fell backward toward the windows.

Grabbing her was like shoving a live electrical cable into myself. Every nerve inside me flared with sudden rough awareness of her Mark slamming into mine. My Mark slammed into hers like a fist into a brick wall. I might have screamed in pain before we smashed into the deck.

I felt the world around us, dimly, at the edge of my perception. The feel of my hands around her neck seemed an incidental afterimage in the face of the steel hands of her Mark crushing my own. My reality became nothing but a point of sensation tumbling through the void of Chaos, demon winds abrading away the parts of me that weren't battered at the hands of Ulrika's Mark. I felt her tear at me and it felt as if she had torn open my belly to feed on my entrails.

Fool, I heard her voice clearly, though she hadn't spoken. Somehow, I was still aware of my fingers locked around her throat. As if it mattered.

Demon claws dug into the invisible substance of my Mark, tearing pieces of it away.

You think you can fight me like this?

I could feel her hard alien touch cut into me, wrap itself around the heart of my Mark, pulling it as if grabbing the base of my spine. Everything inside me flared in agony. Nothing was left but pain and my sister's voice.

You are nothing, a mistake, an obstacle to restoring . . . to restoring . . .

I felt the painful grip slip slightly before digging in deeper. Twisted in pain as I felt, that one slip gave me a sudden resolve. She was feeling it, weakening herself. For all her arrogance, we weren't as mismatched as she'd thought.

Somewhere in the real world, I whispered into the shrieking Chaos. "I. Am. Not. Nothing." I pulled my awareness away from the feeling of her Mark tearing me apart to focus on where we were. My eyes focused on her face staring up at mine. In the periphery of my vision I saw the light on the deck change as the airship fell out of Chaos into a real universe somewhere, my sister unable to maintain the movement between the worlds.

I will kill you! I heard her in my head as her phantom talons pierced the heart of my Mark and yanked it as if she was an eagle ripping the liver out of my body.

"And I'm going to kick your ass!" I screamed, bringing my forehead down to slam into her face. The impact was hard enough to stun me. My grip on her neck slipped and I collapsed on top of her, but the claws of her Mark withdrew from my own, leaving her touch draped across me: inert, suffocating, and impossible to push away.

It took a moment to recover from my own attack, but I managed to move before she recovered. I pushed myself away from her, and the suffocating presence of her Mark receded when I no longer touched her.

She groaned, semiconscious, bleeding from split lips and a broken nose, and I pushed myself to my hands and knees and looked madly around for something I could use as a weapon without touching her. Then I saw the view out the windows.

"Oh, shit."

Nothing was visible out the windows except the surface of the Atlantic Ocean. For one moment all I saw was sunlight glinting off the crests of the waves, sunlight that disappeared as an ominously large shadow grew across the water.

We hit.

FORTY-THREE

THE NOSE OF the airship, above and ahead of us, hit the water first. The impact might have been slow compared to a typical aircraft crash, but it sent shuddering groans through the airframe around us and stopped our forward motion hard enough to throw me from my crouched position to tumble forward. I slammed on my back against the windows, and for a moment it seemed the floor was now vertical, the Shadows and my half-conscious sister falling toward me.

One of the Shadows fell out the broken window next to me. More groans shook the airship, and the floor started falling back down as the gondola slammed into the waves. Water rushed in the open window in a sudden torrent. I grabbed the edge of the window frame to keep the inward rush of water from slamming me into a pulp against the walls.

The water was already chest-high.

I gathered my strength to push my wounded Mark to get out of here. Something grabbed my leg, throwing a crushing weight against my efforts, heavier than the rushing water. I looked down and couldn't see anything but a grinning shadow in the flickering remnants of the surviving electric lights.

You don't escape that easy.

"Fuck you, sister!" I yelled at her, taking in half a lungful of water as I did so. I ran every day, and my legs were not to be trifled with. Barefoot or not, when my free foot connected with her face, I felt flesh give way, and her neck snap back. Her grip weakened enough for the rush of water to carry her off, deeper into the bridge, away from me.

The water slid above my chin, and I took in a last gulp of air as the lights died, plunging me into a cold, wet darkness. My Mark throbbed with the violence done to it, and I felt as if I was bleeding inside. The water rushed over my head, the splashing rush subsiding to a muffled underwater roar.

I felt the current ebb as the pressure equalized. I let go of my anchor and drifted away from the window. I couldn't tell up from down now, in from out. The darkness was complete.

It didn't matter, I just needed to move a small bit. I drifted, and I took my wounded Mark and made it push. The effort felt as if it tore flesh from inside my body, but the darkness changed to dimness.

My lungs ached from holding my breath, and every primal instinct in my brain urged me to panic. It took a supreme effort of will to keep from scrambling madly, swimming in any direction.

I looked around, eyes burning with saltwater, until I saw the direction that seemed lighter, above and behind my left shoulder. I turned myself in the right direction and began kicking toward the light. I was less than twenty feet down, and I broke the surface after three seconds of swimming.

I gasped for air under a cloudless blue sky.

"I'm alive, bitch!" I screamed at the sky. The words were sucked away by the emptiness of the surrounding ocean. I looked around, and saw nothing but water, sky, and horizon.

The starkness of it began sinking in.

"Alive" was a relative term.

THE good news, in terms of schadenfreude anyway, was that my antagonist was in the same boat as I was. In fact, she was probably already dead if my kick had knocked her out. Even if it had stunned her a minute or two, she'd have to Walk out of the wreck underwater, and face the same disorienting panic I had with less air, and from farther down. Even then, she'd end up, at best, in the same position I was, stranded in the middle of an ocean. I didn't care how many universes there might be surrounding me right now, I was certain that all of them looked pretty much like where I was now. Whoever Napoleon might have married, or if Waterloo happened, or who won the Civil War . . . I doubted any of that changed the size or location of the Atlantic Ocean.

I floated for a while, recovering. Minutes passed without incident, no last-minute Shadow popping up to attack me. The water was calm, and there wasn't any sound but the gentle rocking of the waves.

Okay, the fight was over, but I couldn't support myself forever by kicking my legs. I needed something to, at the very least, help me float.

When I felt up to it, I pushed myself back to the only place I thought there might be something like that.

IT was daylight back where the airship had gone down, and it had drifted—or I had—halfway to the horizon. Fortunately, the weather was calm, and I was a good swimmer. It took hours, it seemed, before I started swimming through a grotesque debris field that seemed to be half made of corpses and parts of corpses.

An impractical part of my mind had me look for Ivan in the midst of the dead, until I saw my first shark. After that, I stayed hyperaware of my own location, ready to push myself off into another ocean at the first sign of danger.

Fortunately, there was much easier quarry for the sharks, and none came very close to me.

The airship floated, half-deflated, looming like a half-rotted corpse of a whale, complete with a sky-darkening flock of sea birds looking for an easy meal. The hump of the wreck spilled its shredded envelope to trail in the sea in all directions, and once I was within about ten yards, I had to change from swimming to pulling myself along its flayed skin.

By the time I reached the part of the wreck that still resembled an airship, I was a good five feet above the water, which I could see below me through the occasional tear in the envelope. I couldn't climb any farther, and I sprawled where I was, facing the sky, letting the sun dry the ocean from my skin.

The relief at my survival slowly gave way to dread as my respite from swimming gave me the leisure to think about my situation. I knew enough about the ocean to realize that I was facing death from thirst or exposure. I was most likely the only survivor, and I was probably hundreds of miles from another living soul. Any people who might want to look for me were in another universe.

I lay there, on the skin of a dead airship, and realized that, as isolated I had felt for most of my life, I had never really known what alone was. Nothing like seeing my own death beating down on me from a clear blue sky to put my earlier self-pity into perspective. Especially when I thought that Ivan did not get this far.

Every time I closed my eyes, I saw him falling under the Shadows, out the window and into Chaos . . .

"I hope it was quick," I whispered through lips that were already cracked.

I let my exhaustion play out, and I might have had a few hours of delirious sleep, but I didn't give up. Jacob was still alive, and I promised I would get him back home. So, when I could manage movement again, I crawled out of the sun, through a large tear in the envelope of the airship, and into the wreckage.

It was cool inside, and enough sunlight shone through holes in the skin for me to see the inner skin of a gas cell that had remained remarkably intact; no longer enough to keep this beast in the air, but more than enough to keep it from sinking.

I crawled through the shade and leaned against it. The skin of the gas cell felt clammy and a little damp. I felt thirsty enough that I sucked some of the damp off my fingers. Surprisingly, I didn't taste any salt. I wiped my hand against it again and sucked more moisture to make sure.

I wouldn't call the water fresh. It tasted like old machinery and dirty socks, but it was salt-free. The damp wasn't spray from the ocean, it was condensation.

I wasn't going to die from dehydration at least.

I lived alone in that wreck for about two and a half days. Once I found shelter and a source of water, however foul tasting, I was out of immediate danger. I could have lasted as long as my wreck stayed afloat. I even had a food source, as fish had trapped themselves in the maze of drifting canvas and twisted girders trailing in the water below me. When the morning sun hit the water below me, I saw dozens of silver glints floating between the intact gas cell and the skin of the ship.

By the middle of the third day, I had gotten as far as collecting a small pile of fish near where I made my little camp, but not quite as far as biting into one. Sure, I was hungry, but I wasn't *that* hungry yet though the smell was no longer that unappetizing.

I also spent my time, most of it, crawling through the accessible parts of the wreck and collecting pieces of it that would be useful in putting together a raft. Unlike my late sister, I wasn't up to pushing a whole airship through Chaos, but a raft? That I could manage. If I collected enough water and enough fish, I figured I could probably make it to a coastline somewhere, just using my Mark to keep me in seas that were calm with currents going in the right direction.

My Mark still ached inside from my sister's attack, but I figured I could manage.

I was proud enough of my plan and my budding survival skills that I was almost annoyed when I heard someone calling out to the wreck.

Almost.

I scrambled out of the skin of the airship and waved my arms, screaming to the ship sliding into view around the nose of the dead airship, "Over here!" I was hoarse before I realized I called out in Old English.

SURPRISE number one, the ship was a wooden-clad steamship with long fluted cast-iron stacks emblazoned with the blue-and-gold double eagle of the Empire. Surprise number two, the first person to greet me when they hauled me aboard was Ivan Roskov, Sergeant of the Imperial White Guard.

"You're alive!" we said to each other. Yelled really. I can't say who hugged who, but I know we didn't stop until we were both groaning.

Apparently, the angle of descent of the doomed airship wasn't quite as steep as it had seemed in the heat of combat. By the time Ivan had fallen out the window, we were already close enough to the surface of the water for the fall to be survivable. Ivan had cracked a few ribs, but he'd managed to remain conscious enough to swim to the surface.

It also turned out that we were not as far from the Empire as I had thought. Movement though Chaos was a complicated product of the ability of the Walker, the physical speed at which the Walker moved, and how much mass the Walker moved along with them. My sister had been powerful, powerful enough to drag the airship along, but the airship was huge, and had only been moving barely twenty miles an hour. The net effect was that Ivan had been dropped within swimming distance of the Empire.

So had I, for that matter, not that I'd known it.

The steamship was driven back through Chaos by the coordinated efforts of five members of the Guard, and we returned to Ivan's world in less than twenty minutes.

After that, it was another three days on the cramped steamship before we reached land somewhere on the coast of Greenland. The Emperor's airship had preceded us there, dominating the sky above the little fishing village that served as the steamship's port. I saw the massive beast's silhouette and sighed. I was back where I had started, semiprisoner of an Emperor with an unhealthy interest in marriage as a tool of diplomacy. I would have run as soon as we hit ground, if it wasn't for the fact that Jacob was still on board that thing.

Turns out I needn't have worried. The attack of the Shadows within the Emperor's most secure domain had severely shaken him. And, apparently, the fact that Ivan had returned to report my attack on the Shadows at their source had shaken him more. The man, despite the global Empire, was at heart more cautious than wise. His rescue mission was driven less by a desire to retrieve a potential consort, than it was to ensure that the enemy was, in fact, dead, and no one of any major power was left to plot revenge or a subsequent attack.

The Emperor now seemed much more interested in my goodwill than anything else; enough so that, when I asked for Jacob and me to be returned to my car so we could travel home, he seemed relieved. In the end, I managed to escape simply by signing a formal diplomatic treaty with the Empire.

IT wasn't until nearly a week later, back in DC, that I discovered the catch.

A contingent of the White Guard escorted us to the fringes of the District. Unlike our arrival, this time our carriage had windows, and I was able to see the city as they took us away from the Mall. I watched the Emperor's airship disengage from the Washington Monument and float east. It moved slowly enough that it was still hanging above the skyline when we reached our destination.

One of the Guard opened the door for us and we stepped out next to the train station. The station was a small city unto itself, all brick and glass and cast iron, the air heavy with coal smoke, steam, and the sounds of idling machinery.

I looked at the station and sighed. "I was hoping to get my car back."

Jacob got out next to me and said, "After everything, I'm not going to complain about a train ride back to Cleveland."

"Even if I could, I don't think they'd like me to take one of their trains back."

One of the guards bowed slightly and gestured down a brick-paved street and said, "This way, my Lady."

"Sure," I said, following him.

Jacob and I followed the brightly-uniformed guard, and for a moment I was struck by how the whole scene seemed to have been lifted whole out of some nineteenth century novel—Dickens or Austen. We were dressed for the part: Jacob in a brown tweed suit and bowler hat that made him look like the wealthy client in a Sherlock Holmes story, and I had been given a white dress that someone must have lifted out of a Seurat painting. Our guide was in a Napoleonic dress uniform out of central casting, all blue, red, and white.

As we followed him between the low brick buildings and away from the station platforms, Jacob said, "I wonder if I still have a job."

"I'm sorry I dragged you—"

"Dana, we've been over that."

"I shouldn't have—"

"I agreed to come with you. Stop with the angst about it."

I sighed. "We're probably both out of a job. We've been gone nearly a month."

Jacob laughed.

I gave him a dirty look. "What's so funny about losing our jobs?"

"You have to admit, after facing a horde of cannibal zombies, it doesn't seem like such a big deal."

"It still isn't funny," I said. I had to look away from him and bite my lip to keep from laughing myself.

"Here we are, my Lady." The guard stopped in front of a sliding door in one of the brick buildings. The building looked like a stable, low and long, with half-high windows evenly spaced along the upper part of the wall down its length. The door was heavy, wood, about ten feet square, and painted a deep forest green. It hung on a track mounted on the wall above us.

The guard took out a brass key and removed a heavy padlock from the door before he pulled it aside. It revealed a long brick aisleway between dozens of currently empty stalls.

Something sat between the ranks of stalls, covered by a canvas tarpaulin, something vaguely car-shaped.

"You're kidding!" I said, running up to it.

"Dana?" Jacob made a token protest, for the sake of decorum I guessed. But I didn't really care if I was acting like a six-year-old at Christmas. I yanked the canvas until its own weight started pulling it off the car beneath.

There was my Charger, intact. They'd even washed it. The fenders shone in the light from the open door, the rims practically gleamed.

From behind me, I heard a familiar Russian-accented voice. "Meets with your approval?"

I turned around and saw that Ivan had walked up to the doorway behind us. Unlike his fellow guardsman, he wore civilian clothes, much like Jacob's, except his suit was a forest green and accented with a feathered cap that seemed to have come from an Alp somewhere. He also carried a suitcase.

"Ivan—" I began to say.

"What are you doing here?" Jacob finished the question for me.

He set down the suitcase, reached into the inside of his jacket, and took out a small folded piece of parchment with a prominent wax seal. He walked up and handed it to me.

"What's this?"

"From the Emperor," Ivan told me. "Open it."

I peeled the document open, tearing the seal, feeling the apprehension as I faced another complication. If this was somehow keeping me from leaving, I was probably going to punch someone, starting with Ivan.

I looked at the parchment and saw a short paragraph in French, repeated in English. I read the English one a few times before I started laughing.

"What is it?" Jacob asked.

"The first official diplomatic act between our world and the Empire," I folded the paper and handed it to Jacob. "Keep that safe. It's probably historic or something."

He took the paper, frowning. I looked at Ivan and said, "Grab your suitcase."

I opened the door and was gratified to see that they had left the keys in the ignition. I popped the trunk just in time to hear Jacob say, "*Ambassador?*"